More praise for
A Knight of the Word

"The identity of John's demonic manipulator and the meaning of his dreams are carefully crafted mysteries that build to a climax filled with surprising twists and turns. Brooks's real achievement, however, is his orchestration of the tale's social issues and personal dramas into a scenario with the resonance of myth. Both a sprightly entertainment and a thoughtful allegory of the forces of Good and Evil at large in the modern world, this novel is sure to increase its author's already vast readership."
—*Publishers Weekly* (starred review)

"Brooks has developed in Nest Freemark one of my all-time favorite fictional characters. . . . If you are familiar with Seattle, you will be fascinated by the way the author, who lives there, has nearly made the city a character in the action. If you haven't been to 'the Emerald City,' the book may encourage a trip."
—*Rocky Mountain News*

By Terry Brooks
Published by Ballantine Books:

FIRST KING OF SHANNARA
THE SWORD OF SHANNARA
THE ELFSTONES OF SHANNARA
THE WISHSONG OF SHANNARA

The Heritage of Shannara:
THE SCIONS OF SHANNARA
THE DRUID OF SHANNARA
THE ELF QUEEN OF SHANNARA
THE TALISMANS OF SHANNARA

The Magic Kingdom of Landover:
MAGIC KINGDOM FOR SALE—SOLD!
THE BLACK UNICORN
WIZARD AT LARGE
THE TANGLE BOX
WITCHES' BREW

RUNNING WITH THE DEMON
A KNIGHT OF THE WORD

HOOK

A KNIGHT OF THE WORD

Terry Brooks

A Del Rey® Book
BALLANTINE BOOKS • NEW YORK

A Del Rey® Book
Published by The Ballantine Publishing Group
Copyright © 1998 by Terry Brooks
Excerpt from *Angel Fire East* copyright © 1999 by Terry Brooks

www.randomhouse.com/delrey/

Library of Congress Catalog Card Number: 99-90173

ISBN 0-345-42464-6

Manufactured in the United States of America

First Hardcover Edition: August 1998
First Mass Market Domestic Edition: July 1999
First Mass Market International Edition: August 1999

10 9 8 7 6 5 4 3 2

A KNIGHT OF
THE WORD

PROLOGUE

*H*e stands on a hillside south of the city looking back at the carnage. A long, gray ribbon of broken highway winds through the green expanse of woods and scrub to where the ruin begins. Fires burn among the steel and glass skeletons of the abandoned skyscrapers, flames bright and angry against the washed-out haze of the deeply clouded horizon. Smoke rises in long, greasy spirals that stain the air with ash and soot. He can hear the crackling of the fires and smell their acrid stench even here.

That buildings of concrete and iron will burn so fiercely puzzles him. It seems they should not burn at all, that nothing short of jackhammers and wrecking balls should be able to bring them down. It seems that in this postapocalyptic world of broken lives and fading hopes the buildings should be as enduring as mountains. And yet already he can see sections of walls beginning to collapse as the fires spread and consume.

Rain falls in a steady drizzle, streaking his face. He blinks against the dampness in order to see better what is happening. He remembers Seattle as being beautiful. But that was in another life, when there was still a

1

chance to change the future and he was still a Knight of the Word.

John Ross closes his eyes momentarily as the screams of the wounded and dying reach out to him. The slaughter has been going on for more than six hours, ever since the collapse of the outer defenses just after dawn. The demons and the once-men have broken through and another of the dwindling bastions still left to free men has fallen. On the broad span of the high bridge linking the east and west sections of the city, the combatants surge up against one another in dark knots. Small figures tumble from the heights, pinwheeling madly against the glare of the flames as their lives are snuffed out. Automatic weapons—fire ebbs and flows. The armies will fight on through the remainder of the day, but the outcome is already decided. By tomorrow the victors will be building slave pens. By the day after, the conquered will be discovering how life can sometimes be worse than death.

At the edges of the city, down where the highway snakes between the first of the buildings that flank the Duwamish River, the feeders are beginning to appear. They mushroom as if by magic amid the carnage that consumes the city. Refugees flee and hunters pursue, and wherever the conflict spreads, the feeders are drawn. They are mankind's vultures, picking clean the bones of human emotion, of shattered lives. They are the Word's creation, an enigmatic part of the equation that defines the balance in all things and requires accountability for human behavior. No one is exempt; no one is spared. When madness prevails over reason, when what is darkest and most terrible surfaces, the feeders are there. As they are now, he thinks, watching. Unseen and un-

known, inexplicable in their single-mindedness, they are always there. He sees them tearing at the combatants closest to the city's edges, feeding on the strong emotions generated by the individual struggles of life and death taking place at every quarter, responding instinctively to the impulses that motivate their behavior. They are a force of nature and, as such, a part of nature's law. He hates them for what they are, but he understands the need for what they do.

Something explodes in the center of the burning city, and a building collapses in a low rumble of stone walls and iron girders. He could turn away and look south and see only the green of the hills and the silver glint of the lakes and the sound spread out beneath the snowy majesty of Mount Rainier, but he will not do that. He will watch until it is finished.

He notices suddenly the people who surround him. There are perhaps several dozen, ragged and hollow-eyed figures slumped down in the midday gloom, faces streaked with rain and ash. They stare at him as if expecting something. He does not know what it is. He is no longer a Knight of the Word. He is just an ordinary man. He leans on the rune-carved black staff that was once the symbol of his office and the source of his power. What do they expect of him?

An old man approaches, shambling out of the gloom, stick-thin and haggard. An arm as brittle as dry wood lifts and points accusingly.

I know you, he whispers hoarsely.

Ross shakes his head in denial, confused.

I know you, the old man repeats. Bald and white-bearded, his face is lined with age and by weather and

*his eyes are a strange milky color, their focus blurred. I
was there when you killed him, all those years ago.*

Killed who? Ross cannot make himself speak the
words, only mouth them, aware of the eyes of the others
who are gathered fixing on him as the old man's words
are heard.

The old man cocks his head and lets his jaw drop,
laughing softly, the sound high and eerie, and with this
simple gesture he reveals himself. He is unbalanced—
neither altogether mad nor completely sane, but something in between. He lives in a river that flows between
two worlds, shifting from one to the other, a leaf caught
by the current's inexorable tug, his destiny beyond his
control.

The Wizard! The old man spits, his voice rising bro-
kenly in the hissing sound of the rain. *The Wizard of Oz!
You are the one who killed him! I saw you! There, in
the palace he visited, in the shadow of the Tin Woodman,
in the Emerald City! You killed the Wizard! You killed
him! You!*

The worn face crumples and the light in the milky eyes
dims. Tears flood the old man's eyes and trickle down his
weathered cheeks. He whispers, *Oh, God, it was the end
of everything!*

And Ross remembers then, a jagged-edged, poisonous
memory he had thought forever buried, and he knows
with a chilling certainty that what the old man tells him
is true.

John Ross opened his eyes to the streetlit darkness and
let his memory of the dream fade away. Where had the
old man been standing, that he could have seen it all? He

shook his head. The time for memories and the questions they invoked had come and gone.

He stood in the shadows of a building backed up on Occidental Park in the heart of Pioneer Square, his breath coming in quick, ragged gasps as he fought to draw the cool, autumn night air into his burning lungs. He had walked all the way from the Seattle Art Museum, all the way from the center of downtown Seattle some dozen blocks away. Limped, really, since he could not run as normal men could and relied upon a black walnut staff to keep upright when he moved. Anger and despair had driven him when muscles had failed. Crippled of mind and body and soul, reduced to an empty shell, he had come home to die because dying was all that was left.

The shade trees of the park loomed in dark formation before him, rising out of cobblestones and concrete, out of bricks and curbing, shadowing the sprawl of benches and trash receptacles and the scattering of homeless and disenfranchised that roamed the city night. Some few looked at him as he pushed off the brick wall and came toward them. One or two even hesitated before moving away. His face was terrible to look upon, all bloodied and scraped, and the clothes that draped his lean body were in tatters. Blood leaked from deep rents in the skin of his shoulder and chest, and several of his ribs felt cracked or broken. He had the appearance of a man who had risen straight out of Hell, but in truth he was just on his way down.

Feeders gathered at the edges of his vision, hunch-backed and beacon-eyed, ready to show him the way.

It was Halloween night, All Hallows' Eve, and he was

about to come face-to-face with the most personal of his demons.

His mind spun with the implications of this acknowledgment. He crossed the stone and concrete open space thinking of greener places and times, of the smell of grass and forest air, lost to him here, gone out of his life as surely as the hopes he had harbored once that he might become a normal man again. He had traded what was possible for lies and half truths and convinced himself that what he was doing was right. He had failed to listen to the voices that mattered. He had failed to heed the warnings that counted. He had been betrayed at every turn.

He stopped momentarily in a pool of streetlight and looked off into the darkened spires of the city. The faces and voices came back to him in a rush of sounds and images. Simon Lawrence. Andrew Wren. O'olish Amaneh. The Lady and Owain Glyndwr.

Nest Freemark.

Stefanie.

His hands tightened on the staff, and he could feel the power of the magic coursing through the wood beneath his palms. Power to preserve. Power to destroy. The distinction had always seemed a large one, but he thought now that it was impossibly small.

Was he still, in the ways that mattered, a Knight of the Word? Did he possess courage and strength of will in sufficient measure that they would sustain him in the battle that lay ahead? He could not tell, could not know without putting it to the test. By placing himself in harm's way he would discover how much remained to him of the power that was once his. He did not think that it would be enough to save his life, but he hoped that it might be enough to destroy the enemy who had undone him.

It did not seem too much to ask.

In truth, it did not seem half enough.

Somewhere in the distance a siren sounded, shrill and lingering amid the hard-edged noises that rang down the stone and glass corridors of the city's canyons.

He took a deep breath and gritted his teeth against the pain that racked his body. With slow, measured steps, he started forward once more.

Death followed in his shadow.

SUNDAY,
OCTOBER 28

CHAPTER 1

It was dawn when she woke, the sky just beginning to brighten in the east, night's shadows still draping the trunks and limbs of the big shade trees in inky layers. She lay quietly for a time, looking through her curtained window as the day advanced, aware of a gradual change in the light that warmed the cool darkness of her bedroom. From beneath the covers she listened to the sounds of the morning. She could hear birdsong in counterpoint to the fading hum of tires as a car sped down Woodlawn's blacktop toward the highway. She could hear small creaks and mutterings from the old house, some of them so familiar that she remembered them from her childhood. She could hear the sound of voices, of Gran and Old Bob, whispering to each other in the kitchen as they drank their morning coffee and waited for her to come out for breakfast.

But the voices were only in her mind, of course. Old Bob and Gran were gone.

Nest Freemark rose to a sitting position, drew up her long legs to her chest, rested her forehead against her knees, and closed her eyes. Gone. Both of them. Gran for five years and Old Bob since May. It was hard to believe, even now. She wished every day that she could have

11

them back again. Even for five minutes. Even for five seconds.

The sounds of the house wrapped her, small and comforting, all part of her nineteen years of life. She had always lived in this house, right up to the day she had left for college in September of last year, a freshman on a full ride at one of the most prestigious schools in the country. Northwestern University. Her grandfather had been so proud, telling her she should remember she had earned the right to attend this school, but the school, in turn, had merited her interest, so both of them should get something out of the bargain. He had laughed, his voice low and deep, his strong hands coming about her shoulders to hold her, and she had known instinctively that he was holding her for Gran, as well.

Now he was gone, dead of a heart attack three days before the end of her first year, gone in a moment, the doctor said afterward—no pain, no suffering, the way it should be. She had come to accept the doctor's reassurance, but it didn't make her miss her grandfather any the less. With both Gran and Old Bob gone, and her parents gone longer still, she had only herself to rely upon.

But, then, she supposed in a way that had always been so.

She lifted her head and smiled. It was how she had grown up, wasn't it? Learning to be alone, to be independent, to accept that she would never be like any other child?

She ticked off the ways in which she was different, running through them in a familiar litany that helped define and settle the borders of her life.

She could do magic—had been able to do magic for a

long time. It had frightened her at first, confused and troubled her, but she had learned to adapt to the magic's demands, taught first by Gran, who had once had use of the magic herself, and later by Pick. She had learned to control and nurture it, to find a place for it in her life without letting it consume her. She had discovered how to maintain the balance within herself in the same way that Pick was always working to maintain the balance in the park.

Pick, her best friend, was a six-inch-high sylvan, a forest creature who looked for the most part like something a child had made of the discards of a bird's nest, with body and limbs of twigs and hair and beard of moss. Pick was the guardian of Sinnissippi Park, sent to keep in balance the magic that permeated all things and to hold in check the feeders that worked to upset that balance. It was a big job for a lone sylvan, as he was fond of saying, and over the years various generations of the Freemark women had helped him. Nest was the latest. Perhaps she would be the last.

There was her family, of course. Gran had possessed the magic, as had others of the Freemark women before her. Not Old Bob, who had struggled all his life to accept that the magic even existed. Maybe not her mother, who had died three months after Nest was born and whose life remained an enigma. But her father . . . She shook her head at the walls. Her father. She didn't like to think of him, but he was a fact of her life, and there was enough time and distance between them now that she could accept what he had been. A demon. A monster. A seducer. The killer of both her mother and her grandmother. Dead now, destroyed by his own ambition and hate, by Gran's magic and his own, by Nest's determination, and by Wraith.

Wraith. She looked out the window in the diminishing shadows and shivered. The ways in which she had been different from other children began and ended with Wraith.

She sighed and shook her head mockingly. Enough of that sort of rumination.

She rose and walked into the bathroom, turned on the shower, let it run hot, and stepped in. She stood with her eyes closed and the water streaming over her, lost in the heat and the damp. She was nineteen and stood just under five feet ten inches. Her honey-colored hair was still short and curly, but most of her freckles were gone. Her green eyes dominated her smooth, round face. Her body was lean and fit. She was the best middle-distance runner ever to come out of the state of Illinois and one of the best in history. She didn't think about her talent much, but it was always there, in much the same way as her magic. She wondered often if her running ability was tied in some way to her use of the magic. There was no obvious connection and even Pick tended to brush the suggestion aside, but she wondered anyway. She had been admitted to Northwestern on a full track-and-field scholarship. Her grades were good, but it was her athletic skills that got her in. She had won several middle-distance events at last spring's NCAA track-and-field championships. She had already broken several college records and one world. In two years the summer Olympics would be held in Melbourne, Australia. Nest Freemark was expected to contend for a medal in multiple running events. She was expected to win at least one gold.

She turned off the shower, stepped out onto the mat, grabbed a towel, and dried herself off. She tried not to think about the Olympics too often. It was too distant in time and too mind-boggling to consider. She had learned a hard lesson when she was fourteen and her father had revealed himself for what he was. Never take anything in your life for granted; always be prepared for radical change.

Besides, there were more pressing problems just now. There was school; she had to earn grades high enough to allow her to continue to train and to compete. There was Pick, who was persistent and unending in his demand that she give more of her time and effort to helping him with the park—which seemed silly until she listened to his reasoning.

And, right at the moment, there was the matter of the house.

She dressed slowly, thinking of the house, which was the reason she was home this weekend when her time would have been better spent at school, studying. With her grandfather's death, the house and all of its possessions had passed to her. She had spent the summer going through it, room by room, closet by closet, cataloguing, boxing, packing, and sorting what would stay and go. It was her home, but she was barely there enough to look after it properly and, Pick's entreaties notwithstanding, she had no real expectation of coming back after graduation to live. The Realtors, sensing this, had already begun to descend. The house and lot were in a prime location. She could get a good price if she was to sell. The money could be put to good use helping defray her training and competition expenses. The real estate market was strong just now, a seller's market. Wasn't this the right time to act?

She had received several offers over the summer, and this past week Allen Kruppert had called from ERA Realty to tender one so ridiculously high that she had agreed to consider it. She had come after classes on Friday, skipping track-and-field practice, so that she could meet with Allen on Saturday morning and look over the papers. Allen was a rotund, jovial young man, whom she had met on several occasions at church picnics, and he impressed her because he never tried to pressure her into anything where the house was concerned but seemed content just to present his offers and step back. The house was not listed, but if she was to make the decision to sell, she knew, she would almost certainly list it with him. The papers he had provided on this latest offer sat on the kitchen table where she had left them last night. The prospective buyer had already signed. The financing was in place. All that was needed was her signature and the deal was done.

She put the papers aside and sat down to eat a bowl of cereal with her orange juice and coffee, her curly hair still damp against her face as golden light spread through the curtained windows and the sun rose over the trees.

If she signed, her financial concerns for the immediate future would be over.

Pick, of course, would have a heart attack. Which was not a good thing if you were already a hundred and fifty years old.

She was just finishing the cereal when she heard a knock at the back door. She frowned; it was only eight o'clock in the morning, not the time people usually came calling. Besides, no one ever used the back door, except . . .

She walked from the kitchen down the hall to the porch. A shadowy figure stood leaning into the screen, trying to peer inside. Couldn't be, could it? But, as she stepped down to unlatch the screen door, she could already see it was.

"Hey, Nest," Robert Heppler said.

He stood with his hands shoved deep into the pockets of his jeans and one tennis shoe bumping nervously against the worn threshold. "You going to invite me in or what?" He gave her one of his patented cocky grins and tossed back the shoulder-length blond hair from his angular face.

She shook her head. "I don't know. What are you doing here, anyway?"

"You mean like, 'here at eight o'clock in the morning,' or like, 'here in Hopewell as opposed to Palo Alto'? You're wondering if I was tossed out of school, right?"

"Were you?"

"Naw. Stanford needs me to keep its grade point average high enough to attract similarly brilliant students. I was just in the neighborhood and decided to stop by, share a few laughs, maybe see if you're in the market for a boyfriend." He was talking fast and loose to keep up his confidence. He glanced past her toward the kitchen. "Do I smell coffee? You're alone, aren't you? I mean, I'm not interrupting anything, am I?"

"Jeez, Robert, you are such a load." She sighed and stepped back. "Come on in."

She beckoned him to follow and led him down the

hall. The screen door banged shut behind them and she winced, remembering how Gran had hated it when she did that.

"So what are you really doing here?" she pressed him, gesturing vaguely in the direction of the kitchen table as she reached for the coffeepot and a cup. The coffee steamed in the morning air as she poured it.

He shrugged, giving her a furtive look. "I saw your car, knew you were home, thought I should say hello. I know it's early, but I was afraid I might miss you."

She handed him the coffee and motioned for him to sit down, but he remained standing. "I've been waiting to hear from you," she said pointedly.

"You know me, I don't like to rush things." He looked away quickly, unable to meet her steady gaze. He sipped gingerly from his cup, then made a face. "What is this stuff?"

Nest lost her patience. "Look, did you come here to insult me, or do you need something, or are you just lonely again?"

He gave her his hurt puppy look. "None of the above." He glanced down at the real estate papers, which were sitting on the counter next to him, then looked up at her again. "I just wanted to see you. I didn't see you all summer, what with you off running over hill and dale and cinder track."

"Robert, don't start . . ."

"Okay, I know, I know. But it's true. I haven't seen you since your grandfather's funeral."

"And whose fault is that, do you think?"

He pushed his glasses further up on his nose and screwed up his mouth. "Okay, all right. It's my fault. I haven't seen you because I knew how badly I messed up."

"You were a jerk, Robert."

He flinched as if struck. "I didn't mean anything."

"You didn't?" A slow flush worked its way up her neck and into her cheeks. "My grandfather's funeral service was barely finished and there you were, making a serious effort to grope me. I don't know what that was all about, but I didn't appreciate it one bit."

He shook his head rapidly. "I wasn't trying to grope you exactly."

"Yes, you were. Exactly. You might have done yourself some good, you know, if you'd stuck around to apologize afterward instead of running off."

His laugh was forced. "I was running for my life. You just about took my head off."

She stared at him, waiting. She knew how he felt about her, how he had always felt about her. She knew this was difficult for him and she wasn't making it any easier. But his misguided attempt at an intimate relationship was strictly one-sided and she had to put a stop to it now or whatever was left of their friendship would go right out the window.

He took a deep breath. "I made a big mistake, and I'm sorry. I guess I just thought you needed . . . that you wanted someone to . . . Well, I just wasn't thinking, that's all." He pushed back his long hair nervously. "I'm not so good at stuff like that, and you, well, you know how I feel . . ." He stopped and looked down at his feet. "It was stupid. I'm really sorry."

She didn't say anything, letting him dangle in the wind a little longer, letting him wonder. He looked up at her after a minute, meeting her gaze squarely for the first time. "I don't know what else to say, Nest. I'm sorry. Are we still friends?"

Even though he had grown taller and gotten broader through the shoulders, she still saw him as being fourteen. There was a little-boy look and sound to him that she thought he might never entirely escape.

"Are we?" he pressed.

She gave him a considering look. "Yes, Robert, we are. We always will be, I hope. But we're just friends, okay? Don't try to make it into anything else. If you do, you're just going to make me mad all over again."

He looked doubtful, but nodded anyway. "Okay." He glanced down again at the real estate papers. "Are you going to sell the house?"

"Robert!"

"Well, that's what it looks like."

"I don't care what it looks like, it's none of your business!" Irritated at herself for being so abrupt, she added, "Look, I haven't decided anything yet."

He put his coffee cup in the exact center of the papers, making a ring. "I don't think you should sell."

She snatched the cup away. "Robert . . ."

"Well, I don't. I think you should let some time pass before you do anything." He held up his hands in a placating gesture. "Wait, let me finish. My dad says you should never make any big changes right after someone you love dies. You should wait at least a year. You should give yourself time to grieve, to let everything settle so you know what you really want. I don't think he's right about much, but I think he might be right about this."

She pictured Robert's father in her mind, a spectacled, gentle man who was employed as a chemical engineer but spent all his free time engaged in gardening and lawn care. Robert used to call him Mr. Green Jeans and swore that his father would have been happier if his son had been born a plant.

"Robert," she said gently, "that's very good advice."

He stared at her in surprise.

"I mean it. I'll give it some thought."

She put the coffee cups aside. Robert was annoying, but she liked him anyway. He was funny and smart and fearless. Maybe more to the point, she could depend on him. He had stood up for her five years earlier when her father had come back into her life. If not for Robert, her grandfather would never have found her trussed up in the caves below the Sinnissippi Park cliffs. It was Robert who had come after her on the night she had confronted her father, when it seemed she was all alone. She had knocked the pins out from under him for his trouble, leaving him senseless on the ground while she went on alone. But he had cared enough to follow.

She felt a momentary pang at the memory. Robert was the only real friend she had left from those days.

"I have to go back to school tonight," she said. "How long do you have?"

He shrugged. "Day after tomorrow."

"You came all the way home from California for the weekend?"

He looked uncomfortable. "Well . . ."

"To visit your parents?"

"Nest . . ."

"You can't say it, can you?"

He shook his head and blushed. "No."

She nodded. "Just so you don't think I can't see through you like glass. You just watch yourself, buster."

He looked down at his feet, embarrassed. She liked him like this—sweet and vulnerable. "You want to walk

over to Gran and Grandpa's graves with me, put some
flowers in their urns?"

He brightened at once. "Sure."

She was already heading for the hall closet. "Let me
get my coat, Mr. Smooth."

"Jeez," he said.

CHAPTER 2

They went out the porch door, down the steps, across the yard, and through the hedgerow that marked the back end of the Freemark property, then struck out into Sinnissippi Park. Nest carried a large bundle of flowers she had purchased the night before and left sitting overnight in a bucket of water on the porch. It was not yet nine, and the air was still cool and the grass slick with damp in the pale morning light. The park stretched away before them, broad expanses of lush, new-mown grass fading into distant, shadowy woods and ragged curtains of mist that rose off the Rock River. The bare earth of the base paths, pitcher's mounds, and batting boxes of the ball diamonds cornering the central open space were dark and hard with moisture and the night's chill. The big shade trees had shed most of their leaves, the fall colors carpeting the areas beneath them in a patchwork mix of red, gold, orange, and brown. Park toys dotted the landscape like weird sculpture, and the wooden trestle and chute for the toboggan slide glimmered with a thin coating of frost. The crossbar at the entrance was lowered, the fall hours in effect so that there was no vehicle access to the park until after ten. In the distance, a solitary walker was towed in the wake of a hard-charging

23

Irish setter that bounded through the haze of soft light and mist in a brilliant flash of rust.

The cemetery lay at the west end of the park on the other side of a chain-link fence. Having grown up in the park, they had been climbing that fence since they were kids—Robert and Cass Minter and Brianna Brown and Jared Scott and herself. Best friends for years, they had shared adventures and discoveries and hopes and dreams. Everything but the truth about who Nest was.

Robert shoved his bare hands in his pockets and exhaled a plume of white moisture. "We should have driven," he declared.

He was striding out ahead of her, taking the lead in typical Robert fashion, not in the least intimidated by the fact that she was taller and stronger and far more familiar with where she was going than he was.

She smiled in spite of herself. Robert would lead even if he were blindfolded.

She remembered telling him her deepest secret once, long ago, on the day after she had eluded him on her way to the deadly confrontation with her father. She had done something to him, he insisted, and he wanted to know what it was. That was the price he was demanding for his help in getting into the hospital to see Jared. She told him the truth, that she had used magic. She told him in a way that was meant to leave him in doubt. He could not quite believe her, but not quite ignore her, either. He had never been able to resolve his confusion, and that was a part of what attracted him to her, she supposed.

But there were distances between them that Robert could not even begin to understand. Between her and everyone she knew, now that Gran was gone, because Nest was the only one who could do magic, the only one who would ever be able to do magic, the only one who would probably ever even know that magic was out there. She was the one who had been born to it, a legacy passed down through generations of the Freemark women, but through her demon father, as well. Magic that could come to her in the blink of an eye, could come unbidden at times. Magic that lived within her heart and mind, a part of her life that she must forever keep secret, because the danger that came from others knowing far outweighed the burden of clandestine management. Magic to heal and magic to destroy. She was still struggling to understand it. She could still feel it developing within her.

She looked off into the shadows of the woods that flanked the cliffs and cemetery ahead, where the night still lingered in dark patches and the feeders lurked. She did not see them, but she could sense that they were there. As she had always been able to when others could not. Unseen and unknown, the feeders existed on the fringes of human consciousness. Sylvans like Pick helped to keep them in check by working to maintain a balance in the magic that was invested in and determinative of the behavior of all living things. But humans were prone to adversely affect that balance, tilting it mostly without even knowing, changing it with their behavior and their feelings, altering it in the careless, unseeing way that mudslides altered landscapes.

This was the other world, the one to which Nest alone had access. Since she was very small, she had worked to understand it, to help Pick maintain it, and to find a way to reconcile it with the world that everyone else inhabited and believed fully defined. There, in no-man's-land between the known and the secret, she was an anomaly, never entirely like her friends, never just another child.

"You've lived in your grandparents' house all your life," Robert said suddenly, eyes determinedly fixed in a forward direction. They were crossing the entrance road and moving into the scattering of shade trees and spruce that bordered the picnic grounds leading to the chain-link fence and the cemetery. "That house is your home, Nest. If you sell it, you won't have a home anymore."

She scuffed at the damp grass with her tennis shoes. "I know that, Robert."

"Do you need the money?"

"I could use it. Training and competition is expensive. The school doesn't pay for everything."

"Why don't you take out a mortgage, then? Why sell, if you don't have to?"

She couldn't explain it to him, not if she tried all day. It had to do with being who she was, and that wasn't something Robert could know about without having lived her life. She didn't even want to talk about it with him because it was personal and private.

"Maybe I want a new home," she said enigmatically, giving sudden, unexpected voice to the feelings that churned inside her. It was hard to keep from crying as she thought back upon their genesis.

Her friends were gone, all but Robert. She could still see their faces, but she saw them not as they were at the end, but as they were when they were still fourteen and it seemed as if nothing in their lives would ever change. She saw them as they were during that last summer they were all together, on that last weekend before everything changed—when they were close and tight and believed they could stand up to anything.

Brianna Brown and Jared Scott moved away within a year of that summer. Brianna wrote Nest at first, but the time between letters steadily lengthened, and finally the letters ceased altogether. Nest heard later that Brianna was married and had a child.

She never heard from Jared at all.

Cass Minter remained her oldest and closest friend all through high school. Different from each other in so many ways, they continued to find common ground in a lifetime of shared experiences and mutual trust. Cass planned to go to the University of Illinois and study genetics, but two weeks before graduation, she died in her sleep. The doctor said it was an aneurysm. No one had suspected it was there.

Jared, Brianna, and Cass—all gone. Of her old friends, that left only Robert, and by the end of her freshman year at Northwestern, Nest could already feel herself beginning to drift. Her parents were gone. Her grandparents were gone. Her friends were gone. Even the cats, Mr. Scratch and Miss Minx, were gone, the former dead of old age two years earlier, the latter moved to a neighbor's home with her grandfather's passing. Her future, she thought, lay somewhere else. Her life was going in a different direction, and she could feel Hopewell receding steadily into her past.

They reached the chain-link fence and, without pausing to debate the matter, scrambled over. Holding the flowers for Nest while she completed the climb, Robert gave them a cursory sniff before handing them back. Side by side, the two made their way down the paved road that wound through the rows of tombstones and markers, feeling the October sun grow warmer against their skin as it lifted into a clear autumn sky. Summer might be behind them and winter closing fast, but there was nothing wrong with this day.

She felt her thoughts drift like clouds, returning to the past. She had acquired new friends in high school but they lacked the history she shared with the old, and she couldn't seem to get past that.

Of course, the Petersons still lived next door and Mildred Walker still lived down the street. Reverend Emery still conducted services at the First Congregational Church, and a few of her grandfather's old cronies still gathered for coffee at Josie's each morning to share gossip and memories. Once in a while, she even saw Josie, but she could sense the other's discomfort, and understanding its source, kept her distance. In any event, these were people of a different generation, and their real friendships had been with her grandparents rather than with her.

There was always Pick, though. And, until a year or so ago, there had been Wraith . . .

Robert left the roadway to cut through the rows of markers, bearing directly for the gravesites of her grandparents. Isn't it odd, she thought, trailing distractedly in his wake, that Hopewell should feel so alien to her? Small towns were supposed to be stable and unchanging. It was part of their charm, one of their virtues, that while larger communities would almost certainly undergo some form of upheaval, they would remain the same. But Hopewell didn't feel like that to her. It felt altered in ways that transcended expectation, ways that did not involve population growth or economic peaks. Those were substantially the same as they had been five years earlier. It was something else, an intangible that she believed might have influenced only her.

Perhaps it *was* her, she pondered. Perhaps it was she who had changed and not the town at all.

They walked up to her grandparents' graves and stopped below the markers, looking down at the mounds that fronted them. Gran's was thick and smooth with autumn grass; the grass on Old Bob's was still sparse and the earth less settled. Identical tombstones marked their resting places. Nest read her grandmother's. EVELYN OPAL FREEMARK. BELOVED WIFE OF ROBERT. SLEEP WITH ANGELS. WAKE WITH GOD. Old Bob had chosen the wording for Gran's marker, and Nest had simply copied it for his.

Her mother's gravestone stood just to the left. CAITLIN ANNE FREEMARK. BELOVED DAUGHTER & MOTHER.

A fourth plot, just a grassy space now, was reserved for her.

She studied it thoughtfully for a moment, then set about dividing up the flowers she had brought, arranging them carefully in each of the three metal vases that stood on tripods before the headstones. Robert watched her as she worked, saying nothing.

"Bring some water," she said, pointing toward the spigot and watering can that sat in a small concrete well several dozen yards off.

Robert did, then poured water into each vase, being careful not to disturb Nest's arrangements.

Together, they stood looking down at the plots, the sun streaming through the branches of the old shade trees that surrounded them in curtains of dappled brightness.

"I remember all the times your grandmother baked us cookies," Robert said after a minute. "She would sit us down at the picnic table out back and bring us a plate heaped with them and glasses of cold milk. She was always saying a child couldn't grow up right without cookies and milk. I could never get that across to my mother. She thought you couldn't grow up right without vegetables."

Nest grinned. "Gran was big on vegetables, too. You just weren't there for that particular lecture."

"Every Christmas we had that cookie bake in your kitchen. Balls of dough and cookie sheets and cutters and frosting and little bottles of sprinkles and whatnot everywhere. We trashed her kitchen, and she never blinked an eye."

"I remember making cookies for bake sales." Nest shook her head. "For the church, for mission aid or something. It seemed for a while that I was doing it every other weekend. Gran never objected once, even after she stopped going to church altogether."

Robert nodded. "Your grandmother never needed to go to church. I think God probably told her she didn't have to go, that he would come to see her instead."

Nest looked at him. "That's a very nice thing to say, Robert."

He pursed his lips and shrugged. "Yeah, well, I'm just trying to get back into your good graces. Anyway, I liked your grandmother. I always thought, when things got a little rough at home, that if they got real bad I could move in with you if I really wanted to. Sure, you and your grandfather might object, but your grandmother would have me in an instant. That's what I thought."

Nest nodded. "She probably would have, too."

Robert folded his arms across his chest. "You can't sell your house, Nest. You know why? Because your grandmother's still there."

Nest was silent for a moment. "I don't think so."

"Yes, she is. She's in every room and closet, in every corner, and under every carpet, down in the basement and up in the attic. That's where she is, Nest. Where else would she be?"

Nest didn't answer.

"Up in Heaven playing a harp? I wouldn't think so. Too boring. Not floating around on a cloud either. Not your grandmother. She's in that house, and I don't think you should move out on her."

Nest wondered what Robert would say if he knew the truth of things. She wondered what he would say if he knew that Gran's transgressions years earlier had doomed her family in ways that would horrify him, that Gran had roamed the park at night like a wild thing, that she had run with the feeders and cast her magic in dangerous ways, that her encounter with a demon had brought about both her own death and the death of Nest's mother. Would he think that she belonged in an afterlife of peace and light or that perhaps she should be consigned to a place where penance might be better served?

She regretted the thought immediately, a rumination both uncharitable and harsh, but she found she could not dispel it entirely.

Still, was Robert's truth any less valid in determining the worth of Gran's life than her own?

Robert cleared his throat to regain her attention. She looked at him. "I'll think about it," she said.

"Good. 'Cause there are a lot of memories in that house, Nest."

Yes, there are, she thought, looking off into the sun-streaked trees to where the river was a blue glint through the dark limbs. But not all the memories were ones she wanted to keep, and perhaps memories alone were not enough in any case. There was a lack of substance in memories and a danger in embracing them. You did not want to be tied too closely to something you could never recapture.

"I wouldn't sell if it was me, you know," Robert persisted. "I wouldn't sell unless I didn't have a choice."

He was pushing his luck, irritating her with his insistence on making the decision for her, on assuming she couldn't think it through as carefully as he could and needed his advice. It was typical Robert.

She gave him a look and dared him to speak. To his credit, he didn't. "Let's go," she said.

They walked back through the cemetery in silence, climbed the fence a second time, and crossed the park. The crossbar was raised now, and a few cars had driven in. One or two families were playing on the swing sets, and a picnic was being spread in a sunny spot across from the Sinnissippi burial mounds. Nest thought suddenly of Two Bears, of O'olish Amaneh, the last of the Sinnissippi. She hadn't thought of him in a long time. She hadn't seen him in five years. Now and then she wondered what had become of him. As she wondered what had become of John Ross, the Knight of the Word.

The memories flooded through her.

At the hedgerow bordering her yard, she leaned over impulsively and gave Robert a kiss on the cheek. "Thanks for coming by. It was sweet of you."

Robert looked flustered. He was being dismissed, and he wasn't ready for that. "Uh, are you, do you have any plans for the rest of the day? Or anything?"

"Or anything?" she repeated.

"Well, lunch, maybe. You know what I mean."

She knew exactly. She knew better than he did. Robert

would never change. The best thing she could do for them both was not to encourage him.

"I'll call you if I get some time later, okay?"

It had to be okay, of course, so Robert shrugged and nodded. "If it doesn't work out, I'll see you at Thanksgiving. Or Christmas."

She nodded. "I'll drop you a note at school. Study hard, Robert. I need to know you're out there setting an example for the rest of us."

He grinned, regaining a bit of his lost composure. "It's a heck of a burden, but I try." He began to move away into the park. "See you, Nest." He tossed back his long blond hair and gave her a jaunty wave.

She watched him walk down the service road that ran behind her backyard, then cut across the park toward his home, which lay beyond the woods at the east end. He grew smaller and less distinct as he went, receding slowly into the distance. It was like watching her past fade before her eyes. Even when she saw him again, it would not be the same. She knew it instinctively. They would be different people leading different lives, and there would be no going back to the lives they had lived as children.

Her throat tightened, and she took a deep breath. *Oh, Robert!*

She waited a moment longer, letting the memories flood through her one final time, then turned away.

CHAPTER 3

As Nest pushed through the hedgerow into her back-yard, Pick dropped from the branches onto her shoulder with a pronounced grunt.

"That boy is sweet on you. Sweet, sweet, sweet."

Pick's voice was harried and thin, and when he spoke he sounded like one of those fuzzy creatures on *Sesame Street*. Nest thought he wouldn't be so smug if he could hear himself on tape sometime.

"They're all sweet on me," she said, deflecting his dig, moving toward the picnic table. "Didn't you know?"

"No, I didn't. But if that one were any sweeter, he could be bottled for syrup." Pick sniffed. "Classic case of youthful hormonal imbalance."

She laughed. "Since when did you know anything about 'youthful hormonal imbalance'? Didn't you tell me once that you were born in a pod?"

"That doesn't mean I don't know about humans. I suppose you don't think I've learned anything in my life, is that it? Since I'm roughly ten times your age, it's probably safe to assume I've learned a great deal more than you have!"

She straddled one of the picnic bench seats, and Pick slid down her arm and jumped onto the table in front of

34

her, hands on hips, eyes defiant. At first glance, he looked like a lot of different things. A quick glimpse suggested he was some sort of weird forest flotsam and jetsam, shed by a big fir or blown off an aging cedar. A second look suggested he was a poorly designed child's doll made out of tree parts. A thick layer of bark encrusted him from head to foot, and tiny leaves blossomed out of various nooks and crannies where his joints were formed. He was a sylvan, in fact, six inches high and so full of himself Nest was sometimes surprised he didn't just float away on the wind. He never stopped talking and, in the many years she had known him, had seldom stopped moving. He was full of energy and advice, and he had a tendency to overwhelm her with both.

"Where have you been?" he demanded, clearly agitated that he had been forced to wait on her return.

She brushed back her cinnamon-colored hair and shook her head at him. "We walked over to the cemetery and put flowers on my grandparents' and mother's graves. What is your problem, anyway?"

"*My* problem?" Pick huffed. "Well, since you asked, *my* problem is that I have this entire park to look after, all two-hundred-odd acres of it, and I have to do it *by myself*! Now, you might say, 'But that's your job, Pick, so what are you complaining about?' Well, that's true enough, isn't it? But time was I had a little help from a certain young lady who lived in this house. Now what was her name again? I forget, it's been so long since I've seen her."

"Oh, please!" Nest moaned.

"Sure, it's easy for you to go off to your big school and your other life, but words like 'commitment' and 'responsibility' mean something to some of us." He stamped hard on the picnic table. "I thought the least you could do was to spend *some* time with me this weekend, this *one* solitary weekend in the *whole* of this autumn that you've chosen to come home! But no, I haven't seen you for five minutes, have I? And now, today, what do you do? Go off with that Heppler boy instead of looking for me! I could have gone to the graves with you, you know. I would have liked to go, as a matter of fact. Your grandmother was my friend, too, and I don't forget my friends . . ." He trailed off meaningfully.

"Unlike some people," she finished for him.

"I wasn't going to say that."

"Oh, not for a minute." She sighed. "Robert came by to apologize for his behavior last spring at the funeral."

"Oh, that. Criminy." Pick knew right away. They might fight like cats and dogs, but they confided in each other anyway.

"So I had to spend a little time with him, and I didn't think it would hurt if we walked over to the cemetery. I was saving the rest of the day to work with you, all right? Now stop complaining."

He held up his twiggy hands. "Too late. Way too late."

"To stop complaining?"

"No! To do any work!"

She hunched down so that her face was close to his. It was a little like facing down a beetle. "What are you talking about? It isn't even noon. I don't have to go back until tonight. Why is it too late?"

He folded his stick arms across his narrow chest, scrunched up his face, and looked off into the park. She always wondered how he could make his features move like that when they were made out of wood, but since he had a tendency to regard such questions as some sort of invasion of his personal life, she'd never had the courage to ask. She waited patiently as he sighed and fussed and jittered about.

"There's someone here to see you," he announced finally.

"Who?"

"Well, I think you had better see for yourself."

She studied him a moment. He refused to meet her eyes, and a cold feeling seeped through her. "Someone from before?" she asked quietly. "From when my father . . . ?"

"No, no!" He held up his hands quickly to calm her fears. "No one you've met before. No one from then. But . . ." He stopped. "I can't tell you who it is without getting myself in deeper than I care to go. I've thought about it, and it will be better if you just come with me and ask your questions there."

She nodded. "Ask my questions where?"

"Down by the bayou below the deep woods. She's waiting there."

She. Nest frowned. "Well, when did *she* get here?"

"Early this morning." Pick sighed. "I just wish these things wouldn't happen so suddenly, that's all. I just wish I'd be given a little notice beforehand. It's hard enough doing my job without these constant interruptions."

"Well, maybe it won't take long," she offered, trying to ease his obvious distress. "If it doesn't, we can still get some work done in the park before I have to go back."

He didn't even argue the point. His anger was deflated, his fire burned to ash. He just stared off at nothing and nodded.

Nest straightened. "Pick, it's a beautiful October morning, filled with sunshine. The park has never looked better. I haven't seen a single feeder, so the magic is in some sort of balance. You've done your job well, even without my help. Enjoy yourself for five minutes."

She reached over, plucked him off the tabletop, and set him on her shoulder. "Come on, let's take a walk over to the deep woods."

Without waiting for an answer, she rose and headed for the hedgerow, pushing through the thin branches into the park. Sunshine streamed down out of a cloudless sky, filling the morning air with the pale, washed-out light peculiar to late autumn. There was a nip in the air, a hint of winter on the rise, but there was also the scent of dried leaves and cut grass mingling with the pungent smells of cooking that wafted out of barbecue grills and kitchen vents from the houses bordering the park. Cars dotted the parking lots and turnoffs beneath the trees, and families were setting out picnic lunches and running with dogs and throwing Frisbees across the grassy play areas ahead.

On such days, she thought to herself with a smile, she could almost imagine she would never leave.

"Pick, if we don't get back to it today, I'll come home again next weekend," she announced impulsively. "I know I haven't been as good about working with you as I should. I've let other things get in the way, and I shouldn't do that. This is more important."

He rode her shoulder in silence, apparently not ready to be mollified. She glanced down at him covertly. He didn't seem angry. He just seemed distant, as if he were looking beyond her words to something else.

She traversed the central open space to the parking lot serving the ball diamonds and play areas at the far end of the park, crossed the road, and entered the woods. The

toboggan slide stood waiting for winter, the last sections
of the wooden chute and the ladder that allowed access
to the loading platform still in storage, removed and
locked away as a safeguard against kids' climbing on and
falling off before the snows came. It never seemed to
help much, of course. Kids climbed anything that had
footholds whether it was intended for that purpose or
not, and the absence of stairs just made the challenge that
much more attractive. Nest smiled faintly. She had done
it herself more times than she could count. But she supposed that one day some kid would fall off and the parents would sue and that would be the end of it; the slide
would come down.

She walked through the hilly woods that marked the
beginning of the eastern end of the park, alone now with
Pick, wrapped in the silence of the big hardwoods. The
trees rose bare-limbed and skeletal against the autumn
sky, stripped of their leaves, waiting for winter's approach. Their colors not yet completely faded, the fallen
leaves formed a thick carpet on the ground, still damp
and soft with morning dew. She peered ahead into the
tangled clutter of limbs and scrub and shadow. The forest
had a bristling, hostile appearance. Everything looked as
if it were wrapped in barbed wire.

Her long strides covered the ground rapidly as she
descended to the creek that wound out of the woods
and emptied into the bayou. How much bigger the park
had seemed when she was a child growing up in it.
Sometimes her home felt the same way—too small
for her now. She supposed it was true of her child's
world entirely, that she had outgrown it, that she
needed more room.

"How much farther?" she asked as she crossed the

wooden bridge that spanned the creek bed, and started up the slope toward the deep woods.

"Bear right," he grunted.

She angled toward the bayou, following the tree line. She glanced involuntarily toward the deep woods, just as she always did, any time she came here, remembering what had taken place there five years earlier. Sometimes she could see it all quite clearly, could see her father and John Ross and the maentwrog. Sometimes she could even see Wraith.

"Has there been any sign of him?" she asked suddenly, the words escaping from her mouth before she could think better of them.

Pick understood what she was talking about. "Nothing. Not since . . ."

Not since she turned eighteen two summers ago, she finished as he trailed off. That was the last time either of them had seen Wraith. After so many years of having him around, it seemed impossible that he could be gone. Her father had created the giant ghost wolf out of his dark magic to serve as a protector for the daughter he intended one day to return for. Wraith was to keep her safe while she grew. All the time she had worked with Pick to keep the magic in balance and the feeders from luring children into the park, Wraith had warded her. But Gran had discerned Wraith's true purpose and altered his makeup with her own magic in such a way that when her father returned to claim her, Wraith destroyed him.

She could see it happening all over again through the dark huddle of the trees. Night cloaked the deep woods, and on the slopes of the park, over by the toboggan slide, Fourth of July fireworks were exploding in a shower of bright colors and deep booms. The white oak that had

imprisoned the maentwrog was in shreds, and the maentwrog itself was turned to ash. John Ross lay motionless
upon the charred earth, damaged and exhausted. Nest
faced her father, who approached with hand outstretched
and soothing, persuasive words. *You belong to me. You
are my blood. You are my life.*

And Wraith, come out of the night like an express train
exploding free of a mountain tunnel . . .

She was fourteen when she learned the truth about her
father. And her family. And herself. Wraith had stayed as
her protector afterward, a shadowy presence in the park,
showing himself only occasionally as the next few years
passed, but always when the feeders came too close.
Now and then she would think that he seemed less substantive than she remembered, less solid when he loomed
out of the darkness. But that seemed silly.

However, as she neared her eighteenth birthday, Wraith
turned pale and then ethereal and finally disappeared completely. It happened quickly. One day he was just as he had
always been, his thick body massive and bristling, his gray
and black tiger-stripe facial markings wicked and men-
acing, and the next he was fading away. Like the ghost he
had always seemed, but finally become.

The last time she saw him, she was walking the park at
sunset, and he had appeared unexpectedly from the
shadows. He was already so insubstantial she could see
right through him. She stopped, and he walked right up
to her, passing so close that she felt his rough coat brush
against her. She blinked in surprise at the unexpected
contact, and when she turned to follow him, he was already gone.

She hadn't seen him since. Neither had Pick. That was
almost a year and a half ago.

"Where do you think he's gone?" she asked quietly.

Pick, riding her shoulder in silence, shrugged. "Can't say."

"He was disappearing though, there at the end, wasn't he?"

"It looked that way, sure enough."

"So maybe he was all used up."

"Maybe."

"Except you told me magic never gets used up. You told me it works like energy; it becomes transformed. So if Wraith was transformed, what was he transformed into?"

"Criminy, Nest!"

"Have you noticed anything different about the park?"

The sylvan tugged at his beard. "No, nothing."

"So where did he go then?"

Pick wheeled on her. "You know what? If you spent a little more time helping me out around here, maybe you could answer the question for yourself instead of pestering me! Now turn down here and head for the riverbank and stop asking me stuff!"

She did as he asked, still pondering the mystery of Wraith, thinking that maybe because she was grown up and Wraith had served his purpose, he had reverted to whatever form he had occupied before he was created to be her protector. Yes, maybe that was it.

But her doubts lingered.

She reached the riverbank and stopped. The bayou spread out before her, a body of water dammed up behind the levy on which the railroad tracks had been built to carry the freight trains west out of Chicago. Reeds and cattails grew in thick clumps along the edges of the water, and shallow inlets that eroded the riverbank were filmed with stagnation and debris. There was little movement in the water, the swift current of the Rock River absent here.

She looked down at Pick. "Now what?"

He gestured to her right without speaking.

She turned and found herself staring right at the tatterdemalion. She had seen only a handful in her life, and then just for a few seconds each time, but she knew this one for what it was right away. It stood less than a dozen yards away, slight and ephemeral in the pale autumn light. Diaphanous clothing and silky hair trailed from its body and limbs in wispy strands, as if on the verge of being carried off by the wind. The tatterdemalion's features were childlike and haunted. This one was a girl. Her eyes were depthless in dark-ringed sockets and her rosebud mouth pinched against her sunken face. Her skin was the color and texture of parchment. She might have been a runaway who had not eaten in days and was still terrified of what she had left behind. She had that look. But tatterdemalions were nothing of the sort. They weren't really children at all, let alone runaways. They weren't even human.

"Are you Nest Freemark?" this one asked in her soft, lilting childlike voice.

"I am," Nest answered, risking a quick glance down at Pick. The sylvan was mired in the deepest frown she had ever seen on him and was hunched forward on her shoulder in a combative stance. She had a sudden, inescapable premonition he was trying to protect her.

"My name is Ariel," said the tatterdemalion. "I have a message for you from the Lady."

Nest's throat went dry. She knew who the Lady was. The Lady was the Voice of the Word.

"I have been sent to tell you of John Ross," Ariel said.

Of course. John Ross. She had thought of him earlier that morning for the first time in weeks. She pictured him anew, enigmatic and resourceful, a mix of light and dark, gone from Hopewell five years earlier in the wake of her father's destruction, gone out of her life. Maybe she had inadvertently wished him back into it. Maybe that was why the mention of him seemed somehow inevitable.

"John Ross," she repeated, as if the words would make of his memory something more substantial.

Ariel stood motionless in a mix of shadow and sunlight, as if pinned like a butterfly to a board. When she spoke, her voice was reed-thin and faintly musical, filled with the sound of the wind rising off trees heavy with new leaves.

"He has fallen from grace," she said to Nest Freemark, and the dark eyes bore into her. "Listen, and I will tell you what has become of him."

CHAPTER 4

As with almost everything since John Ross had become a Knight of the Word, his disintegration began with a dream.

His dreams were always of the future, a future grim and horrific, one where the balance of magic had shifted so dramatically that civilization was on the verge of extinction. The Void had gained ascendancy over the Word, good had lost the eternal struggle against evil, and humanity had become a pathetic shadow of the brilliant ideal it had once approached. Men were reduced to hunters and hunted, the former led by demons and driven by feeders, the latter banded together in fortress cities and scattered outposts in a landscape fallen into ruin and neglect. Once-men and their prey, they were born of the same flesh, but changed by the separate and divisive moral codes they had embraced and by the indelible patterns of their lives. It had taken more than a decade, but in the end governments had toppled, nations had collapsed, armies had broken into pieces, and peoples worldwide had reverted to a savagery that had not been in evidence since well before the birth of Christ.

The dreams were given to John Ross for a purpose. It was the mission of a Knight of the Word to change the

course of history. The dreams were a reminder of what
the future would be like if he failed. The dreams were
also a means of discovering pivotal events that might be
altered by the Knight on waking. John Ross had learned
something of the dreams over time. The dreams always
revealed events that would occur, usually within a matter
of months. The events were always instigated by men
and women who had fallen under the sway of the demons
who served the Void. And the men and women who
would perpetrate the monstrous acts that would alter in
varying, cumulative ways the direction in which humanity drifted could always be tracked down.

But even then there was a limit to what a Knight of
the Word could do, and John Ross discovered the full
truth of this at San Sobel.

In his dream, he was traveling through the nightmare landscape of civilization's collapse on his way to
an armed camp in San Francisco. He had come from
Chicago, where another camp had fallen to an onslaught
of demons and once-men, where he had fought to save
the city and failed, where he had seen yet another small
light smothered, snuffed out in an ever-growing darkness. Thousands had died, and thousands more had been
taken to the slave pens for work and breeding. He had
come to San Francisco to prevent this happening again,
knowing that a new army was massing and moving west
to assault the Bay Area fortress, to reduce humanity's
tenuous handhold on survival by yet another digit. He
would plead with those in charge once again, knowing
that they would probably refuse to listen, distrustful of
him, fearful of his motives, knowing only that their past
was lost and their future had become an encroaching
nightmare. Now and again, someone would pay heed.

Now and again, a city would be saved. But the number of his successes was dwindling rapidly as the strength of the Void's forces grew. The outcome was inevitable; it had been foreordained since he had become a Knight of the Word years ago. His failure then had writ in stone what the future must be. Even in his determined effort to chip away the hateful letters, he was only prolonging the inevitable. Yet he went on, because that was all that was left for him to do.

The dream began in the town of San Sobel, west and south of the Mission Peak Preserve below San Francisco. It was just another town, just one more collection of empty shops and houses, of concrete streets buckling with wear and disuse, of yards and parks turned to weeds and bare earth amid a jumble of debris and abandoned cars. Wild dogs roamed in packs and feral cats slunk like shadows through the midday heat. He walked past windows and doors that gaped broken and dark like sightless eyes and voiceless mouths. Roofs had sagged and walls had collapsed; the earth was reclaiming its own. Now and again he would spy a furtive figure making its way through the rubble, a stray human in search of food and shelter, another refugee from the past. They never approached him. They saw something in him that frightened them, something he could not identify. It was in his bearing or his gaze or perhaps in the black, rune-scrolled staff that was the source of his power. He would stride down the center of a boulevard, made whole now with the fulfillment of the Word's dark prophecy, his ruined leg healed because his failure had brought that prophecy to pass, and no one would come near him. He was empowered to help them, and they shunned him as anathema. It was the final irony of his existence.

In San Sobel, no one approached him either. He saw them, the strays, hiding in the shadows, skittering from one bolt-hole to the next, but they would not come near. He walked alone through the town's ruin, his eyes set on the horizon, his mind fixed on his mission, and he came upon the woman quite unexpectedly. She did not see him. She was not even aware of him. She stood at the edge of a weed-grown lot and stared fixedly at the remains of what had once been a school. The name was still visible in the crumbling stone of an arch that bridged a drive leading up to the school's entry. SAN SOBEL PREPARATORY ACADEMY. Her gaze was unwavering as she stood there, arms folded, body swaying slightly. As he approached, he could hear small, unidentifiable sounds coming from her lips. She was worn and haggard, her hair hung limp and unwashed, and she looked as if she had not eaten in a while. There were sores on her arms and face, and he recognized the markings of one of the cluster of new diseases that were going untreated and killing with increasing regularity.

He spoke to her softly, and she did not reply. He came right up behind her and spoke again, and she did not turn.

When finally he touched her, she still did not turn, but she began to speak. It was as if he had turned on a tape recorder. Her voice was a dull, empty monotone, and her story was one that quite obviously she had told before. She related it to him without caring whether he heard her or not, giving vent to a need that was self-contained and personal and without meaningful connection to him. He was her audience, but his presence served only to trigger a release of words she would have spoken to anyone.

He was my youngest child, she said. *My boy, Teddy. He was six years old. We had enrolled him in kindergarten the year before, and now he was finishing first grade. He was so sweet. He had blond hair and blue eyes, and he was always smiling. He could change the light in a room just by walking into it. I loved him so much. Bert and I both worked, and we made pretty good money, but it was still a stretch to send him here. But it was such a good school, and we wanted him to have the best. He was very bright. He could have been anything, if he had lived.*

There was another boy in the school who was a little older, Aaron Pilkington. His father was very successful, very wealthy. Some men decided to kidnap him and make his father pay them money to get him back. They were stupid men, not even bright enough to know the best way to kidnap someone. They tried to take him out of the school. They just walked right in and tried to take him. On April Fools' Day, can you imagine that? I wonder if they knew. They just walked in and tried to take him. But they couldn't find him. They weren't even sure which room he was in, which class he attended, who his teacher was, anything. They had a picture, and they thought that would be enough. But a picture doesn't always help. Children in a picture often tend to look alike. So they couldn't find him, and the police were called, and they surrounded the school, and the men took a teacher and her class hostage because they were afraid and they didn't know what else to do, I suppose.

My son was a student in that class.

The police tried to get the men to release the teacher and the children, but the men wouldn't agree to the terms the police offered and the police wouldn't agree to the terms the men offered, and the whole thing just fell to pieces. The men grew desperate and erratic. One of them kept talking to someone who wasn't there, asking, What should he do, what should he do? They killed the teacher. The police decided they couldn't wait any longer, that the children were in too much danger. The men had moved the children to the auditorium where they held their assemblies and performed their plays. They had them all seated in the first two rows, all in a line facing the stage. When the police broke in, they started shooting. They just . . . started shooting. Everywhere. The children . . .

She never looked at him as she spoke. She never acknowledged his presence. She was inaccessible to him, lost in the past, reliving the horror of those moments. She kept her gaze fixed on the school, unwavering.

I was there, she said, her voice unchanging, toneless and empty. *I was a room mother helping out that day. There was going to be a birthday party at the end of recess. When the shooting began, I tried to reach him. I threw myself . . . His name was Teddy. Theodore, but we called him Teddy, because he was just a little boy. Teddy . . .*

Then she went silent, stared at the school a moment longer, turned, and walked off down the broken sidewalk. She seemed to know where she was going, but he could not discern her purpose. He watched after her a moment, then looked at the school.

In his mind, he could hear the sounds of gunfire and children screaming.

When he woke, he knew at once what he would do. The woman had said that one of the men spoke to someone who wasn't there. He knew from experience that it would be a demon, a creature no one but the man could see. He knew that a demon would have inspired this event, that it would have used it to rip apart the fabric of the community, to steal away San Sobel's sense of safety and tranquillity, to erode its belief that what happened in other places could not happen there. Once such seeds of doubt and fear were planted, it grew easier to undermine the foundations of human behavior and reason that kept animal madness at bay.

It was late winter, and time was already short when he left for California. He reached San Sobel more than a week before April 1, and he felt confident that he had sufficient time to prevent the impending tragedy. There had been no further dreams of this event, but that was not unusual. Often the dreams came only once, and he was forced to act on what he was given. Sometimes he did not know where the event would happen, or even when. This time he was lucky; he knew both. The demon would have set things in motion already, but Ross had come up against demons time and again since he had taken up the cause of the Word, and he was not intimidated. Demons were powerful and elusive adversaries, relentless in their hatred of humans and their determination to see them subjugated, but they were no match for him. It was the vagaries of the humans they used as their tools that more often proved troubling.

There were the feeders to be concerned about, too. The feeders were the dark things that drove humans to madness and then consumed them, creatures of the mind and soul that lived mostly in the imagination until venal behavior made them real. The feeders devoured the dark emotions of the humans they preyed upon and were sustained and given life by. Few could see them. Few had any reason to. They appeared as shadows at the corner of the eye or small movements in a hazy distance. The demons stirred them into the human population as they would a poison. If they could infect a few, the poison might spread to the many. History had proved that this was so.

The feeders would delight in a slaughter of innocents, of children who could barely understand what was wanted of them by the men John Ross would confront. He could not search out these men; he had no way to do so. Nor could he trace the demon. Demons were changelings and hid themselves with false identities. He must wait for the men and the demons who manipulated them to reveal themselves, which meant that he must be waiting at the place he expected them to strike.

So he went to San Sobel Preparatory Academy to speak with the headmaster. He did not tell the head-master of his dream, or of the demon, or of the men the demon would send, or of the horror that waited barely a week away. There was no point in doing that because he had no way to convince the headmaster he was not insane. He told the headmaster instead that he was the parent of a child who would be eligible for admission to the academy in the fall and that he would like some information on the school. He apologized for his appearance—he was wearing jeans and a blue denim shirt under his corduroy jacket with the patches on the el-bows and a pair of worn walking shoes—but he was a nature writer on assignment, and he was taking half a day off to make this visit. The headmaster took note of his odd walking staff and his limp, and his clear blue eyes and warm smile gave evidence of the fact that he was both sympathetic and understanding of his visitor's needs.

He talked to John Ross of the school's history and of its mission. He gave Ross materials to read. Finally, he took Ross on a tour of the buildings—which was what Ross had been waiting for. They passed down the shadowed corridors from one classroom to the next and at last to the auditorium where the tragedy of the dream would occur. Ross lingered, asking questions so that he would have time to study the room, to memorize its layout, its entries and exits and hiding places. A quick study was all it took. When he was satisfied, he thanked the headmaster for his time and consideration and left.

He found out later in the day that a boy named Aaron Pilkington attended the academy, that he was enrolled in the third grade, and that his parents had been made enormously wealthy through his father's work with microchips.

That night, he devised a plan. It was not complicated. He had learned that by keeping his plans simple, his chances of successfully implementing them improved. There were small lives at stake, and he did not want to expose them to any greater risk than necessary.

It seemed to him, thinking the matter through in his motel room that night, that he had everything under control.

He waited patiently for the days to pass. On the morning of April 1, he arrived at the school just before sunrise. He had visited the school late in the afternoon of the day before and left a wedge of paper in the lock of one of the classroom windows at the back of the main building so the lock would not close all the way. He slipped through the window in the darkness, listening for

the movement of other people as he did so. But the maintenance staff didn't arrive for another half hour, and he
was alone. He worked his way down the hallway to
the auditorium, found one of the storage rooms where
the play props were kept at the rear and side of the stage,
and concealed himself inside.

Then he waited.

He did not know when the attack would come, but he
did know that until the moment of his intervention, history would repeat itself and the events of the dream
would transpire exactly as related by Teddy's mother. It
was up to him to choose just when he would try to alter
the outcome.

He crouched in the darkness of his hiding place and
listened to the sounds of the school about him as the day
began. The storage room had sufficient space that he was
able to change positions and move around so his leg
didn't stiffen up. He had brought food. Time slipped
away. No one came to the auditorium. Nothing unusual
occurred.

Then the doors burst open, and Ross could hear the
screams and cries of children, the pleas of several women,
and the angry, rough voices of men fill the room. Ross
waited patiently, the storage door cracked open just far
enough that he could see what was happening. A hooded
figure bounded onto the stage between the half-closed
curtains, glanced around hurriedly, and began barking
orders. A second figure joined him. The women and children filed hurriedly into the front rows of the theater in
response to the men's directions.

Still Ross waited.

One of the men had a cell phone. It rang, and he began
talking into it, growing increasingly angry. He jumped

down off the stage, screaming obscenities into the mouth-piece. Ross slipped out of the storage room, the black staff gleaming with the magic's light. He moved slowly, steadily through the shadows, closing on the lone man who stood at the front of the stage. The man held a handgun, but he was looking at his captives. Ross could see a third man now, one standing at the far side of the room, looking out the door into the hallway.

Ross came up to the man standing on the stage and leveled him with a single blow of the staff. He caught a glimpse of the other two, the one on the phone still yelling and screaming with his back turned, the other wheeling in surprise as he caught sight of Ross. The chil-dren's eyes went wide as Ross appeared, and with a sweep of his staff Ross threw a heavy blanket of magic over the children, a weighted net that forced them to lower their heads and shield their eyes. The man at the door was swinging his AK-47 around to fire as Ross hit him with a bolt of bright magic and knocked him senseless.

The third man dropped the phone, still screaming, and brought up a second AK-47. But Ross was waiting for him as well, and again the magic lanced from the staff. A burst from the man's weapon sprayed the ceiling harm-lessly as he went down in a heap.

Ross scanned the room swiftly for other kidnappers. There were none. Just the three. The children and their teacher and two other women were still crouched in their seats, weighted down by the magic. Ross lifted it away, setting them free. No one was hurt. Everything was all right . . .

Then he saw the feeders, dozens of them, oozing through cracks in the windows and doors, sliding out of corners and alcoves, dark shadows gathering to feast, sensing something that was hidden from him.

Ross wheeled about in desperation, searching everywhere at once, his heart pounding, his mind racing . . .

And police burst through the doors and windows, shattering wood and glass. Someone was yelling, Throw down your weapons! Now, now, now! The women and children were screaming anew, scrambling out of their seats in terror, and someone was yelling, He's got a gun! Shoot him, shoot him! Ross was trying to tell them, No, no, it's all right, it's okay now! But no one was listening, and everything was chaotic and out of control, and the feeders were leaping about in a frenzy, climbing over everything, and there were weapons firing everywhere, catching the kidnapper who was just coming to his knees in front of the stage, still too stunned to know what was happening, lifting him in a red spatter and dropping him back again in a crumpled heap, and small bodies were being struck by the bullets as well, hammered sideways and sent flying as screams of fear turned to shrieks of pain, and still the voice was yelling, He's got a gun, he's got a gun! Even though Ross still couldn't see any gun, couldn't understand what the voice was yelling about, the police kept firing, over and over and over into the children . . .

He read about it in the newspapers in the days that followed. Fourteen children were killed. Two of the kidnappers died. There was considerable debate over who fired the shots, but informed speculation had it that several of the children had been caught in a crossfire.

There was only brief mention of Ross. In the confusion that followed the shooting, Ross had backed away into the shadows and slipped out through the rear of the auditorium into a crowd of parents and bystanders and disappeared before anyone could stop him. The teacher who had been held hostage told of a mysterious man who had helped free them, but the police insisted that the man was one of the kidnappers and that the teacher was mistaken about what she had seen. Descriptions of what he looked like varied dramatically, and after a time the search to find him waned and died.

But John Ross was left devastated. How had this terrible thing happened? What had gone wrong? He had done exactly as he intended to do. The men had been subdued. The danger was past. And still the children had died, the police misreading the situation, hearing screams over the kidnapper's dropped cell phone, hearing the AK-47 go off, bursting in with weapons ready, firing impulsively, foolishly . . .

Fourteen children dead. Ross couldn't accept it. He could tell himself rationally that it wasn't his fault. He could explain away everything that had happened, could argue persuasively and passionately to himself that he had done everything he could, but it still didn't help. Fourteen children were dead.

One of them, he discovered, was a blond, blue-eyed little boy named Teddy.

He saw all of their pictures in magazines, and he read their stories in papers for weeks afterward. The horror of what had happened enveloped and consumed him. It haunted his sleep and destroyed his peace of mind. He could not function. He sat paralyzed in motel rooms in small towns far away from San Sobel, trying to regain his sense of purpose. He had experienced failures before, but nothing with consequences that were so dramatic and so personal. He had thought he could handle anything, but he wasn't prepared for this. Fourteen lives were on his conscience, and he could hardly bear it. He cried often, and he ached deep inside. He replayed the events over and over in his mind, trying to decide what it was he had done wrong.

It was weeks before he realized his mistake. He had assumed that the demon who sought to inspire the killings had relied on the kidnappers alone. But it was the police who had killed the children. Someone had yelled at them to shoot, had prompted them to fire, had put them on edge. It took only one additional man, one further intent, one other weapon. The demon had seduced one of the police officers as well. Ross had missed it. He hadn't even thought of it.

After a time, he began to question everything he was doing in his service to the Word. What was the point of it all if so many small lives could be lost so easily? He was a poor choice to serve as a Knight of the Word if he couldn't do any better than this. And what sort of supreme being would permit such a thing to happen in the first place? Was this the best the Word could do? Was it necessary for those fourteen children to die? Was that the message? John Ross began to wonder, then to grow certain, that the difference between the Word and the Void was small indeed. It was all so pointless, so ridiculous. He began to doubt and then to despair. He was servant to a master who lacked compassion and reason, whose poor efforts seemed unable to accomplish anything of worth. John Ross looked back over the past twelve years and was appalled. Where was the proof that anything he had done had served a purpose? What sort of battle was it he fought? Time after time he had stood against the forces of the Void, and what was there to show for it?

There was a limit to what he could endure, he decided finally. There was a limit to what he could demand of himself. He was broken by what had happened in San Sobel, and he could not put himself back together again. He no longer cared who he was or what he had pledged himself to do. He was finished with everything.

Let someone else take up the Word's cause.

Let someone else carry the burden of all those lives.

Let someone else, because he was done.

CHAPTER 5

Ariel paused, and Nest found that she couldn't keep quiet any longer.

"You mean he quit?" she demanded incredulously. "He just quit?"

The tatterdemalion seemed to consider. "He no longer thinks of himself as a Knight of the Word, so he has stopped acting like one. But he can never quit. The choice isn't his to make."

Her words carried a dark implication that Nest did not miss. "What do you mean?"

Ariel's childlike face seemed to shimmer in the midday sun as she shifted her stance slightly. It was the first time she had moved, and it almost caused her to disappear.

"Only the Lady can create a Knight of the Word, and only the Lady can set one free." Ariel's voice was so soft that Nest could barely hear her. "John Ross is bound to his charge. When he took up the staff that gives him his power, he bound himself forever. He cannot free himself of the staff or of the charge. Even if he no longer thinks of himself as a Knight of the Word, he remains one."

Nest shook her head in confusion. "But he isn't doing anything to be a Knight of the Word. He's given it all up, you said. So what difference does it make whether or not he really is a Knight of the Word? If he's not only stopped thinking of himself as a Knight, but he's stopped functioning as one, he might as well be a bricklayer."

Ariel nodded. "This is what John Ross believes, as well. This is why he is in so much danger."

Nest hesitated. How much of this did she really want to know? The Lady hadn't sent Ariel just to bring her up to date on what was happening to John Ross. The Lady wanted something from her, and where Ross was concerned, she wasn't at all sure it would be something she wanted to give. She hadn't seen or heard from Ross in five years, and they hadn't parted under the best of circumstances. John Ross had come to Hopewell to accomplish one of two things—to help thwart her father's intentions for her or to make certain she would never carry them out. He had seen her future, and while he would not describe it to her, he made it clear that it was dark and horrific. So she would live to change it or she would die. That was his mission in coming to Hopewell. He had admitted it at the end, just before he left. She had never quite gotten over it. This was a man she had grown to like and respect and trust. This was a man she had believed for a short time to be her father—a man she would have liked to have had for a father.

And he had come to kill her if he couldn't save her. The truth was shattering. He was not a demon, as her real father had been, but he was close enough that she was still unable to come to terms with how she felt about him.

"The difficulty for John Ross is that he cannot stop being a Knight of the Word just because he chooses to," Ariel said suddenly.

She had moved to within six feet of Nest. Nest hadn't

seen her do that, preoccupied with her thoughts of Ross. The tatterdemalion was close enough that Nest could see the shadowy things that moved inside her semi-transparent form like scraps of stray paper stirred by the wind. Pick had told her that tatterdemalions were made up mostly of dead children's memories and dreams, and that they were born fully grown and did not age afterward but lived only a short time. All of them took on the aspects of the children who had formed them, becoming something of the children themselves while never achieving real substance. Magic shaped and bound them for the time they existed, and when the magic could no longer hold them together, the children's memories and dreams simply scattered into the wind and the tatterdemalion was gone.

"But the magic John Ross was given binds him forever," Ariel said. "He cannot disown it, even if he chooses not to use it. It is a part of him. It marks him. He cannot be anything other than what he is, even if he pretends otherwise. Those who serve the Word will always know him. More importantly, those who serve the Void will know him as well."

"Oh, oh," muttered Pick, sitting up a little straighter.

"He is in great danger," Ariel repeated. "Neither the Word nor the Void will accept that he is no longer a Knight. Both seek to bind him to their cause, each in a different way. The Word has already tried reason and persuasion and has failed. The Void will try another approach. A Knight who has lost his faith is susceptible to the Void's treachery and deceit. The Void will seek to turn John Ross through subterfuge. He will have begun to do so already. John Ross will not know that it is happening. He will not see the truth of things until it is too late. It does not happen all at once; it does not happen in a recognizable way. It will begin with a single misstep. But once that first step is taken, the second becomes much easier. The path is a familiar one. Knights have been lost to the Void before."

Nest brushed at a few stray strands of hair that had blown into her eyes. Clouds were moving in from the west. She had read that rain was expected later in the day. "Does he know this will happen?" she asked sharply, almost accusatorily. She was suddenly angry. "How many years of his life has he given to the Word? Doesn't he at least deserve a warning?"

Ariel's body shimmered, and her eyes blinked slowly, flower petals opening to the sun. "He has been warned. But the warning was ignored. John Ross no longer trusts us. He no longer listens. He believes himself free to do as he chooses. He is a prisoner of his self-deception."

Nest thought about John Ross, picturing him in her mind. She saw a lean, rawboned, careworn man with haunted eyes and a rootless existence. But she saw a fiercely determined man as well, hardened of purpose and principle, a man who would not be easily swayed. She could not imagine how the Void would turn him. She remembered the strength of his commitment; he would die before he would betray it.

Yet he had already given it up, hadn't he? By shedding his identity as a Knight of the Word, he had given it up. She knew the truth of things. People changed. Lives took strange turns.

"The Lady sent me to ask you to go to John Ross and warn him one final time."

Ariel's words jarred her. Nest stared in disbelief. "Me? Why would he listen to me?"

"The Lady says you hold a special place in his heart." Ariel said it in a matter-of-fact way, as if Nest ought to know what this would mean. "She believes that John Ross will listen to you, that he trusts and respects you, and that you have the best chance of persuading him of the danger he faces."

Nest shook her head stubbornly. "I wouldn't know what to say. I'm not the right choice for this." She hesitated. "Look, the truth is, I'm not even sure how I feel about John Ross. Where is he, anyway?"

"Seattle."

"Seattle? You want me to go all the way out to Seattle?" Nest was aghast. "I'm in school! I've got classes tomorrow!"

Ariel stared at her in silence, and suddenly Nest was aware of how foolish she sounded. The tatterdemalion was telling her John Ross was in danger, his life was at risk, she might have a chance to help him, and she was busy worrying about missing a few classes. It was more than that, of course, but it hadn't come out sounding that way.

"This is a lot of nonsense!" Pick stormed suddenly, leaping to his feet on her shoulder. "Nest Freemark is needed here, with me! Who knows what could happen to her out there! After what she went through with her father, she shouldn't have to go anywhere!"

"Pick, relax," Nest soothed.

"Criminy!" Pick was not about to relax. "Why can't the Lady go herself? Why can't she speak to Ross? She's the one who recruited him, isn't she? Why can't she send one of her other people, another Knight, maybe?"

"She has already done what she could," Ariel answered, her strange voice calm and distant, her slight form ephemeral in the changing light. "She has sent others to speak for her. He ignores them all. He is lost to himself, locked away by his choice to abandon his charge, and given over to his doom." Her childlike hand gestured. "There is only Nest."

"Well, she's not going!" Pick declared firmly. "So that's it for John Ross, I guess. Thanks for coming, but I think you'd better be on your way."

"Pick!" Nest admonished, surprised at his vehemence. "Be nice, will you?" She looked at Ariel. "What happens if I don't go?" she asked.

Ariel's strange eyes, clear as stream water, locked on her own. "John Ross has had a dream. The events of the dream will occur in three days. On the last day of October. On Halloween. Ross will be a part of these events. To the extent that he is, there is a very great chance he will become ensnared by the Void and will begin to turn. The Lady cannot know this for certain, but she suspects it. She will not let that happen. She has already sent someone to see that it doesn't."

Nest felt a chill sweep through her. *Like she sent Ross to me, five years ago. If Ross is subverted, he will be killed. Someone has been sent to see to it.*

"You are his last chance," Ariel said again. "Will you go to him? Will you speak to him? Will you try to save him?"

Her thin voice drifted on the autumn breeze and was lost in a rustle of dry leaves.

Nest walked back through the park, lost in thought. Pick rode her shoulder in silence. The afternoon was lengthening out from midday, and the park was busy with fall picnickers, hikers, a few stray pickup ballplayers, and parents with kids and dogs. The blue skies were still bright with sunshine, but the sun was easing steadily west toward a large bank of storm clouds that were rolling out of the plains. Nest could smell the coming rain in the soft, cool air.

"What are you going to do?" Pick asked finally.

She shook her head. "I don't know."

"You're seriously thinking about going, aren't you?"

"I'm thinking about it."

"Well, you should forget about it right here and now."

"Why do you feel so strongly about this?" She slowed in the shadow of a large oak and looked down at him. "What do you know that you're not telling me?"

Pick's wooden face twisted in an expression of distaste, and his twiggy body contorted into a knot. His eyes looked straight ahead. "Nothing."

She waited, knowing from experience that there would be more.

"You remember what happened five years ago," Pick said finally, still not looking at her. "You remember what that was like—with John Ross and your grandparents and your . . . You remember?" He shook his head. "It wasn't any of it what it seemed to be at first glance. It wasn't any of it what you thought it was. There were things you didn't know. Things I didn't know, for that matter. Secrets. It was over before you found out everything."

He paused. "It will be like that with this business, too. It always is. The Word doesn't reveal everything. It isn't His nature to do so."

Something was being hidden from her; Pick could sense it, even if he couldn't identify what it was. Maybe so. Maybe it was even something that could hurt her. But it didn't change what was happening to John Ross. It didn't change what was being asked of her. Did she have the right to use it as a reason for not going?

She tried a different tack. "Ariel says she will go with me, that she will help me."

Pick snorted. "Ariel is a tatterdemalion. How much help can she be? She's made out of air and lost memories. She's only alive for a heartbeat. She doesn't know anything about humans and their problems. Tatterdemalions come together mostly by chance, wander about like ghosts, and then disappear again. She's a messenger, nothing more."

"She says she can serve as a guide for me. She says that the Lady has sent her for that purpose."

"The blind leading the blind, as your grandmother used to say." Pick was having none of it.

Nest angled through the trees, bypassing the picnickers and ballplayers, turning up the service road that ran along the backside of the residences bordering the park. Her mind spun in a jumble of concerns and considerations. This was not going to be an easy decision to make.

"Would you come with me?" she asked suddenly.

Pick went still, stiffening. He didn't say anything for a moment, then muttered in a barely audible voice, "Well, the fact of the matter is, I've never been out of the park."

She was surprised, although she shouldn't have been. Why would Pick ever have gone anywhere else? What would have taken him away? The park was his home, his work, his life. He was telling her, without quite speaking the words, that the idea of leaving was frightening to him.

She had embarrassed him, she realized.

"Well, I'm being selfish asking you to go," she said quickly, as if brushing her suggestion aside. "Who would look after the park if you weren't here? It's bad enough that I'm gone so much of the time. But if you left, there wouldn't be anyone to keep an eye on things, would there?"

Pick shook his head quickly. "True enough. No one at all. It's a big responsibility."

She nodded. "Just forget I said anything."

She turned down the service road toward home. Shadows were already beginning to lengthen, the days growing shorter with winter's approach. They spread in black pools from the trees and houses, staining the lawns and roadways and walks. A Sunday type of silence cloaked the park, sleepy and restful. Sounds carried a long way. She could hear voices discussing dinner from one of the houses to her right. She could hear laughter and shouts from off toward the river, down below the bluff where children were playing. She could hear the deep bark of a dog in the woods east.

"I could do this trip in a day and be back," she said, trying out the idea on him. "I could fly out, talk to him, and fly right back."

Pick did not respond. She walked down the roadway with him in silence.

She sat inside by herself afterward, staring out through the curtains, thinking the matter over. Clouds masked the sky beyond, and rain was starting to fall in scattered drops. The people in the park had gone home. Lights were beginning to come on in the windows of the houses across Woodlawn Road.

What should I do?

John Ross had always been an enigma. Now he was a dilemma as well, a responsibility she did not want. He had been living in Seattle for over a year, working for a man named Simon Lawrence at a place called Fresh Start. She remembered both the man and the place from a report someone had done in one of her classes last year. Fresh Start was a shelter for battered and homeless women, founded several years ago by Lawrence. He had also founded Pass/Go, a transitional school for homeless children. The success of both had been something of a celebrity cause for a time, and Simon Lawrence had been labeled the Wizard of Oz. Oz, because Seattle was commonly known as the Emerald City. Now John Ross was there, working at the shelter. So Ariel had informed her.

Nest scuffed at the floor idly with her tennis shoe and tried to picture Ross as a Munchkin in the employ of the great and mighty Oz.

Oh, God. What should I do?

She had told Ariel she would think about it, that she would decide by evening. Ariel would return for her answer then.

She got up and walked into the kitchen to make herself a cup of hot tea. As she stood by the stove waiting for the kettle to boil, she glanced over at the real estate papers for the sale of the house. She had forgotten about them. She stared at them, but made no move to pick them up. They didn't seem very important in light of the John Ross matter, and she didn't want to think about them right now. Allen Kruppert and ERA Realty would just have to wait.

Standing at the living room picture window, holding her steaming cup of tea in front of her, she watched the rain begin to fall in earnest, streaking the glass, turning the old shade trees and the grass dark and shiny. The feeders would come out to prowl in this weather, bolder when the light was poor and the shadows thick. They preferred the night, but a gloomy day would do just as well. She still watched for them, not so much afraid anymore as curious, always thinking she would solve their mystery somehow, that she would discover what they were. She knew what they did, of course; she understood their place in nature's scheme. No one else even knew they were out there. But there was so much more—how they procreated, what they were composed of, how they could inflict madness, how they could appear as shadows and still affect things of substance. She remembered them touching her when her father had made her a prisoner in the caves below the park. She remembered the horror and disgust that blossomed within her. She remembered how badly she had wanted to scream.

But her friends and her grandparents had been there to save her, and now only the memory remained.

Maybe it was her turn to be there for John Ross.

Her brow furrowed. No matter how many ways she looked at the problem, she kept coming back to the same thing. If something happened to John Ross and she hadn't tried to prevent it, how could she live with herself? She would always wonder if she might have changed things. She would always live in doubt. If she tried and failed, well, at least she would have tried. But if she did nothing . . .

She sipped at her tea and stared out the window fixedly. John Ross, the Knight of the Word. She could not imagine him ever being different from what he had been five years ago. She could not imagine him being anything other than what he was. How had he fallen so far away from his fierce commitment to saving the world? It sounded overblown when she said it, but that was what he was doing. Saving the world, saving humanity from itself. O'olish Amaneh had made it plain to her that such a war was taking place, even before Ross had appeared to confirm it. We are destroying ourselves, Two Bears had told her; we are risking the fate of the Sinnissippi—that we shall disappear completely and no one will know who we were.

Are we still destroying ourselves? she wondered. *Are we still traveling the road of the Sinnissippi?* She hadn't thought about it for a long time, wrapped up in her own life, the events of five years earlier behind her, buried in a past she would rather forget. She had been only a girl of fourteen. Her world had been saved, and at the time she had been grateful enough to let it go at that.

But her world was expanding now, reaching out to places and people beyond Hopewell. What was happening in that larger world, the world into which her future would take her? What would become of it without John Ross?

Rain coated the windows in glistening sheets that turned everything beyond into a shimmering haze. The park and her backyard disappeared. The world beyond vanished.

She walked to the phone and dialed Robert Heppler. He answered on the fourth ring, sounding distracted. "Yeah, hello?"

"Back on the computer, Robert?" she asked teasingly.

"Nest?"

"Want to go out for a pizza later?"

"Well, yeah, of course." He was alert and eager now, if surprised. "When?"

"In an hour. I'll pick you up. But there's a small price for this."

"What is it?"

"You have to drive me to O'Hare tomorrow morning. I can go whenever you want, and you can use my car. Just bring it back when you're done and park it in the drive."

She didn't know how Ariel would get to Seattle, but she didn't think it was something she needed to worry about. The Lady's creatures seemed able to get around just fine without any help from humans.

She waited for Robert to say something. There was a long pause before he did. "O'Hare? Where are you going?"

"Seattle."

"Seattle?"

"The Emerald City, Robert."

"Yeah, I know what it's called. Why are you going there?"

She sighed and stared off through the window into the rainy gloom. "I guess you could say I'm off to see the Wizard." She paused for effect. "Bye, Robert."

Then she hung up.

Monday,
October 29

CHAPTER 6

John Ross finished the closing paragraph of Simon's Seattle Art Museum speech, read it through a final time to make certain it all hung together, dropped his pen, and leaned back in his chair with a satisfied sigh. Not bad. He was getting pretty good at this speech-writing business. It wasn't what Simon had hired him for, but it looked like it was a permanent part of his job description now. All those years he had spent knocking around in graduate English programs were serving a useful purpose after all. He grinned and glanced out the window of his tiny office. Morning rain was giving way to afternoon sun. Overhead, the drifting clouds were beginning to reveal small patches of blue. Just another typical Seattle day.

He glanced at the clock on his desk and saw that it was nearing three. He had been at this since late morning. Time for a break.

He pushed back his chair and levered himself to his feet. He was three years beyond forty, but when rested he could easily pass for ten years less. Lean and fit, he had the sun-browned, rawboned look of an outdoorsman, his face weathered, yet still boyish. His long brown hair was tied back with a rolled bandanna, giving him the look of a man who might not be altogether comfortable with the idea of growing up. Pale green eyes looked out at the world as if still trying to decide what to make of it.

And, indeed, John Ross had been working on deciphering the meaning of life for a long time.

He stood with his hand gripping the polished walnut staff that served as his crutch, wondering again what would happen if he simply cast it away, if he defied the warning that had accompanied its bestowal and cut loose his final tie to the Word. He had considered it often in the last few months, thinking there was no reason for further delay and he should simply make the decision and act on it. But he could never quite bring himself to carry through, even though he was no longer a Knight of the Word and the staff's power was no longer a part of his life.

He ran his fingers slowly up and down the smooth wood, trying to detect whether he was still bound to it. But the staff revealed nothing. He did not even know if the magic it contained was still his to command; he no longer felt its warmth or saw its gleam in the wood's dark surface. He no longer sensed its presence.

He closed his eyes momentarily. He had wanted his old life back, the one he had given up to become a Knight of the Word. He had been willing to risk everything to regain it. And perhaps, he thought darkly, he had done exactly that. The Word, after all, was the Creator. What did the Creator feel when you told Him you wanted to back out of an agreement? Maybe Ross would never know. What he did know was that his life was his own again, and he would not let go of it easily. The staff, he reasoned, looking warily at it, was a reminder of what it would mean for him if he did.

Raised voices, high-pitched and tearful, chased Della Jenkins down the hall. Della swept past his doorway, muttering to herself, giving him a frustrated shake of her head. She was back a moment later, returning the way she had come, a clutch of papers in one hand. Curious, he trailed after her up the hallway to the lobby at the front of the old building, taking his time, leaning on his staff for support. Della was working the reception desk today, and Mondays were always tough. More things seemed to happen over the weekend than during the week— confrontations of all sorts, exploding out of pressure cookers that had been on low boil for weeks or months or even years. He could never understand it. Why such things were so often done on a weekend was a mystery to him. He always thought a Friday would do just as well, but maybe weekends for the battered and abused were bridges to the new beginnings that Mondays finally required.

By the time Ross reached the lobby, the voices had died away. He paused in the doorway and peeked out guardedly. Della was bent close to a teenage girl who had collapsed in a chair to one side of the reception desk and begun to cry. A younger girl was clinging tightly to one arm, tears streaking her face. Della's hand was resting lightly on the older girl's shoulder, and she was speaking softly in her ear. Della was a large woman with big hair, skin the color of milk chocolate, and a series of dresses that seemed to come only in primary colors. She had both a low, gentle voice and a formidable glare, and she was adept at bringing either to bear as the situation demanded. In this instance, she seemed to have abandoned the latter in favor of the former, and already the older girl's sobs were fading. A handful of women and children occupied chairs in other parts of the room. A few were looking over with a mix of curiosity and sympathy. New arrivals, applying for a bed. When they saw Ross, the women went back to work on their application forms and the children shifted their attention to him. He gave them a smile, and one little girl smiled back.

"There, now, you take your time, look it all over, fill out what you can, I'll help you with the rest," Della finished, straightening, taking her hand from the older girl's shoulder. "That's right. I'll be right over here, you just come on up when you're ready."

She moved back behind the desk, giving Ross a glance and a shrug and settling herself into place with a sigh. Like all the front-desk people, she was a trained professional with experience working intake. Della had been at Fresh Start for something like five years, almost from its inception, according to Ray Hapgood, so she had pretty much seen and heard it all.

Ross moved over to stand beside her, and she gave him a suspicious frown for his trouble. "You at loose ends, Mr. Speechwriter? Need something more to do, maybe?"

"I'm depressed, and I need one of your smiles," he answered with a wink.

"Shoo, what office you running for?" She gave him a look, then gestured with her head. "Little lady over there, she's seventeen, says she's pregnant, says the father doesn't want her or the baby, doesn't want nothing to do with none of it. Gangbanger or some such, just eighteen himself. Other girl is her sister. Been living wherever, the both of them. Runaways, street kids, babies making babies. Told her we could get them a bed, but she had to see a doctor and if there were parents, they had to be notified. Course, she doesn't want that, doesn't trust doctors, hates her parents, such as they are. Good Lord Almighty!"

Ross nodded. "You explain the reason for all this?"

Della gave him the glare. "Course I explained it! What you think I'm doing here, anyway—just taking up space? Who's been here longer, you or me?"

Ross winced. "Sorry I asked."

She punched him lightly on the arm. "No, you ain't."

He glanced around the room. "How many new beds have come in today?"

"Seven. Not counting these." Della shook her head ruefully. "This keeps up, we're going to have to start putting them up in your office, having them sleep on your floor. You mind stepping over a few babies and mothers while you work—assuming you actually do any work while you're sitting back there?"

He shrugged. "Wall-to-wall homeless. Maybe I can put some of them to work writing for me. They probably have better ideas about all this than I do."

"They probably do." Della was not going to cut him any slack. "You on your way to somewhere or did you just come out here to get underfoot?"

"I'm on my way to get some coffee. Do you want some?"

"No, I don't. I got too much work to do. Unlike some I know." She returned to the paperwork on her desk, dismissing him. Then she added, "Course, if you brought me some—cream and sugar, please—I guess I'd drink it all right."

He went back down the hall to the elevator and pressed the button. The staff's coffee room was in the basement along with a kitchen, storage rooms for food and supplies,

maintenance equipment, and the water heaters and furnace. Space was at a premium. Fresh Start sheltered anywhere from a hundred and fifty to two hundred women
and children at any given time, all of them homeless,
most of them abused. Administrative offices and a first-
aid room occupied the ground floor of the six-story
building, and the top five floors had been converted into a
mix of dormitories and bedrooms. The second floor also
housed a dining hall that could seat up to a hundred
people, which worked fine if everyone ate in shifts. Just
next door, in the adjacent building, was Pass/Go, the alternative school for the children housed at Fresh Start.
The school served upward of sixty or seventy children
most of the time. The Pass/Go staff numbered twelve, the
Fresh Start staff fifteen. Volunteers filled in the gaps.

No signs marked the location of the buildings or gave
evidence of the nature of the work conducted within. The
buildings were drab and unremarkable and occupied
space just east of Occidental Park in the Pioneer Square
district of Seattle. The International District lay just to
the south above the Kingdome. Downtown, with its ho-
tels and skyscrapers and shopping, lay a dozen blocks
north. Elliott Bay and the waterfront lay west. Clients
were plentiful; you could find them on the streets nearby,
if you took the time to look.

Fresh Start and Pass/Go were nonprofit corporations
funded by Seattle Public Schools, various charitable
foundations, and private donations. Both organizations
were the brainchild of one man—Simon Lawrence.

John Ross looked down at his feet. Simon Lawrence.
The Wizard of Oz. The man he was supposed to kill in
exactly two days, according to his dreams.

The elevator doors opened and he stepped in. There

were stairs, but he still walked with difficulty, his resignation from the Word's service notwithstanding. He supposed he always would. It didn't seem fair he should
remain crippled after terminating his position, given that
he had become crippled by accepting it, but he guessed
the Word didn't see matters that way. Life, after all,
wasn't especially fair.

He smiled. He could joke about it now. His new life allowed for joking. He wasn't at the forefront of the war
against the creatures of the Void, wasn't striving any
longer to prevent the destruction of humanity. That was
in the past, in a time when there was little to smile about
and a great deal to fear. He had served the Word for the
better part of fifteen years, a warrior who had been both
hunter and hunted, a man always just one step ahead of
Death. He had spent each day of the first twelve years
trying to change the horror revealed in his dreams of the
night before. San Sobel had been the breaking point, and
for a while he thought he might never recover from it.
Then Stef had come along, and everything had changed.
Now he had his life back, and his future was no longer
determined by his dreams.

His dreams? His nightmares. He seldom had them
now, their frequency and intensity diminishing steadily
from the time he had walked away from being a Knight
of the Word. That much, at least, suggested his escape
had been successful. The dreams had come every night
when he was a Knight of the Word, because the dreams
were all he had to work with. But now they almost never
came, and when they did, they were vague and indistinct,
shadows rather than pictures, and they no longer suggested or revealed or threatened.

Except for his dream about Simon Lawrence, the one

in which the old man recognized him from the past, the one in which he recognized that the old man's words were true and he had indeed killed the Wizard of Oz. He'd had that same dream three times now, and each time it had revealed a little bit more of what he would do. He had never had a dream three times, even when he was a Knight of the Word; he had never had a dream more than once. It had frightened him at first, unnerved him so that even though he was already living in Seattle and working for Simon he had thought to leave at once, to go far, far away from even the possibility of the dream coming to pass.

It was Stef who had convinced him that the way you banish the things you fear is to stand up to them. He had decided to stay finally, and it had been the right choice. He wasn't afraid of the dream anymore. He knew it wasn't going to happen, that he wasn't going to kill Simon. Simon Lawrence and his incredible work at Fresh Start and Pass/Go was the future John Ross had chosen to embrace.

Ross stepped out of the elevator into the coffee room. The room was large but bare, save for a couple of multi-purpose tables with folding chairs clustered about, the coffee machine and cups sitting on a cabinet filled with coffee-making materials, a small refrigerator, a micro-wave, and a set of old shelves containing an odd assortment of everyday china pieces, silverware, and glasses.

Ray Hapgood was sitting at one of the tables as Ross appeared, reading the *Post-Intelligencer*. "My man, John!" he greeted, glancing up. "How goes the speech-writing effort? We gonna make the Wiz sound like the Second Coming?"

Ross laughed. "He doesn't need that kind of help

from me. Most people already think he *is* the Second Coming."

Hapgood chuckled and shook his head. Ray was the director of education at Pass/Go, a graduate of the University of Washington with an undergraduate degree in English literature and years of teaching experience in the Seattle public school system, where he had worked before coming to Simon. He was a tall, lean black man with short-cropped hair receding dramatically toward the crown of his head, his eyes bright and welcoming, his smile ready. He was a "black" man because that was what he called himself. None of that "African American" stuff for him. Black American was okay, but black was good enough. He had little time or patience for that political-correctness nonsense. What you called him wasn't going to make any difference as to whether or not he liked you or were his friend. He was that kind of guy—blunt, open, hardworking, right to the point. Ross liked him a lot.

"Della sends you her love," Ross said, tongue firmly in cheek, and moved over to the coffee machine. He would have preferred a latte, but that meant a two-block hike. He wasn't up to it.

"Yeah, Della's in love with me, sure enough," Ray agreed solemnly. "Can't blame the woman, can you?"

Ross shook his head, pouring himself a cup and stirring in a little cream. "But it isn't right for you to string her along like you do. You have to fish or cut bait, Ray."

"Fish or cut bait?" Ray stared at him. "What's that, some sort of midwestern saying, something you Ohio homeboys tell each other?"

"Yep." Ross moved over and sat down across from

him, leaning the black staff against his chair. He took a sip. "What do you Seattle homeboys say?"

"We say, 'Shit or get off the pot,' but I expect that sort of talk offends your senses, so I don't use it around you." Ray shrugged and went back to his paper. After a minute, he said, "Damn, why do I bother reading this rag? It just depresses me."

Carole Price walked in, smiled at Ross, and moved over to the coffee machine. "What depresses you, Ray?"

"This damn newspaper! People! Life in general!" Ray Hapgood leaned back and shook the paper as if to rid it of spiders. "Listen to this. There's three stories in here, all of them the same story really. Story one. Woman living in Renton is depressed—lost her job, ex-husband's not paying support for the one kid that's admittedly his, boyfriend beats her regularly and with enough disregard for the neighbors that they've called the police a dozen times, and then he drinks and totals her car. End result? She goes home and puts a gun to her head and kills herself. But she takes time first to kill all three children because—as she says in the note she so thoughtfully leaves—she can't imagine them wanting to live without her."

Carole nodded. Blond, fit, middle-aged, a veteran of the war against the abuse of women and children, she was the director of Fresh Start. "I read about that."

"Story two." Hapgood plowed ahead with a nod of satisfaction. "Estranged husband decides he's had enough of life. Goes home to visit the wife and children, two of them his from a former marriage, two of them hers from same. Kills her, 'cause she's his wife, and kills *his* children, 'cause they're *his*, see. Lets *her* children live, 'cause they aren't his and he doesn't see them as his responsibility."

Carole shook her head and sighed.

"Story three." Hapgood rolled his eyes dramatically before continuing. "Ex-husband can't stand the thought of his former wife with another man. Goes over to their trailer with a gun, shoots them both, then shoots himself. Leaves three small children orphaned and homeless in the process. Too bad for them."

He threw down the newspaper. "We could have helped all these people, damn it! We could have helped if we could have gotten to them! If they'd just come to us, these women, just come to us and told us they felt threatened and . . ." He threw up his hands. "I don't know, it's all such a waste!"

"It's that, all right," agreed Carole. Ross sipped his coffee and nodded, but didn't say anything.

"Then, right on the same page, like they can't see the irony of it, is an article about the fuss being created over the Pirates of the Caribbean exhibit in Disney World!" Ray looked furious. "See, these pirates are chasing these serving wenches around a table and then auctioning them off, all on this ride, and some people are offended. Okay, I can understand that. But this story, and all the fuss over it, earns the same amount of space, and a whole lot more public interest, than what's happened to these women and children. And I'll bet Disney gives the pirates more time and money than they give the homeless. I mean, who cares about the homeless, right? Long as it isn't you or me, who cares?"

"You're obsessing, Ray," said Jip Wing, a young volunteer who had wandered in during the exchange. Hapgood shot him a look.

"How about the article on the next page about the kid who won't compete in judo competition anymore if she's required to bow to the mat?" Carole grinned wolfishly. "She says bowing to the mat has religious connotations, so she shouldn't have to do it. Mat worship or something. Her mother backs her up, of course. That story gets half a page, more than the killings or the pirates."

"Well, the priorities are all skewed, that's the point." Ray shook his head. "When the newspapers start thinking that what goes on at Disney World or at a judo competition deserves as much attention as what goes on with homeless women and children, we are in big trouble."

"That doesn't even begin to address the amount of coverage given to sports," Jip Wing interjected with a shrug.

"Well, politically incorrect pirates and mat worship, not to mention sports, are easier to deal with than the homeless, aren't they?" Carole snapped. "Way of the world, Ray. People deal with what they can handle. What's too hard or doesn't offer an easy solution gets shoved aside. Too much for me, they think. Too big for one man or woman. We need committees, experts, organizations, entire governments to solve this one. But, hey, mat worship? Pirates chasing wenches? I can handle those."

Ross stayed quiet. He was thinking about his own choices in life. He had given up the pressures of trying to serve on a far larger and more violent battlefield than anything that was being talked about here. He had abandoned a fight that had become overwhelming and not a little incomprehensible. He had walked away from demons and feeders and maentwrogs, beings of magic and darkness, creatures of the Void. Because after San Sobel he felt that he wasn't getting anywhere with his efforts to destroy them, that he couldn't control the results anymore, that it was dumb luck if he ended up killing the monsters instead of the humans. He felt adrift and ineffective and dangerously inadequate. Children had died because of him. He couldn't bear the thought of that happening again.

Even so, it seemed as if Ray were speaking directly to him, and in the other man's anger and frustration with humanity's lack of an adequate response to the problem of homeless and abused women and children, he felt the sharp sting of a personal reprimand.

He took a deep breath, listening as Ray and Carole continued their discussion. *How much good do you think we're doing?* he wanted to ask them. *With the homeless. With the people you're talking about. Through all our programs and hard work. How much good are we really doing?*

But he didn't say anything. He couldn't. He sat there in silence, contemplating his own failures and shortcomings, his own questionable choices in life. The fact remained that he liked what he was doing here and he did think he was doing some good—more good than he had done as a Knight of the Word. Here, he could see the results on a case-by-case basis. Not all of his efforts—their efforts—were successful, but the failures were easier to live with and less costly. If change for the better was achieved one step at a time, then surely the people involved with Fresh Start and Pass/Go were headed in the right direction.

He took a fresh grip on his commitment. The past was behind him and he should keep it there. He was not meant to be a Knight of the Word. He had never been more than adequate to the undertaking, never more than satisfactory. It required someone stronger and more fit, someone whose dedication and determination eclipsed his own. He had done the best he could, but he had done as much as he could, as well. It was finished after San Sobel. It was ended.

"Time to get back to work," he said to no one in particular.

The talk still swirled about him as he rose. A couple of other staffers had wandered in, and everyone was trying to get a word in edgewise. With a nod to Ray, who glanced up as he moved toward the elevator, he crossed the room, pressed the button, stepped inside the empty cubicle when it arrived, and watched the break room and its occupants disappear as the doors closed.

He rode up to the main floor in silence, closing his eyes to the past and its memories, sealing himself in a momentary blackness.

When the elevator stopped and he stepped out, Stefanie Winslow was passing by carrying two latte containers, napkins, straws, and plastic spoons nestled in a small cardboard tray.

"Coffee, tea, or me?" she asked brightly, tossing back her curly black hair, looking curiously girlish with the gesture.

"Guess." He pursed his lips to keep from smiling. "Whacha got there?"

"Two double-tall, low-fat, vanilla lattes, fella."

"One of those for me?"

She smirked. "You wish. How's the speech coming?"

"Done, except for a final polish. The Wiz will amaze this Halloween." He gestured at the tray. "So who gets those?"

"Simon is in his office giving an interview to Andrew Wren of *The New York Times*. That's Andrew Wren, the *investigative* reporter."

"Oh? What's he investigating?"

"Well, sweetie, that's the sixty-four-thousand-dollar question, isn't it?" She motioned with her head. "Out of my way, I have places to go."

He stepped obediently aside, letting her pass. She glanced back at him over her shoulder. "I booked dinner at Umberto's for six. Meet you in your office at five-thirty sharp." She gave him a wink.

He watched her walk down the hall toward Simon's office. He was no longer thinking about the homeless and abused, about Ray and Carole, about his past and its memories, about anything but her. It was like that with Stef. It had been like that from the moment they met. She was the best thing that had ever happened to him. He loved her so much it hurt. But the hurt was pleasurable. The hurt was sweet. The way she made him feel was a mystery he did not ever want to solve.

"I'll be there," he said softly.

He had to admit, his new life was pretty good. He went back to his office smiling.

CHAPTER 7

Andrew Wren stood looking out the window of the Wiz's corner office at the derelicts occupying space in Occidental Park across the way. They slouched on benches, slept curled up in old blankets in tree wells, and huddled on the low steps and curbing that differentiated the various concrete and flagstone levels of the open space. They drank from bottles concealed in paper sacks, exchanged tokens and pennies, and stared into space. Tourists and shoppers gave them a wide berth. Almost no one looked at them. A pair of cops on bicycles surveyed the scene with wary eyes, then moved over to speak to a man staggering out of a doorway leading to a card shop. Pale afternoon sunlight peeked through masses of cumulous clouds on their way to distant places.

Wren turned away. Simon Lawrence was seated at his desk, talking on the phone to the mayor about Wednesday evening's festivities at the Seattle Art Museum. The mayor was making the official announcement of the dedication on behalf of the city. An abandoned apartment building just across the street had been purchased by the city and was being donated to Fresh Start to provide additional housing for homeless women and children. Donations had been pledged that would cover needed renovations to the interior. The money would bring the building up to code and provide sleeping rooms, a kitchen, dining room, and administrative offices for staff and volunteers. Persuading the city to dedicate the building and land had taken the better part of two years. Raising the money necessary to make the dedication meaningful had taken almost as long. It was, all in all, a terrific coup.

Andrew Wren looked down at his shoes. The Wizard of Oz had done it again. But at what cost to himself and the organizations he had founded? That was the truth Wren had come all the way from New York to discover.

He was a burly, slow-moving man with a thatch of unruly, grizzled brown hair that refused to be tamed and stuck out every which way no matter what was done to it. The clothes he wore were rumpled and well used, the kind that let him be comfortable while he worked, that gave him an unintimidating, slightly shabby look. He carried a worn leather briefcase in which he kept his notepads, source logs, and whatever book he was currently reading, together with a secret stash of bagged nuts and candy that he used to sustain himself when meals were missed or forgotten in the heat of his work. He had a round, kindly face with bushy eyebrows, heavy cheeks, and he wore glasses that tended to slide down his nose when he bent forward to listen to compensate for his failing hearing. He was almost fifty, but he looked as if he could just as easily be sixty. He could have been a college professor or a favorite uncle or a writer of charming anecdotes and pithy sayings that stayed with you and made you smile when you thought back on them.

But he wasn't any of these things. His worn, familiar

teddy-bear look was what made him so effective at what he did. He looked harmless and mildly confused, but how he looked was dangerously deceptive. Andrew Wren was a bulldog when it came to ferreting out the truth. He was relentless in getting to the bottom of things. Investigative reporting was a tough racket, and you had to be both lucky and good. Wren had always been both. He had a knack for being in the right place at the right time, for sensing when there was a story worth following up. His instincts were uncanny, and behind those kindly eyes and rumpled look was a razor-sharp mind that could peel away layers of deception and dig down to that tiny nugget of truth buried under a mound of bullshit. More than one overconfident jackass had been undone by underestimating Andrew Wren.

Simon Lawrence was not likely to turn into one of these unfortunates, however. Wren knew him well enough to appreciate the fact that the Wiz hadn't gotten where he was by underestimating anyone.

Simon hung up the phone and leaned back in his chair. "Sorry about that, Andrew, but you don't keep the mayor waiting."

Wren nodded benignly, shrugging. "I understand. Wednesday's event means a lot to you."

"Yes, but more to the point, it means a lot to the mayor. He went out on a limb for us, persuading the council to pass a resolution dedicating the building, then selling the idea to the voters. I want to be certain that he comes out of this experience feeling good about things."

Wren walked over to the easy chair that fronted Simon's desk and sat down. Even though they had met only once before, and that was two years ago, Simon Lawrence felt comfortable enough with Wren to call him by his first name. Wren wouldn't do anything to discourage that just yet.

"I should think just about everyone is feeling pretty good about this one, Simon," he complimented. "It's quite an accomplishment."

Simon leaned forward and put his elbows on his desk and his chin in his hands, giving Wren a thoughtful look. He was handsome in a rugged sort of way, with nicely chiseled features, thick dark hair, and startling blue eyes. When he walked, he looked like a big cat, sort of gliding from place to place, slow and graceful, never hurried, with an air of confidence about him that suggested he would not be easily surprised. Wren placed him at a little over six feet and maybe two hundred pounds. His birth certificate, which Wren had ferreted out by searching the records in a suburb of St. Louis two years earlier in an unsuccessful attempt to learn something about his childhood, put him at forty-five years of age. He was unmarried, had no children, had no living relatives that anyone could identify, lived alone, and was the most important voice of his generation in the fight against homelessness.

His was a remarkable story. He had come to Seattle eight years ago after spending several years working for nationally based programs like Habitat for Humanity and Child Risk. He worked for the Union Gospel Mission and Treehouse, then, after three years, founded Fresh Start. He began with an all-volunteer staff and an old warehouse on Jackson Street. Within a year, he had secured sufficient funding to lease the building where Fresh Start was presently housed, to hire a full-time staff of three, including Ray Hapgood, and to begin generating seed money for his next project, Pass/Go. He wrote a book on homeless women and children, entitled *Street*

Lives. A documentary filmmaker became interested in his work and shot a feature that won an Academy Award. Shortly afterward, Simon was nominated for the prestigious Jefferson Award, which honors ordinary citizens who do extraordinary things in the field of community service. He was one of five statewide winners, was selected as an entry for national competition, and was subsequently a winner of the Jacqueline Kennedy Onassis Award.

From there, things really took off. The media began to cover him regularly. He was photogenic, charming, and passionate about his work, and he gave terrific interviews. His programs became nationally known. Hollywood adopted him as a cause, and he was smart enough to know how to make the most of that. Money poured in. He purchased the buildings that housed Fresh Start and Pass/Go, increased his full-time staff, began a volunteer training program, and developed a comprehensive informational program on the roots of homelessness, which he made available to organizations working with the homeless in other cities. He held several high-profile fund-raisers that brought in national celebrities to mingle with the locals, and with the ensuing contributions established a foundation to provide seed money for programs similar to his own.

He also wrote a second book, this one more controversial than the first, but more critically acclaimed. The title was *The Spiritual Child*. It was something of a surprise to everyone, because it did not deal with the homeless, but with the spiritual growth of children. It argued rather forcibly that children were possessed of an innate intelligence that allowed them to comprehend the lessons of spirituality, and that adults would do better if they were to spend less time trying to impose their personal religious and secular views and more time encouraging children to explore their own. It was a controversial position, but Simon Lawrence was adept at advancing an argument without seeming argumentative, and he pretty much carried the day.

By now he was being referred to regularly as the Wizard of Oz, a name that had been coined early on by *People* magazine when it ran a fluff piece on the miracles he had performed in getting Fresh Start up and running. Wren knew Simon Lawrence wasn't overly fond of the tag, but he also knew the Wiz understood the value of advertising, and a catchy name didn't hurt when it came to raising dollars. He lived in the Emerald City, after all, so he couldn't very well complain if the media decided to label him the Wizard of Oz. Or the Wiz, more usually, for these days everyone seemed to think they were on a first-name basis with him. Simon Lawrence was hot stuff, which made him news, which made Andrew Wren's purpose in coming to see him all the more intriguing.

"An accomplishment," Simon said softly, repeating Wren's words. He shook his head. "Andrew, I'm like the Dutch boy with his finger in the hole in the dike and the sea rising on the other side. Let me give you some statistics to think about. Use them or not when you write your next story, I don't care. But remember them.

"There are two hundred beds in this facility. With the new building, we should be able to double that. That will give us four hundred. Four hundred to service homeless women and children. There are twelve hundred school-age homeless children, Andrew. That's children, not women. Twenty-four percent of all our homeless are under the age of eighteen. And that number is growing every day.

"Ours is a specific focus. We provide help to homeless women and children. Eighty percent of those women and children are homeless because of domestic violence. The problem of domestic violence is growing worldwide, but especially here, in the United States. The statistics regarding children who die violently are all out of proportion with the rest of the world. An American child is five times more likely to be killed before the age of eighteen than a child living in another industrialized nation. The rate of gun deaths and suicides among our children is more than twice that of other countries. We like to think of ourselves as progressive and enlightened, but you have to wonder. Homelessness is an alternative to dying, but not an especially attractive one. So it is difficult for me to dwell on accomplishments when the problem remains so acute."

Wren nodded. "I've seen the statistics."

"Good. Then let me give you an overview of our response as a nation to the problem of being homeless." Simon Lawrence leaned back again in his chair. "In a time in which the homeless problem is growing by leaps and bounds worldwide—due, to varying extents, to increases in the population, job elimination, technological advances, disintegration of the family structure, violence, and the rising cost of housing—our response state by state and city by city has been an all-out effort to look the other way. Or, as an alternative, to try to relocate the problem to some other part of the country. We are engaged in a nationwide effort to crack down on the homeless by passing new ordinances designed to move these people to where we can't see them. Stop them from panhandling, don't let them sleep in our parks and public places, conduct police sweeps to round them up, and get them the hell out of town—that's our solution. Is there a concerted effort to get at the root problems of homelessness, to find ways to rehabilitate and reform, to address the differences between types of homelessness so that those who need one kind of treatment versus another can get it? How many tax dollars are being spent to build shelters and provide showers and hot meals? What efforts are being made to explore the ways in which domestic violence contributes to the problem, especially where women and children are concerned?"

He folded his arms across his chest. "We have thousands and thousands of people living homeless on the streets of our cities at the same time that we have men and women earning millions of dollars a year running companies that make products whose continued usage will ruin our health, our environment, and our values. The irony is incredible. It's obscene."

Wren nodded. "But you can't change that, Simon. The problem is too indigenous to who we are, too much a part of how we live our lives."

"Tell me about it. I feel like Don Quixote, tilting at windmills." Simon shrugged. "It's obviously hopeless, isn't it? But you know something, Andrew? I refuse to give up. I really do. It doesn't matter to me if I fail. It matters to me if I don't try." He thought about it a moment. "Too bad I'm not really the Wizard of Oz. If I were, I could just step behind the old curtain and pull a lever and change everything—just like that."

Wren chuckled. "No, you couldn't. The Wizard of Oz was a humbug, remember?"

Simon Lawrence laughed with him. "Unfortunately, I

do. I think about it every time someone refers to me as the Wiz. Do me a favor, Andrew. Please refrain from using that hideous appellation in whatever article you end up writing. Call me Toto or something; maybe it will catch on."

There was a soft knock, the door opened, and Stefanie Winslow walked in carrying the lattes Simon had sent her to purchase from the coffee shop at Elliott Bay Book Company. Both men started to rise, but she motioned them back into their seats. "Stay where you are, gentlemen, you probably need all your energy for the interview. I'll just set these on the desk and be on my way."

She gave Wren a dazzling smile, and he wished instantly that he was younger and cooler and even then he would probably need to be a cross between Harrison Ford and Bill Gates to have a chance with this woman. Stefanie Winslow was beautiful, but she was exotic as well, a combination that made her unforgettable. She was tall and slim with jet-black hair that curled down to her shoulders, cut back from her face and ears in a sweep so that it shimmered like satin in sunlight. Her skin was a strange smoky color, suggesting that she was of mixed ancestry, the product of more than one culture, more than one people. Startling emerald eyes dominated an oval face with tiny, perfect features. She moved in a graceful, willowy way that accentuated her long limbs and neck and stunning shape. She seemed oblivious to how she looked and comfortable within herself, radiating a relaxed confidence that had both an infectious and unsettling effect on the people around her. Andrew Wren would have made the journey to Seattle just to see her in the flesh for ten seconds.

She set the lattes before them and started for the door.

"Simon, I'm going to finish with the SAM arrangements, then I'm out of here. John has your speech all done except for a once-over, so we're going out for a long, quiet, intimate dinner. See you tomorrow."

"Bye, Stef." Simon waved her out.

"Nice seeing you, Mr. Wren," she called back.

The door closed behind her with a soft click. Wren shook his head. "Shouldn't she be a model or an actress or something? What sort of hold do you have over her, Simon?"

Simon Lawrence shrugged. "Will you be staying for the dedication on Wednesday, Andrew, or do you have to get right back?"

Wren reached for his latte and took a long sip. "No, I'm staying until Thursday. The dedication is part of what I came for. It's central to the article I'm writing."

Simon nodded. "Excellent. Now what's the other part, if you don't mind my asking? Everything we've talked about has been covered in the newspapers already—ad nauseam, I might add. *The New York Times* didn't send its top investigative reporter to interview me for a rerun, did it? What's up, Andrew?"

Wren shrugged, trying to appear casual in making the gesture. "Well, part of it is the dedication. I'm doing a piece on corporate and governmental involvement—or the lack thereof—in the social problems of urban America. God knows, there's little enough to write about that's positive, and your programs are bright lights in a mostly shadowy panorama of neglect and disinterest. You've actually done something where others have just talked about it—and what you've done works."

"But?"

"But in the last month or so the paper has received a

series of anonymous phone calls and letters suggesting
that there are financial improprieties in your programs
that need to be investigated. So my editor ordered me to
follow it up, and here I am."

Simon Lawrence nodded, his face expressionless. "Financial improprieties. I see." He studied Wren. "You
must have done some work on this already. Have you
found anything?"

Wren shook his head. "Not a thing."

"You won't, either. The charge is ridiculous." Simon
sipped at his latte and sighed. "But what else would I say,
right? So to set your mind at ease, Andrew, and to
demonstrate that I have nothing to hide, I'll let you have
a look at our books. I don't often do this, you understand,
but in this case I'll make an exception. You already
know, I expect, that we have accountants and lawyers
and a board of directors to make certain that everything
we do is above reproach. We're a high-profile operation
with important donors. We don't take chances with our
image."

"I know that," Wren demurred, looking vaguely embarrassed to deflect the implied criticism. "But I appreciate your letting me see for myself."

"The books will show you what comes in and what
goes out, everything but the names of the donors. You
aren't asking for those, are you, Andrew?"

"No, no." Wren shook his head quickly. "It's what
happens to the money after it comes in that concerns me.
I just want to be certain that when I write my article ex-
tolling the virtues of Fresh Start and Pass/Go and Toto
the Wonder Wizard, I won't be shown up as an idiot later
on." He tacked on a sheepish smile.

Simon Lawrence gave him a cool look. "An idiot? Not

you, Andrew. Not likely. Besides, if there's something crooked going on, I want to know about it, too."

He stood up. "Finish your latte. I'll have Jenny Parent, our bookkeeper, bring up the records. You can sit here and look them over to your heart's content." He glanced down at his watch. "I've got a meeting with some people downtown at five, but you can stay as long as you like. I'll catch up with you in the morning, and you can give me your report then. Fair enough?"

Wren nodded. "More than fair. Thank you, Simon."

Simon Lawrence paused midway around his desk. "Let me be honest with you about my feelings on this matter, Andrew. You are in a position to do a great deal of harm here, to undo an awful lot of hard work, and I don't want that to happen. I resent the hell out of the implication that I would do anything to subvert the efforts of Fresh Start and Pass/Go and the people who have given so much time and effort and money in support of those programs, but I understand that you can't ignore the possibility that the rumors and innuendos have some basis in fact. You wouldn't be doing your job if you did. So I am trusting you to be up front with me on anything you find—or, more to the point, don't find. Whatever you need, I'll try to give it to you. But I'm giving it to you in the belief that you won't write an article where rumors and accusations are repeated without any basis in fact."

Wren studied Lawrence for a moment. "I don't ever limit the scope of an investigation by offering conditions," he said quietly. "But I can also say that I have never based a report on anything that wasn't backed up by solid facts. It won't be any different here."

The other man held his gaze a moment longer. "See you tomorrow, Andrew."

He walked out the door and disappeared down the hallway, leaving Wren alone in his office. Wren sat where he was and finished his latte, then stood up and walked over to the window again. He admired the Wiz, admired the work he had done with the homeless. He hoped he wouldn't find anything bad to write about. He hoped the phone calls and letters were baseless—sour grapes from a former employee or an errant shot at troublemaking from an extremist group of "real Americans." He'd read the letters and listened to the tapes of the phone calls. It was possible there was nothing to them.

But his instincts told him otherwise. And he had learned from twenty-five years of experience that his instincts were seldom wrong.

The demon gave Andrew Wren the better part of an hour with the foundation's financial records, waiting patiently, allowing the reporter enough time to familiarize himself with the overall record of donations to Fresh Start and Pass/Go, then checked to make certain the hallway was empty and slipped into the room behind him. Wren never heard the demon approach, his back to the door, his head lowered to the open books as he ran his finger across the notations. The demon stood looking at him for a moment, thinking how easy it would be to kill him, feeling the familiar hunger begin to build.

But now was not the time and Wren had not been lured to Seattle to satisfy the demon's hunger. There were plenty of others for that.

The demon moved up behind Andrew Wren and placed its fingers on the back of the man's exposed neck.

Wren did not move, did not turn, did not feel anything as the dark magic entered him. His eyes locked on the pages before him, and his mind froze. The demon probed his thoughts, drew his attention, and then whispered the words that were needed to manipulate him.

I won't find what I'm looking for here. Simon Lawrence is much too clever for that. He wouldn't be stupid enough to let me look at these books if he thought they were incriminating. I have to be patient. I have to wait for my source to contact me.

The demon spoke in Andrew Wren's voice, in Andrew Wren's mind, in Andrew Wren's thoughts, and it would seem to the reporter as if the words were his own. He would do as the demon wanted without ever realizing it; he would be the demon's tool. He would think that the ideas the demon gave him were his own and that the conclusions the demon reached for him were his. It was easy enough to arrange. Andrew Wren was an investigative reporter, and investigative reporters believed that everyone was covering up something. Why should Simon Lawrence be different?

Andrew Wren hesitated a moment as the demon's words took root, and then he closed the book before him and began to stack it with the others.

The demon smiled in satisfaction. It wouldn't be long now until everything was in place. Another two days was all it would take. John Ross would be turned. A Knight of the Word would become a servant of the Void. It would happen so swiftly that it would be over before Ross even realized what was taking place. Even afterward, he would not know what had been done to him. But the demon would know, and that would be enough. A single step was all that was required to change John Ross's life,

a step away from the light and into the dark. Andrew
Wren would help make that happen.

The demon lifted its fingers from Andrew Wren's
neck, slipped back out the door, and was gone.

CHAPTER 8

In the aftermath of San Sobel, John Ross decided to return to the Fairy Glen and the Lady.

It took him a long time to reach his decision to do so. He was paralyzed for weeks following the massacre, consumed with despair and guilt, replaying the events over and over in his mind in an effort to make sense of them. Even after he had reached his conclusion that the demon had subverted a member of the police rescue squad, he could not lay the matter to rest. To begin with, he could never know for certain if his conclusion was correct. There would always be some small doubt that he still didn't have it right and might have done something else to prevent what had happened. Besides, wasn't he just looking for a way to shift the blame from himself? Wasn't that what it all came down to? Whatever the answer, the fact remained that he had been responsible for preventing the slaughter of those children, and he had failed.

So, after a lengthy deliberation on the matter, he decided he could no longer serve as a Knight of the Word.

But how was he to go about handing in his resignation? He might have decided he was quitting, but how did he go about giving notice? He had already stopped

105

trying to function as a Knight, had ceased thinking of himself as the Word's champion. He had retreated so far from who and what he had been that even the nature of his dreams had begun to change. Although he still dreamed, the dreams had turned vague and purposeless. He still wandered a grim and desolate future in which his world had been destroyed and its people reduced to animals, but his part in that world was no longer clear. When he dreamed, he drifted from landscape to landscape, encountering no one, seeing nothing of value, discovering nothing of his past that he might use as a Knight of the Word. It was what he wanted, not to be burdened with knowledge of events he might influence, but it was vaguely troubling as well. He still carried the staff bequeathed to him by the Word, the talisman that gave him his power, but he no longer used it for its magic, only as a walking stick. He still felt the magic within, a small tingling, a brief surge of heat, but he felt removed and disconnected from it.

He no longer saw himself as a Knight of the Word, had quit thinking of himself as one, but he needed a way to sever his ties for good. He decided finally that to do this he must go back to where it had all begun.

To Wales, to the Fairy Glen, and to the Lady.

He had not been back in more than ten years, not since he had traveled to England in his late twenties, a graduate student permanently mired in his search for his life's purpose, not since he had drifted from postgraduate course to postgraduate course, a prisoner of his own indecision. He had gone to England to change the direction of his life, to travel and study and find a path that had meaning for him. In the course of that pursuit, he had journeyed into Wales to stay at the cottage of a friend's parents in the village of Betwys-y-Coed in Gwynedd in the heart of the Snowdonia wilderness. He had been studying the history of the English kings, particularly of Edward Longshanks, who had built the iron ring of fortresses to subdue the Welsh in the Snowdonia region, and so was drawn to the opportunity to travel there. Once arrived, he began to fall under the spell of the country and its people, to become enmeshed in their history and folklore, and to sense that there was a purpose to his being there beyond what was immediately apparent.

Then he found the Fairy Glen and the ghost of Owain Glyndwr, the Welsh patriot, who appeared to him as a fisherman and persuaded him to come back at midnight so that he could see the fairies at play. Skeptical of the idea of fairies and a little frightened by the encounter, but captivated as well by the setting and the possibility that there was some truth to the fisherman's words, he eventually did as he was asked. It was there, in the blackness of the new moon and the sweep of a thousand stars on a clear summer night, that the Lady appeared to him for the first and only time. She told him of her need for his services as a Knight of the Word. She revealed to him his blood link to Owain Glyndwr, who had served her as a Knight in his lifetime. She showed to him a vision of the future that would be if her Knights failed to prevent it. She persuaded him to accept her, to accept the position she offered him, to accept a new direction in his life.

To accept the way of the Word.

Now, to abandon that way, to sever the ties that bound him to the Word's path, he decided he must return to her.

He bought a ticket, packed a single bag, and flew east. He arrived at Heathrow, boarded a train, and traveled west to Bristol and then across the border into Wales. He found the journey nostalgic and unsettling; his warm memories of the past competed with the harsh reality of his purpose in the present, and his emotions were left jumbled, his nerves on edge. It was late fall, and the countryside was beginning to take on a wintry cast as the colors of summer and autumn slowly drained away. The postage-stamp fields and meadows lay fallow, and the livestock huddled closer to the buildings and feeding troughs. Flowers had disappeared, and skies were clouded and gray with the changing weather.

He reached Betwys-y-Coed after expending several days and utilizing various forms of transportation, and he booked himself at a small inn. It began to rain the day he arrived, and it kept raining afterward. He waited for the rain to stop, spending time in the public rooms of the inn and exploring various shops he remembered from his visit before. A few of the residents remembered him. The village, he found, was substantially unchanged.

He spent time thinking about what he would say to the Lady when he came face-to-face with her. It would not be easy to tell her he could no longer be in her service. She was a powerful presence, and she would try to dissuade him from his purpose. Perhaps she would even hurt him. He still remembered how she had crippled him. After his return to his parents' home in Ohio, her emissary, O'olish Amaneh, had come to him with the staff, and he had sensed immediately that his life would change irrevocably if he accepted it. His determination and conviction had been eroding steadily since his return from England, but now there was no time left to equivocate. The staff was thrust upon him, and the moment his hands touched the polished wood, his foot and leg cramped and withered, the pain excruciating, and he was bound to the talisman forever.

Would that change now? he wondered. If he was no longer a Knight of the Word, would his leg be healed, be made whole and strong again? Or would his decision to abandon his charge cost him even more?

He tried not to dwell on the matter, but the longer he waited, the harder it became to convince himself to carry through on his resolve. His imagination was working overtime after a week of deliberation, stimulated by the rain and the gray and his own fears, turned gloomy and despairing of hope. This was a mistake, he began to believe. This was stupid. He should not have come here. He should have stayed where he was. It was sufficient that he refused to act as a Knight of the Word. His decision did not require the Lady's validation. He barely dreamed at all anymore, his dreams so indistinct by now that they lacked any recognizable purpose. They were closer to real dreams, to the ones normal people had that involved bits and pieces of events and places and people, all of it disjointed and meaningless. He was no longer being shown a usable future. He was no longer being given clues to a past he might act upon. Wasn't that sufficient proof that he was severed from his charge as a Knight of the Word?

But in the end he decided that he was being cowardly. He had come a long way just to turn around and go home again, and he should at least give it a try. He put on a slicker and boots and hitched a ride out to the Fairy Glen. He went at midday, thinking that perhaps the daylight would lessen his trepidation. But it was a slow, steady rain that fell, turning everything gray and misty, and the world had taken on a hazy, ephemeral look in which nothing seemed substantive, but was all made of shadows and the damp.

His ride dropped him right next to the white board sign with black letters that read FAIRY GLEN. Ahead, a rutted lane led away from the highway and disappeared over a low rise, following a wooden fence. A small parking lot was situated on the left with a box for donations, and a wooden arrow pointed down the lane, saying TO THE GLEN.

It was all as he remembered.

The car drove away, and he was left alone. The forest about him on both sides of the road was deep and silent and empty of movement. He could see no houses. Fences ran along the road at various points, bent with its curves, and disappeared into the gray. He took a long moment to stare at the signs, the donation box, the parking lot, and the rutted lane, and then at the countryside about him, recalling what it had been like when he had come here for the first time. It had been magical. Right from the beginning, he had felt it. He had been filled with wonder and expectation. Now he was weary and uncertain and burdened with a deep-seated sense of failure. As if all he had accomplished had gone for nothing. As if all he had given of himself had been for naught.

He walked up the rutted lane to find the break in the fence line that would lead him down into the glen. He walked slowly, placing his feet carefully, listening to the patter of the rain and the silence behind it. The branches of the trees hung over him like giants' arms, poised to sweep him up and carry him off. Shadows moved and drifted with the clouds, and his eyes swept the haze uneasily.

At the opening in the fence, he paused again, listening.

There was nothing to hear, but he kept thinking there should be, that something of what he remembered of his previous visit would reveal itself. But everything seemed new and different, and while the terrain looked as he remembered, it didn't feel the same. Something was missing, he knew. Something was changed.

He went through the gate in the fence and started down the pathway that wound into the ravine. Leaning heavily on his staff, he worked his way slowly ahead. The Fairy Glen was a jumble of massive boulders and broken rock and isolated patches of wildflowers and long grasses. A waterfall tumbled out of the high rocks to become a meandering stream of eddies and rapids, with pools so clear and still he could see the colored pebbles they collected. Rain dripped from the trees and puddled on the trail and ran down the steep sides of the ravine in rivulets that eroded the earth in intricate designs. No birdsong disturbed the white noise of the water's rush or the fall of the rain. No movement disrupted the deep carpet of shadows.

As he reached the floor of the ravine, he glanced back to where the waterfall spilled off the rocks, but there was no sign of the fairies. He slowed and looked around carefully. The Lady was nowhere to be seen. The Fairy Glen was cloaked in shadow and curtained by rain, and it was empty of life. It was as he remembered, but different, too. Like before, he decided, when he had stood at the gate opening, it seemed changed. He took a long moment to figure out what the nature of that change might be.

Then he had it. It was the absence of any magic. He couldn't feel any magic here. He couldn't feel anything.

His hand tightened on the staff, searching. The magic

failed to respond. He stood staring at the Fairy Glen in disbelief, unable to accept that this could be so. Were the Lady and the fairies gone from the glen? Was that why he could not sense the magic? Because the magic was no longer here?

He walked along the rugged bank of the rain-choked stream, picking his way carefully over the litter of broken rock and thick grasses. On a flat stone shelf, he knelt and peered down into a still pool. He could see his reflection clearly. He looked for something more, for something different, for a sign. Nothing revealed itself. He watched the rain pock his reflection with droplets that sent glistening, concentric rings arcing away, one after the other. His image grew shimmery and distorted, and he looked quickly away.

When he lifted his head, a fisherman was standing on the opposite shore a dozen yards away, staring at him. For a moment, Ross couldn't believe what he was seeing. He had convinced himself that the Fairy Glen was abandoned; he had given up hope of finding anyone here. But he recognized the fisherman instantly. His clothes and size and posture were unmistakable. And his look. Because he was a ghost and was not entirely solid, his body shifted and changed as the light played over it. When he tilted his head, as he did now, a slight movement of his broad-brimmed hat, his familiar features were revealed. It was Owain Glyndwr, his ancestor, the Welsh patriot who had fought against the English Bolingbroke, Henry IV—Owain Glyndwr, dead now for hundreds of years, but given new life in his service to the Lady. He looked just as he had years earlier, when Ross had first come upon him in the Fairy Glen.

Seeing him like this, materialized unexpectedly, would

have startled John Ross before, but not now. Instead, he felt his heart leap with gratitude and hope.

"Hello, Owain," he greeted with an anxious wave of his hand.

The fisherman nodded, a spare, brief movement. "Hello, John. How are you?"

Ross hesitated, suddenly unsure of what he should say. "Not well. Something's happened. Something terrible."

The other man nodded and turned away, working his line carefully through the rapids that swirled in front of where he stood. "Terrible things always happen when you are a Knight of the Word, John. A Knight of the Word is drawn to terrible things. A Knight of the Word stands at the center of them."

Ross adjusted the hood of his slicker to ward off the rain that blew into his eyes. "Not any longer. I'm not a Knight of the Word anymore. I've given it up."

The fisherman didn't look at him. "You cannot give it up. The choice isn't yours to make."

"Then whose choice is it?"

The fisherman was silent.

"Is she here, Owain?" Ross asked finally, coming forward to the very edge of the rock shelf on which he stood. "Is the Lady here?"

The fisherman gave a barely perceptible nod. "She is."

"Good. Because I couldn't feel her, couldn't feel anything of the magic when I walked down." Ross groped for the words he needed. "I suppose it's because I've been away for so long. But . . . it doesn't feel right." He hesitated. "Maybe it's because I'm here in the daylight, instead of at night. You told me, the first day we met, that if it was magic I was looking for, if I wanted to see the fairies, it was best to come at night. I'd almost forgotten

about that. I don't know what I was thinking. I'll come
back tonight—"

"John." Owain's soft voice stopped him midsentence.
"Don't come back. She won't appear for you."

John Ross stared. "The Lady? She won't? Why not?"

The fisherman took a long time before answering.
"Because the choice isn't yours to make."

Ross shook his head, confused. "I don't understand
what you're saying. Which choice? The one for her to
appear or the one for me to stop being a Knight of the
Word?"

The other man worked his pole and line without looking
up. "Do you know why you can't feel the magic, John?
You can't feel it because you don't admit that it's inside
yourself anymore. Magic doesn't just happen. It doesn't
just appear. You have to believe in it."

He looked over at Ross. "You've stopped believing."

Ross flushed. "I've stopped believing in its useful-
ness. I've stopped wanting it to rule my life. That's not
the same thing."

"When you become a Knight of the Word, you give
yourself over to a life of service to the Word." Owain
Glyndwr ran his big, gnarled hands smoothly along the
pole and line. Shadows from passing clouds darkened
his features. "If it was an easy thing to do, anyone would
be suitable to the task. Most aren't."

"Perhaps I'm one of them," Ross argued, anxious to
find a way to get his foot in the door the Lady had apparently closed on him. "Perhaps the Word made a mistake
with me."

He paused, waiting for a response. There was none.
This was stupid, he thought, arguing with a ghost. Pointless. He closed his eyes, remembering San Sobel. "Listen

to me, Owain. I can't go through it anymore. I can't live with it another day. The dreams and the killing and the monsters and the hate and fear and all of it endless and purposeless and stupid! I can't do it. I don't know how you did it."

The big man turned to face him again, taking up the pole and line, looking away from the stream. "I did it because I had to, John. Because I was there. Because maybe there was no one else. Because I was needed to do it. Like you."

Ross clenched his hands on the walnut staff. "I just want to return the staff," he said quietly. "Why don't I give it to you?"

"It doesn't belong to me."

"You could give it to the Lady for me."

The fisherman shook his head. "If I take it from you, how will you leave the Fairy Glen? You cannot walk without the staff. Will you crawl out on your hands and knees like an animal? If you do, what will you find waiting for you at the rim? When you became a Knight of the Word, you were transformed. Do you think you can be as you were? Do you think you can forget what you know, what you've seen, or what you've done? Ever?"

John Ross closed his eyes against the tears that suddenly welled up. "I just want my life back. I just want this to be over."

He felt the rain on his hands, heard the sound of the drops striking the rocks and trees and stream, small splashes and mutterings that whispered of other things. "Please, help me," he said quietly.

But when he looked up again, the ghost of Owain Glyndwr was gone, and he was alone.

* * *

He climbed out of the Fairy Glen and returned—walking more than half the distance before he found a ride—to his inn. He ate dinner in the public rooms and drank several pints of the local ale, thinking on what he would do, on what he believed must happen. The rain continued to fall, but as midnight neared it eased off to a slow, soft drizzle that was more mist than rain.

The innkeeper let him borrow his car, and Ross drove out to the Fairy Glen and parked in the little parking lot and walked once more to the gap in the fence. The night was clouded and dark, the world filled with shadows and wet sounds, and the interlaced branches of the trees formed a thick net that looked as if it were poised to drop over him. He eased his way through the gap and proceeded carefully down the narrow, twisting trail. The Fairy Glen was filled with the sound of water rushing over the rocks of the rain-swollen stream, and the rutted trail was slick with moisture. Ross took a long time to reach the floor of the ravine, and once there he stood peering about cautiously for a long time. When nothing showed itself, he walked to the edge of the stream and stood looking back at the falls.

But the fairies, those pinpricks of scattered, whirling bright light he remembered so well, did not appear. Nor did the Lady. Nor did Owain Glyndwr. He stood in the darkness and rain for hours, waiting patiently and expectantly, willing them to appear, reaching out to them with his thoughts, as if by the force of his need alone he could make them materialize. But no one came.

He returned to his rooms in disappointment, slept for most of the day, rose to eat, waited anew, and went out again the following night. And again, no one appeared.

He refused to give up. He went out each night for a week and twice more during the days, certain that someone would appear, that they could not ignore him entirely, that his determination and persistence would yield him something.

But it was as if that other world had ceased to exist. The Lady and the fairies had vanished completely. Not even Owain returned to speak with him. Not a hint of the magic revealed itself. Time after time he waited at the edge of the stream, a patient supplicant. Surely they would not abandon him when he needed help so badly. At some point they would speak to him, if only to reject his plea. His pain was palpable. They must feel it. Wasn't he entitled to at least the reassurance that they understood? The rain continued to fall in steady sheets, the forests of Snowdonia stayed dark and shadowy, and the air continued damp and cold in the wake of fall's passing and the approach of winter.

Finally he went home to America. He despaired of giving up, but there seemed to be no other choice. It was clear he was to be given no audience, to be offered no further contact. He was wasting his time. He packed his bags, bussed and trained his way back to Heathrow, boarded a plane, and flew home. He thought more than once to turn around and go back to the Fairy Glen, to try again, but he knew in his heart it was futile. By choosing to give up his office, he had made himself an outcast. Perhaps Owain Glyndwr was right, that once you gave up on the magic, it gave up on you, as well. He no longer felt a part of it, that much was certain. Even when he touched the rune-scrolled length of his staff, he could find no sign of life. He had wanted to distance himself from the magic, and apparently he had done so.

He accepted that this was the way it must be if he was to stop being a Knight of the Word. Whatever ties had bound him to the Word's service were apparently severed. The magic was gone. The dreams had nearly ceased. He was a normal man again. He could go about finding a normal life.

But he remembered Owain Glyndwr's words about how, by becoming a Knight of the Word, he had been transformed and things could never be the same again. He found himself thinking of a time several years earlier in Hopewell, Illinois, when Josie Jackson had made him feel for just a few hours of his nightmarish existence what it was like to be loved, and of how he had walked away from her because he knew he had nothing to give her in return. He recalled how Nest Freemark had asked him in despair and desperation if he was her father, and he remembered wishing so badly he could tell her that he was.

He thought of these things, and he wondered if anything even remotely resembling a normal life would ever be possible again.

CHAPTER 9

It was already dark when John Ross and Stefanie
Winslow exited the offices of Fresh Start, turned
down Main Street, and headed for Umberto's. Daylight
saving time was over for another year, and all the clocks
had been reset Sunday morning in an effort to conserve
daylight—spring forward, fall back—but the approach
of winter in the northwest shortened Seattle days to not
much more than eight hours anyway. Streetlights threw
their hazy glare on the rough pavement of the roadways
and sidewalks, and the air was sharp and crisp with cold.
It had rained earlier in the day, so shallow puddles dotted
the concrete and dampness permeated the fall air. Traffic
moved sluggishly through a heavy concentration of mist,
and the city was wrapped in a ghostly pall.

Ross and Stefanie crossed Second Avenue and continued west past Waterfall Park, a strange, secretive
hideaway tucked into an enclosure of brick walls and
iron fences that abutted the apartment building where
they lived. One entire wall and corner of the park's enclosure was devoted to a massive waterfall that tumbled
over huge rocks with such a thunderous rush that conversation attempted in its immediate vicinity was drowned
out. A walkway dropped down along a catchment and

circled back around to a narrow pavilion with two additional features involving a spill of water over stone, and a cluster of tables and chairs settled amid a collection of small trees and flowering vines. In better weather, people employed in the vicinity would come into the park on their lunch breaks to watch the waterfall and to eat. John and Stefanie did so frequently. From their bedroom window, they could look down on the park and across at the offices of Fresh Start.

Adjoining Waterfall Park was Occidental Park, a broad open space paved with cobblestones that overlapped Main from Jackson to Yesler and fronted a series of shops and restaurants and a parking lot that serviced the entire Pioneer Square area. The new Seattle was built on the old Seattle, the earlier version of the city having burned to the ground in a turn-of-the-century fire. An underground tour of portions of the old city began just a few blocks to the north. By passing through a nondescript door and descending a steep, narrow flight of stairs, you could step back in time.

But the present was above ground, and that was what most people came to see. Pioneer Square was an eclectic collection of art galleries, craft outlets, bookstores, bars, restaurants, souvenir shops, and oddities, funky and unassuming and all-embracing, and John Ross had felt at home from the day he arrived.

He had come to Seattle with Stef more than a year ago. They had been together for several months by then, were drifting more or less, and had read about Fresh Start and thought it would be a good place for them to work. They had come on a whim, not even knowing if there might be jobs available, and there hadn't been, not at first, but they had fallen in love with the city and particularly with Pio-

neer Square. They had rented a small apartment to see
how things would go, and while he had been pessimistic
about their chances of catching on at Fresh Start—they
had been told, after all, that there were no paid openings
and none expected anytime soon—Stef had just laughed
and told him to be patient. And sure enough, within a week
Simon Lawrence had called her back and said he had
something, and within a month after that, after spending
his time doing volunteer work at the shelter, Ross had
been offered full-time employment, too.

He glanced over at Stef surreptitiously as they crossed
Occidental Park. He was wearing his greatcoat with the
huge collar turned up and his heavy wool scarf with
the fringed ends trailing behind, and as he limped along
with the aid of his heavy walking staff, he looked a little
like a modern-day Gandalf. Stefanie matched her pace to
his, all sleek and smooth and flawless with her shimmering black hair and long limbs. She seemed entirely
out of place amid the jumble of old buildings, antique
street lamps, and funky people. She looked odd walking
past the trolley that was stopped at the little island across
from The Paper Cat, as if she had gotten off at the wrong
stop on her way to the glass and steel towers of the high-
rent district uptown. You might have thought she was
slumming amid the homeless men who were clustered
together next to the carved wooden totems and on the
benches and under the mushroom-shaped pavilion across
the way.

But you would have been wrong. If there was one
thing Ross had learned about Stefanie Winslow, it was
that notwithstanding how she looked and dressed, she
was right at home anywhere. You might think you could
tell something about her by just looking at her, but you

couldn't. She was comfortable with herself in a way that astonished him. Stef was one of those rare people who could walk into any situation, anyplace, anytime, and find a way to deal with it. It was a combination of presence and attitude and intelligence. It was the reason Simon Lawrence had hired her. And subsequently hired him, for that matter. Stefanie made you feel she was indispensable. She made you believe she was up to anything. It was, in large part, he knew, why he was in love with her.

They rounded the corner at Elliott Bay Book Company and walked down First Avenue to King Street, then turned into the door of Umberto's Ristorante. The hostess checked off their names, smiled warmly at Stef, and said that their table was ready. She led them down several steps to the dining area, past the salad island toward the neon sign that said IL PICCOLO, which was the tiny corner bar, then turned right down a hallway covered with posters of upcoming Seattle arts events. Ross looked at Stef in surprise. The dining room was behind them now; where were they going? Stef gave him a wink.

At the end of the hallway was the wine cellar, a small room closed away behind an iron gate in which a single table had been set for dinner. The hostess opened the wrought-iron door and seated them inside. A white tablecloth, green napkins, and silver and china seemed to glow in soft candlelight amid the racks of wines surrounding them.

"How did you manage this?" Ross asked in genuine amazement as the hostess left them alone.

Stef tossed back her long hair, reached for his hand, and said, "I told them it was for you."

* * *

He had been back from Wales for almost a month when he met her. He had returned defeated in spirit and bereft of hope. He had failed in his effort to speak with the Lady or return the staff of power. His parents were dead, and his childhood home sold. He had lost contact with his few relatives years earlier. He had nowhere to go and no one to go to. For lack of a better idea, he went up from New York to Boston College, where he had studied years earlier, and began auditing classes while he worked out his future. He was offered a position in the graduate-studies program in English literature, but he asked for time to think about it, uncertain if he wanted to go back into academia. What he really wanted was to do something that would allow him to make a difference in people's lives, to take a job working with people he could help. He needed human contact again. He needed validation of his existence. He worked hard at thinking of himself as something other than a Knight of the Word. He struggled bravely to develop a new identity.

Each day he would take his lunch in the student cafeteria, sitting at a long table, poring through his study books and staring out the windows of the dining hall. It was winter, and snow lay thick and white on the ground, ice hung from the eaves, and breath clouded in the air like smoke. Christmas was approaching, and he had nowhere to spend it and no one to spend it with. He felt incredibly lonely and adrift.

That was when he first saw Stefanie Winslow. It was early December, only days before the Christmas break. He wasn't sure if she had been coming there all along and he just hadn't noticed her or if she had suddenly appeared. Once he saw her though, he couldn't look away. She was easily the most beautiful woman he had ever seen—exotic, stunning, and unforgettable. He couldn't find words to give voice to what he was feeling. He watched her all through the lunch hour and stayed afterward when he should have been auditing his class, continuing to stare at her until she got up and walked away.

The next day she was back, sitting at the same table, off to one side, all alone. He watched her come in and sit down to have her lunch for five days, thinking each time that he had to go over to her and say something, had to introduce himself, had to make some sort of contact, but he always ended up just sitting there. He was intimidated by her. But he was compelled, as well. No one else tried to sit with her; no one else even tried to approach. That gave him pause. But his connection with her was so strong, so visceral, that he could not ignore it.

Finally, at the beginning of the following week, he just got up and walked over, limped over really, feeling stupid and inadequate with his heavy staff and rough look, and said hello. She smiled up at him as if he were the most important thing in her life, and said hello back. He told her his name, she told him hers.

"I've been watching you for several days," he said, giving her a deprecatory shrug.

"I know," she said, arching one eyebrow speculatively.

He flushed. "I guess I overdid it if I was that obvious. I was wondering if you were a student at the college."

She shook her head, her black hair catching the winter light. "No, I work in administration."

"Oh. Well, I'm auditing some classes." He let the words trail away. He didn't know where else to go with it. He felt suddenly awkward about what he was doing, sitting here with her. He glanced about. "I didn't mean to intrude, I just . . ."

"John," she interrupted gently, drawing his eyes back to hers, holding them. "Do you know why I've been sitting here alone every day?"

He shook his head slowly.

"Because," she said, drawing out the word, "I've been waiting for you to join me."

She always knew the right thing to say. He had been in love with her from the beginning, and his feelings had just grown stronger over time. He sat watching her now as she gave their order to the waiter, a young man with long sideburns and a Vandyke beard, holding his attention with her eyes, with her voice, with her very presence. The waiter wouldn't look away if a bomb went off, Ross thought. When he left with the order, the wine steward, who had been by earlier, reappeared with the bottle of Pinot Grigio Stef had ordered. He poured it for Ross to taste, but Ross indicated Stef was in charge. She tasted it, nodded, and the wine steward filled their glasses and disappeared.

They sat close within the dim circle of candlelight and stared at each other without speaking. Silently Ross hoisted his glass. She responded in kind, they clinked crystal softly, and drank.

"Is this some sort of special occasion?" he asked finally. "Did I forget an important date?"

"You did," she advised solemnly.

"And you won't tell me what it is, will you?"

"As a matter of fact, I will. But only because I don't

want to see how long it takes you to remember." She cocked her head slightly in his direction. "It was one year ago today, exactly, that Simon Lawrence hired you to work at Fresh Start."

"You're kidding."

"I don't kid. Josh, yes. Tease, now and then. Never kid." She took a sip of her wine and licked her lips. "Cause for celebration, don't you think? Who would have thought you would end up writing speeches for the Wizard of Oz?"

Ross shook his head. "Who would have thought I would have ended up living with Glinda the Good?"

Stef arched her eyebrows in mock horror. "Glinda the Good? Wasn't she a witch?"

"A good witch. That's why she was called Glinda the Good."

Stef gave him a considering look. "John, I love you deeply, madly, truly. But don't call me Glinda the Good. Don't call me anything that smacks of the Wizard of Oz or the Emerald City or Munchkins or Dorothy or the yellow brick road. I get quite enough of that at work. Our life is separate and distinct from all this Wiz business."

He leaned back, looking hurt. "But it's the date of my hiring. Isn't the analogy appropriate under those circumstances?"

The waiter returned with their salads, and they began to eat. The sounds of the main dining room seemed distant and disconnected from their little haven. Ross thought about all the years he had dreaded night's coming and sleep, plagued by the knowledge that when he slept he was condemned to dream of the future he must prevent and of the horror he must live if he failed. Once, he had thought he would never escape that life, and that even if he did, its memories would haunt him forever. Stefanie had saved him from that, helped him find his way free of the labyrinth of his past, and brought him back into the light of possibility and hope.

"Have you finished your polish of the Wiz's speech?" she asked. "Hmm, good salad. I like the bits of walnuts and blue cheese."

"It's all done," he replied with a sigh. "Another masterpiece. Simon will be quoted for weeks afterward." He grinned. "I shall live vicariously through him, his words my own."

"Yes, well, I don't know how much of this vicarious-living business you want to indulge in," she mused, lifting her wineglass and studying it speculatively. "He seemed pretty on edge after Andrew Wren's visit."

Ross looked up from his salad. "Really? What was that all about anyway, did you ever find out?"

She shook her head. "But it's never good news for a public figure when an investigative reporter comes calling."

"No, I suppose not."

"Jenny told me Simon asked for the books cataloguing donations and expenditures to be brought up for Wren to look at. What does that suggest to you?"

"Financial impropriety." Ross shrugged. "Wren will hunt a long time before he'll find evidence of that. Simon's a fanatic about keeping clean books. He can account for every penny received or spent."

He went back to eating his salad. Stef continued to study her wineglass, finally taking a sip from it. "I just don't like the way Simon is behaving," she said finally. "He isn't himself lately. Something is bothering him."

Ross finished chewing, kept his eyes lowered, then

forced himself to look up at her and smile. "Something is bothering almost everyone, Stef. The thing to remember is, mostly we have to work these things out by ourselves."

John Ross dreams. It is the same dream, the only dream he has anymore that he can remember upon waking. It is a dream of the future he was sworn to prevent as a Knight of the Word, and each time it reoccurs it is a little darker than it was before.

This time is no exception.

He stands on a hillside south of Seattle, watching as the city burns. Hordes of once-men and demons pour through gaps in the shattered defenses and drive the defenders steadily back toward the water that hems them in on all sides but his. Feeders cavort through the carnage and drink in the terror and frenzy and rage of the dying and wounded. It is a nightmarish scene, the whole of the scorched and burning landscape awash in rain and mist, darkened by clouds and gloom, wrapped in a madness that finds voice in the screams and cries of the humans it consumes.

But the feelings that fill Ross are unfamiliar ones. They are not of frustration or anger, not of despair or sadness, as they have been each time before. His feelings now are dull and empty, devoid of anything but irritation and a faint boredom. He stands with a group of the city's survivors, but he has no regard for them either. Rather, he is a shell, armored and invulnerable, but emotionless. He has no idea how he became this way, but it is a transcending experience to realize it has happened. He is no longer a Knight of the Word; he is something else en-

tirely. The humans he stands with are not a part of him. They do not meet his gaze as he looks over at them speculatively. They cower in his presence and huddle submissively before him. They are frightened of him. They are terrified.

Then the old man approaches and whispers that he knows him, that he remembers him from years earlier. His hollow-eyed gaze is vacant, and his voice is flat and toneless. He looks and speaks as if he is disconnected from his body. He repeats the familiar words. You were there, in the Emerald City! You killed the Wizard of Oz! It was Halloween night, and you were wearing a mask of death! They were celebrating his life, and you killed him!

He shoves the old man away roughly. The old man collapses in a heap and begins to sob. He lies helpless in the dirt and rainwater, his ragged clothes and beard matted with mud, his frail body shaking.

Ross looks away. He knows the words the old man speaks are true, but he does not care. He has walled away all guilt long since, and killing no longer means anything to him.

He realizes in that moment that he is no longer part of the humans clustered at his feet. He has shed his humanity; he has left it behind him in a past he can barely remember.

Suddenly, he understands why the humans look at him as they do.

He is the enemy who has come to destroy them.

Ross and Stef walked slowly back along First Avenue after leaving Umberto's, arms linked, shoulders hunched against the cold. The air was still hazy and damp and the sky still gray, but there was no rain yet. The street lamps of Pioneer Square blazed above them, casting their shadows on the sidewalk as they passed, dark human patterns lengthening and then fading with each bright new circle.

The dream had come again last night, for the first time in several weeks, and Ross was still wrestling with its implications. In this latest version of the future, Simon Lawrence was still dead, and Ross was still his killer. But now Ross was one of the bad guys, no longer a Knight of the Word, no longer even a passive observer as he had been every time the dream came to him before. He was some sort of demon clone, a creature of the Void and only barely recognizable as having ever been human.

He frowned into the upturned collar of his coat. It was ridiculous, ludicrous to think that any of this could ever come to pass.

So why was he having this dream?

Why was he being plagued with visions of a future he would never let happen?

"The state legislature is going to pass a bill before the end of the week that will cut back on state funding for welfare recipients to match what the federal government has already done in cutting back its funding to the state." Stef's voice was soft and detached in the gloom. "Maybe that's what has got Simon so upset."

"Well, by all means, let's put more people back on the streets." Ross shook his head, thinking of other things.

"Welfare encourages people not to work, John. You know that. You hear it all the time. Cutting off their aid will force them to get out there and get a job."

"Good thing it's all so simple. We can just ignore the culture of poverty. We can just pretend that poor people are just rich people without money. We can tell ourselves that educational, social, and cultural opportunities are the same for everyone. We can ignore the statistics on domestic violence and teen pregnancy and rate of exposure to crime and disease and family stability. Cut off welfare and put 'em to work. I don't know why anyone didn't think of it before. We can have everyone off the street and working by the end of the month, I bet."

"Yep. Then we can tackle a cure for cancer and get that out of the way, too." She snuggled her face into his shoulder, her dark hair spilling over him like silk.

"I liked our dinner," he ventured, trying to take the edge off his frustration.

She nodded into his coat. "Good. I liked it, too."

They rounded the corner of Main at Elliott Bay Book Company and started for home. Occidental Park sprawled ahead of them, empty of life, watched over by the wooden totems, spectral sentinels in the gloom. The homeless had moved on to warmer spots for the night, abandoning their daytime haunt. Some would find a bed in one of the shelters. Some would make their bed on the streets. Some would wake up in the morning. Some would not.

"There are just not enough of us," Ross said quietly.

She lifted her head to look at him. "Not enough of who?"

"Not of who. Of what. I misspoke. Not enough shelters for the homeless. Not enough schools for displaced children. Not enough food banks. Not enough care facilities. Not enough churches working with the needy. Not enough charities. Not enough programs or funding or answers. Not enough of anything."

She nodded. "There's a lot of competition for people's money and time, John. The choices aren't always easy."

"Maybe it would be easier if people remembered there's a lot of competition for their souls, as well."

She stared hard at him for a moment. "Then everyone should be able to figure out what to do, shouldn't they?"

They crossed Main to Waterfall Park, peering into the blackness where the sound of rushing water welled up and reverberated off the brick walls. Amid the cluster of rocks and trees and garden tables, shadows shifted with barely perceptible movements. Ross thought he caught a glimpse of lantern eyes peering out at him. He didn't see the feeders much anymore—only brief glimpses. It bothered him sometimes that he couldn't see them better. He had wanted to remove himself from their world, and it didn't help knowing they were there and not being able to see them.

It reminded him of something Owain Glyndwr had asked of him.

Do you think you can ever be as you were?

He found himself thinking of the dream again, of the way he had appeared in it, of the way it made him feel. He might not ever be as he was, but at least he could keep himself from being like that. He could manage that much, couldn't he?

He stared into the shadows in silence, Stefanie clinging to his arm, and dared the things that lurked within to come into the light. It seemed to him as he did so that he could feel them daring him, in turn, to come into the dark.

CHAPTER 10

Even though its hunger had become all-consuming, the demon waited until after midnight to hunt.

It crept from its lair as silent as the death that awaited its victims and slipped out onto the empty streets of Pioneer Square. The weeknight city had closed its eyes early, and even the bars and restaurants had shuttered their doors and clicked off their lights. The air was damp and heavy with mist and the beginnings of a fresh rain, and the moisture glistened on the concrete in a satiny sheen. Cars eased past in ones and twos, carrying their occupants to home and bed, strays following in the wake of the early evening rush. The demon watched from the shadows close by Occidental Park, wary of being seen. But the park and sidewalks and streets were empty and still. The demon was alone.

It crept from its hiding place in human form, standing upright, maintaining its guise as it made its way to the place where the hunt would begin. It wore running shoes and sweats to mask the sound of its passing, keeping to the shadows as much as possible, sliding along the walls of the darkened buildings, across the shadowed stretches of the park, and through the blackened tunnels of the alleys and walkways. The homeless who spent their days in the park had all gone elsewhere, and the Indian totems loomed above the empty stone spaces like hunters in search of prey, eyes fearsome and staring, beaks and talons at the ready.

But the demon's hunt was not for food. Its hunger was of a different sort. Its hunger was more primal and less easily understood. The demon hunted because it needed to kill. It hunted to feel the struggles of its victims as it rent their flesh, cracked their bones, and spilled their blood. It hunted to experience that exquisite moment of fulfillment when its efforts claimed another human life—that last shudder of consciousness, that final exhalation of breath, that concluding gasp as death arrived. The demon's need for killing humans was indigenous to its makeup. It had been human itself once, long ago, and to continue to be what it was, it was necessary for it to keep killing its human self over and over again. It accomplished this through the killing of others. Its own humanity was drowned completely in the madness that drove it, but it was necessary that it pretend at being human so that it could move freely among its victims, and there was danger in this. Killing kept the pretense from ever threatening to become even a momentary reality.

At the corner of First Avenue and Yesler, the demon paused a final time in the shadows to look about. Seeing neither cars nor people approaching, it slipped quickly across First to the line of old doorways and basement windows that fronted the street, and hunkered down beside a set of concrete steps that led into a kite and banner shop. Again, it paused to look about and listen. Again, it saw and heard nothing.

Scooting forward like a crab, it paused in front of an old, wood-frame basement window with its glass painted out, levered the window open with practiced ease, slithered through the opening into the darkness beyond, and was gone.

Inside, it dropped softly to the basement floor and waited for its eyes to adjust. It took only a moment, for the demon's sight was as keen in darkness as in light. It saw with all its senses, unlike the human it had once been, unlike the humans it hunted. It despised the weaknesses of flesh and blood and bone it had long ago discarded. It despised the humanity that it had shed like a snake's skin. It was not burdened by moral codes or emotional balance or innate sensibility or anything even approaching responsibility. The demon functioned in its service to the Void without any restrictions save one—to survive. It did not question that it served the Void; it did so because it could not conceive of any other way to be and because the Void's interests were a perfect fit with its own. The demon's purpose in life was to destroy the humans of whom it had once been part. Its purpose was to wipe them from the face of the earth. That it served the Void in doing so seemed mostly chance.

It stood motionless in the darkness for a long moment, then began to strip off its clothes. It would hunt better once it had transformed. Its human guise was uncomfortable and restrictive, and it served only to remind the demon of the shell it had been trapped inside for so many years. All demons were mutable and, given time, could become whatever they chose. But this demon was particularly adept. It could change forms effortlessly, which was not usually the case. Most demons were required to keep to the form they adopted because it took so long to build another. But this demon was different. It could change forms with the speed of a chameleon changing colors, rebuilding itself in moments. Its ability had served it well as a creature of the Void. It specialized in ferreting out and subverting the more powerful servants of the Word. It had destroyed many of them. It was working now at destroying John Ross.

Of course, it was only the part of Ross that was human that the demon sought to destroy. It would keep the rest. It would keep his magic. It would keep his knowledge. It would set free the dark underside that he worked so hard to contain and give it mastery over what remained of his spirit.

When its clothes lay on the floor, the demon began to change. Its human form disappeared as its body swelled and knotted with muscle and its skin sprouted thick, coarse hair. Its head lengthened, its jaws widened, and its teeth grew long and sharp. It took on the appearance of something that was a cross between a huge cat and a massive dog, but it resembled most closely a monstrous hyena—all powerful neck and sinewy shoulders and fanged muzzle.

Altered, it dropped down on all fours and began to make its way through the darkness. It passed from the basement down a set of open stairs to another level. Now it was inside the burned-out shell of old Seattle, of the ruin that served as the foundation for the city above. This was not a part of the old city that was covered by the underground tour. It was a part that was closed off, inaccessible to most. The streets and alleyways ran on for hundreds of yards, mysterious and empty. Parts of it collapsed from time to time, and sometimes its darkened corridors flooded with runoff from the streets and sewers during heavy rains. Few knew it even existed. No one ever came down at night.

Except for the homeless.

And the demon who liked to hunt them.

The demon was thinking of John Ross, imagining what it would be like to close its massive jaws about his throat, to crush the life from him, to feel the blood spurt from his torn body. The demon hated Ross. But the demon was attracted to him, too. All that magic, all that power, the legacy of a Knight of the Word. The demon would like to taste that. It would like to share it. It hungered for killing, but it hungered for the taste of magic even more.

Its feral eyes cast about in the black as it loped through the darkness on silent paws, ears pricked forward, listening. All about, feeders kept pace. There would be killing, they sensed. There would be terror and rage and desperation, and they were anxious to taste them all. Just as the demon hungered after magic and killing, the feeders hungered for the residual emotions in humans that both evoked.

John Ross belongs to me, the demon was thinking. *He belongs to me because I have found him, claimed him, and understand his uses. I will subvert him, and I will set him free. I will make him over as I have made myself over. It will happen soon, so soon. The wheels of the machine that will make it possible are in motion. No one can stop them. No one can change what I intend.*

John Ross is mine.

Ahead, distant still through the seemingly unending darkness, the faint sound of voices rose. The demon's jaws hung open and its tongue lolled out. The eyes of the feeders gleamed more brightly and their movements grew more intense.

Head lowered, nose sniffing expectantly at the cobblestones of the underground city's abandoned streets, the demon began to creep forward.

Above ground and unaware of the demon's presence, Nest Freemark was less than two blocks away.

It had taken her all day to get to Seattle, and she had arrived too late to make a serious effort at contacting John Ross until tomorrow—which, by now, was today, because it was after midnight. Fending off endless questions regarding her travel plans and misguided offers of help, she had booked a United flight leaving O'Hare at three-fifteen in the afternoon and, as planned, ridden into Chicago that morning with Robert. Robert meant well, but he still didn't know when to back off. She avoided telling him exactly what it was she was doing or why she was going. It was an unexpected trip, a visit to some relatives, and that was all she would say. Robert was beside himself with curiosity, but she thought it would do him good to have to deal with his frustration. Besides, she wasn't entirely unhappy with the idea of letting him suffer a little more as penance for his behavior at her grandfather's funeral.

He dropped her at the ticketing entrance to United, still offering to come along, to accompany her, to meet her, to do whatever she asked. She smiled, shook her head, said good-bye, picked up her bag, and walked inside. Robert drove away. She waited to make sure.

She hadn't seen Ariel since the night before and had no idea how the tatterdemalion planned to reach Seattle, but that wasn't her problem. She checked her bag, received her boarding pass, and was advised that the departure time had been moved back to five o'clock due to a problem with the plane.

She walked down to the assigned gate, took a seat, and resumed reading the book she had begun the night before. It was titled *The Spiritual Child*, and it was written by Simon Lawrence. She was drawn to the book for several reasons—first, because it made frequent reference to the writing of Robert Coles, and to his book *The Spiritual Life of Children* in particular, which she had read for a class in psychology last semester and enjoyed immensely, and second, because she was on her way to find John Ross, who was working for Lawrence at Fresh Start, and she wanted to know something about the thinking of the man with whom a failed Knight of the Word would ally himself. Of course, it might be that this was only a job for Ross and nothing more, but Nest didn't think so. That didn't sound like John Ross. He wasn't the sort to take a job indiscriminately. After abandoning his service to the Word, he would want to find something he felt strongly about to commit to.

In any case, she had whiled away the time reading Simon Lawrence, the airplane still hadn't shown, the weather had begun to deteriorate with the approach of a heavy thunderstorm, and the departure time had been pushed back yet again. Growing concerned that she might not get out at all, Nest had gone up to the gate agent and asked what the chances were that the flight might not leave. The agent said she didn't know. Nest

retraced her steps to customer service and asked the
agent on duty if she could transfer to another flight. The
agent looked doubtful until Nest explained that a close
friend was dying, and she needed to get to Seattle right
away if she was to be of any comfort to him. It was close
enough to the truth that she didn't feel too bad about
saying it, and it got her a seat on a flight to Denver connecting on to Seattle.

The flight had left a little after five, she was in
Denver by six forty-five, mountain time, and back on a
second plane to Seattle by seven-fifty. The flight up
took another two hours and something, and it was approaching ten o'clock Pacific time before the plane
touched down at Sea-Tac. Nest disembarked carrying
her bag, walked outside to the taxi stand, and caught a
ride downtown. Her driver was Pakistani or East Indian,
a Sikh perhaps, wearing one of those turbans, and he
didn't have much to say. She still hadn't seen a sign of
Ariel, and she was beginning to worry. She could find
her way around the city, locate John Ross, and make
her pitch alone if she had to, but she would feel better
having someone she could turn to for advice if she came
up against a problem. She was already composing what
she would say to Ross. She was wondering as well why
he would pay any attention to her, the Lady's assur-
ances notwithstanding.

She missed Pick terribly. She hadn't thought their
separation would be so bad, but it was. He had been with
her almost constantly from the time she was six years
old; he was her best friend. She had been able to leave
him to go off to school, but Northwestern University was
only a three-hour drive from Hopewell and it didn't feel
so far away. She supposed her grandfather's death con-

tributed to her discomfort as well; Pick was the last link to her childhood, and she didn't like leaving him behind. It was also the first time she had done anything involving the magic without him. Whatever the reason, not having him there made her decidedly uneasy.

The taxi driver had taken her to the Alexis Hotel, where she had booked a room the night before by phone. The Alexis was situated right at the north end of Pioneer Square, not far from the offices of Fresh Start. It was the best hotel in the area, and Nest had decided from the start that if she was going to travel to a strange city, she wanted to stay in a good place. She had been able to get a favorable rate on a standard room for the two-night stop-over she had planned. She checked in at the front desk, took the elevator to her room, dropped her bag on the bed, and looked around restlessly.

Despite the fact that she had been traveling all day, she was not tired. She unpacked her bag, glanced through a guide to Seattle, and walked to the window and looked out. The street below glistened with dampness, and the air was hazy with mist. All of the shops and offices she could see were closed. There were only a few cars passing and fewer people. It was just a little after eleven-thirty.

She had decided to go for a walk.

Nest was no fool. She knew about cities at night and the dangers they presented for the unwary. On the other hand, she had grown up with the feeders in Sinnissippi Park, spending night after night prowling the darkness they favored, avoiding their traps, and surviving confrontations far more dangerous than anything she was likely to encounter here. Moreover, she had the magic to protect her, and while she hadn't used it in a while and didn't know what stage of growth it was in at the moment, she had confidence that it would keep her safe.

So she had slipped on her heavy windbreaker, ridden the elevator back down to the lobby, and gone out the door.

She was no sooner outside and walking south along First Avenue toward the banks of old-fashioned street lamps that marked the beginning of Pioneer Square than Ariel had appeared. The tatterdemalion materialized out of the mist and gloom, filling a space in the darkness beside Nest with her vague, transparent whiteness. Her sudden appearance startled Nest, but she didn't seem to notice, her dark eyes cast forward, her silken hair flowing out from her body as if caught in a breeze.

"Where are you going?" she asked in her thin child-like voice.

"Walking. I can't sleep yet. I'm too wound up." Nest watched the shadows whirl and spin inside the tatterdemalion's gauzy body. "How did you get here?"

Ariel didn't seem to hear the question, her dark eyes shifting anxiously. "It isn't safe," she said.

"What isn't safe?"

"The city at night."

They had crossed from the hotel and walked into the next block. Nest looked around cautiously at the darkened doorways and alcoves of the buildings. There was no one to be seen.

"I remember about cities," Ariel continued, her voice small and distant. She seemed to float across the pavement, a ghostly hologram. "I remember how they feel and what they hide. I remember what they can do to you. They are filled with people who will hurt you. They are places in which children can disappear in the blink of an eye. Sometimes they lock you away in dark places and no one comes for you. Sometimes they wall you up forever."

She was speaking from the memories of the children she had been once, of the only memories she had. Nest decided she didn't want to know about those memories, the memories of dead children.

"It will be all right," she said. "We won't go far."

They walked quite a distance though, all the way down First Avenue under Pioneer Square's turn-of-the-century street lamps past shuttered shops and galleries to where they could see the Kingdome rising up against the night sky in a massive hump. The mist thickened and swirled about them, clinging to Nest's face and hands in a thin, cold layer of moisture. Nest drew her windbreaker tighter about her shoulders. When the character of the neighborhood began to change, the shops and galleries giving way to warehouses and industrial plants, Nest turned around again, with Ariel hovering close, and started back.

They were approaching a small, concrete, triangular park with benches and shade trees fronting a series of buildings that included one advertising Seattle's Underground Tour when the screams began.

They were so faint that at first Nest couldn't believe she was hearing them. She slowed and looked around doubtfully. She was all alone on the streets. There was no one else in sight. But the screams continued, harsh and terrible in the blackness and mist.

"Something hunts," Ariel hissed as she shimmered brightly, darting left and right.

Nest wheeled around, looking everywhere at once.

"Where are they coming from?" she demanded, frantic now.

"Beneath us," Ariel said.

Nest looked down at the concrete sidewalk in disbelief. "From the sewers?"

Ariel moved close, her childlike face smooth and expressionless, but her eyes filled with terror. "There is an old city beneath the new. The screams are coming from there!"

The demon worked its way ahead slowly through the blackness of the underground city, following the scent of the humans and the sound of their voices. It wound through narrow streets and alleyways and in and out of doors and gaps in crumbling walls. It was filled with hunger and flushed with a need to kill. It was driven.

Scores of feeders trailed after it, lantern eyes glowing in the musky gloom.

After a time, the demon saw the first flicker of light. The voices of the humans were clear now; it could hear their words distinctly. There were three of them, not yet grown to adulthood, a girl and two boys. The demon crept forward, eyes narrowing, pulse racing.

"What's that?" one of them said suddenly as stone and earth scraped softly under the demon's paw.

The demon could see them now, huddled about a pair of candles set into broken pieces of old china placed on a wooden crate. They were in a room in which the doors and windows had long since fallen away and the walls had begun to collapse. The ceiling was ribbed with pipes and conduits from the streets and buildings above, and the air was damp and smelled of rotting wood and earth.

The boys and the girl had made a home of sorts in the open space, furnishing it with several wooden crates, a couple of old mattresses and sleeping bags, several plastic sacks filled with stuff they had scavenged, and a few books. Where they had come from was anybody's guess. They must have found their way down from the streets where they spent their days, taking shelter each night as so many did in the abandoned labyrinth of the older city.

The demon rounded the corner of a building across from them and paused. Feeders crowded forward and hovered close. The older of the two boys came to his feet and stood looking out into the dark. The other two crouched guardedly to either side. There was only one way in or out of their shelter. The demon had them trapped.

It advanced slowly into the light, showing itself gradually, letting them see what it was. Fear showed on their faces and in their eyes. Frantic exclamations escaped their lips—low, muttered curses that sounded like prayers. The demon was filled with joy.

The older boy produced a long-bladed knife. "Get away!" he warned, and swore violently at the demon. The demon came forward anyway, the feeders trailing in its wake. The girl and the younger boy shrank from it in terror. The girl was already crying. Neither would challenge it; the demon could tell from what it saw in their eyes. Only the older boy would make a stand. The demon's tongue licked out across its hooked teeth, and its jaws snapped hungrily at the air.

The demon crept through the doorway in a crouch, eyes fixed on the knife. All three of its intended victims retreated toward the back wall of the room. Foolish choice, the demon thought. They had let it inside, let it block their only escape.

Then the younger boy wheeled away in a flurry of arms and legs and threw himself toward one of the broken windows, intent on breaking free that way. But the demon was too quick. It lunged sideways and caught the unfortunate boy in a single bound. It dragged him to the earthen floor, closed its massive jaws on his neck as he screamed and thrashed frantically, and crushed the life from him with a single snap.

The boy fell back lifelessly. Feeders piled onto the body, tearing at it. The demon swung its bloodied muzzle toward the other two, showing all its teeth. The girl was screaming now, and the older boy was cursing and shouting and brandishing the knife more as a talisman than as a weapon. They might have made a run for the open doorway while the demon was engaged in killing their companion, but they had failed to do so. Or even to try. The girl was on her knees with her arms about her head, keening. The older boy was standing his ground, but it seemed to the demon that he was doing so because he could not bring himself to move.

The demon advanced on the older boy, stiff-legged, alert. When it was close enough, it waited until the boy lunged with the knife, then hurled itself under the gleaming blade, jaws closing on the hand that wielded it. Bones crunched and muscles tore, and the boy screamed in pain. The demon knocked the boy backward against the wall and tore out his throat while he was still staring at his ruined hand.

Feeders sprang out of the darkness in knots of black shadow, falling on the dying boy, lapping up the life that drained away from him, feeding on the raw feelings of terror and despair and pain.

The girl had begun to crawl toward the open door, a futile attempt to get free. The demon moved quickly to intercept her. She crouched before it in a shivering heap, her arms clasped over her head, her eyes closed. She was crying and screaming and begging—*Don't, please, don't, please, don't*—over and over again. The demon studied her for a moment, intrigued by the way the madness had enveloped her. It was no longer in a hurry, its hunger appeased with the killing of the boys. It felt languorous and sleepy. It watched the girl through lidded eyes. There were feeders crawling all over her, savoring the emotions she expended, licking them up anxiously. Perhaps she could feel them, perhaps even see them by now, with death so close. Perhaps she sensed what death held in store for her. The demon wondered.

Then it closed its jaws almost tenderly about the back of the girl's exposed white neck and crushed the slender stalk to pulp.

Abruptly, the screams faded to silence. Nest froze, staring into the mist and gloom, into the faint pools of streetlight, listening. She couldn't hear a thing.

Ariel drifted close. The tatterdemalion hung suspended on the air, spectral, barely a presence at all. "It is over."

Nest blinked. Over. So quickly. Her mind spun. "What was it?" she asked quietly.

"A creature of the Void."

Nest stared into the tatterdemalion's eyes and knew

exactly which creature. She felt a chill sweep through her body and settle in her throat. "A demon," she whispered.

"Its stink is in the air," Ariel said.

"What was it hunting?"

"The humans who live under the streets."

Homeless people. Nest closed her eyes in despair. Could she have helped them, if she had been quicker, if she had known where to go, if she had summoned her magic? If, if, if. She took a deep breath. She wondered suddenly if these killings were connected in some way with John Ross. Was this monster hunting for him, as well? Mustn't it be, if it was here, so close to where he was working?

"We have to go," said Ariel. Her childlike voice was a ripple of breeze in the silence. "It isn't safe for us to remain here."

Because it might come for us next, Nest thought. She stood her ground a moment longer, tempted to invite it to try, riddled with anger and disgust. But staying would be foolish. Demons were too strong for her. She had learned that lesson from her father five years earlier.

She began to walk, Ariel skimming the air beside her, moving toward the hotel once more. She had been searching the shadows for feeders the entire time they had walked, a habit she would never break, but she hadn't seen any. Now she understood why. They were all underground with the demon, drinking in the detritus of its kills.

She stared off into the night, down the darkened corridors of side streets and alleyways, into blackened doorways and landings, and along shadowy eaves and overhangs. It isn't safe for us to remain here, Ariel had said, urging her to move quickly away, to flee.

Maybe so, she thought. Not with a demon present. But demons seemed to be everywhere in her life. Demons and dark magic, the workings of the Void.

It isn't safe for us here.

But maybe it was no longer safe anywhere.

TUESDAY, OCTOBER 30

CHAPTER 11

W hen Nest Freemark awoke the following morning, the sun was streaming so brightly through her window that she thought she must have overslept. The clock radio she had set the night before was playing softly, which meant that the alarm had gone off, and she leaned over quickly to check the time. But it was only nine o'clock, the hour she had chosen for her wake-up, so she was right on schedule. She glanced over at the window, and she realized that the reason it was so bright was that she had forgotten to draw the blinds.

She laid her head back on her pillow sleepily for a moment, still disoriented from her sudden awakening. She could hear the sounds of traffic on the street below, brash and jarring, but her room was a bright cocoon of silence and warmth. She had read somewhere that it rained a lot in Seattle, but apparently that wasn't going to be the case today.

She closed her eyes and then opened them again, searching her mind. Last night's memories of her walk into Pioneer Square seemed distant and vague, almost as if they were part of a dream. She stared at the ceiling and forced herself to remember. Walking alone with Ariel.

Hearing the screams. Feeling frightened and helpless. Hearing Ariel's words.

Something hunts.

A demon, she had replied.

She rose and walked to the window and looked down at the street. Same street as last night, only brighter and more populated in the daylight. She watched the people and cars for a few minutes, organizing her scattered thoughts and gathering up the shards of confusion and uncertainty that littered her mind. Then she went into the bathroom and showered. She stood beneath the hot stream of water for a long time, eyes closed, thinking. She was a long way from home, and she was still uncertain of her purpose in coming to find John Ross. She wished she had a better idea of what she was going to do when she found him. She wished she knew what she was going to say. She wished she were better prepared.

She toweled dry and dressed, thinking once again of the demon. She would tell Ross of last night; she knew that much, at least. She would tell him of the Lady's concern, of her warning to him. She would try to convince him of his danger. But what else could she do? What did she really know about all this, after all? She knew what Ariel had told her, but she couldn't say for certain that it was the truth. If Pick's response was any measure of things, it probably wasn't. The truth wasn't something you got whole cloth from the Word anyway; it came in bits and pieces, riddles and questions, and self-examination and deductive reasoning that, if you were lucky, eventually led to some sort of revelation. She had learned that much from her father. The truth wasn't simple; it was complex. Worse, it wasn't easily decipherable, and it was often difficult to accept.

She sighed, looking about the room, as if the answer to her dilemma might be hidden there. It wasn't, of course. There were no answers here; the answers all lay with John Ross.

She went down to the lobby for her breakfast, pausing to stare out through large plate-glass doors at the busy city streets. Although the day was bright and sunny, people out walking were bundled up in coats and scarves, so she knew it must be cold. She continued on to the dining room and ate alone at a table near the back, sipping at her coffee and nibbling on her toast and scrambled eggs as she formulated her plan for the day.

She would have preferred to talk things over with Ariel, but there was no sign of the tatterdemalion. Nor was there likely to be. She remembered Ariel saying to her last night, just before she went back into the hotel, "Don't worry. I'll be close to you. You won't see me, but I'll be there when you need me."

Reassuring, but not particularly satisfactory. It made her wish Pick was with her. Pick would have appeared whether she needed him or not. Pick would have talked everything over with her. She still missed him. She found herself comparing the sylvan and the tatterdemalion and decided that, given the choice, she still preferred Pick's incessant chatter to Ariel's wraithlike presence.

She tried to remember the rest of what Pick had told her about tatterdemalions. It wasn't much. Like sylvans they were born fully formed, but unlike sylvans they lived only a short time and didn't age. Both were forest creatures, but sylvans never went beyond the territory for which they were given responsibility, while tatterdemalions rode everywhere on the back of the wind and went all over the world. Sylvans worked at managing the magic, at its practical application, at keeping the balance in check. Tatterdemalions did none of that, cared nothing for the magic, were as insubstantial in their work as they were in their forms. They served the Word, but their service was less carefully defined and more subject to change than that of sylvans. Tatterdemalions were like ghosts.

Nest finished the last of her orange juice and stood up. Tatterdemalions were strange, even as fairy creatures went. She tried to imagine what it must be like to be Ariel, to have lived without experiencing a childhood and with no expectation of ever becoming an adult, to know you would be alive only a short time and then be gone again. She supposed the concept of time was a relative one, and some creatures had no concept of time at all. Maybe that was the way it was with tatterdemalions. But what would it be like to live your entire life with the memories of dead children, of lives come and gone before your own, to have only their memories and none of your own?

She gave it up. She would never be able to put herself in Ariel's place, not even in the most abstract sense, because she had no reference point to help her gain any real insight. They were as different as night and day. And yet they both served the Word, and they were both, in some sense, creatures of magic.

Nest stopped thinking about it, went back to her room, brushed her teeth, put on her heavy windbreaker and scarf, and went out to greet the day.

She had looked up the address to Fresh Start and consulted a map of Pioneer Square, so she pretty much knew where she was going. The map was tucked in her pocket

for ready reference. She walked down First Avenue, re-
tracing her steps from the night before, until she reached
the triangular open space where she had heard the death
screams of the demon's victims. She stood in the center of
the little concrete park and looked around. No one acted
as if anyone had died. No one seemed to think anything
was amiss. People came and went along the walk—
workers, shoppers, and tourists. A few sad-looking homeless people sat with their backs to the walls of buildings
fronting the street, holding out hand-lettered cardboard
signs and worn paper cups as they begged for a few coins.
The former mostly ignored the latter, looking elsewhere
as they passed, engaging in conversations that kept their
eyes averted, acting as if they didn't see. In a way, she
supposed, they didn't. She thought that was an accurate
indicator of how the world worked, that people frequently managed to find ways of ignoring what troubled
them. Out of sight, out of mind. Maybe that was how the
demon got away with killing homeless people; everyone
was ignoring them anyway, so when a few disappeared,
no one even noticed.

Maybe that was the cause that John Ross had taken up
in joining forces with Simon Lawrence. Maybe that was
his passion now that he was no longer a Knight of the
Word. The thought appealed to her.

She walked on, doing her best to turn away from the
gusts of cold wind that blew at her. Winter was coming;
she didn't like to think of her world turning to ice and
snow and temperature drops and wind-chill factors. She
didn't like thinking of everything turning white and gray
and mud-streaked. She glanced back at the people begging. How much worse it would be for them.

At the corner of Main, she turned east and walked

through a broad open space that was marked on her map as Occidental Park. It wasn't much of a park, she thought. Cobblestones and concrete steps, with a few shade trees planted in squares of open earth, a scattering of bushes, a few scary totem poles, some benches, and a strange steel and Plexiglas pavilion. Clusters of what looked to be homeless were gathered here, many of them Native Americans, and a couple of police officers on bicycles. She followed the sidewalk east and found herself at the entrance to an odd little enclosure formed of brick walls and iron fencing with a sign that identified it as Waterfall Park. The space was filled with small trees, vines, and tables and chairs, and was backed by a thunderous man-made waterfall that cascaded into a narrow catchment over massive rocks stacked up against the wall of the building it attached to.

She glanced back at Occidental Park, then into Water-fall Park once again. The parks here weren't much like the parks she was familiar with, and nothing like Sinnis-sippi Park, but she supposed you made do with what you had.

She crossed Second Avenue and began to read the numbers on the buildings. There was no sign identifying Fresh Start, but she found the building number easily enough and went through the front door.

Once inside, she found herself in a lobby that was mostly empty. A heavyset black woman sat at a desk facing the door, engaged in writing something on a clip-board, and a Hispanic woman sat holding her baby on one of a cluster of folding chairs that lined the window-less walls of the room. Behind the black woman and her desk, a hallway led to what looked like an elevator.

Almost immediately, Nest experienced an odd feeling

of uneasiness. She glanced around automatically in an effort to locate its source, but there was nothing to see.

Shrugging it off, she walked up to the desk and stopped. The black woman didn't look up. "Can I help you, young lady?"

"I'm looking for John Ross," Nest told her. "Does he work here?"

The black lady's eyes lifted, and she gave Nest a careful once-over. "He does, but he's not here right now. Would you like to wait for him? He shouldn't be gone long."

Nest nodded. "Thanks." She looked around at the empty seats, deciding where to sit.

"What's your name, young lady?" The black woman regained her attention.

"Nest Freemark."

"Nest. Now, that's an unusual name. Nest. Very different. I like it. Wish I had a different name like that. I'm Della, Nest. Della Jenkins."

She stuck out her hand and Nest shook it. The handshake was firm and businesslike, but warm, too. "Nice to meet you," Nest said.

"Nice to meet you, too," Della said, and smiled now. "I work intake here at the center. Been at it from the start. How do you know John? Isn't anyone ever came in before that knows John. I was beginning to think he didn't have a life before he came here. I was beginning to think he was one of those pod people." She laughed.

Nest grinned. "Well, I don't know him very well. He was a friend of my mother's." She shaded the truth deliberately, unwilling to give anything away she didn't have to. "I was in town, and I thought I ought to stop in and say hello."

Della nodded. "Well, how about that? John was a friend of your mother's. John doesn't talk much about his past life with us. Hardly at all. A friend of your mother's. How about that." She seemed amazed. Nest blushed. "Oh, now, don't you be embarrassed, Nest. I'm just making conversation to hide my surprise at anybody knowing John from before him coming here. You know, really, he spends all his time with Stef—that's Stefanie Winslow, his . . . oh, what do you call it, I always forget? Oh, that's right, his 'significant other.' Sounds so awkward, saying it like that, doesn't it? His significant other. Anyway, that's what Stefanie is. Real pretty girl, his sweetheart. Do anything for him. They came here together about a year ago, and neither one of them talks hardly at all about what went on before."

Nest nodded, distracted. The uneasiness was stealing over her again, a persistent tugging that refused to be ignored. She couldn't understand where it was coming from. She had never experienced anything like it.

Della stood up abruptly. "You want a cup of coffee while you wait, Nest? Tell you what. Why don't you come with me, and I'll introduce you to a few of the people who work here, some of John's friends, let them catch you up on what he's been doing? He's downtown at the Seattle Art Museum checking things out for tomorrow night. Big dedication party. Simon's giving a speech John wrote, thanking the city and so forth for the building, their support and all. You probably don't know about that, but John can fill you in later. C'mon, young lady, right this way."

She led Nest around the intake desk and down the hallway toward the elevator. Nest followed reluctantly, still trying to sort out the reason for her discomfort. Was

Ariel responsible? Was the tatterdemalion trying to communicate with her in some way?

As they reached the elevator doors, a tall, lean, mostly balding black man walked through a doorway from further down the hall and came toward them.

"Ray!" Della Jenkins called out to him at once. "Come over here and meet Nest Freemark. Nest is an old friend of John's, come by to say hello."

The black man strolled up, grinning broadly. "We talking about John Ross, the man with no past? I didn't think he had any old friends. Does he know about this, Nest, about you being his old friend? Or are you here to surprise him with the news?"

He held out his hand and Nest took it. "Ray Hapgood," he introduced himself. "Very pleased to meet you, and welcome to Seattle."

"Ray, you take Nest on down and get her some coffee, will you? Introduce her to Stef and Carole and whoever, and keep her company until John gets back." Della was already looking over her shoulder at the lobby entrance as the elevator doors opened. "I got to get back out front and keep an eye on things. Go on now."

She gave Nest a smile and a wave and walked away. The doors closed, leaving Nest alone with Ray Hapgood.

"What brings you to Seattle, Nest?" he asked, smiling.

She hesitated. "I was thinking of transferring schools," she said, inventing a lie to suit the situation.

He nodded. "Lot of good schools in Washington. You'd like it out here. So tell me. You know John a long time? I meant what I said; he never talks about his past, never mentions anything about it."

"I don't know him all that well, actually." She glanced up at the floor numbers on the reader board. "Mostly, my mother knows him. Knew him. She's dead. I didn't know him until a few years ago, when he came to visit. For a few days, that's all."

She was talking too much, giving up too much, but her uneasiness was increasing with every passing moment. She was beginning to hear voices—vague whispers that might be coming from her, but might also be coming from someone else.

"Oh, I'm sorry about that. About your mother." Ray Hapgood seemed genuinely embarrassed. "Has she been gone a long time?"

Nest suddenly felt trapped in the elevator. She thought that if she didn't get out right away, right this instant, she might start to scream. She was racked with shivers and her skin was crawling and her breathing was coming much too quickly. "She's been dead since I was little," she managed.

The elevator doors opened, and she burst through in a near panic, feeling stupid and frightened and confused all at the same time. Ray Hapgood followed, looking at her funnily. "I don't like close places," she lied.

Oh, he mouthed silently, nodded, and gave her a reassuring smile.

They were in a basement room filled with long, multipurpose tables and folding chairs, a coffee machine, shelves with dishes, and storage cabinets. There were mingled smells of cooking and musty dampness, and she could hear a furnace cranking away from behind a closed door at the back of the room. Fluorescent lighting from low-hung fixtures cast a brilliant white glare over the whole of the windowless enclosure, giving it a harsh, unnatural brightness. A young man sat alone at a table to one side, poring through a sheaf of papers. Two women sat together at another table close to the coffee machine, talking in low voices. The women looked up as Nest appeared with Ray Hapgood. One was middle-aged and unremarkable, with short blond hair and a kind face. The other was probably not yet thirty and strikingly beautiful. Nest knew at once that she was Stefanie Winslow.

"Ladies," Ray greeted, steering Nest toward their table. "Say hello to Nest Freemark, an old friend of John's. Nest, this is Carole Price, our director of operations here at Fresh Start, and Stefanie Winslow, the boss's press secretary and all-around troubleshooter."

Nest shook hands with each in turn, noting the looks of surprise that appeared on both faces when Ray mentioned her connection to Ross. It was becoming clear that when John Ross had ceased to be a Knight of the Word, he had turned his back on his past entirely. The women smiled at Nest, and she smiled back, but this whole business of her relationship with Ross was growing awkward, and she wished he would just hurry up and get back so that she could get this visit over with.

"Sit down, Nest," Carole Price suggested, pulling out a chair. "I can't believe we have someone here who actually knows John from . . . well, from when?"

"A long time ago," Nest answered, trying not to sound evasive. She sat down. "It was my mother who knew him, really."

"Your mother?" Carole Price prompted.

"They went to school together."

"Good heavens!" Carole Price seemed amazed. "Even Stef doesn't know much about our boy from those days."

Stefanie Winslow shook her head in quick agreement. "He never talks about himself, about what he was doing or who he was before we met." Her smile was dazzling.

"Tell us something about him, Nest. Before he gets back. Tell us something he won't tell us himself."

"Yeah, go on," Ray Hapgood urged, drawing up a chair across from her.

What Nest Freemark wanted to do most right then was to get out of there. The room felt impossibly close and airless, the fluorescent light hot and revealing, and the presence of these people she didn't know a weight she could barely shoulder. What was happening inside her was indescribable. The uneasiness had taken on a life of its own, and it was careening about in her chest and throat like a pinball, shrieking unintelligibly and battering her senses. It was taking all her energy to keep it from getting completely out of control, to prevent it from breaking free in a form she could only begin to imagine. She had never experienced anything like it before. She was frightened and confused. She was wishing she had never come looking for John Ross.

"Come on, Nest, tell us something," Stefanie Winslow urged cheerfully.

"He was in love with my mother," she blurted out, saying the first thing that came to mind, not caring if it was true or not, just wanting to shift their focus to something else. What in heaven's name was wrong with her?

There was a flicker of uncertainty in Stefanie Winslow's eyes. Then Ray Hapgood said, "Her mother died some years ago, Stef. This was a college romance, I'd guess."

"It was," Nest agreed quickly, realizing what Stefanie Winslow must be thinking. "It happened a long time ago."

"Let's get you some coffee, Nest," Hapgood announced. "I don't want Della on my case for not keeping my promises."

He stood up and walked over to the coffee machine and drew down a cup and filled it. "Cream or sugar?"

Nest shook her head. She no longer wanted the coffee. She thought if she drank it, she would throw it right back up. She was physically sick to her stomach, her head was throbbing, and there was a buzzing in her ears. But it was the uneasiness that roiled through her like a riptide that commanded her focus.

"Nest, you don't look well," Carole Price said suddenly, concern shadowing her blunt features.

"I am a little queasy," she admitted. "I think maybe it was something I ate at breakfast."

"Do you want to lie down for a little while? We've got some beds that aren't in use, up on two."

Nest shook her head. "No, I just need to . . . you know, maybe what I need is to go back up and get some fresh air for a moment."

Carole Price was on her feet instantly. "Here, I'll take you right up. Ray, forget about that coffee. I don't think it's what she needs just now. C'mon, Nest, come with me."

She took Nest's arm and led her toward the elevator. "Nice meeting you, Nest," Stefanie Winslow called after her. "Maybe I'll see you later."

"Bye, Nest," Ray Hapgood said. "You take care."

Carole Price had her almost to the elevator when the doors opened and Simon Lawrence stepped out. She knew him right away from his pictures in the magazine articles and books. He was dressed in jeans with the sleeves of his plain blue workshirt rolled up, but there was something polished and elegant about the way he held himself as he stepped out of the lift and smiled at her.

He held out his hands. "Here, here, what's this? Carole, where are you taking her? She just got here. I haven't even met her yet. Is everything all right?"

"She's feeling a little queasy, that's all," Carole replied, slowing. "I was taking her up for some air."

Simon Lawrence took Nest's hands in his own and held them. "Well, we can't have you getting sick," he said. "You go on upstairs, Nest, and we'll talk later. I want you to know that I'm very pleased you've come to see us. I didn't realize you were a friend of John's, but I certainly know who you are."

Everyone stared at them, confused. Simon Lawrence laughed. "You don't recognize her, do you?" He shook his head. "I have got to get you out of the office more, all of you. Or at least reading the papers about something besides the homeless once in a while. Ray, I'm especially disappointed in you." He squeezed Nest's hands. "This young lady is the best college distance runner in the nation—maybe in the world. She's been written up in any number of articles as the next Mary Decker Slaney—except that Nest isn't going to fall when she runs in the next Olympics, are you, Nest? You're going to win."

Nest knew she was expected to say something, but she couldn't think of what it should be. Finally she said, "It's a long way off yet."

Simon Lawrence laughed and released her hand. "Good point, young lady. We shouldn't get ahead of ourselves. But you'll do fine, I know. It's very nice to meet you. Now you go on up with Carole, and I'll see you later."

He walked past Nest with a smile, already back to kidding Ray Hapgood about his failure to recognize Nest Freemark when he was such an avid sports fan. Stefanie

Winslow was on her feet, grinning and joking, as well. Nest stepped into the elevator with Carole Price and let the doors close behind them.

She rode back up to the ground floor with something approaching panic, but she made it down the hall past a wondering Della Jenkins and out the front door, where she stood with Carole holding on to her while she took huge gulps of fresh air in an effort to steady herself. The deep breathing seemed to work. The nausea and headache went away. Her uneasiness lingered, but gradually it began to lessen. Her insides quit churning, and the whispers and buzzing receded into the sounds of the city about her.

"Are you feeling better?" Carole asked her after a few minutes.

Nest nodded. "I am, thanks. Much better." She straightened, gently freeing herself from Carole's proprietorial grip. She tried out a fresh smile. "I didn't come here to get underfoot. I know you must have work to do, and I'm fine now. I'll just wait out here for John. Maybe I'll come back inside in a few minutes."

Carole seemed uncertain, but Nest reassured her, and the other woman left her alone. Nest leaned against the wall of the building and stared out at the people and traffic, trying to make sense of what had happened. She could not account for it. This odd uneasiness was an entirely new experience. It was like having a sudden bout of flu coupled with a good scare. It didn't make any sense. The feeling had started when she entered the building and talked with the people who worked there. Was it something connected with that? Was it her magic, reacting to something? If so, her magic was taking a new direction; it hadn't ever done anything like this before.

She whispered Ariel's name as she stood with her back against the building wall, thinking that the tatter-demalion might appear and reveal to her the source of her discomfort. But Ariel stayed hidden.

Nest stood to one side of the doorway and considered the matter from every angle she could imagine, but the answer she was seeking eluded her.

She was still deliberating when a taxi pulled up in front of her and the man she had come to Seattle to find stepped out.

CHAPTER 12

John Ross.

She recognized him immediately. Even though it had been five years since she had seen him last and she had been only a girl at the time, she recognized him. He didn't look as if he had changed at all. His boyish face was still weathered and rugged, still all planes and angles, still the face of the boy next door grown up. He still wore jeans and a blue denim shirt with worn walking shoes and a silver-buckled belt, looking as if he might be one meal or one paycheck from being homeless himself. He still wore his long brown hair tied back from his face with a bandanna, and he still carried the heavy black staff.

It was as if he had been frozen in time, and while she had changed, grown into a young woman, he had remained exactly the same.

She watched him climb gingerly from the taxi, leaning heavily on the staff, reach back to pay the driver, then start toward the front door of Fresh Start. She straightened and moved away from the wall. He looked at her without recognition and smiled pleasantly.

Then surprise shadowed his face and turned quickly to astonishment mingled with something else. He stared at

her, slowing, then came forward again, an uncertain
smile chasing the feelings back into hiding.

"Nest?" he asked carefully. "Is that you?"

"Hello, John," she greeted.

"I don't believe it," he said.

He stopped in front of her and stood there awkwardly,
shaking his head, the smile broadening. His clear green
eyes looked her up and down, assessing her, comparing
her with what he remembered. She could read everything in his expression—how much she had changed,
and at the same time, how familiar he found her.

She started to extend her hand, then stopped, feeling it
wasn't enough. He glanced down, then up again, meeting her gaze, and their arms extended toward each other
at the same moment and they embraced warmly.

"Nest, Nest, Nest," he whispered, and he said it with
such tenderness that it made her want to cry.

She drew back after a moment and grinned. "Guess
I've changed a bit from what you remember."

He returned her grin. "Guess you have. You look
good, Nest. You look . . . terrific."

She blushed in spite of herself. "Well, gee." She shook
her head in embarrassment. "You look pretty terrific
yourself."

They stood in the middle of the sidewalk staring at each
other. People walked by, a few glancing over curiously,
but neither one paid the least attention. For Nest, it was as
if time had stopped completely. She wasn't prepared for
how good it was to see him. She wasn't prepared for how
good it made her feel. She had come looking for John Ross
because she believed she must if she did not want his death
on her conscience, and not because she felt she needed to
see him. She had lived five years with such ambivalent

feelings about him that she could not come to terms with whether she ever wanted to see him again. Now, in an instant's time, five years of uncertainty were swept away, and she knew that coming to find him, that seeing him, was exactly the right thing.

"I just can't believe that you're standing here." He opened his arms to emphasize the extent of his amazement. "I suppose I should have written you or called, but I wasn't sure . . . well, that you would want to speak to me."

She smiled sadly. "Neither was I. Not until right now."

"How did you ever find me?"

She shrugged. "I had some help."

"I didn't think anyone knew where I was. I haven't talked to anyone, told anyone here about . . ."

"I know. They told me you've kept your life a mystery."

"You've been inside already?" He glanced toward the doorway. "You met Simon?" She nodded. "And Stef?" She nodded again. "Ray, Carole, all the others?"

"Some of them, anyway. The lady at the reception desk, Della, sent me downstairs to wait for you. I met everyone there. They were amazed you had any friends from the past." She gave him a meaningful look. "They were amazed you even had a past."

He nodded slowly. "I expect so. I don't ever talk about it." He hesitated. "I don't know what to say. Or where to begin. Things have changed for me, Nest. A lot of things."

"I know that, too," she said.

He looked closely at her now, and suddenly there was suspicion as well as curiosity mirrored in his eyes. "I've read some articles about you," he said, his words tentative, cautious. "I know you're a student at Northwestern

University, that you're still running competitively, that you're good enough that you're expected to represent the United States in the next Olympics." He hesitated. "Is that why you're here?"

She waited a heartbeat, meeting his intense gaze. "No. I came here looking for you. I was sent. By the Lady."

He stared at her, astonishment filling his eyes. When he spoke, his voice was unsteady. "The Lady sent you?"

"Is there somewhere we could talk about it?" she asked, no longer comfortable standing out in the open where they could be heard. "Just for a little while."

He seemed distracted, uncertain. "Sure, of course." He glanced toward the building.

"No, not in there," she said quickly. "Somewhere else, please."

He nodded slowly. "All right. It's almost noon. Why don't we go down to the waterfront, and I'll buy you a northwest kind of lunch. Some clam chowder, some fish and chips. How would that be?"

"That would be good," she said.

He didn't bother with going in to tell anyone he was leaving. He didn't even pause to consider doing so. He simply motioned her toward the direction from which she had come, and they began to walk. They crossed Second Avenue, passed by Waterfall Park, and moved over to the island platform in the center of Main where the trolley stopped on its way down to the waterfront. They sat together on the wrought-iron bench and stared out over the cobblestones of Occidental Park, waiting.

"Do you know what I do now?" he asked after a minute. His tone of voice was distant and weary, as if he were at the start of a long journey.

"I know you work for Simon Lawrence at Fresh Start," she replied. "I know about the work Fresh Start does."

He nodded. "It's important work, Nest. The most important work I've done in a long time. Maybe ever." He paused. "Did the Lady tell you about me?"

Nest nodded, saying nothing.

"Then you know I'm no longer a Knight of the Word?"

She nodded a second time. *It's what you believe anyway,* she thought, but she didn't speak the words.

They didn't say anything further for a time, wrapped in their separate thoughts amid the jumbled noise of traffic and people's voices. *This is going to be hard,* Nest thought. He was not going to want to hear what she had to say. Maybe he would simply refuse to listen. Maybe he would just walk away. She could see him doing that. He had walked away already from the most important part of his life.

"Do you still live on the park?" he asked finally.

"Yes." She glanced at him. "But Grandpa died last May, so I live there alone."

She could see the pain reflect in his face. He was remembering the time he had spent in their house, pretending to be someone he was not. He was remembering how he had left things with her grandfather. "I'm sorry he's gone," he said finally. "I liked him very much."

Nest nodded. "Everybody did. Pick is still there, looking after the park. He wants me to come back and help him like I used to."

"That would be very hard for you now, I expect," he said.

"It is," she agreed.

"Things change. Life changes. Nothing stays the same."

She wasn't sure she agreed with this, but she nodded anyway, not wanting to get into a debate about it.

A few moments later, the trolley arrived and they boarded. Ross gave the conductor two tokens, and they took a seat near the front. They rode the trolley down a hill between rows of buildings, under a two-tiered viaduct that supported an expressway, over some railroad tracks, and then turned right on Alaskan Way to follow the waterfront north. It was too noisy inside the open-air trolley for conversation, so they rode in silence.

At the Madison Street stop, they got off and walked across Alaskan Way to the piers. Orange cranes stretched steel limbs skyward at the edges of the loading docks along Elliott Bay, dominating the skyline. Huge container ships piled with freight sat at rest beneath their cabled lifts, some being unloaded of the shipments they had brought from abroad and others loaded with whatever was being exported. Trawlers were tied up at the ends of several piers, winches cinched, nets drawn up and folded. To their immediate left, a terminal buttressed by huge clumps of wooden pilings provided docking slips for the ferries that serviced the islands and the Olympic Peninsula. Tour boats filled with passengers nosed their way along the waterfront, poking into the channels that ran back to the ends of the docking slips of Harbor Island and into the Duwamish River. Small sailboats with brightly colored, wind-filled spinnakers rode the crest of the silver-tipped blue waves, and tiny fishing boats dotted the bay, straddling the shipping lanes on the open water.

The piers closest to where they departed the trolley were dominated by long, wooden buildings housing shops and restaurants. The one to which John Ross took

Nest was painted yellow with red letters that identified it as Pier 56. They navigated the noonday crowd strolling the walkways out front and pushed through the doors of a glassed-in entryway beneath a sign that announced they were guests of Elliott's Oyster House. The entryway was stuffy and hot. A hostess greeted them and led them to a booth near the back of the dining area, further out on the pier toward the water. Nest seated herself across from Ross and looked out at the view. The sun shone brightly through scattered clouds, and the sky was azure and depthless. In the distance, beyond the bay and the sound, the peaks of the Olympics gleamed whitely against the horizon.

The waitress brought them water and menus and asked if they were ready to order. Nest glanced at the menu, then at Ross, arching one eyebrow. "Two bowls of chowder, two orders of the fish and chips, and two iced teas," he told the waitress, and she picked up the menus and left.

Nest looked out the window again. "This is a wonderful city," she told him.

"People who visit when it's not raining always say that," he advised, shrugging.

"I guess I'm lucky to be here now."

"Stay a few more days, and you can see what it's like the rest of the time."

She looked out at the tour boats, which were anchored right next to where they were sitting. A small crowd of tourists was boarding one of two tied up in the docking slips, filing through the interior and out onto the upper and lower decks. They were bundled up against the chill, and they all carried cameras at the ready. Nest thought she would like to be going out with them. She would like to look back at the city from the water, see if the view was as spectacular from that direction. Maybe she would do so later.

"So you like your new life," she said to him, looking for a place to start.

He nodded slowly. "I like what I do at Fresh Start. I like Simon Lawrence and the others who work for him. I've met someone I'm very much in love with, and who is very much in love with me—something I thought would never happen. Yes, I like my life. I'm happy."

"Stefanie is beautiful," she said.

"She is. But she's more than that. A lot more. She saved me when I thought there wasn't anything left worth saving. After San Sobel."

Nest wondered suddenly if he ever thought about Josie Jackson. Early on, not long after he left, Josie had asked Nest if she had heard from him; from the way she asked, Nest had known that there had been something between them. But that was a long time ago. He probably didn't think of Josie at all these days. Maybe she had stopped thinking about him, too. "What happened at San Sobel must have been awful," she said.

"It was, but it's over." He looked up as the waitress reappeared with their iced teas. When she left again, he took a careful sip of his, and then said, "Why did the Lady send you to find me, Nest?"

Nest shook her head doubtfully. "To talk with you. To tell you something you probably already know. I'm not sure." She looked away from him, out over the water. "The truth is, I came because I don't want to hear later that something bad has happened to you and find myself wishing I'd tried to prevent it."

He grinned cautiously. "What is it you think might happen?"

She sighed. "Let me start at the beginning, all right? Let me tell it my way, maybe work up to the part about what might happen. I'm not really sure about any of this myself. Maybe you can fill in the gaps for me. Maybe you can even persuade me I came here for no better reason than to see you again. That would be all right."

She told him then about Ariel's appearance in the park two days earlier, the tatterdemalion's purpose in coming as a messenger, and the Lady's request that Nest come to Seattle to find him in the hope he might heed her warning that his life was in peril.

Nest paused. "So I gather you've already been told that you're in some kind of danger."

He seemed to consider the statement, to weigh it in a way she didn't understand. Then he nodded. "I've been told. I don't know that any warning is necessary."

She shrugged. "I don't know that it is, either. But here I am, delivering the message anyway. I guess you don't have any concerns about it, huh?"

He smiled unexpectedly. "Nest, let me tell you what happened at San Sobel."

And he did so, retelling the story from his perspective, recounting it carefully and thoroughly, obviously trying to make her understand how terrible it was for him, to help her see why he had been unable to continue as a Knight of the Word. She listened attentively, for he kept his voice low and his words shielded from the people eating around them, pausing once when he came to the aftermath of the killings to gather his thoughts so that he could relate clearly what the experience had done to his psyche, pausing a second time when the bowls of clam chowder arrived and the waitress was standing over them.

At the conclusion of his tale, he told her something he had never been able to tell anyone. He told her how close to suicide he had been when he realized the fault might be his. He had managed to get past that, but only by determining he could never revisit that place in his mind, could never again put himself in a position where he might have to hold himself responsible for people dying.

Nest let him finish, then shook her head doubtfully. "If you do nothing, people die anyway, John. What would have happened to me if you hadn't come to Hopewell? I don't know that you can say any of it is your fault."

"It feels like it is. That's enough." He looked down at the soup cooling before him. He hadn't eaten a bite. "I don't mean to argue with you on this, but you can't know what it's like if you're not me. You don't have to live with the dreams. You don't have to live with the responsibility for what happens if they come true." He shook his head. "It's a special kind of hell."

"I know," she said. "I wouldn't even try to put myself in your shoes. I wouldn't presume."

She finished her soup. All the bad feelings she had experienced at Fresh Start had evaporated, and she found herself hungrier than expected.

"I drifted afterward, looking for something to do, some place to be, a reason for being alive." Ross began to eat a little. "Then I found Stef, and everything changed. She gave me back what I had lost at San Sobel. Or maybe lost even before that. She made me feel good about something again. So here we are, working at Fresh Start with the Wizard of Oz, and doing something important. I don't want to go back to what I was. Let's face it; I can't go back. How could I? It would change everything."

He shrugged. "I don't know what to tell you about being in danger, Nest. I don't feel as if I'm in any danger. I'm not part of that life anymore. I don't have any connection to what I was or did. I don't even dream anymore—or hardly ever, anyway. It's all in the past."

The fish and chips arrived, and they paused while the waitress set down their plates, asked if there was anything else she could get them, and walked away. Nest picked up a piece of deep-fried halibut and bit into it. "Mmmm, this is wonderful," she said.

"Told you." He picked up a piece of his own fish and began eating.

"Ariel said the Lady thinks the Void will try to subvert you, whether or not you think you're still involved in its battle with the Word." Nest studied his face. "She says you can't stop being a Knight of the Word. She says you can't quit unless the Word allows it."

He nodded soberly. "I've heard it all before. I don't think I believe it. What have I been doing for the past year if she's right? Haven't I quit, if I haven't served? What else do I have to do? Write a letter of resignation? I don't dream, I don't use the magic, I don't go out looking for demons. I'm done with all of it."

"She says you can't ever be done with it." Nest paused, moving a french fry around in a paper cup filled with ketchup. "Here's the part that bothers me—the reason I came looking for you, I guess. She says you've had a dream, and the events of the dream will take place on Halloween. She says your involvement with the dream will place you in danger of becoming ensnared by the Void."

She watched his reaction closely. He said nothing, but she could tell at once that he knew what she was talking about, that in fact there had been a dream, and that in some way he was a part of it.

"The Lady told Ariel something else, John. She told her she will never let that happen, she will never allow a Knight of the Word to be subverted. She has sent someone to prevent it."

A flicker of recognition crossed his lean face.

"The way you were sent to me maybe, five years ago," she finished quietly.

For an instant she thought he would tell her everything. She could see in his eyes that he wanted to, that a part of him was looking for a way. But he stayed silent. She watched him a moment longer, then went back to eating. The voices around them filled the sudden silence.

"She told you all this?" His anger was laced with irony. "When I went back to Wales and the Fairy Glen to ask her to release me from my duty, she wouldn't even speak to me."

Nest said nothing, didn't even look up at him, continuing to eat.

"All the times I waited for her to come to me, to tell me what I had to do, to help me . . ." He trailed off, staring fixedly at her. "Nothing is going to happen," he said finally.

She nodded. "But you know about the dream, don't you?"

"It's only a dream. It won't happen. It can't happen, because I won't let it."

She straightened and locked her eyes on his. "You taught me about being strong, John. I learned that from you in Hopewell. But I learned about caution, as well.

You don't seem cautious enough to me. You think you can't be hurt, no matter what, unless you do something to invite it. But I don't think that's how life works."

"I think I can control what I do," he snapped. "That's all I'm saying."

She shook her head. "What if Stefanie's life is threatened, and you have to choose between doing what the Void wants or letting her die? What will you do? If you love her as much as you say, what will you do? I don't think you can just shrug this off."

Pushing back his lunch, he shook his head emphatically. "I'm not shrugging anything off. I'm not taking this lightly. But there's no reason for the Void to try to subvert me. I'm worthless. I have nothing left to give. I gave up everything already."

She looked at him. "Did you?" She looked over very deliberately at the black staff, resting against the window ledge beside him.

"It doesn't work," he insisted quietly, but she could tell from the way he said it that he was hedging.

"What if the Lady has sent someone to kill you, just to be sure you don't switch sides?" She flushed. "Are we going to pretend that what happened five years ago couldn't happen again today? That war between the Word and the Void is still going on, and the creatures that fight in it still exist. There are still feeders out there, multiplying in the wake of the bad things that happen. Humans are still working hard at destroying themselves. Nothing has changed, John. You act as if it has. The fact that your life is different doesn't mean the world is. And it doesn't mean your connection to it has stopped having significance. Some things you can't walk away from. Wasn't that the lesson you taught me?"

He stared at her for a moment without replying, then shook his head. "It isn't the same."

He was lying to himself, and he didn't even realize it. She saw it clearly, a truth so obvious that she was appalled. Why was he refusing to listen to her? She remembered him as being so clearheaded, so focused on the reality of the world's harsh demands and unexpected treacheries. What had happened to him?

"Did you know there's a demon in Pioneer Square?" she asked quietly.

That got his attention. She watched his reaction with satisfaction, a quick shifting of the pale green eyes, a hint of shock and disbelief on the angular face. "It was hunting homeless people last night in the catacombs of the old city. I was out walking with Ariel, after midnight, because I couldn't sleep. We could hear its victims screaming."

"You didn't see it?"

She shook her head. "Ariel could smell it. She wouldn't let me go after it. She was terrified."

He glanced down at his food. "Maybe she was mistaken."

Nest gave him a moment to consider what he had said, then replied, "Maybe she wasn't."

She could tell what he was thinking. He was wondering what a demon would be doing so close to home. He was wondering why he hadn't known, then deciding it was because he had given up his position as a Knight of the Word, then realizing how vulnerable that made him. She let him work it through, saying nothing.

"If there is a demon, it has nothing to do with me," he said after a moment, sounding like a man trying hard to convince himself.

She finished her iced tea and looked over at him. "You don't believe that for a moment." She paused. "You wouldn't care to tell me about your dream, would you?"

He shook his head.

She smiled. "Okay, John. I did my good deed. I came here to warn you, and I've warned you. The rest is up to you. I'm here until tomorrow. We can talk about this some more, if you'd like. Just give me a call. I'm staying at the Alexis."

She rose. It was better to leave things where they were, not to say anything more, to let him think about it. He stared at her, perplexed by her abruptness. She reached for her purse. "Can I help pay for the lunch?"

He shook his head quickly. "Wait, I'll walk back with you."

"I'm not going back," she said. "I'm staying down on the waterfront for a while, have a look around."

They stared at each other, neither saying anything. She could see the indecision mirrored in his green eyes. "You believe what she's saying about me, don't you?" he asked finally. "What the Lady's saying?"

"I don't know that I do," she answered him. "I don't know what I believe. It's difficult to decide. But I think you have to look carefully at the possibility that she might be telling you the truth. I think you have to protect yourself."

He reached for his staff and levered himself to his feet. The waitress saw them rise, and she came over to give them the check. Ross took it, thanking her. When she was gone, he held out his hand to Nest.

"I'm glad you came, Nest. Whether or not it turns out there was a good reason for it, I'm glad you came. I've wondered about you often."

She nodded, brushing back her curly hair. "I've wondered about you, too."

"I didn't like leaving things with you in Hopewell the way I did. I've always felt bad about that."

She smiled. "It's over with, John."

"Sometimes it doesn't feel as if any of it will ever be over, as if the past will ever really be the past." He stepped around the table and bent to kiss her cheek. "I'll think about what you've told me, I promise. I'll think about it carefully. And I'll talk with you before you leave."

"All right," she said, content to leave it at that.

They left together, walking out into the brilliant afternoon sunshine and coolish fall air, and he left her standing on the sidewalk in front of the harbor tours ticket booth, then limped across the street for the trolley. He looked older to her then, as if he had aged all at once, his movements more studied, his stoop more pronounced. She wished she could do more to help him with this, but she had done everything she could think to do.

Even so, she could not shake the feeling that it wasn't enough.

CHAPTER 13

Nest was debating what to do with the rest of her day when Ariel unexpectedly reappeared. The tatterdemalion was gossamer thin and spectral in the sunlight, and she floated close against Nest, as if human contact had become suddenly necessary. Nest glanced around quickly to see if passersby were looking, but no one was. It was clear they couldn't see Ariel. Only Nest could.

"Where have you—" she began, but the tatterdemalion cut her short with a sudden rush of movement.

"Did you say everything to John Ross that you came to say?" the forest creature hissed in her soft, childlike voice.

Nest stared in surprise. "Yes, I guess so, pretty much."

Ariel was hunched close against her, and Nest could feel her small, transparent body vibrating as if it were a cord pulled taut in a high wind.

"Then stay away from him." The tatterdemalion's dark eyes were wide and staring as she watched John Ross depart. "Stay far away."

Nest followed Ariel's gaze across the roadway to where Ross was boarding the trolley. "What do you mean, *stay away*?"

The tatterdemalion darted behind her as the trolley

moved down the tracks, and Nest realized that she was trying to conceal herself. Nest didn't think Ariel was even conscious of the movement, that she was reacting to something instinctual. The vibrating had increased, turned to a violent trembling, and Ariel was pressed so closely against her that parts of them were beginning to blend together. Nest shuddered at the feeling of invasion, inundated by a wave of dark emotions and terrifying memories. She realized that she was reliving with Ariel snippets of the lives of the children the magic had assimilated to create the tatterdemalion, caught in their overpowering flow. She tried to close her mind against them, to seal herself away, but Ariel's closeness made it impossible. Nest recoiled with the impact of their assault and stepped back in revulsion. She tried to move away from Ariel, to free herself of the other's presence, and she nearly collided with an elderly couple passing behind her.

"Sorry, I'm sorry," she said hastily, then turned away and walked to the railing overlooking the slips where the tour boats docked. She took several deep gulps of air, staring down at the choppy waters, waiting for her mind to clear, for the dizziness to pass.

Ariel reappeared at her side, but did not try to touch her. "I didn't mean to do that," she said.

Nest nodded. "I know. But it was so, so . . ."

"Sometimes, I forget myself. Sometimes, all the children inside me come together in a knot and claim me. They want to be alive again. They want to be who they were. Their memories are so strong that they overwhelm me. I can feel everything they feel. I can remember everything they knew. They fight to get out of me, to become free. They need to touch another human being.

They want to be inside a human body, to feel it warm and alive around them, to be real children again."

Her small voice faded away in a whisper, and her dark eyes seemed to lose their focus. "It scares me when that happens. I think that if they succeed, there will be nothing left of me."

Nest swallowed the dryness in her throat. "It's all right, I wasn't hurt. And you're still here." She forced herself to look into the tatterdemalion's opaque eyes. "Tell me, Ariel. What is it that bothers you about John Ross? Why did you tell me to stay away from him?"

"He is lost," the tatterdemalion replied softly.

"Lost?" Nest shook her head. "Lost how? I don't understand."

"You can't save him. Nothing you can do can save him. It is too late."

Nest stared in confusion. "Why would you say that? Why is it too late?"

The strange childlike face looked at her wonderingly. "Because he has demon stink all over him. He is already claimed."

They stood facing each other in the shadow of the overhang that protected the pier walkway, eyes locked. Nest started to speak again and then stopped. There were people moving all around them, passing on their way to someplace else, talking, laughing, unaware. She did not want to draw attention to herself; she did not want them to hear.

The sun broke through the high clouds and blinded her. She turned away. Demon stink? On John Ross? She shook her head slowly. This wasn't making sense.

"We have to go," Ariel said suddenly, and she started to move away.

"Wait!" Nest called out to her, saying the word so loudly that heads turned. She tried to look nonchalant as she detached herself from the pier railing and walked over to where Ariel hovered, glancing out at the boats as she did so. "Go where?" she whispered fiercely.

Ariel pointed north, down the trolley line, away from the direction they had come. "Someone is waiting to see you."

"Who?"

"Someone you know. Hurry, we have to go."

Ariel moved out to the sidewalk and Nest followed reluctantly. They turned north along the waterfront, passing Elliott's on Pier 56 and the shops on Pier 57. The wind whipped off the bay, cold and sharp, and in spite of the sunshine, Nest hunched down into her windbreaker, wishing she had brought something warmer.

Her mind raced as her eyes followed the movement of her feet. She spoke without looking up. "Ariel, were you in the building with me at Fresh Start, when I talked to John's friends?"

The tatterdemalion nodded. "I was."

"Was the demon stink there, too?"

"Yes, everywhere."

"Was it as strong?"

"Yes, as strong."

Nest tried to decide what this meant. Something had made her violently ill inside the rooms of Fresh Start. Could it be demon stink? If there was demon stink all over John Ross, wouldn't she have felt sick around him, too? Besides, she hadn't been able to detect demon stink five years ago, when her demon father had come back into her life, so why should she be able to detect it now?

Had something changed since then?

Maybe something about her?

She walked up Alaskan Way, keeping pace with Ariel, her head lowered against the bite of the October wind. The tatterdemalion seemed unaffected by the cold and wind, her ephemeral form a steady presence, her light silken coverings hanging limp and unruffled. Ariel did not look at her, but kept her gaze directed ahead, toward wherever it was they were going.

They crossed Alaskan Way at Pier 59, which housed the Seattle Aquarium, passed under the viaduct, and moved toward the broad, concrete steps of a hillclimb that led up to the city. There was another possibility, she realized, still thinking about what Ariel had said. Maybe what had happened at Fresh Start had nothing to do with demon stink. Maybe it had to do with the demon itself. If there was demon stink all over Fresh Start and John Ross, then it stood to reason the demon made its home close to both. So maybe the reason she became sick at Fresh Start was that the demon had been right there beside her.

One of Ross's friends and coworkers.

One of the people he trusted.

It made sense. The Lady said that the Void would send someone to subvert Ross, that maybe it had already happened. Ariel seemed to think it had. Ross did not. But maybe Ross couldn't see what was happening and that was the whole problem. Maybe her job in coming to find him was to make him take a closer look at himself.

Had she done that by speaking to him as she had? Had she given him enough cause to reexamine his situation? She couldn't be sure. But she knew now that she had to find out.

She climbed the steps past a small Mexican restaurant and a series of shops to Western Avenue, then turned up

toward Pike Place Market. She knew where she was
from the time she had spent studying the map of Seattle.
Pike Place Market was a Seattle landmark, a long, low
building that consisted of stalls and kiosks and display
tables that were leased by vendors of fresh fish, fruits and
vegetables, flowers, and crafts. Western ran below the
market through warehouses and buildings that had been
converted into microbreweries, restaurants, retail shops,
and parking garages. The street sloped steadily upward
from where she left the hillclimb, passing beneath several overpasses that connected the waterfront to the
market and the surrounding shops. The crowds had dissi-
pated to a scattering of people working their way between
the parking lots and shopping areas. She wondered anew
where it was that Ariel was taking her.

They passed a ramp leading down into an open-sided
parking garage that abutted the expressway, and the
sound of passing cars was a dull whine of tires on concrete. Then a park came into view. It was a small park,
barely more than an open space with a grassy knoll at its
center, clusters of small trees, and a sidewalk winding
out from the street to a railing that overlooked Elliott
Bay. Wooden benches lined the sidewalk and quarter-
slot telescopes pointed out toward the Olympics. A juncture of streets leading down to the Market from the city
fronted the little park, and traffic crawled past sluggishly
in the afternoon sun.

A blue and red sign at the edge of the lawn proclaimed
that this was Victor Steinbrueck Park.

"Here," said Ariel.

Nest walked up into the park for a closer look, drawn
by the vista of the bay and the distant mountains, by the
bright, sunny mix of blue water, green trees, and white-

capped mountain peaks. She glanced around at the people in the park. They were an eclectic group. There were schoolchildren clustered at the railing with their supervising teachers and parents. There were shoppers on their way to and from the market. Businessmen and women were reading newspapers and magazines in the warmth of the sun as they munched sandwiches and sipped coffee.

But mostly there were Native Americans. They occupied the majority of the benches, particularly those fronting Western. They sat together in small groups on the grassy knoll. One or two lay sleeping in the sunshine, wrapped in old blankets or coats. They were a ragged, sullen group, their copper faces weathered, their black hair lank, and their clothes shabby. The ones sitting on the benches fronting the sidewalk on Western had placed paper cups and boxes in front of them to solicit handouts from passersby. They kept their faces lowered and their eyes on each other, seldom bothering even to look up at the people they begged from. Some drank from bottles wrapped in brown paper sacks. Most were men, but there were a few women, as well.

Nest turned to find Ariel, to ask who it was that they had come to meet, but the tatterdemalion was gone.

"Hello, little bird's Nest," someone growled from behind.

She knew the voice instantly, and even so she couldn't quite believe it. She turned around, and there stood Two Bears. The Sinnissippi was as ageless and unchanging as John Ross, his copper-colored features blunt and smooth, his long hair ink black and woven into a single braid, and his eyes so dark they seemed depthless. He wore the familiar army fatigue pants and boots, but here, where it was cooler, he also wore a heavy jacket over a checked flannel shirt. The silver buckle of his belt was tarnished and the leather scarred. He was as big and imposing as she remembered, with huge shoulders and thick, gnarled fingers. He was a solid and immutable presence.

"O'olish Amaneh." She spoke his Indian name carefully, as if it were made of glass.

"You remember," he said approvingly. "Good."

"Are you the one I'm supposed to meet?"

He cocked his head. "I don't know. Have you come here to meet someone, little bird's Nest?"

She nodded. "My friend Ariel brought me. She said . . ."

"Your friend? Have you come with a friend? Where is she?"

Nest looked around. "Gone, I guess. Hiding."

"Ah, just like your friend in the park five years ago. Mr. Pick." Two Bears seemed amused. His broad face creased with his smile. "All your friends want to hide from me, it seems."

She colored slightly. "Maybe you frighten them."

"Do you think so?" He shrugged, as if disclaiming responsibility. "You've changed, little bird's Nest. Maybe I can't call you that anymore. Maybe you're too old, too grown up."

"You haven't changed," she replied. "You look just the same. What are you doing here?"

He looked around speculatively. "Maybe I've come to be with my brothers and sisters. The Sinnissippi are gone, but there are still plenty of other tribes. Some of them have prospered. They run casinos and sell fireworks. They have councils to govern their people and rules to enforce their proclamations. The government in Washington recognizes their authority. They call them Native Americans and pass laws that give them special privileges. They don't call them Indians or Redskins anymore. At least, not to their faces."

He cocked an eyebrow at her. "There is even a segment of the population who believes that my people were wronged once, long ago, when white Europeans took away their land and their way of life. Can you imagine that?"

Nest shook her head noncommittally. "Are you sure Ariel didn't bring me here to see you?"

His face remained expressionless. "Why don't we sit down and talk, little bird's Nest?"

He led her to a bench facing out toward the water. A group of weathered men was sitting there, passing around a bottle and speaking in low voices. Two Bears said something to them in another language, and they rose at once and moved away. Two Bears took their place on the bench, and Nest sat down next to him.

"What did you say to them?" she asked.

He shrugged. "I told them they have no pride in themselves and should be ashamed." The copper skin of his blunt features tightened around his bones. "We are such a sad and hopeless people. Such a lost people. There are some of us, it is true, who have money and property. There are some who have found a way of life that provides. But most of us have nothing but empty hearts and alcohol and bad memories. Our pride in ourselves was stripped away a long time ago, and we were left hollow. It is a sad thing to see. Sadder to live."

He looked at her. "Do you know what is wrong with us, little bird's Nest? We are homeless. It is a bad way to

be in the world. But that is how we are. We are adrift, tiny
boats in a large ocean. Even those of us who have land
and houses and friends and neighbors and some sort of
life. It is a condition indigenous to our people. We bear a
legacy of loss passed down to us by our ancestors. We
bear the memory of what we had and what was taken. It
haunts us."

He shook his head slowly. "You can be homeless in
different ways. You can be homeless like those of my
people you see here, living on the streets, surviving on
handouts, marking time between the seasons. But you
can be homeless in your heart, too. You can be empty inside yourself because you have no spiritual center. You
can wander through life without any real sense of who
you are or where you belong. You can exist without purpose or cause. Have you ever felt like that, little bird's
Nest?"

"No," she said at once, wondering where he was going
with this.

"Indians know," he said softly. "We have known for a
long time. We are homeless in the streets and we are
homeless in our hearts as well. We have no purpose in
the world. We have no center. Our way of life was
changed for us long ago, and it will never return. Our
new life is someone else's life imposed on us; it is a false
life. We struggle to find our home, our center, but it is as
faded as the Sinnissippi. A building is a home if the
people who inhabit it have memories and love and a
place in the world. Otherwise, it is just a building, a
shelter against the elements, and it can never be anything
more. Indians know."

He bent close to her, pausing. "There are others who
know this, too. A few, who have been uprooted and dis-

placed, who have been banished to the road and a life of wandering, who have lost any sense of who they are. Some of these are like us—men and women whose way of life has been taken from them. Some of them are looking for a way back home again. Maybe you even know one."

Nest stared at him in silence.

"Do you still have your magic?" he asked suddenly.

Caught off guard by the question, she fumbled for an answer. "I think so."

"Not sure, are you? Perhaps it has changed as you have grown?" He nodded his understanding. "It may be so. Everything changes with time's passage. Only change itself is constant. So you must adapt and adjust and re-member to keep close what is important and not to forget its purpose. Remember when we sat in the park and watched the spirits of the Sinnissippi dance?"

She did. On the Fourth of July weekend five years ear-lier, at midnight, she had gone into the park she had grown up in, the park that Pick warded, to see if the spirits would speak to her. The spirits had come on Two Bears' summons, and they had danced in the starlit dark-ness and shown to Nest in a vision a secret her family had hidden from her. It had been the catalyst for her terri-fying confrontation with her father, and it had probably saved her life. She had not understood it that way at the time; she had not understood much of what had hap-pened to her that weekend until much later.

"We were searching for truths, you and I—me, about my people, and you, about your father." He shook his head. "Hard questions were needed to uncover those truths. But the truths define who we are. They measure our place in the world. That is why they have worth. We search and we learn. It is how we grow."

He looked out over the bay. "Do you think this country has changed much since we spoke last, little bird's Nest? Since you were a girl, living in the park of the Sinnissippi? This is a hard question to answer, but the truth it masks needs uncovering. As a country, as a people, have we changed? On the surface we might appear to have done so, but underneath I think we are still the same. Our change is measurable, but not significant. We remain bent on destroying ourselves. We still kill each other with alarming frequency and for foolish reasons, and we begin the killing at a younger age. We have much to celebrate, but we live in fear and doubt. We are pessimistic about our own lives and the lives of our children. We trust almost no one.

"It is the same everywhere. We are a people under siege, walled away from each other and the world, trying to find a safe path through the debris of hate and rage that collects around us. We drive our cars as if they were weapons. We use our children and our friends as if their love and trust were expendable and meaningless. We think of ourselves first and others second. We lie and cheat and steal in little ways, thinking it unimportant, justifying it by telling ourselves that others do it, so it doesn't matter if we do it, too. We have no patience with the mistakes of others. We have no empathy for their despair. We have no compassion for their misery. Those who roam the streets are not our concern; they are examples of failure and an embarrassment to us. It is best to ignore them. If they are homeless, it is their own fault. They give us nothing but trouble. If they die, at least they will provide us with more space to breathe."

His smile was bitter. "Our war continues, the war we fight with one another, the war we wage against ourselves. It has its champions, good and bad, and sometimes one or the other has the stronger hand. Our place in this war is often defined for us. It is defined for many because they are powerless to choose. They are homeless or destitute. They are a minority of sex or race or religion. They are poor or disenfranchised. They are abused or disabled, physically or mentally, and they have forgotten or never learned how to stand up for themselves.

"But you and me, little bird's Nest, we are different. We have advantages others do not. We have magic and knowledge and insight. We know of the ways men destroy themselves and of the reasons they do so. We know the enemy who threatens us all. Because we know these truths, we are empowered and we can choose the ground we would defend. We have an obligation and a responsibility to decide where we will stand."

He paused. "I chose my ground a long time ago, when I returned from the Nam. I did so because after I died and came back to life, I was no longer afraid. I did so because even though I was the last of my people, I was made strong by the fire that tested me, and I was given purpose. You have been tested and given purpose, as well. You have been made strong. Now it is your turn to choose where you will stand."

Nest waited, impatient for the rest, guarded and edgy. On the sidewalk in front of her, close by the railing, the schoolchildren shrieked as a seagull dove over their heads in a wide sweep and soared away.

Two Bears locked her eyes with his. "Let me tell you a story. It is just a story, but maybe it will speak to you. A long time ago, a servant of a very powerful lady carried a talisman to a man who had agreed to become her champion. This man was conscripted to fight in a good and necessary cause. He was to wield the talisman as a weapon in an effort to help turn aside an evil that threatened to destroy all. He was fearful of his responsibilities, but he was determined as well. He took the talisman from the servant and bore it into battle, and for many years he fought bravely. His task was not easy, because the people he fought to protect often acted badly and foolishly, and by doing so they did harm to themselves. But he remained their champion nevertheless.

"Then something happened to him, and he lost faith in his cause. He abandoned hope; he gave up his fight. He became one of those who are homeless in their hearts. He despaired of who he was, and he thought to change everything about himself. He ran away to find a place to start over."

Two Bears looked around speculatively. "He might even have come to a city like this. This is the kind of city a man might flee to, if he were looking to begin again, don't you think, little bird's Nest?"

Her heart was hammering in her chest.

"Now the lady who had sent her servant to give this man her talisman was very disappointed in his failure to keep his promise to her. Shhhh, listen now, don't interrupt. Ask yourself what you would do if you were the lady in question. Your talisman is in the hands of a man who will not use it, but cannot give it back. A talisman once given cannot be returned. The magic does not allow for it."

He smiled. "Or so the story goes. At any rate, the lady

sent someone to talk to this man, a young woman. As a matter of fact, she was someone very much like you. She was the man's friend, and the lady thought she might be able to persuade him of the danger he faced if he continued to ignore who he was and what he had promised. The lady thought the young woman was his best hope."

His eyes glistened. "Picture how this must be for the young woman. She is faced with a difficult task. She must find a way to help her friend, even though he does not wish her help. She must help him, because he has no one else and no other hope. The young woman is like you, little bird's Nest. She has magic at her command, and she has been tested by fire. She has a strength and purpose lacking in others."

He paused. "And so she must decide where she will stand. Because of who she is. Because, as with you and me, she has an obligation and a responsibility to do so."

Nest shook her head in dismay. "But I don't know what . . ."

A big hand came up swiftly to cut her short. "Because, if the young woman does not help him," he said carefully, his rough voice leaning heavily on each word, "he will be lost forever."

She nodded, her breath tight in her throat.

"Because, if the young woman fails, the lady has made other arrangements." Two Bears leaned so close that his broad face was only inches from her own. His voice became a whisper. "She cannot allow her champion to serve another cause, one that would be harmful to her own. She cannot allow her talisman to fall into the hands of her enemies."

There was no mistaking his meaning. It was the same

message the Lady had given Ariel. If John Ross succumbed to the Void, he would be killed. But how did you kill a Knight of the Word? Who was strong enough? Who had a weapon more powerful than his?

Two Bears rose abruptly, and she with him. They stood close, looking out over the bay. The wind blew in chilly gusts off the water, causing Nest to shiver.

"As I said, it is only a story. Who knows if it is true? There are so many stories like it. Fairy tales. But the young woman reminded me of you." Two Bears folded his massive arms. "Tell me. If you were the young woman in this story, what would you do?"

She looked up at him, tall, broad-shouldered, and implacable. She was suddenly frightened. "I don't know."

He smiled at her, and the smile was warm. "Don't be so sure of that. Maybe you know better than you think."

She took hold of his arm. "If this is only a story, then it must have an ending. Tell it to me."

He said nothing, and his smile turned chilly. Her hands fell away. "There are many endings to this story. They change over time and with the teller. The stories of the Sinnissippi were all changed when my people perished. The endings would be different if they had survived, but they did not. I know this much. If you make the story your own, then the ending becomes yours to tell as you wish."

He was leaving, and when he did so she would lose any chance of gaining his help. She fought down the desperation that flooded through her. "Don't go," she begged.

"Our paths have crossed twice now, little bird's Nest," the Sinnissippi said. "I would not be surprised if they were to cross again."

"You could help me," she hissed, pleading with him.

He shook his head and placed his big hands on her slender shoulders. "Perhaps it is for you to help me. If I were the lady in the story, in the event all else failed, I would send someone to take back the talisman from my fallen champion, someone strong enough to do so, someone who knew much about death and did not fear it, because he had embraced it many times before." He paused. "Someone like me."

Nest's throat knotted in horror. Images of the past flooded through her mind. In Sinnissippi Park, on the Fourth of July, five years earlier, when he had appeared so mysteriously and done so much to help her find the courage she needed to face her father, she had seen nothing of this. She stared at him in disbelief, unable to give voice to what she was thinking.

"Speak my name," the big man said softly.

"O'olish Amaneh," she whispered.

He nodded. "It sounds good when you say it. I will remember that always."

One hand pointed. "Look. Over there, where the mountains and the forests and the lakes shine in the sunlight. Look closely, little bird's Nest. It will remind you of home."

She did as he asked, compelled by his voice. She stared out expectantly at a vista of white and green and blue, at a panorama that extended for miles, at a sweep of country that was so beautiful it took her breath away. Ferry boats churned through the bay below. Sailboats tacked into the wind. The late afternoon sun beat down on the foaming waters, reflecting in bright silver bursts off the wave caps. The forests of the islands and peninsula were lush and inviting. The mountains shone.

Two Bears was right, she thought suddenly. It did make her think of home.

But when she turned to tell him so, he was gone.

CHAPTER 14

John Ross had told Nest he had already been warned of the consequences of his refusal to continue as a Knight of the Word. What he hadn't told her was that the warning had been delivered by O'olish Amaneh.

As he rode the trolley back up to Pioneer Square and the offices of Fresh Start, thinking through everything Nest had said, he recalled anew the circumstances of that visit.

It was not long after he met Stef and before they started living together. He was still residing in Boston and auditing classes at the college. It was just after Christmas, sometime in early January, and a heavy snow had left everything blanketed in white. The sky was thickly clouded, and a rise in the temperature following a deep cold spell had created a heavy mist that clung to the landscape like cotton to Velcro and slowed traffic to a crawl. It was the perfect day to stay indoors, and that was what he was doing. He was in his apartment, finished with his classes, working his way through a book on behavioral science, when the door (which he was certain he had locked) opened and there stood the Indian.

Ross remembered his panic. If he had been able to do so, he would have bolted instantly, run for his life, consequences and appearances be damned. But he was settled back in his easy chair, encumbered by his book and various notepads, so there was no possibility of leaping up to escape. His staff lay on the floor beside him, but he didn't bother to reach for it. He knew, without having ever been given any real proof of it, that trying to use the staff's magic against O'olish Amaneh, even in self-defense, would be a big mistake.

"What do you want?" he asked instead, fighting to keep his voice steady.

O'olish Amaneh stepped inside and closed the door softly behind him. He was wearing a heavy winter parka, which he unzipped and removed. Underneath, he wore fatigue pants and combat boots, a checked flannel shirt with the sleeves rolled up, and a fisherman's vest with mesh pockets. A wide leather belt with a silver buckle bound his waist, metal bracelets encircled his wrists, and a beaded cord held back his long, black hair. His blunt features were wind-burnt and raw with the cold, and his dark eyes were flat and empty as they fixed on Ross.

He crossed his arms over his massive chest with the parka folded between them, but made no move to come closer. "You are making a mistake," he rumbled.

Ross put aside the book and notepads and straightened slightly. "Did the Lady send you?"

"What did I tell you, John Ross, about trying to cast off the staff?"

"You told me not to. Ever."

"Did you not believe me?"

"I believed you."

"Did you fail to realize that when I told you not to cast off the staff, I meant spiritually as well as physically?"

Ross's mouth and throat went dry. This was the Lady's

response to his attempt to return the staff at the Fairy Glen. This was her answer to his abdication of his responsibilities as a Knight of the Word. She had sent O'olish Amaneh to discipline him. He still remembered the Indian delivering the staff to him fifteen years earlier, forcing him to take it against his will. He remembered the pain when he had touched the staff for the first time and the magic had bound them as one, joining them irrevocably and forever. He was terrified then. And now.

"What are you going to do?" he asked.

O'olish Amaneh studied him expressionlessly. "What should I do?"

Ross took a deep breath. "Take back the staff. Return it to the Lady."

The Indian shook his head. "I cannot do that. It is not permitted. Not while you remain a Knight of the Word."

Ross leaned forward in the chair and pushed himself to his feet. Whatever was going to happen, he wanted to be standing for it. He reached for the staff and used it to lean upon as he faced the big man. "I am no longer a Knight of the Word. I quit. I tried to tell the Lady, but she wouldn't speak to me. Maybe you can tell her. I just can't do it anymore. The truth is, I don't want to do it."

O'olish Amaneh sighed impatiently. "Listen closely to me. When you become a Knight of the Word, you become one forever. You cannot stop. The choice is not yours to make. You accepted a charge, and the charge is yours until it is lifted. That has not been done. The staff cannot be returned. You cannot send it back. That is the way things are."

Ross came forward a step, stumbling against a pile of books and magazines and nearly falling. "Do you know what happened to me?" he asked angrily. "At San Sobel?"

The Indian nodded. "I know."

"Then why is it so hard for you to understand that I want to quit? I don't want to have what happened at San Sobel ever happen again! I can't stand for it to happen again! So I quit, now, forever, and that's the end of it, and I don't care what the rules are!"

He knew he had crossed some line, but he didn't care. Even his fear could not control him. He hated who and what he had been. He had met Stefanie, and there was something special happening there. For the first time in years, he was feeling alive again.

The Indian walked right up to him, and Ross flinched in spite of himself, certain he was about to be struck. But the big man stopped before reaching him, and the flinty eyes bore deep into his own.

"Did you think, when you accepted your charge, you would make no mistakes in carrying it out? Did you think no innocents would die as a result of your actions? Did you think the world would change because you had agreed to serve, and the strength of your convictions alone would be enough to save the lives you sought to protect? Is that what you thought, John Ross? Were you so full of pride and arrogance? Were you such a fool?"

Ross flushed, but held his tongue.

"Let me tell you something about yourself." The Indian's words were as sharp as knives. "You are one man serving a cause in which many have given their lives. You are one man in a long line of men and women, one only, and not so special that you could ever afford to hope you might make a significant difference. But you have done the best you could, and no more was ever asked. The war between the Word and the Void is a long and difficult one, and it has been waged since the beginning of time. It is in the nature of all life that it must be waged. That you were chosen to take up the Word's cause is an honor. It should be enough that you have been given a chance to serve.

"But you disgrace yourself and our cause by denigrating its purpose and abdicating your office. You shame yourself by choosing to renounce your calling. Who do you think you are? The burden of those children's deaths is not yours to bear. Yours is not the hand that took their lives; yours was not the will that decreed those lives must be sacrificed. Such choices and acts belong to a power higher than your own."

Ross felt the tendons in his neck go taut with his rage. "Well, it feels as if they are my responsibility, and I'm the one who has to live with the consequences of their dying because of my efforts or lack thereof, and blaming it on the Word or fate or whatever is a whole lot of bullshit! Don't try to tell me it isn't something I should think about! Don't try to tell me that! I do think about it! I think about it every day of my life. I see the faces of those children, dying in front of me. I see their eyes . . ."

He wheeled away, tears blurring his vision. He felt defeated. "I can't do it anymore, and that's all there is to it. You can't make me do it, O'olish Amaneh. No one can."

He went silent, waiting for whatever was going to happen next, half believing this was the end for him and not caring if it was.

But the Indian did not move. He was so still he might have been carved from stone.

"The consequences of accepting responsibility for the

lives of others are not always pleasant. But neither are the consequences of abdicating that same responsibility. What is certain is that you cannot pretend to be someone other than who you are. You made a choice, John Ross. Failure and pain are a part of the price of your choice, but you cannot change that by telling yourself the choice was not binding. It was. It is."

The big man's voice dropped to a whisper. "By behaving as you do, you present a danger to yourself. Your self-deception places you at great risk. Whatever you believe, you are a Knight of the Word. You cannot be otherwise. The creatures of the Void know this. They will come for you. They will steal your soul away. They will make you their own."

Ross shook his head slowly. "No, they won't. I won't let them."

"You won't be able to stop it."

Ross met his gaze. "If they make the attempt, I will resist. I will resist to the point of dying, if that's what it takes. I may no longer be in service to the Word, but I will never serve the Void. I will never do that."

O'olish Amaneh looked out the window into the snow-covered landscape, into the somnolent white. "The Void wants your magic at its service, and it will do what it takes to obtain it. Subverting you will take time and effort and will require great deception, but it will happen. You may not even realize it until it is too late. Think, John Ross. Do not lie to yourself."

Ross held out the black staff. "If you take this from me now, the Void can do nothing. The solution is simple."

The Indian made no move. He kept his gaze directed away, his body still. "Others have suffered a loss of faith. Others have tried to abandon their charges. Others like you. They have been warned. Some thought they were strong. They have all been lost. One way or the other, they have been lost."

He looked at Ross, solemn-faced and sad-eyed. "You will go down the same path if you do not heed me."

They faced each other in silence, eyes locked. Then O'olish Amaneh turned without a word and went out the door and was gone, and John Ross did not see him again.

But he thought about him now, riding the trolley to Pioneer Square, stepping off onto the platform at Main, and walking back to the offices of Fresh Start. He thought about everything Two Bears had told him. The Indian and Nest had given him essentially the same warning, a veiled suggestion that the danger he posed by refusing to continue as a Knight of the Word would not be ignored and that measures would be taken to bring him back in line.

But did those measures include eliminating him? Would the Lady really send someone to kill him? He thought maybe she would. After all, five years ago he had been sent to kill Nest Freemark in the event she failed to withstand the assault of her demon father. Why should it be any different now, with him? They could not chance losing him to the Void. They could not let him become a weapon for their enemy.

Lost in thought, he slowed as he approached the entry to the shelter. Why did everyone think such a thing could happen? What could the Void possibly do to subvert him that he wouldn't recognize and resist? There was his dream, of course, and the danger that it might somehow come to pass and he would kill Simon Lawrence. But the events of that dream would never happen. There was no reason for them to happen. And in any case, he didn't really believe his dream and the Lady's warning were connected.

He shook his head stubbornly. Only one thing bothered him about all this. Why had the Lady sent Nest to warn him? She could just as easily have sent Ariel. He would have given the tatterdemalion's warning the same consideration he was giving Nest's. Why send the girl? The Lady couldn't possibly believe that Nest would have a greater influence on him than O'olish Amaneh. No, something else was going on, something he didn't understand. His instincts told him so.

He walked into the reception area at Fresh Start, said hello to Della, gave Ray Hapgood a perfunctory wave on his way back to the office, and closed the door behind him. He sat in his chair with his elbows on his desk and his chin in his hands, and tried to think it through.

What was he missing? What was it about Nest's coming to find him that was so troubling?

He was getting exactly nowhere when Stefanie Winslow walked in.

"You're back," she said. "How did it go?"

He blinked. "How did what go?"

She gave him an incredulous look. "Your lunch with your old flame's daughter. I assume that's where you've been." She took the chair across from him. "So tell me about it."

He shrugged, uncomfortable with the subject. "There's nothing to tell. She was in town and decided to look me up. I don't know how she even knew I was here. I haven't seen or spoken with her in five years. And that stuff about her mother is—"

"I know, I know. It was a long time ago, and her mother is dead. She told us before you came back." Stef brushed back her dark hair and crossed her long legs. "It must have been quite a shock to see her again."

"Well, it was a surprise, anyway. But we had a nice talk."

He had never told Stef anything about his past or the people in it, save for stories about his boyhood when he was growing up in Ohio. He had never told her about his service as a Knight of the Word, about the Lady or Owain Glyndwr or O'olish Amaneh. She did not know about his dreams. She did not know of the war between the Word and the Void or the part he had played in it. She did not know of his magic. As far as he knew, she had no concept of the feeders. Having Nest Freemark appear unexpectedly, come out of a past he had so carefully concealed from her, was unnerving. He did not want to tell her about any of that. He traced his present life to the moment he had met her, and everything that went before to another life entirely.

Stef studied his face. "Simon says she's some kind of world-class runner, that she might even win a gold medal in the next Olympics. That's pretty impressive."

He nodded noncommittally. "I gather she's pretty good."

"Is she in town for very long? Did you think to ask her to have dinner with us?"

He took a deep breath, wishing she would stop talking about it. "I mentioned dinner, but she said she might have other plans. She said she would call later. I don't think she's here for very long. Maybe only a day or so."

Stef looked at him. "You seem uneasy about this, John. Is everything all right? This girl hasn't announced that she's your love child or something, has she?"

The words shocked Ross so that he started visibly.

Five years earlier Nest had indeed thought he was her father, had wished it were so. He had wished it were so, too.

He laughed quickly to mask his discomfort. "No, she didn't come here to tell me that. Or anything like that." He pushed back in his chair, feeling trapped. "I guess I'm just a little nervous about the speech. I haven't heard back from Simon on it. Maybe it wasn't so good."

Stef smirked. "The speech was fine. He told me so himself." Her smile brightened the whole room. "Matter of fact, he loved it. He'll tell you himself when he sees you again, if the two of you are ever in the office at the same time. He's gone again just now. There's a lot of preparation left for tomorrow night."

He nodded. "I suppose so." He fidgeted with his pens and paper, gathering his thoughts. "You know, I don't feel so well. I think I'm going to go back to the apartment and lie down for a while. You think they can get along without me for an hour or so?"

She reached across and took his hand in her own. "I think they can get along just fine. It's me I'm not sure about."

"Then come back with me."

"I thought you were sick."

"I'll get better."

She smirked. "I'll bet. Well, you're out of luck. I have work to do. I'll see you later." She frowned. "Or maybe not. I just remembered, I'm supposed to go with Simon to the KIRO interview, then maybe to some press things after that. He hasn't given me the final word yet. Sorry, sweetie, but duty calls. Ring me if you hear from Nest, okay? I'll try to break free to join you."

She smiled and went out the door, blowing him a kiss. He stared after her without moving, then pushed the pens and paper away and got to his feet. Might as well follow through on his plan and get out of there, he decided. He was already back to thinking about something else Nest had said—that a demon in Pioneer Square was killing homeless people in the underground city. No one would miss them; no one would know. Except the feeders, of course. And he didn't see the feeders much anymore, so he couldn't tell if their current behavior reflected the demon's presence or not.

He stared down at his desk, unseeing. Sometimes he was tempted to try out his magic, just for a minute, just to see if he still had the use of it. If he did that, he might see the feeders clearly and maybe be able to determine if there was a demon in their midst.

But he refused to do that. He had sworn an oath that he wouldn't, because using magic was integral to acting as a Knight of the Word, and he had given all that up.

He walked out of his office, down the hall, past Della and a cluster of new arrivals huddled about her desk, and through the front door. The midday sunshine was fading, masked by heavy clouds blown in from the west on a sharp wind. The air had turned cold and brittle, and the light was autumn gray and pale. He glanced skyward. A storm was moving in. There would be rain by tonight.

His thoughts drifted.

A demon in Pioneer Square.

Someone sent to kill him.

Someone sent to subvert him.

The Word and the Void at play.

He crossed the street and moved past Waterfall Park

toward the doorway to his apartment building. The waterfall tumbled down over the massive rocks and filled the walled enclosure with white noise. The park was empty, the afternoon shadows falling long and dark over the tables and chairs, benches and planters, and fountains. He didn't like how the emptiness made him feel. He didn't care for the thoughts it provoked. It seemed to reflect something inside.

In the shadows pooled among the boulders of the waterfall, something moved. The movement was quick and furtive, but unmistakable. Feeders. He paused to look more closely, to spy them out, but he could not do so. Those days were gone. He was someone different now. Something rough-edged brushed up against his memory—a reluctance, a wistfulness, a regret. The past had a way of creeping into the present, and his attempts at separating the two were still difficult. Even now. Even here.

Why had Nest Freemark been sent to him?

For just a moment he experienced an almost overpowering urge to flee. Just pack his bags, pick up Stefanie, and catch the first bus out of town. He stood facing into the park, and the movement in the shadows seemed to be reaching for him. He felt trapped in his life and by his decisions, and he could feel his control over things slipping away.

Then the moment passed. He took a deep breath and exhaled slowly, and he was all right again. He studied the shadows and saw nothing. The park was still and empty. He felt foolish and slightly embarrassed. He supposed he was not yet entirely free of the emotional fallout of San Sobel. He guessed that's what it was.

That was what he told himself as he turned away from

the park and went down the sidewalk. That was how he dismissed the matter.

But deep inside, where hunches and instinct kept separate counsel, he wasn't really sure.

CHAPTER 15

After Two Bears disappeared, Nest Freemark sat back down on the bench they had shared and stared out at the bay. Her thoughts kept returning to five years ago when she had first met him. She kept trying to reconcile what she remembered from then with what she knew from now. She kept trying to make the parts fit.

I fought in Vietnam. I walked and slept with death; I knew her as I would a lover. I was young before, but afterward I was very old. I died in the Nam so many times, I lost count. But I killed a lot of men, too.

He had told her that right after he had told her his name. He had told her he was a killer. But nothing else he had told her had made him seem so. There had been no hint of violence about him. He had gone out of his way to dispel her concerns.

I am a stranger, a big man, a combat veteran who speaks of terrifying things. You should be afraid. But we are friends, Nest. Our friendship was sealed with our handshake. I will not hurt you.

But he might hurt John Ross. He might have to, because that was what he had been sent to do. She pondered the idea, thinking that in some strange way they had all changed places from five years ago. John Ross was on trial instead of her, and Two Bears might become his executioner. Ross now stood in her shoes, and Two Bears stood in his.

But where did she stand?

She was aware after a while that there were eyes watching her, and she glanced around cautiously. The shabby, sad-eyed Native Americans whom Two Bears had dismissed from their bench were staring at her from a short distance away. They huddled together on the grass, sitting cross-legged, their coats pulled over their shoulders, their heads hunched close, their dark eyes haunted. She wondered what they were thinking. Maybe they were wondering about her. Maybe about Two Bears. Maybe they just wanted their bench back.

I'm afraid, she had said five years ago to Two Bears. And he had replied, *Fear is a fire to temper courage and resolve. Use it so.*

She was afraid again, and she wondered if she could use her fear now as he had taught her to use it then.

Speak my name once more, he had asked her, and she had done so. *O'olish Amaneh. Yes,* he had said. *Say it often when I am gone, so that I will not be forgotten.*

Speak my name, he asked her again, just moments ago. As if by saying it, she could keep him alive.

The last of his kind, the last of the Sinnissippi, appearing and disappearing like a ghost. But his connection to her, while she didn't pretend to understand it completely, was as settled as concrete. They were linked in a way that transcended time and distance, and she felt her kinship to him so strongly it seemed as if they had been joined always. She wondered at its meaning. She knew now he was a servant of the Word, just like John Ross. So he shared with her a knowledge of the war with

the Void, and they were possessed of magic, and they
knew of demons and feeders, and they walked a line between two worlds that others didn't even know existed.

But there was more. In some strange way, she knew,
they needed each other. It was hard to explain, but it was
there. She took strength from him, but he took something from her, as well. Something. Her brow furrowed.
Something.

She rose and walked to the railing, abandoning the
bench. She stared out over the bay to the mountains, their
jagged peaks cutting across the horizon. What was it he
took from her? A hope? A comfort? A companionship?
Something. It was there, a shape, a form at the back of
her mind, but she could not quite put a name to it.

The afternoon was lengthening. Already the sun was
sliding rapidly toward the horizon, its light tinting the
clouds that masked it in myriad colors of purple and rose.
It would be dark soon. She glanced at her watch. Four-
fifteen. She wondered what she should do. She had already decided to meet John Ross for dinner, to tell him of
her conversation with O'olish Amaneh, to try again to
persuade him of the danger he was in. But it was too
early yet to go back to the hotel and call him.

She walked out of the park and through the market,
ambling along through the stalls of fruits and vegetables,
fish and meats, and flowers and crafts, pausing now and
again to look, to listen to the itinerant musicians, and to
talk with the vendors. Everyone was friendly, willing to
spend a few minutes with a visitor to the city. She bought
a jar of honey and a fish pin, and she tasted a cup of apple
cider and a slice of fresh melon. She reached the brass
pig that marked the far end of the market, turned around,
and walked back again.

When she had made the circuit, she went back into the park and looked around. The park was almost empty, dappled with shadows and splashed with light from the street lamps. Even the Indians had moved on, all but one who was asleep on the grass, wrapped head to foot in an old green blanket, long black hair spilling out of the top like silk from an ear of corn.

Nest looked around. She kept thinking that Ariel would reappear, but so far there was no sign of her. She checked her watch again. It was five o'clock. Maybe she should call Ross. She had the phone number of Fresh Start written on a slip of paper in her pocket. She could probably reach him there. She looked around for a phone and didn't see one. But there were several restaurants close at hand, and there would be phones inside.

Then she heard her name called in an excited whisper. "Nest! Come quickly!"

Ariel was right next to her, hovering in the fading light, a pale shimmer of movement.

"Where have you been?" she demanded.

The tatterdemalion's face brushed against her own, and she could feel the other's urgency. "Out looking. There are sylvans everywhere, and sometimes they can tell you things. I went to find the ones who live here. There are three in the city, and all of them make their homes in its parks. One is east in the Arboretum, one is north in Discovery, and one is west in Lincoln."

She paused, and then the words exploded out of her in a rush. "The one in Lincoln," she hissed, "has seen the demon!"

* * *

"Some kids set fire to a homeless man under the viaduct last night," Simon Lawrence announced, looking into his tonic and lime as if it were a crystal ball. "They doused him with gasoline and lit him up. Then they sat around and watched him burn. That's how the police caught them; they were so busy watching, they forgot to run." He shook his head. "Just when you think some measure of sanity has been restored to the world, people find a way to prove you wrong."

Andrew Wren sipped at his scotch and water and nodded. "I thought that sort of thing only happened in New York. I thought Seattle was still relatively civilized. Goes to show."

They were sitting across from each other in easy chairs on the upper level of the lobby bar in the Westin. It was five o'clock, and the hotel was bustling with activity. Participants from a handful of conferences the hotel was hosting were streaming in, identified by plastic badges that announced their company name in abbreviated block letters, one tag indistinguishable from another. With the day's meetings and seminars concluded, drinks and dinner and evening entertainment were next on the agenda, and the attendees were ready to rock and roll. But the corner of the bar in which Simon Lawrence and Andrew Wren sat was an island of calm.

Wren watched the Wiz check his watch. He seemed distracted. He had seemed so since his arrival, as if other things commanded his attention and he was just putting in his time here until he could get to them. They had agreed to meet for drinks after Simon had been detained earlier in the day at a meeting with the mayor and been unable to keep their noon appointment. When he was done here, the Wiz had a TV interview scheduled.

Maybe that was what he was thinking about. No rest for the wicked, Wren thought sourly, then immediately regretted it. He was being perverse because he hadn't found anything bad to write about Simon Lawrence. No skeletons had emerged from the closet. No secrets had revealed themselves. The anonymous tips had not panned out. His instincts had failed him. He sipped at his drink some more.

"I appreciate your meeting me, Andrew," Simon said, smiling now. He was dressed in a dark shirt, slacks, and sport coat, and he looked casually elegant and very much at ease amid the convention suits. Wren, in his familiar rumpled journalist's garb, looked like something the cat had dragged in. "I know I haven't been able to give you as much time as you would like, but I want to make sure you feel you've been given full access to our records."

Wren nodded. "I've got no complaints. Everyone has been very cooperative. And you were right. I didn't find so much as a decimal point out of place."

The smile widened. "You sound a tad disappointed. Does this mean you will be forced to write something good about us?"

Wren pushed his glasses up on his nose. "Looks that way. Damned disappointing to have it end like this. When you're an investigative reporter, you like to find something to investigate. But you can't win them all."

Simon Lawrence chuckled. "I've found that to be true."

"Not lately, I'll wager." Wren cocked an eyebrow expectantly. "Lately, you've been winning them all. And you're about to win another."

The Wiz looked unexpectedly skeptical. "The shelter? Oh, that's a victory all right. It counts for something. But

I wonder sometimes what it is that I'm winning. Like that general, I keep thinking I'm winning battles, but losing the war."

Wren shrugged. "Wars are won one battle at a time."

Simon Lawrence hunched forward, his dark eyes intense. The distracted look was gone. "Sometimes. But some wars can't be won. Ever. What if mine against homelessness is one?"

"You don't believe that."

The Wiz nodded. "You're right, I don't. But some do, and they have cogent arguments to support their position. A political scientist named Banfield posited back in the early seventies that the poor are split into two groups. One is disadvantaged simply because it lacks money. Give them a jump start and their middle-class values and work ethic will pull them through. But the second group will fail no matter how much money you give them because they possess a radically present-oriented outlook on life that attaches no value to work, sacrifice, self-improvement, or service. If that's so, if Banfield was right, then the war effort is doomed. The problem of homelessness will never be solved."

Wren frowned. "But your work is with women and children who have been disenfranchised through circumstances not of their own making. It's not the same thing, is it?"

"You can't compartmentalize the problem so easily, Andrew. There aren't any conditions of homelessness specifically attributable to particular groups that would allow us to apply different solutions. It doesn't work like that. Everything is connected. Domestic violence, failed marriages, teen pregnancy, poverty, and lack of education are all a part of the mix. They all contribute, and ultimately you can't solve one problem without solving them all. We fight small battles on different fronts, but the war is huge. It sprawls all over the place."

He leaned back again. "We treat homelessness on a case-by-case basis, trying to help the disadvantaged get back on their feet, to reclaim their lives, to begin anew. But you have to wonder sometimes how much good we are really doing. We shore up people in need, and that's good. But how much of what we do is actually solving the problem?"

Wren shrugged. "Maybe that's best left to somebody else."

Simon Lawrence chuckled. "Who? The government? The church? The general population? Do you see anyone out there addressing the specific causes of homelessness or domestic violence or failed marriages or teen pregnancy in any meaningful way? There are efforts being made to educate people, but the problem goes way beyond that. It has to do with the way we live, with our values and our ethics. And that's exactly what Banfield wrote decades ago when he warned us that poverty is a condition that, to a large extent at least, we cannot alleviate."

They stared at each other across the little table, the din of the room around them closing in on the momentary silence, filling up the space like water poured in a glass. Wren was struck suddenly by the similarity of their passion for their work. What they did was so different, yet the strength of their commitment and belief was much the same.

"I'm sounding pessimistic again," the Wiz said, making a dismissive gesture. "You have to ignore me when I'm like this. You have to pretend that it's someone else talking."

Wren drained the last of his drink and sat back. "Tell me something about yourself, Simon," he asked the other man suddenly.

Simon Lawrence seemed caught off guard. "What?"

"Tell me something about yourself. I came out here for a story, and the story is supposed to be about you. So tell me something about yourself that you haven't told anyone else. Give me something interesting to write about." He paused. "Tell me about your childhood."

The Wiz shook his head immediately. "You know better than to ask me about that, Andrew. I never talk about myself except in the context of my work. My personal life isn't relevant to anything."

Wren laughed. "Of course it is. You can't sit there and tell me how you grew up doesn't have anything to do with how you came to be who you are. Everything connects in life, Simon. You just said so yourself. Homelessness is tied to domestic violence, teen pregnancy, and so forth. Same with the events of your life. They're all tied together. You can't pretend your childhood is separate from the rest of your life. So tell me something. Come on. You've disappointed me so far, but here's a chance to redeem yourself."

Simon Lawrence seemed to think about it a moment, staring across the table at the journalist. There was a dark, troubled look in his eyes as he shook his head. "I've got a friend," he said slowly, reflecting on his choice of words. "He's the CEO of a big company, an important company, that does some good work with the disadvantaged. He travels the same fund-raising circuits I do, talks to some of the same people. They ask him constantly to tell them about his background. They want to know all about him, want to take something personal away with them, some piece of who he is. He won't give it to them. All they can have, he tells me, is the part that deals directly with his work—with the present, the here and now, the cause to which he is committed.

"I asked him about it once. I didn't expect him to tell me anything more than he told anyone else, but he surprised me. He told me everything."

The Wiz reached for his empty glass, studied it a moment, and set it down. A server drifted over, but he waved her away. "He grew up in a very poor neighborhood in St. Louis. He had a brother and a sister, both younger. His parents were poor and not well educated, but they had a home. His father had a day job at a factory, and his mother was a housewife. They had food on the table and clothes on their backs and a sense of belonging somewhere.

"Then, when he was maybe seven or eight, the economy went south. His father lost his job and couldn't get rehired. They scraped by as long as they could, then sold their home and moved to Chicago to find work there. Within months, everything fell apart. There was no work to be found. They used up their savings. The father began to drink and would sometimes disappear for days. They drifted from place to place, often living in shelters. They started taking welfare, scraping by on that and the little bit of income the father earned from doing odd jobs. They got some help now and then from the churches.

"One day, the father disappeared and didn't come back. The mother and children never knew what happened to him. The police searched for him, but he never turned up. The younger brother died in a fall shortly afterward. My friend and his little sister stayed with their mother in a state-subsidized housing project. There wasn't enough food. They ate leftovers scavenged from garbage cans. They slept on old mattresses on the floor. There were gangs and drugs and guns in the projects. People died every day in the rooms and hallways and sidewalks around them."

He paused. "The mother began to go out into the streets at night. My friend and his sister knew what she did, even though she never told them. Finally, one night, she didn't come home. Like the father. After a time, the state came looking for the children to put them in foster homes. My friend and his sister didn't want that. They preferred to stay on the streets, thinking they could stay together that way.

"So that was how they lived, homeless and alone. My friend won't talk about the specifics except to say it was so terrible that he still cries when he remembers it. He lost his sister out there. She drifted away with some other homeless kids, and he never saw her again. When he was old enough to get work, he did so. Eventually, he got himself off the streets and into the schools. He got himself a life. But it took him a lot of hard years."

Simon Lawrence shrugged. "He had never told this to anyone. He told it to me to make a point. What difference did any of this make, he asked me, to what he did now? If he told this story to the people from whom he sought money—or if he told the press—what difference would it make? Would they give him more money because he'd had a hard life? Would they give him more money because they felt sorry for him? Maybe so. But he didn't want that. That was the wrong reason for them to want to help. It was the cause he represented that mattered. He wanted them to help because of that, not because of who he was and where he came from. He did not want to come between the donors and the cause. Because if that happened, then he risked the possibility he would become more important than the cause he represented. And that, Andrew, would be a sin."

He stood up abruptly, distracted anew. "I'm sorry, but I've got to run. You're staying over for the dedication tomorrow night, aren't you?"

Wren nodded, rising with him. "Yes, but I'd like to . . ."

"Good." Simon took his hand and gave it a firm shake. "If the newspaper's paying, try Roy's, here at the hotel, for a good dinner. It's first-rate. I'll see you tomorrow."

He was gone at once, striding across the lobby toward the front door, tall form scything through the crowd with catlike grace and determination. Andrew Wren stared after him, and it wasn't until he was out of sight that it occurred to the journalist that maybe, just maybe, Simon Lawrence had been talking about himself.

Nest Freemark found a phone booth across from the park and dialed the number for Fresh Start. It was after five now, the sun slipped below the horizon, the last color fading fast in a darkening sky. Ariel was hovering invisibly against the building walls behind her, and the streets were filling with traffic from people on their way home from work. The park had emptied long ago, and the grassy rise was a shadowed hump against the skyline.

It was beginning to rain, a slow, chilly misting that clung to Nest's skin. On the sound, a bank of fog was beginning to build over the water.

The lady who answered the phone was not Della, and she did not know Nest. She said John Ross wasn't there and wasn't expected back that day and she couldn't give out his home number. Nest told her it was important she speak to him. The lady hesitated, then asked her to hold on a minute.

Nest stared off into the gathering darkness, itching with impatience.

"Nest? Hi, it's Stefanie Winslow." The familiar voice sounded rushed and out of breath. "John's gone home, and I think he's shut off the phone, because I just tried to call him a little while ago and I couldn't reach him. Are you calling about dinner?"

Nest hesitated. "Yes. I don't think I can make it."

"Well, neither can I, but I think maybe John was planning on it. Will you be by tomorrow?"

"I think so." Nest thought furiously. "Can you give John a message for me?"

"Of course. I have to go by the apartment for a few minutes. I could even have him call you, if you want."

"No, I'm at a pay phone."

"All right. What should I tell him?"

For just an instant Nest thought about dropping the whole matter, just hanging up and leaving things the way they were. She could explain it all to Ross later. But she was uncomfortable with not letting him know there was new reason for him to be concerned about his safety, that something was about to happen that might change everything.

"Could you just tell him I'm meeting a friend of Pick's over in West Seattle who might know something about that trouble we were talking about at lunch? Tell him Pick's friend might have seen the one we were looking for."

She paused, waiting. Stefanie Winslow was silent. "Have you got that, Stefanie?" she pressed. "I know it's a little vague, but he'll know what I'm talking about. If I get back in time, I'll call him tonight. Otherwise, I'll see him tomorrow."

"Okay. Listen, are you all right? This sounds a little . . . mysterious, I guess. Do you need some help?"

Nest shook her head at the phone. "No, everything's fine. I have to go now. I'll see you tomorrow. Thanks for helping."

She hung up the phone and went looking for a taxi.

The demon walked into the lobby of the Westin through a side door, paused to look around, then moved quickly to the elevators across from the lobby bar. It didn't have much time; it had to hurry. An empty elevator was waiting, doors open, and the demon rode alone to the sixth floor. It stepped off into a deserted hallway, checked the wall numbers for directions, and turned left.

Seconds later, it stood before Andrew Wren's room. It listened carefully for a moment to make certain the room was empty, then slipped a thin manila envelope under the door. When Wren returned, he would find all the evidence he needed to confront the Wiz with the threat of exposure and a demand for an explanation that the latter would be unable to provide. The consequences of that would be inescapable. By tomorrow night, the Wiz would be history and John Ross would have taken his first step toward entering into the service of the Void.

There was only one additional matter to be settled.

Nest Freemark was a threat to everything. The demon had sensed her magic when they had talked earlier that day at Fresh Start. It was raw and unrealized, but it was potent. She could prove dangerous. Moreover, she had a tatterdemalion with her, and the tatterdemalion, if given the right opportunity, could expose the demon. If that happened, everything would be ruined.

The demon was not about to allow that. It didn't know what the girl and the forest creature were doing here, if they had been sent by the Word or come on their own, but it was time to be rid of them.

The demon turned and walked to the exit sign above the stairs and descended the six flights to the lobby. No one saw it leave.

In the parking garage, it claimed its car and headed for West Seattle.

CHAPTER 16

The night was cool and dark. As Nest Freemark rode through the city, rain misted on the windshield of the taxi, smearing the glass, blurring the garish neon landscape beyond. The taxi passed back down First Avenue in front of the Alexis Hotel, then climbed a ramp to the viaduct. Suspended above the waterfront, with the piers and ferries and colored lights spread out below and the orange cranes lifting skyward overhead, the taxi wheeled onto the lower tier of the expressway and sped south.

It had taken longer to find transportation than Nest had expected. She couldn't find anything in the market area, so she had walked down to a small hotel called the Inn at the Market, situated just above the Pike Place Market sign, and had the doorman call for her. Ariel had disappeared again. How the tatterdemalion would reach their destination was anybody's guess, but since she had gotten there once already, Nest guessed she would manage this time, too.

The canopy of the northbound viaduct lowered and leveled to join with the southbound, and Nest was back out in the rain again. The taxi eased around slower cars, its tires making a soft, steady hiss on the damp pavement.

Nest watched the cranes and loading docks appear and fade on her right, prehistoric creatures in the gloom. The driver was a motionless shape in front of her. Neither of them spoke. Brightly lit billboards whizzed by, advertisements for beer, restaurants, sports events, and clothing. She read them swiftly and forgot them even quicker, her thoughts tightly focused on what lay ahead.

The taxi took the off-ramp onto the West Seattle Bridge, and headed west. Nest settled back in the seat, thinking. Ariel had found a sylvan in one of the parks who had seen the demon a few months ago and gotten a good look at it. More important, at least from Ariel's point of view, was the story behind that sighting. She wouldn't elaborate when Nest asked for details. She wanted the sylvan to tell the story. She wanted Nest to hear for herself.

The freeway took a long, sweeping turn up a hill past a sign announcing their arrival in West Seattle. Residential lights shone through the rain. Fog cloaked the wooded landscape, clinging in thick patches to the heavy boughs of the conifers. Nest peered into the deepening gloom as the city dropped away behind her. They crested the hill and passed through a small section of shops and fast-food outlets. Then there were only residences and streetlights, and the city disappeared entirely.

The taxi wound its way steadily down the far side of the hill, took a couple of wide turns, then straightened out along a broad, straight, well-lit roadway. Ahead, she could see the dark wall of her destination. Lincoln Park was south of West Seattle proper, bordering Puget Sound just above the Vashon Island Ferry terminal. She found it on the map while she was riding in the taxi, checking its location, situating herself so that she wouldn't become turned around. When she was satisfied that she knew where she was, she stuck the map back in her pocket.

The taxi passed a park sign, then pulled into an empty parking area fronting a thick mass of trees. Nest could just make out the flat, earthen threshold of a trailhead next to it. There was no one in sight. Within the trees, nothing moved.

She paid the driver and asked him where she could call a taxi to get back into the city. The driver told her there was a pay phone at the gas station they had passed just up the road. He gave her a business card with the phone number of his company.

She stepped out into the mist and gloom, pulling up the hood of her windbreaker as the taxi drove away. Standing alone at the edge of the park, she glanced around uncertainly. For the first time that night, she began to have doubts.

Then Ariel was next to her, appearing out of nowhere. "This way, Nest! Follow me!"

The silken white image floated onto the trailhead, and Nest Freemark dutifully followed. They entered the wall of trees, and within seconds the parking lot and its lights disappeared behind them. Nest's eyes adjusted slowly to this new level of darkness. There were no lights here, but the low ceiling of clouds reflected the lights of the city and its homes to provide a pale, ambient glow. Nest could pick out the shapes of the massive conifers—cedar, spruce, and fir—interspersed with broad-leaved madrona. Thick patches of thimbleberry and salal flanked the pathway, and fern fronds drooped in feathery clusters. Rain carpeted the grass and leaves in crystal shards, and mist worked its way through the branches and trunks of the trees in snakelike tendrils. The park was silent and empty-feeling. It could have been Sinnissippi Park on a cold, wet fall night, except that the limbs of the northwest conifers, unlike their deciduous midwest cousins, were still thick with needles and did not lift bare, skeletal limbs against the sky.

The trail branched ahead, but Ariel chose the way without hesitation, her slender childish body wraithlike in the gloom. Nest glanced right and left at every turn, her senses pricked for movement and sound, wary of this dark, misty place. The uneasiness she had felt earlier was still with her. At times like these, she wished she had Wraith to protect her. The big ghost wolf had been a reassuring presence. She did not think often of him these days, not since he had disappeared. She was surprised to discover now that she missed him.

The trail climbed and she went with it, working her way through heavy old growth, fallen limbs, and patches of thick scrub. Clearings opened every so often to either side, filled with dull, gray light reflected off the heavy clouds. The rain continued to mist softly, a wetness that settled on her face and hands and left the air tasting of damp earth and wood. Now and again, her shoes slipped on patches of mud and leaves, causing her to lose her balance. Each time, she righted herself and continued, keeping Ariel in sight ahead of her.

They topped a rise, and Nest could just make out the black, choppy surface of Puget Sound through the trees. They were atop a bluff that dropped away precipitously beyond a low rail fence. The trail they followed branched yet again, following the edge of the cliff both ways along the fence into the darkness.

Ariel turned left and led Nest to a small clearing with a

rain-soaked wooden bench that looked out over the sound.

"Here," she said, stopping.

Nest drew even with her and looked around doubtfully. "What happens now?"

Ariel was insistent. "We wait."

The minutes ticked by as they stood in the chilly darkness, listened to the rain falling softly through the trees, and watched the mist float in and out of the damp, shiny trunks in shifting forms. Wind rustled the topmost branches in sudden gusts that showered them with water. Out on the sound, ferry boats and container ships steamed by, their lights steady and bright against the black waters.

Nest hugged herself with her arms and dug the toe of her shoe into the wet earth, growing impatient.

Then a familiar shadow flitted across the darkness, appearing abruptly from out of the woods. It swept down to the bench in a long glide and settled on the back rest, folding into itself. It was an owl, and on its back rode a sylvan, twiggy legs and arms entwined within the feathers of the great bird's neck.

The sylvan jumped off the owl with a quick, nimble movement, slid down the back rest, and stood facing her on the bench seat. She peered through the gloom in an effort to make out his features. He was younger than Pick, his wooden face not so lined, his beard not so mossy, and his limbs not so gnarled. He wore a bit of vine strapped about his waist, and from the vine dangled a small tube.

"You Nest?" he asked perfunctorily.

She nodded, coming forward several steps, closing the distance between them to six feet.

"I'm Boot, and this is Audrey." The sylvan indicated the owl. It was a breed with which she was not familiar, something a little larger and lighter colored than the barn owls she was used to. "We're the guardians of this park."

"Pleased to meet you," she said.

"You grew up in a park like this, I understand. You're friends with another sylvan."

"His name is Pick."

"You can do magic, too. That's unusual for a human. What sort of magic can you do?"

Nest hesitated. "I'm not sure I can do any magic. I haven't used it for a while. I have some problems with it. It hurts me to use it sometimes."

Ariel came forward, a delicate white presence in the night, dark eyes shifting from one to the other. "Tell her about the demon, Boot," she whispered anxiously.

The sylvan nodded. "Don't rush me. There's plenty of time to do that. All night, if we need it, and we don't. Where demons are concerned, you don't want to rush things. You want to step carefully. You want to watch where you go."

"Tell her!"

The sylvan harrumphed irritably. Nest thought of Pick. Apparently sylvans became curmudgeons at a young age.

Audrey ruffled her feathers against a rush of wind and damp, and resettled herself on the bench back, luminous round eyes fixing on Nest. Boot folded his skinny arms and muttered inaudibly into his beard and gave every appearance of refusing to say another word.

"I have a friend who is in danger from this demon," Nest announced impulsively, not wanting to lose him to a mood swing. "Whatever you can tell me might help save his life."

Boot stared at her. "All right. No reason not to, I guess. You've come a long way, haven't you? Well, then."

The arms unlocked and dropped to his sides. "The demon came to this park about three months ago. I'd never seen it before. I'd seen others from time to time, but they were always passing through on their way to somewhere else, and they were cloaked in their human guise and had been for a long time. But this one came deliberately. This one came with a purpose. It was night, midsummer, and it walked into the park just after sunset and came up to the cliffs and waited in the trees where the paths don't go. It was hiding, waiting for something. I was patrolling the park on Audrey and saw it from the air. I knew what it was right away. So Audrey and I circled back behind it, keeping to the high limbs, and found a place to watch."

"What did it look like?" Nest asked quickly.

"I'm getting to that, if you please," the sylvan informed in a no-nonsense tone of voice. "Don't rush me." He cleared his throat. "It was a man. He was tall and thin, rather different looking—dark hair and small features. He wore a long coat, no hat. I got a good look at him through the scope." He held up the tube tied to his waist. "Spyglass. Lets me see everything. Anyway, he stood there in the shadows for a long time. Maybe an hour or more. The park emptied out. It was a bright, moonlit night, so I could see what happened next very clearly."

He paused meaningfully. "Another demon appeared. It crawled up the cliff face from somewhere below, from the shoreline. I don't know where it came from before that. This one was huge, barely recognizable as human, its disguise sort of thrown together. It was thick-limbed and hunched over and all hairy and twisted. It looked more like an animal than a human, but a human is what it was trying to play at being, sure enough.

"So the first demon steps out from its hiding place to talk to the second. I have good ears, so I could hear them. 'What are you doing here?' the first one asks. 'I've come to kill him,' says the second. 'You can't kill him, he's mine, he belongs to me, and I want him alive,' says the first. 'It doesn't matter what you want. He's too dangerous to be allowed to live, and besides, I want to taste his magic. I want to make it my own,' says the second.

"Then they begin shrieking at each other, making threatening gestures, calling each other names." Boot shook his leafy head. "Well, you can imagine. I'm watching all this and wondering what in the world is going on. Two demons fighting over a human! I'd never heard of such a thing! Why would they do that when there's a whole world full of them, and more than a few ready, willing, and eager to be made victims?"

The sylvan came forward to the very edge of the bench, head inclined conspiratorially. "So then the first demon says, 'You have no right to interfere in this. The Knight belongs to me. His magic and his life are mine.' Well, now I know what they're talking about. They're quarreling over a Knight of the Word. For some reason, they seem to think there's one out there waiting to be claimed! I've heard of this happening. Rarely, but now and then. But I don't know about this Knight. I don't know much of anything that happens outside the park, so I'm a little surprised to hear about this. I pay close attention."

Boot glanced around at the darkness as if someone else might be listening. "So this is what happens next. The second demon pushes the first and says, 'I was sent to make certain of him. I tracked him before you, in other cities and other towns. You stole him from me. I want him back.' The first demon backs away. 'Don't be stupid! You don't have a chance with him! I'm the one who can turn him! I can make him one of us! I have already started to do so!'

"But the second demon isn't listening. Its hair is bristling and its eyes are narrowed and hard. I can feel Audrey trembling next to me, her talons digging into the limb from which we watch. 'He has made you weak and foolish. You think like the humans you pretend to be,' says the second demon, advancing again on the first. 'You are not strong enough to do what is needed. I must do it for you. I must kill him myself.'

"Then the second demon pushes the first demon hard and sends it sprawling into the brush."

Nest felt the skin on the back of her neck crawl with the idea of two demons fighting over possession of John Ross. She should have taken the time to find him and bring him with her. He should be listening to this. If he were, he would be hard-pressed to argue that he wasn't in any real danger.

Boot nodded, as if reading her mind. "It was a bad moment. The first demon gets back to his feet and says, 'All right, he's yours. Take him. I don't care anymore.' The second demon grunts and sneers at the first, then turns and moves off down the path. The first demon waits until the second is out of sight, then starts to undress. It takes off its coat and the clothes underneath. Then it begins to transform into something else. It happens quickly. I have heard of creatures like this, but I have never seen one—a changeling, a special kind of demon, able to shift from one form to another in moments where it takes the others days or even weeks to assume a new disguise."

The sylvan took a deep breath. "It becomes a four-legged creature, a monster, a predator like nothing I've ever seen. It has these huge jaws and this massive neck and shoulders. A hellhound. A raver. It lopes off into the brush after the second demon. Audrey and I take to the air and follow, watching. The changeling catches up to the second demon in seconds. It doesn't hesitate. It attacks instantly, charging out of the brush. It knocks the second demon to the ground despite its size and holds it there with its body weight. It tears the bigger demon's head from its shoulders, then rips its body down the middle and fastens on the dark thing inside that is its soul. There is a horrible shriek, and the second demon thrashes and goes limp. It begins to dissolve. It turns to ash and blows away in the summer's night breeze.

"The first demon says—growls, actually, and I can hear it even from atop the trees where Audrey and I watch it begin to change again—'He belongs to me, he is mine.' "

Rain gusted suddenly through the trees, blown on a fresh wind, and Nest started as the cold droplets blew into her face. The weather was worsening, the mist turning to a steady downpour. Nest tried to make sense of what the sylvan was telling her, why it was that the first demon would be so desperate to protect its interest in John Ross, to keep him alive so that he could be subverted. Something in the back of her mind nudged at her, a memory of something that had happened before, but she could not quite manage to identify it.

Ariel floated past her in the dark, her childlike form looking frail and exposed against the rush of wind and rain. "Is that all?" she asked Boot. "Is that the end of the story?"

"Not quite," replied the sylvan, dark eyes bright. "Like I said, the demon begins to change again, but—it's the strangest thing—this time it changes into . . ."

Something huge tore through the woods. Thick masses of brush shivered suddenly, shedding water and scattering shadows. Boot wheeled toward the movement in frightened recognition, his voice faltering and his dark eyes blinking in shock. Ariel gasped sharply and screamed at Nest.

Then the brush exploded in a shower of branches and leaves, and a massive black shape hurtled out of the night.

On the advice of Simon Lawrence, Andrew Wren enjoyed a leisurely dinner at Roy's, topping it off with the chocolate soufflé because everyone around him seemed to be doing the same. He was not disappointed. Then he went back out into the lobby for a nightcap. He drank a glass of port and engaged in conversation with a computer-software salesman from California who was in town to do a little business with Microsoft, picking up a few new tidbits of information on Bill Gates in the process (he never knew what was going to prove useful in his business). So it was nearing nine o'clock when he went up to his room to turn in.

He saw the manila envelope as soon as he opened the door, a pale square packet lying on the dark carpet. Wary of strange deliveries and having known more than one investigative journalist who had been the recipient of a letter bomb, he switched on the light and knelt to examine it. After a careful check, and noting how thin it was, he decided it was safe and picked it up. No writing on it anywhere. He carried it over to the small table by the window and set it down. Then he walked to the closet and hung his coat, turned on a few more lights, called the message service to retrieve a call that had come in over the dinner hour from his editor, and finally went back to the table, sat down in the straight-backed chair tucked under it, and picked up the envelope once more.

He knew what it was before he opened it. His intuition told him in a loud, clear voice. It was the material he had been looking for on Simon Lawrence. It was the evidence he had come to find. Maybe it was from his mysterious source. Maybe it was from someone else. Whoever it was from, it was either going to propel the stalled investigation of the Wiz to a new level or it was going to end it once and for all.

Wren separated the flap from the envelope and slipped out the sheaf of papers nestled inside. He set the envelope aside and began to read. It took him a long time because the material consisted mostly of photocopies of bank accounts, transfer slips, records of deposits and withdrawals, and ledger pages, and it was difficult to follow. Besides, he didn't want to jump to conclusions. After a while, he loosened his tie and rolled up his sleeves. His glasses slid down his nose, and his face assumed an intense, professorial look that accompanied deep thought. His burly body slouched heavily in the hard-backed chair, but he paid no attention to his discomfort. Outside, on the rain-slicked streets below, a stream of traffic crawled by, and every so often someone would forget what city they were in and honk their horn in irritation.

When he was done reading, he picked up the phone and called down for a bottle of scotch, a bottle of Evian, and some ice. He was treating himself, but he was fortifying himself as well. He knew what he had here, but it was going to take him half the night to sort it out. He wanted everything in order when he went to see Simon Lawrence in the morning. He wanted it all clear in his own head as well as on paper, so that he could analyze quickly any explanations that the Wiz chose to give. Not that he was likely to give any, if Wren was reading this right. Not that he was likely to want ever to see Andrew Wren again.

Because what someone had uncovered was evidence of a systematic siphoning of funds from the accounts of Fresh Start and Pass/Go, an elaborate and intricate series of transfers from accounts set up to receive charitable donations that dispersed them to other accounts within the corporations, applied them to payments of charges that didn't actually exist, and eventually deposited them in noncorporate accounts. The corporate books he had reviewed yesterday, and which presumably the corporate auditors reviewed as well, disguised the transfers in various ways, none of which could be uncovered readily in the absence of a comprehensive audit, the kind you didn't usually get unless the IRS came calling.

That hadn't happened as yet, and there was no reason to think it would happen anytime soon. The embezzling had been going on for less than a year, and from what Andrew Wren could tell, it involved only two people.

Or maybe only one.

Wren paused, rethinking the matter. Two, if they were both participating. One, if the second was being used as a front. Wren couldn't tell which from the photocopies alone. It would require an analysis of the signatures on the deposits and withdrawals. It would require an extensive investigation.

He shook his head. The photocopies showed the stolen funds being deposited into the private accounts of two people. One was Simon Lawrence. But why would the Wiz steal from his own foundation? Stranger things had happened, sure. But Simon Lawrence was so committed to his work, and his work had brought him nationwide recognition. If all he wanted out of this was more money, he could quit tomorrow and go to work as a CEO for any number of corporations. The thefts were recent. Why would the Wiz decide now, after achieving so much, to start stealing from his company? The thefts were clever, but they weren't perfect. Sooner or later, someone would find out what was happening in any event, and the Wiz would be exposed. He had to know that.

Wren poured two fingers of scotch into a glass of ice and sipped at it thoughtfully. The alcohol burned pleasantly as it slipped down his throat. Something wasn't right about this. The Wiz wouldn't steal from himself without a very strong reason, and then he would steal more than this because he had to know he wouldn't be able to get away with it for very long, so he had to make his killing early.

Wren stared out the window into the night. It was more likely the second man was the one doing all the stealing, and he had siphoned some of the funds into Simon's account so that if he were discovered, he could always claim he was just a flunky acting on orders. The public outcry would pass right over him and settle directly on the Wiz, a high-profile figure just ripe for lynching.

Andrew Wren nodded slowly. Yes, that made better sense. The second man was doing all the real stealing, and the Wiz was guilty merely of bad judgment in hiring him. That was what he believed. That was what his instincts told him was the truth. Of course, he would write the article based on the facts and let the chips fall where they may, because that was his job. So it might be the end of Simon Lawrence in any event. In the wake of a scandal like this, the Wiz would be hard-pressed to escape the fallout.

He sighed. Sometimes he hated being right so often, having those infallible instincts that prodded him on and on until he uncovered the harsh truth of things. Of course, it hadn't been so difficult this time. He wondered who his source was. It had to be someone inside the organization, someone who resented Simon and wanted to see him brought down.

Or possibly, he acknowledged with a lifting of his glass and a small sip of the scotch, someone who wanted to see John Ross brought down as well.

CHAPTER 17

Nest Freemark sprang aside at the sound of Ariel's warning, skidding headfirst across a slick of mud and dead needles as the dark shape hurtled past. In a rain-streaked blur she watched it catapult into Boot and Audrey. The sylvan was back astride the owl, and the owl was lifting away into the night. Both disappeared in a shower of blood and feathers and bits of wood, there one second and gone the next. The dark shape went right through them, bearing them away like a strong wind, the force of its momentum carrying it back into the night.

"Demon!" Ariel was screaming as she fled. "Demon! Demon!"

Nest scrambled to her feet and began to run after the tatterdemalion. She had no idea where she was going, only that she had to get away. She tore down the dirt path that paralleled the cliffs, tennis shoes slipping and sliding on the muddied track. She was nearly blind in the darkness and rain, and she was riddled with fear. Boot and Audrey were gone, dead in one terrible second, and the image of them exploding apart burned in the air before her as she ran, raw and terrible.

"Faster, Nest!" Ariel cried frantically.

Nest could hear the demon behind her, pursuing them.

She could hear the wet sound of its paws on the muddy path over the steady thrum of the rain. What sort of creature had it made itself into? She had only caught a glimpse, and she had never seen anything like it before. Her heart pounded in her chest, and her breath was fiery in her throat. She was deep in the woods and there was nowhere to hide, but if she didn't reach a place of safety in the next few seconds, the demon would have her.

Her eyes flicked left and right, and a new well of fear opened within. Running with her were dozens of feeders, come out of nowhere in the rainy gloom, faceless squat shapes keeping pace as they darted through the trees, eyes filled with excitement and anticipation.

She glanced over her shoulder and saw the demon closing fast, its black shape stretched out low to the ground and hurtling forward. A surge of adrenaline propelled her ahead, and for a few seconds she managed to increase her speed enough to put a little more distance between them. But then the beast was closing on her again, and she could see the gleam of its teeth and eyes in the misty gloom.

Ahead and to her left, there were only more trees and darkness. To her right, beyond the low rail fence, the cliff fell away into a void. There were lights from houses and streets, but they were distant pinpricks through the woods, still far, far away.

She knew she was not going to escape. She was fit and strong; she was a world-class distance runner. But the thing pursuing her was too much for any human. She faltered slightly, preparing to turn and fight. The demon burst out of the night, a silent black predator, gathering itself to strike. She saw it clearly, revealed for just an instant in a patch of gray light, some sort of monstrous

hyena, all neck and blunt muzzle, with huge jaws and
rows of teeth. She swerved through the trees and out
again, scattering feeders everywhere, trying to throw the
demon off, but it was quick and agile, and it followed her
easily.

"Nest, no!" she heard Ariel scream a final time,
turning.

The demon caught up to her at a wide spot where the
trail took a slow bend to the left, away from the cliff.
She looked back and saw that it was right on top of her.
She watched it gather itself, preparing to bear her struggling and helpless to the ground. Her fear enveloped her
like a death shroud, choking off her breath, suffocating
her. Something wild and fierce blossomed inside her in
response, and for just an instant she thought it was her
magic, trying to break free. But her mind was frozen by
the demon's closeness, by the gleam of its yellow eyes
and the certainty of what was going to happen next, and
she could not find a way to help it.

Feeders streamed through the trees, leaping wildly,
shadows with eyes, gathered for the kill.

But as the demon lunged for Nest, rising up against
the night, Ariel threw herself into its path, a white blur
against the dark, and collapsed around its head like a
child's bedsheet. Demon and tatterdemalion went down
in a tangled heap, rolling over and over on the muddied
earth. Nest backed away, staring in horror at the thrashing dark knot. In seconds all that remained of Ariel was a
silken white shroud that clung tenaciously to the momentarily blinded demon.

Then even that was gone, and the demon was clawing
its way back to its feet, snarling in fury.

Nest, momentarily transfixed by the struggle taking

place before her, wheeled to flee once more. But she had lost her sense of direction entirely, forgetting the bend in the trail and the low rail fence at her back. She took one quick stride and toppled right over the fence. She was up again instantly, thrashing at the heavy brush, trying to escape its clinging embrace. Then the ground disappeared beneath her feet, and she was falling head over heels down a rain-slicked slope. She groped futilely for something to hang on to, skidding and sliding along slick bare earth and through long grass, careening off bushes and exposed tree roots, the darkness whirling about her in a kaleidoscope of distant lights and falling rain. Her stomach lurched with each sudden change of direction, and she tucked in her arms and legs and covered her head with her hands, waiting for something to slow her.

When she hit the base of the precipice, the breath was knocked from her lungs and her head was left spinning. She lay where she was for an instant, listening to the sound of the rain. Then she was back on her feet and running, dazed and battered, but otherwise unhurt. A wide, grassy embankment stretched along the base of the cliffs, fronting the dark, choppy waters of Puget Sound, and a concrete path paralleled the water's edge. She wheeled left down the path, heading for the lights of the residences that lay closest.

Already she could hear the sounds of the demon's pursuit. It was coming down the cliff face after her, scrambling through the brush and grasses, branches and roots snapping as it tore through them. She gritted her teeth against her fear and rage. Feeders ran at her side, an unshakable presence. Her windbreaker was muddied and torn, pieces of it flapping wildly against her body. If she could reach the houses outside the park, she would have a chance. Her lungs burned as she forced herself to run faster. Again she thought to turn and face the thing that chased her, to summon up the magic that had protected her so often before. But she had no way of knowing if she still had the use of it, and no time to find out.

Her feet splashed loudly through the rain that puddled on the concrete, spraying surface water everywhere. Her clothing was soaked through, and her curly hair was plastered to her head. She could no longer see or hear the demon, but she knew it was back there. She thought of Ariel, and tears filled her eyes. Dead because of her. All of them—Boot, Audrey, and Ariel—dead because of her. She ran faster, sweeping past grassy picnic areas with tables and iron cookers, swing sets and benches, and a small pavilion with a wooden roof and a concrete floor. To her right, the sound lapped against the shoreline, driven by the wind. The world about her was a vast, empty, rain-swept void.

She wished desperately that Wraith was there. Wraith would protect her. Wraith would be a match for the demon. A part of her, deep inside, shrieked defiantly that he *was* still there and would come if she summoned him. She almost thought to do so, to wheel back and call for him, to bring him to her side once more. But Wraith was gone, disappeared over a year ago, and there was no reason to think he would come to her now, after so long.

She cast aside the last of her futile wishes for what couldn't be, and concentrated on gaining the safety of the city streets. She could see the residences clearly now, bulky shapes hunkered down against the misty gloom, lights a blurry yellow through rain-streaked windows. She could see cars moving on the street further south, distant still, but recognizable.

She risked a quick glance over her shoulder. In the darkness, beyond the feeders trailing after her, the demon's larger shape was visible.

The concrete path rose ahead of her, leading out of the park's lower regions. She swept up the rise without slowing, ignoring the hot, raw feeling in her lungs and the cramping in her stomach. She was not going to give up. She was not going to die. She gained the summit of the rise, broke through the empty parking lot, and was on the street.

She crossed in a gust of wind and rain that blew sideways at her, making for the houses on the other side. The park was a black mass behind her, an impenetrable wall of darkness, the jagged tips of the ancient trees piercing the skyline. The street was momentarily empty of cars; she would find no help there. The feeders stayed with her, keeping pace easily, yellow eyes gleaming in the night. She ignored them, concentrating on the houses ahead. Several were dark or poorly lit, and there was no sign of life. She passed them by. *Please,* she prayed silently, *let someone be home!* Out of the corner of her eye, she saw movement behind her at the head of the pathway leading out of the park. The demon was coming.

There was a brightly lit picture window in a brick cottage that lay ahead, and she could see a man reading a newspaper in an easy chair. She crossed the lawn in a rush, leaped onto the cement steps, and tried to wrench open the screen door. It was locked. She pounded on it wildly, looking over her shoulder as she did. The demon was in the middle of the street, its massive body stretched out as it ran, coming straight for her. All around her the feeders leaped and scrambled anxiously. She hissed at them and pounded on the door again.

The heavy inner door opened and the man stood there, staring at her through the screen with a mix of irritation and surprise that quickly changed to shock when he got a better look.

"Please, let me in," she begged, trying to keep her voice even, to keep the fear out of it. She could see herself reflected in his glasses, disheveled, muddied, scraped, and bruised.

"Good Lord, young lady!" he exclaimed, wide-eyed. He was an older man, white-haired and slightly stooped. He peered at her doubtfully. "What happened to you?"

He was still talking to her through the screen. She felt her desperation threaten to overwhelm her, felt the demon's breath on her neck, its claws and teeth on her body. "An accident!" she gasped. "I need to call for help! Please!"

He unfastened the latch now, finally, and the moment he began to crack the door, she wrenched it open and rushed inside, ignoring his startled surprise as she pushed him aside, slamming the screen door, then the inner door, and locking them both.

The man stared at her. "Young lady, what in the world . . ."

"There's something chasing me . . ." she began.

The demon slammed into the screen door from the other side with such force that it tore it off entirely. Then it hammered into the inner door, once, twice, and the hinges began to loosen.

"What in God's name?" gasped the older man as he stumbled backward in fright.

"Get out of here!" she shouted, racing past him for the back of the house. "Call the police!"

The demon was hammering into the door, pounding at it in fury. It meant to have her, and it didn't care what stood in its way. She raced down a hall into a kitchen, where an older woman stood washing dishes at a sink. The woman looked up in surprise, blinked, and stared at her with the same look of shock as the man.

"Get out of the house now!" Nest screamed at her.

Sorry, sorry, sorry! she apologized silently as she raced out the back door into the night.

Rain and wind beat at her. The storm was growing worse. She glanced left and right into the darkness, then broke across the backyard, heading north once more. If she could reach the service station the taxi driver had told her about, she could call for help there. Porch lights came on in a few of the houses around her. She could no longer hear the sound of the demon trying to break down the door of the house she had abandoned. That meant it knew she was gone and was coming for her again.

She crossed through several backyards before coming to a fence. She would have to climb it or go back out front. Rain and sweat streaked her forehead and spilled into her eyes. Her strength was ebbing. She wheeled left along the fence and raced for the street once more.

When she broke into the open, she was alone but for one or two feeders; the rest had fallen away. There was no sign of the demon. She felt a moment of elation, then saw a flicker of movement behind her. In a panic, she raced toward the street. A car swept out of the darkness, its tires throwing up spray, and she ran for it, waving her arms and yelling. But the car never slowed, and a moment later she was alone again. In the fading sweep of the car's headlights, she caught a momentary glimpse of the demon charging toward her. She turned back to the houses, searching. There was a two-story with a glassed-in porch and lights in almost every window. She made for that one. Cars lined the curbing in front. A party was in progress. She felt a hot rush of satisfaction. This time she would find the help she needed.

She raced up the steps and yanked on the handle of the porch door. The door opened easily, and she was inside in the blink of an eye. She slammed the door behind her, threw the lock, rushed to the front door, and began to pound. Inside, she could hear the sound of laughter and music. She pounded harder.

The door opened. A young woman dressed in a sweater and jeans stood there, holding a drink in her hand and staring in disbelief.

"Please let me in!" Nest began once more. "There's someone after me, and I need to call—"

A storm window flew apart in an explosion of jagged shards as the demon crashed onto the porch and slammed into the front wall of the house, snarling and snapping at the air with its massive jaws and hooked teeth. The young woman screamed in terror, and Nest shoved her back inside the house, followed her in, slammed the door shut, and threw the bolt lock. The young woman went down in a heap and lay there, sobbing. They were in a hallway leading to a series of rooms, the nearest of which was filled with other young people who stared out at them in surprise. Laughter and light conversation gave way to exclamations. Nest went past them down the hall in a rush. Behind her, the demon was tearing at the door, stripping away the wooden facade as if it were cardboard.

Party-goers spilled out into the entry to help the young

woman back to her feet, some calling after Nest, some staring wide-eyed toward the sounds coming from outside the door. "Don't open it!" Nest shouted back at them. Not that anyone was that stupid, she thought in a sudden moment of giddiness.

At the end of the hallway lay the kitchen. Inside, she found a phone and dialed 911. Maybe the old couple down the block had already done so, but maybe not. She told the operator there was a forcible entry in progress at a house just north of Lincoln Park. She said there was screaming. She gave the phone number of the house and then hung up. That ought to bring someone.

There was a new sound of glass breaking, this time from somewhere at the side of the house. The demon was trying to get in another way. She leaned against the kitchen counter, listening to the sounds, staring into space. If she remained where she was, she was risking the safety of the people in the house. If she went out again, she was risking her own safety. She closed her eyes and tried to think. She was so tired. But she was alive, too, and that was more than she could say about Boot and Audrey and Ariel. She pushed away from the counter and went through a laundry room to a back door. The demon was still trying to break in from the other side of the house. She could hear the party-goers shouting and screaming, crowding down the hallway, trying to get away from the intruder. She could hear the phone begin to ring.

She yanked open the door and fled once more into the night.

She was running through a tall hedge into a neighbor's backyard when she heard the boom of a gun. Maybe the shooter would get lucky. You couldn't kill a demon with a gun, but you could destroy its current guise and force it to take time to re-form. If that happened, it would be done chasing after her.

But she knew she couldn't count on that. She couldn't count on anything except that the demon would keep coming. She crossed through several more backyards, then caught sight of something that might save her. A transit bus was just pulling to a stop down the street. She broke from between the houses and raced for it, yelling at the top of her lungs, waving her arms wildly. She saw the bus driver turn and look at her. The look was a familiar one by now. She didn't care. She raced around the front of the bus and through the open door.

"Hey, what's going on?" the driver demanded as she dug frantically into her pockets for some change.

"Just close the door and start driving," she ordered, glancing quickly over her shoulder.

Whatever he saw on her face convinced him not to argue. He closed the doors and put the bus in gear. The bus swung away from the curb and into the street, rain beating against its wide front windows.

She had just begun to make her way down the aisle when something heavy crashed into the doors, causing the metal to buckle and the glass to splinter. There were only three other passengers on the bus, and all three froze, eyes bright with shock and fear. The driver cursed and stepped on the gas. Nest wheeled back toward the damaged doors, hanging on the metal bar of a seat back for support, searching the darkness beyond.

A huge, wolfish shadow was running next to the bus, eyes gleaming brightly in the night.

Then a police car crested the hill in front of them,

coming fast, lights flashing. It swept past without slowing, searchlight cutting through the rainy dark.

The shadow disappeared.

Nest exhaled slowly and slipped into the seat beside her, heart pounding in her chest. When she looked down at her hands, she saw that they were shaking.

The ride back into the city was a blur. Once she determined that the bus was going in the right direction, she quit paying attention. People got on and off, but she didn't look at their faces. She stared out the window into the darkness, thinking.

It took a long time for the fear to subside, and when it did she was filled with cold rage. Three lives had been snuffed out quicker than a candle's flame, and no one but she even knew about it and no one but she cared. Boot, Audrey, and Ariel—a sylvan, an owl, and a tatterde-malion. Creatures of the forest, of magic and imagina-tion. Humans didn't even know they existed. What difference did their loss make to anything? The unfair-ness of it burned inside her. She struggled for a time with the possibility that she was to blame for what had hap-pened, that she had brought the demon down on them. But there was no reason to believe this was so, and her guilt stemmed mostly from the fact they were dead and she was alive. But barely alive, she kept reminding her-self. Alive, because she had been fortunate enough to step off a cliff and survive the fall. Alive, because she had evaded a handful of serious attempts by a monster to rip her to shreds.

She blinked in the sudden glare of a passing truck's headlights. How had the demon found out about her meeting? There was a question that screamed for an answer. She stared harder at the darkness and tried to reason it through. The demon might have followed her. But to do so, it must have been following her all day. Was that possible? Could it have done so without Ariel or Two Bears knowing? Without her feeling something, a twinge of warning initiated by her dormant magic? Maybe. The magic wasn't so dependable anymore. But if the demon hadn't been following her, then it must have intercepted her message to John Ross. It must have been listening in when she called. Or learned something from Stefanie Winslow or from John himself.

She gritted her teeth at the idea that she had been caught so unaware, so vulnerable, and that she had run—*run!*—rather than stand and fight. She hated what had happened, and she was not pleased with how she had behaved. It didn't matter that she could explain it away by telling herself what she had done had kept her alive and that she had reacted on instinct. She had fled and not stood her ground, while three other lives had been taken, and no amount of rationalization could change how that made her feel.

As she rode through the darkness and the rain, struggling with the rush of emotions churning inside, she was reminded of how she had felt at Cass Minter's funeral. She had stood there during the graveside services on a beautiful, sun-filled day trying to make herself believe that her best and oldest friend was gone. It hadn't seemed possible. Not Cass, who was only eighteen and had lived so little of her life. Nest had stood there and tried to will her friend alive again, furious at having had her taken away so unexpectedly and abruptly and pointlessly. She had stood in a rage as the minister read from his Bible in a soft, comforting voice, trying in vain to make sense of the arbitrary nature of one young woman's life and death.

She felt like that now, thinking back on the events in Lincoln Park. She had been in Seattle for less than twenty-four hours. She had come with simple expectations and a single purpose to fulfill. But it had all gotten much more complicated than anything she might have imagined. It had become rife with madness.

She watched the lights and the buildings of the downtown rise out of the darkness, sitting sodden, muddied, and exhausted in her seat. West Seattle fell away behind her, disappearing into the dark, and her rage faded with her fear, and both were replaced by an immense sadness. She began to cry. She cried softly, soundlessly, and no one around her appeared to notice. She wanted to go home again. She wanted none of this ever to have happened. A huge, empty well opened inside, echoing with the sounds of voices she would never hear again. Some came from Lincoln Park and the present. Some came from Hopewell and the past. She felt abandoned and alone. She could not find a center for the downward spiral in which she was caught.

She left the bus at a downtown stop and walked through the mostly empty streets of the city to her hotel. She wondered vaguely if the demon might be tracking her still, but she no longer cared. She almost hoped it was, that it would come for her again and she would have another chance to face it. It was a perverse wish, unreasonable and foolish. Yet it made her feel better. It gave her renewed strength. It told her she was still whole.

But no one approached her or even tried to speak to her. She reached the hotel and went into the lobby and up to her room, locking the door behind her, throwing the deadbolt and fastening the chain. She stripped off her ruined clothes, showered, and climbed into bed.

There, in the warm enfolding dark, just before she fell asleep, with images of Ariel and Boot and Audrey spinning in a wash of streetlight shining brightly through her bedroom window, she made herself a promise that she would see this matter through to the end.

WEDNESDAY, OCTOBER 31

CHAPTER 18

When Stefanie Winslow woke him at midnight, John Ross was so deeply asleep that for a few seconds he didn't know where he was. The bedside clock flashed the time at him, so he knew that much, but his brain was fuzzy and muddled and he could not seem to focus.

"John, wake up!"

He blinked and tried to answer, but his mouth was filled with cotton, his tongue was glued to the roof of his mouth, and there was a buzzing in his ears. He blinked in response to her words, recognizing her voice, hearing the urgency in it. She was shaking him, and the room swam as he tried to push himself up on one elbow.

He felt as if he were drugged.

"John, there's something wrong!"

His memory returned through a haze of confusion and sluggishness. He was in his bedroom—their bedroom. He had come back there after his lunch with Nest, to think things over, to be alone. He had thought about her warning, about the possibility of a demon's presence, about the danger that might pose to him. The afternoon had passed away into evening, the weather outside slowly deteriorating, sunshine fading to clouds as the rain moved in. Stef had come in from work, stopping off to deliver a message from Nest and to see how he was. She had made him pasta and tea and gone out again. That was the last he remembered.

He blinked anew, struggling with his blurred vision in the darkness, with the refusal of his body to respond to the commands from his brain. Stefanie bent over him, trying to pull him upright.

The message from Nest . . .

That she was going to West Seattle for a meeting with a sylvan. That the sylvan had seen the demon she was looking for. That this was her chance to prove to him her warning was valid. Her words were coded, but unmistakable. Stef had asked him if he knew what they meant, and he had, but couldn't tell her, so he had been forced to concoct an explanation.

The message had been very upsetting. He didn't like the idea of Nest wandering around the city looking for a demon. If there actually was one and it found out what she was doing, it would try to stop her. She was resourceful and her magic gave her a measure of protection against creatures of the Void, but she was no match for a demon.

But when he had started to go after her, Stef had quickly intervened. She had felt his forehead and advised him he had a fever. When he insisted he was going anyway, she had insisted with equal fervor that at least he would have something to eat first, and she had made him the pasta. Then she had left for her press conference with Simon, promising to be home soon, and he had moved to the sofa to finish his tea, closed his eyes for just a moment, and . . .

And woken now.

Except that he had a vague memory of Simon Lawrence being there, too, coming in through the door right after Stef had gone, saying something . . . he couldn't remember . . .

He rubbed his eyes angrily and forced his body into a sitting position on the side of the bed, Stef helping to guide him into position.

"John, damn it, you have to wake up!" she hissed almost angrily, shaking him.

His head drooped, heavy and unresponsive. What in the world was wrong with him?

He slept like this often these days, ever since the dreams had stopped and he had ceased to be a Knight of the Word. He had given up his charge and his responsibilities and his search, and the dreams had faded and sleep had returned. But his sleep had turned hard and quick; it frequently felt as if he were awake again almost immediately. There was no sense of having rested, of slumbering as he once had. He was gone and then he was back again, but there had been no journey. Stef marveled at the soundness of his sleep, commenting more than once on how peaceful he seemed, how deeply at rest. But he felt no peace or rest on waking, and save for the few times he had dreamed of the old man and the burning of the city, he had no memory of having slept at all.

"What's wrong?" he managed to ask finally, his head lifting.

She bent close, a black shape in the room's darkness. Streetlight silhouetted her against the curtained window. "I think there's a fire at Fresh Start."

His mind was still clouded, and her words rolled through its jumbled landscape like thick syrup. "A fire?"

"Will you just get up!" she shouted in frustration. "I

don't want to call it in unless I'm sure! I called over to the night manager and no one answered! John, I need you!"

He lurched to his feet, an effort that left him dizzy and weak. It was as if all the strength had been drained from his body. He was like a child. She helped him over to the window, and he peered out into the rainy darkness.

"There," she said, pointing, "at the back of the building, in the basement windows."

Slowly his vision focused on the dark, squarish bulk of the shelter. At first he didn't see anything. Then he caught a flicker of something bright and angry against a pane of glass, low, at ground level. He waited a moment, saw it again. Flames.

He braced himself on the windowsill and tried to shake the cobwebs from his mind. "Call 911. Tell them to get here right away." He squinted against the gloom, peering down the empty streets of Pioneer Square. "Why hasn't the fire alarm gone off?"

She was on the phone behind him, lost in the dark. "That's what I wondered. That's why I didn't call it in right away. You'd think if there was a fire, the alarm . . . Hello? This is Stefanie Winslow at 2701 Second Avenue. I want to report a fire at Fresh Start. Yes, I can see it from where I'm standing . . ."

She went on, giving her report to the dispatcher. John Ross moved away from the window to find his clothes. He tried a light switch and couldn't get it to work, gave up, and dressed in the dark. He was still weak, still not functioning as he should, but the rush of adrenaline he had experienced on realizing what was happening had given him a start on his recovery. He pulled on jeans, shirt, and walking shoes, not bothering with socks or underwear, anxious to get moving. There should be someone on duty at the center. Whoever it was should have detected the smoke—should have answered the phone, too, when Stef called over to see what was wrong.

She was hanging up the phone behind him and heading for the door. "I've got to get over there, John!" she called back to him as she swept out into the living room.

"Stef, wait!"

"Catch up to me as quick as you can! I'll wake as many people as I can find and try to get them out!"

The door slammed behind her. Cursing softly, he finished tying the laces of his shoes, stumbled through the darkness to the front closet, pulled on his all-weather coat, grabbed the black walking stick, and followed her out.

He didn't waste time on the elevator, which was notoriously slow, heading instead for the stairs, taking them as quickly as he could manage with his bad leg, hearing her footsteps fading ahead of him followed by the closing of the stairway door below. His mind was clearer now, and his body was beginning to come around as well. He limped down the stairs in a swift shamble, using the walking stick and the railing for support, and he was into the entryway and out the front door in moments.

Rain beat down in torrents, and the streetlights were murky and diffuse in the storm-swept gloom. Second Avenue was deserted and eerily quiet. Where were the fire engines? He left the sidewalk and crossed through the downpour, head lowered against gusts of wind that blew the rain into his face with such force that he could barely make out where he was going.

Ahead, he watched Stefanie's dark figure pause at the front door of the shelter, pounding at it, then fumbling with her keys to release the lock. The building was dark, save for a glimmer of night-lights in the upper dormitories and front lobby. Inside, everything was silent and still.

Then the front door was open and Stef was inside, disappearing into the gloom. As he drew nearer, he saw rolling gray smoke leaking from the basement windows and the front entry, escaping the building to mix with the mist and rain outside. His chest tightened with fear. In an old building like this, a fire would spread quickly. He shouted after Stefanie, trying to warn her, but his words were blown away on the wind.

He reached the front door, still open from Stef's entry, and rushed inside. The interior was murky with smoke, and he could barely see well enough to make his way across the lobby to the hallway and the offices beyond. The stairway door to the upper floors was open, and he could hear shouts and cries from above. He coughed violently, covered his mouth with his wet sleeve, and tried to find some sign of the night manager. He couldn't remember who had the duty this week, but whoever it was, was nowhere to be found. He searched the length of the hallway and all the offices without success.

The basement door was closed. Smoke leaked from its seams, and it was hot to the touch. He ignored his instincts and wrenched it open. Clouds of smoke billowed forth, borne on a wave of searing heat. He shouted down the stairs, but there was no response. He started down, but the heat and smoke drove him back. He could see the flames spreading along the walls, climbing to the higher floors. Wooden tables, filing bins and cabinets, records and charts, and even the stairway were burning.

He slammed the door shut again, backing away.

There were footsteps on the stairway behind him, the women and children coming down from the upper floors. He limped over to meet them so that he could direct them to the front door. They appeared out of the gloom, dim shapes against the haze of smoke. They stumbled down in ones and twos, coughing and crying and cursing in equal measure, the children clinging to their mothers, the mothers clinging back, the women without children helping both, the whole bunch wrapped in robes and coats and even sheets. The smoke was growing thicker and the heat increasing. He shouted at them to hurry, urging them on. He tried to count heads, to determine how many had come out so he could know how many were still inside. But he couldn't remember the number in residence, and he didn't know how many might have been admitted that afternoon after he left. Twenty-one, twenty-two, twenty-three—they were filing past him in larger groups now, bumping up against one another in their haste to get out. Thirty-five, thirty-six. There had to be at least ninety, probably more like a hundred.

He peered through the haze, feeling the heat grow about him, seeing red flickers from down the hallway at the back of the building. The fire was climbing through the air vents.

There was still no sign of Stef.

Sirens screamed up to the front doorway, and fire-fighters clad in flame-retardant gear rushed inside in a knot. Ross was down on one knee now, coughing violently, eyes burning with the smoke, head spinning. They reached out for him and pulled him to his feet. He was too weak to resist, barely able to keep hold of his staff.

Hoses were being dragged through the doorway, and he could hear the sound of glass being broken.

"Who else is in here?" he heard someone ask.

He shook his head. "More women and children . . . upstairs. Stef is up there . . . helping them." He retched violently and doubled over. "A night manager . . . somewhere."

They hauled him outside into the cool, rainy night, propped him against the side of an ambulance, and gave him oxygen. He gulped it down greedily, his eyes gradually beginning to clear, his sight to return. Knots of women and children huddled all around him, shivering in the cold night air.

His gaze settled on Fresh Start. Flames were climbing the exterior of the walls, shooting out of the second- and third-story windows.

Stef!

He lurched to his feet and tried to push his way back inside, but hands closed tightly on his arms and shoulders and pulled him back again. "You can't do that, sir," a voice informed him quickly. "Get back now, please."

Windows exploded, showering the street with shards of glass. "But she's still in there!" he gasped frantically, trying to make them understand, fighting to break free.

More women and children were being hustled out, escorted by firefighters. A hook and ladder truck had rolled into position, and the extension was being run up toward the roof. Police cars had arrived to protect the firefighters and control traffic, and there were flashing lights everywhere. At the fringe of the action, a crowd was gathering to watch from behind cordoned lines. The mix of rain and hydrant water had turned the streets to rivers.

Still struggling, Ross was moved back to the makeshift shelter, overpowered by the combined weight of his protectors. Fear and anger swept through him in a red haze, and he felt himself losing control.

Stef! He had to go back in for Stef!

And then she appeared, stumbling out the smoke-filled doorway of the shelter, a small child clutched in her arms. Firefighters clustered around her, taking charge of the child, moving both of them away from the blaze, the building behind them bright with flames.

Ross broke free of the restraining hands and went to her. She collapsed into his arms, and they sank to the rain-soaked pavement.

"Stef," he murmured in relief, hugging her tightly.

"It's all right, John," she whispered, nodding into his shoulder, firefighters rushing past them in dark knots, hoses trailing after like snakes. "It's all right."

Fresh Start burned for another hour before the fire was extinguished. The blaze did not spread to the nearby buildings, but was contained. The shelter was a total loss. All of the women and children housed in the building were safely evacuated, in large part because of Stef's quick action in getting to them before the blaze spread to the sleeping rooms.

Only the night manager did not escape. His ruined body was found in the basement, lying near the charred filing cabinets and records bins. It took only a short time to make a tentative identification. It was a man, not a woman, and Ray Hapgood had been on duty and was unaccounted for.

It was three in the morning when Ross and Stef re-entered their apartment and closed the door softly behind them. They stood holding each other in the darkness for a long time, breathing into each other's shoulders in the silence, saying nothing. Ross could not stop thinking about Ray.

"How could this have happened?" he whispered finally, his voice still tight with shock.

Stef shook her head and said nothing.

"What was Ray doing there?" he pressed, lifting his head away from her shoulder to look at her. "It wasn't his duty. He was supposed to go out to his sister's in Kent. He told me so."

Her fingers tightened on his arms. "Let it go, John."

A stubborn determination infused him. "I don't want to let it go. Who had the duty tonight? Who?"

She lifted her head slightly and he could see the angry welts and bruises on her face. "Simon makes up the list, John. Ask him."

"I'm asking you. Who had the duty?"

She blinked back the tears that suddenly filled her eyes. "You did. But when you went home sick, Ray offered to fill in."

He stared at her in disbelief. He had the duty? He couldn't remember it. Why hadn't he known? Even before he was sick, why hadn't he known? It should have been posted. It must have been. He was certain he had looked at the list. So why didn't he remember seeing his name?

He felt worn and defeated. He stood in the dark holding Stef and looking into her eyes, and for the first time in a long time he was uncertain about everything. "Did you see my name?"

"John . . ."

"Did you, Stef?"

She nodded. "Yes." She touched his face. "This isn't

your fault, John. Just because you weren't there and Ray was doesn't mean it's your fault."

He nodded because that was what she expected him to do, but he was thinking that it felt like it was his fault, just as it had felt like it was his fault at San Sobel. Any failure of responsibility or neglect of duty belonged to him, and nothing could change that. He closed his eyes against what he was feeling. Ray Hapgood had been his friend, his good friend, and he had let him die.

"John, listen to me." Stef was speaking again, her face close to his, her body pressing against him in the darkness. "I don't know why this happened. I don't know how it happened. No one does. Not yet. So don't go jumping to conclusions. Don't be shouldering the blame until you know the facts. I'm sorry Ray is dead. But you didn't kill him. And if it had to be someone, I would rather it was him than you."

He opened his eyes, surprised by her vehemence. "Stef."

She shook her head emphatically. "I'm sorry, but that's how I feel."

She kissed him hard, and he kissed her back and held her tightly against him. "I just can't believe he's gone," he whispered, his hand stroking her slender back.

"I know."

They held each other for a long moment, and then she led him to the bedroom. They undressed in the dark and crawled into the bed and held each other again in the cool of the sheets. The streets beyond their window were silent and empty. All the fire trucks, police cars, ambulances, and bystanders were gone. The rain had faded away, and the air was damp and cold in the wake of its passing. Ross hugged Stef's smooth body against his own and listened to the soft, velvet sound of her breathing.

"I could have lost you tonight," he whispered.

She nodded. "But you didn't."

"I was scared I had." He took a long, slow breath and let it out. "When you were inside, bringing out the last of those children, and I saw the flames climbing the walls, I thought for sure I had."

"No, John," she whispered, kissing him gently, over and over, "you won't lose me ever. I promise. No matter what, you won't lose me."

The dream comes swiftly, a familiar acquaintance he wishes now he had never made. He stands once more on the hillside south of Seattle, watching as the city burns, as the hordes of the Void swarm through the collapsed defenses and begin their ritual of killing and destruction. He sees the battle taking place on the high bridge where a last, futile defense has been mounted. He sees the steel and glass towers swallowed in flames. He sees the bright waters of the bay and sound turn red in the reflected glare.

He finds he is cold and indifferent to what he witnesses. He is detached in a way he cannot explain, but seems perfectly normal in his dream, as if he has been this way a long time. He is himself and at the same time he is someone else entirely. He pauses to examine this phenomenon and decides he has changed dramatically from when he was a Knight of the Word. He is a Knight no longer, but he remembers when he was. Oddly, his memories are tinged with a wistfulness he can't quite escape.

Before him, Seattle burns. By nightfall, it will have ceased to exist. Like his old life. Like the person he once was.

There are people huddled about him, and they glance at him fearfully when they think he is not looking. They are right to fear him. He holds over them the power of life and death. They are his captives. They are his to do with as he chooses, and they are anxious to discover what he has planned for them. The exercise of such power is a curious feeling because it both attracts and repels him. He wonders in a vague sort of way how he got to this point in his life.

From the long, dark span of the high bridge, bodies tumble into an abyss of smoke and fire like rag dolls. Their screams cannot be heard.

The old man approaches, as he has approached each time in the dream, and points his bony finger at Ross and whispers in his hoarse, ruined voice, I know you.

Get away from me, Ross orders in disgust and dismay, not wanting to hear the words he will speak.

I know you, the old man repeats, undeterred, the bright light of his madness shining in his strange, milky eyes. You are the one who killed him. I was there.

Ross stands his ground because he cannot afford to turn away. His captives are watching, listening, waiting for his response. They will measure his strength accordingly. The old man sways as if he were a reed caught in a stiff wind, stick-thin and ragged, his mind unbalanced, his laughter filled with echoes of his shattered life.

Get away from me, Ross says once more.

The Wizard of Oz! You killed him! I remember your face! I saw you! There, in the glass palace, in the shadow of the Tin Woodman, in the Emerald City, on All

Hallows' Eve! You killed the Wizard of Oz! You killed him! You!

The words fade and die, and the old man begins to cry softly. Oh, God, it was the end of everything!

Ross shakes his head. It is a familiar litany by now. He has heard it before, and he turns away in curt dismissal. It is all in the past, and the past no longer matters to him.

But the old man presses closer, insistent. I saw you. I watched you do it. I could not understand. He was your friend. There was no reason!

There was a reason, he thinks to himself, though he cannot remember it now.

But, the young woman! The old man is on his knees, his head hanging doglike between his slumped shoulders. What reason did you have for killing her?

Ross starts, shaken now. What young woman?

Couldn't you have spared her? She was just trying to help. She seemed to know you . . .

Ross screams in fury and shoves the old man away. The old man tumbles backward into the mud, gasping in shock. Shut up! Ross screams at him, furious, dismayed, because now he remembers this, as well, another part of the past he had thought buried, a truth he had left behind in the debris of his conversion . . .

Shut up, shut up, shut up!

The old man tries to crawl away, but he has crossed a line he should not have, and Ross cannot forgive him his trespass. He strides to where the old man cringes, already anticipating the punishment he will deliver, and he lifts the heavy black staff and brings it down like a hammer . . .

* * *

Ross jerked upright in the darkness of his bedroom, eyes snapping open, body rigid, awash in terror. His breath came in quick, ragged gulps, and he could hear the pounding of his heart in his ears. Stef lay sleeping next to him, unaware of his torment. The bedside clock read five-thirty. He could hear a soft patter against the window glass. Outside, it was raining again.

He held himself motionless beneath the sheet, staring at nothing, remembering. The dream had been real. The memories were his. He squeezed his eyes shut in dismay. He knew who the young woman was. He knew who it must be.

And for the first time since the dream had come to him, he was afraid it might really happen.

CHAPTER 19

When the phone rang, Nest was buried beneath her blankets where it was pitch-black, and she was certain it was still the middle of the night. She let the phone ring a few times, her mind and body warm and lazy with sleep. Then memories of last night's horror at Lincoln Park flooded through her, and she crawled from under the covers into shockingly bright daylight.

Squinting uncertainly against the glare, she picked up the phone. "Hello?"

"Nest, it's me. Are you all right?"

John Ross. She recognized his voice. But what an odd question. Unless he knew what had happened to her in the park, of course, but she didn't know how he could. She hadn't spoken to anyone afterward. She'd come back and fallen asleep almost immediately.

"I'm fine," she answered, her mouth and throat dry and cottony. What time was it? She glanced at the bedside clock. It was almost noon. She had forgotten to set the alarm and slept more than ten hours.

"Did I wake you?" he asked quickly. "I'm sorry if I did, but we have to talk."

She nodded into the phone. "It's okay. I didn't mean to sleep this late." She could feel the pain begin even as she spoke the words. Her entire body was throbbing, an ache building steadily from a low whine to a sharp scream. "Where are you?"

"Downstairs, in the lobby." He paused. "I called earlier and there was no answer. I was afraid something had happened to you, so I decided to come over. Can you come down?"

She took a deep breath, still working at waking up. "In about a half hour. Can you wait?"

"Yes." He hesitated a long time. "I've been thinking. Maybe you were right about some of the things we talked about. Maybe I was wrong."

She blinked in surprise. "I'll be down as quick as I can."

She returned the receiver to its cradle and rolled onto her back. Whatever had happened to him must have been every bit as significant as what had happened to her. She didn't know for sure that he was ready to concede the point, but it sounded as if he might be. She stared at the sunlight pooling on the floor in a golden rectangle in front of the tall window. Not only had she forgotten to set the alarm, she hadn't even bothered to close the drapes. She looked out at the sliver of blue sky visible through the walls of the surrounding buildings. Last night's storm had given way to better weather, it seemed.

She rolled slowly out of the big bed, her joints and muscles groaning in protest. Every part of her body ached from last night's encounter, and when she looked down at herself, she found bruises the size of Frisbees on her ribs and thighs, and scratches on her hands and arms that were caked with dried blood. She could hardly wait to see what her face looked like. She glanced at the blood-streaked sheets and pillow cases and grimaced.

She was grateful she wouldn't have to explain all this to the day maids when they came around to clean up.

She went into the bathroom and showered. She was reminded by the heap of damp towels and washcloths that she had showered just last night, but she needed to perform the ritual again to prepare for her encounter with John Ross. Last night seemed far away, and the deaths of Ariel, Boot, and Audrey more distant in time than they actually were. At first, as she stood beneath the stream of hot water, they didn't even seem real to her, as if she had dreamed them, as if they were imagined. But as the details recalled themselves, the images sharpened and solidified, and by the time she was pulling on her jeans and an NU sweatshirt, she was surprised to find she was crying.

She picked up the dirty clothes, stuffed them into a laundry bag, and shoved the bag into her suitcase. Her windbreaker was in tatters, so she dropped it into the wastebasket. She would have to buy a new one before she went outside. She paused, wondering exactly where she was going out to. She had taken the room for two nights, and her plane ticket home was for four-thirty that afternoon. Was she really leaving? Was her part in all of this over? She remembered her promise to herself the night before that she would see things through to the end. She had made that promise for Ariel and Audrey and Boot, but for herself, as well.

She looked around the room. Well, what she would do next depended on what John Ross had to say.

The long, dark, feral shape of the demon chasing her through the park flashed unexpectedly in the back of her mind. She hugged herself and set her jaw determinedly. She was done with running out of fear and a lack of preparation. She would be ready if the demon came at her again. She would find a way to deal with it.

But it was John Ross who needed strengthening. It was Ross the demon was really after, not her. She was just a distraction, an annoyance, a threat to its plans for him. Once Ross was subverted, it wouldn't matter what she did.

She went out the door and rode the elevator down to the lobby. Ross was sitting in a chair across from her when she stepped out, and he came to his feet immediately, leaning heavily on the walking stick.

"Good morning," he said as she came up to him. She saw the shock in his expression as he got a closer look at her face.

"Good morning," she replied. She gave him a wry smile. "The rest of me looks just as bad, in case you're wondering."

He looked distraught. "I was. Did this happen at Lincoln Park? I got your message from Stef."

"I'll tell you everything over breakfast. Or lunch, if you prefer. I'm starving. I haven't eaten since yesterday about this same time. Come on."

She led him into the dining room and asked for a table near the back wall, some distance apart from those that were occupied. They sat down facing each other and accepted menus from the waitress. Nest studied hers momentarily and put it aside.

"You said something's happened," she prodded, studying his face.

He nodded. "Fresh Start burned down last night. Ray Hapgood was killed. They made a positive identification this morning." His voice sounded stiff and uncomfortable. "Ray was working the night shift for me, it turns out. I didn't know this. I didn't even know I was scheduled to work it this week. I don't know why I didn't know, but that's the least of what's bothering me." He shook his head. "Ray was a good friend. I'm having a lot of trouble with that."

"When did this happen?" she asked right away. "What time, I mean?"

"Sometime after midnight. I was asleep. Stef woke me, got me up to take a look out the window, to make sure of what she was seeing. We called 911, then rushed over to wake the people in the building. Stef went all the way to the top floor. She got everyone out but Ray."

Nest barely listened to him as he filled in the details, her mind occupied with working out the logistics of the demon's movements between Lincoln Park and Pioneer Square. It couldn't have been both places at once if the events happened concurrently, but there was an obvious gap in time between when it was chasing her and when it would have set the fire. It would have had to rush right back after she had escaped, but it could have done so.

But why would it bother setting fire to Fresh Start? What reason could it possibly have for doing that?

"I know what you're thinking," he said suddenly. "I've been thinking it, too. But the fire marshall's office says the fire started because of frayed or faulty wiring in the furnace system. It wasn't arson."

"You mean, they don't have any evidence it was arson," she said.

He studied her carefully. "All right. I don't believe it was an accident either. But why would a demon set fire to Fresh Start?"

Same question she was asking herself. She shook her head. The waitress returned to take their order and left again. Nest tried to think the matter through, to discover what it was she had missed, because her instincts told her she had missed something.

"You said on the phone you'd been thinking about what I told you," she said finally. "You said that maybe you were wrong. What made you change your mind? It wasn't just the fire, was it? It must have been something else." She paused. "You said you came over because you thought maybe something had happened to me. Why did you think that?"

He looked decidedly uncomfortable, but there was a hard determination reflected in his eyes. "Do you remember the dream I told you about?"

"I remember you didn't exactly tell me about it at all."

He nodded. "I didn't think it was necessary then. I do now."

She studied him silently, considering what this meant. It couldn't be good. "All right," she said. "Tell me."

Her face was so battered and scraped that it was all he could do to keep his voice steady. He could not help feeling responsible, as if by having had last night's dream he had set in motion the events prophesied for today. He wanted to know what had happened to her, but he knew she would not tell him until she was satisfied he was reconsidering his position on the Lady's warning. He felt a sense of desperation grip him as he began his narrative, a growing fear that he could not accomplish what he had come here to do.

"I've been having this dream for several months," he began. "It's always the same dream, and it's the only dream I ever have. That's never happened to me before.

For a long time after I stopped being a Knight of the Word, there were no dreams—not of the sort I used to have, just snippets of the sort everyone has. So when I began having this dream, I was surprised. It was the same dream, but it changed a little every time, showing me a little bit more of what was to happen.

"The dream goes like this. I'm standing on a hill south of Seattle watching the city burn. Like all the old dreams I had as a Knight of the Word, it takes place in the future. The Void has besieged the city and taken it. There is a battle going on. I am not a Knight of the Word in this dream, and I am not involved in the fighting. But I am standing there with captives all around me, and in the dreams of late, I am their captor. I don't understand why this is, but I am.

"Then an old man approaches, and he accuses me of killing someone long ago. He says he was there, that he saw me do it. He says I killed Simon Lawrence, the Wizard of Oz, in Seattle, on Halloween. He says I killed him at the art museum. He doesn't say it exactly that way. He says it happened in the Emerald City, in the glass palace, in the shadow of the Tin Woodman. But I know what he means. The art museum is mostly glass and outside there is a piece of sculpture called *Hammering Man*, a metal giant pounding his hammer on a plate. There's no mistaking what he means. Besides, in the dream I can remember it happening, too. I can't remember the details—maybe because I don't know them. But I know he is telling the truth."

He stopped talking as the waitress arrived with their food. When she departed, he bent forward to continue.

"I didn't learn this all at once. It was revealed in pieces. But I put the pieces together. I knew what the dream was telling me. But I didn't believe it. There is no reason for me to kill Simon Lawrence. I respect and admire him. I want to work for him as long as he'll let me. Why would I ever even consider killing him? When you asked me yesterday about the dream, I didn't see any point in going into it. Whether or not I was a Knight of the Word, I wouldn't let the events of the dream ever happen. To tell you the truth, I was afraid that the dream was a tactic by the Word to bring me back into line, to scare me into changing my mind about serving. I even considered the possibility that it was the work of the Void. It didn't matter. I wasn't going to allow it to affect me."

She was wolfing down her club sandwich as he talked, but her eyes were fixed on him. He glanced down at his own food, which he had not touched. He took a sip of his iced tea.

"Last night, after the fire, I had the dream again." He shook his head. "I don't know why. I never do. The dreams just come. It was the same dream, with the same troubling aspects. But this time there was a new wrinkle. The old man reminded me of something else. He said that I had killed another person at the same time as I killed Simon Lawrence. He said it was a young woman, someone I knew."

She stopped eating and stared at him. "I know," he said quietly. "I felt the same way. The shock woke me. I was awake after that until it was light, thinking. I don't believe it could ever happen. I don't think I would let it." His voice thickened. "But in the dream, it had, so I can't discount the possibility that I might be wrong. I also remember what I was sent to do in Hopewell five years ago. If I was prepared for it to happen once . . ."

He trailed off, his hands knotting before him, his eyes shifting away. "I've gambled as much as I dare to with this business. I don't know if there's a demon out there or not. I don't know if the Void is setting a trap for me. I don't know what's going on. But whatever it is, I don't want you involved. At least not any further than you already are. I want you to get on a plane right now and get out of here. Get far away, so far away you can't possibly be a part of whatever happens next."

She nodded slowly. "And what happens to you?"

He shook his head. "I don't know yet. I have to figure that out. But I can tell you one thing. I'm not so sure anymore I'm not in danger."

She finished the last of her sandwich and wiped her mouth carefully, wincing as she brushed one of the deeper cuts on her chin. "Good for you," she said. There was neither approval nor condemnation in her voice. Her gaze was steady. "But you don't know the half of it. Let me tell you the rest."

She was shaken by the revelations of his dream and more than a little frightened and angered by the idea that she might be his target once again, but she kept it all hidden. She could not afford to let her feelings interfere with her purpose in coming to him in the first place. She could stew about the ramifications of his having had such a dream later, but for now she must concentrate on convincing him he needed to do something to protect himself.

"I watched three forest creatures die last night," she began. "One of them was Ariel, one was a sylvan named Boot, and the third was an owl named Audrey. A demon killed them, a demon that is attempting to claim your soul, John. Ariel, Audrey, and Boot died trying to stop that from happening. So please pay close attention to what I have to say."

She told him everything that had happened. She started with Ariel's appearance in the market, summoning her to West Seattle and Lincoln Park, where Boot and Audrey lived. Boot had seen the demon and had a story to tell. She called to let him know what she was doing, perhaps to persuade him to come, as well. But she couldn't reach him, so she left a message with Stef that she believed only he would understand. She took a taxi to the park and went in. At the rim of the cliffs overlooking Puget Sound and the park embankment, the sylvan and the owl appeared.

She related Boot's tale, repeating the conversation that had taken place between the two demons as accurately as she could remember it, then telling of how the first demon had killed the second to protect its claim on Ross. Boot was about to tell her more, she finished, when the attack occurred that snuffed out Boot's and Audrey's lives and led to the chase along the heights that ended up costing Ariel her life, as well.

"I went over the cliff by mistake or I would be dead, too," she finished. "I fell all the way to the base of the embankment, but I didn't break anything. I got up and ran out of the park with the demon still chasing me. There were houses where I thought I could get help. Twice I managed to get inside and twice the demon broke down doors and windows to get at me. I was lucky, John. It almost had me several times. In the end, I managed to get on a bus just ahead of it. Even then, it slammed into the bus doors with such force that the glass broke and the metal bent. It was in such a frenzy it didn't seem to care what it had to do. If the police hadn't arrived, I think it would have kept coming. It has to be really worried about me to go to such efforts. Maybe it thinks I know something. Maybe I do, but the truth is I haven't figured out what it is yet."

She watched the skin grow taut across his face and his eyes lose their focus, as if he was looking at something beyond her. "I wanted to come after you, and then something happened and I couldn't," he said softly.

She waited. His eyes came back to her. "The demon has to be someone I know, doesn't it?"

She nodded. "I guess so. Someone you know well, for that matter. Someone at Fresh Start, if you want my further opinion. When Ariel appeared to me after our lunch, she said I should stay away from you, that you were lost, that there was demon stink all over you. She said it was all over Fresh Start, as well. I was there earlier, and I was physically sick while I was inside the building. It might have been demon stink or it might have been the demon itself. This is all new to me. But it isn't idle speculation anymore. It's real. Something is after you."

He didn't say anything for a moment, thinking it through. "Who was at Fresh Start yesterday morning when you were there?"

She shook her head. "I can't be sure. Stef, Simon Lawrence, Ray Hapgood, Carole someone, Della Jenkins, some others. There were a lot of people. I don't think we can pin it down that way."

"You're right, it's too hard. How about the park? How did the demon manage to track you there? It must have followed you . . ."

"Or intercepted my message," she finished. "I already

thought of that. Who besides Stef and yourself would have known where I was going?"

He hesitated. "I don't know. Stef took the message at Fresh Start and gave it to me. I don't think she would have told anyone else, but she might have."

Nest took a deep breath, not liking what she was about to say. "So the demon might be Stef."

The look John Ross gave her was unreadable. "That isn't possible," he said quietly.

She didn't say anything.

Ross looked around, took in the nearby diners. "Let's continue this somewhere else."

She charged the bill to her room, and they went out into the lobby. There was a small library bar on the other side and no one inside. They went in and took a table at the back on the upper level. The bartender, who was working the bar alone, came up and took their order for two iced cappuccinos and left. Surrounded by shelves of books and a cloud of suspicion and doubt, they faced each other anew.

"She saved all those people last night," Ross insisted. "She risked her life, Nest. A demon wouldn't do that."

"A demon would do anything that suited its purpose."

"It isn't possible," he said again.

"This demon is a changeling. A very adept changeling."

Ross shook his head. "I would know. I could be fooled, but not that completely."

She wasn't going to change his mind. Besides, she wanted to believe him. "So the demon found out where I was going and what I was doing some other way. What way would that be?"

Ross rubbed his lean jaw with one hand and shook his

head slowly. "I don't know. None of this makes much sense. There's something not right about all of it. If the Void wanted to turn me, why wouldn't it take a more direct approach? Just suppose for a moment the dream comes to pass, and I do kill Simon Lawrence. That would be a terrible thing, but it wouldn't persuade me to begin serving the Void. It would probably do just the opposite."

Nest looked at him doubtfully. "But the Lady said it begins with a single misstep. You don't change all at once. You change gradually."

They stared at each other some more, neither speaking. Nest thought suddenly of Two Bears, and the reason he was in Seattle. Perhaps she should tell Ross. But what would that accomplish? How would it help him at this point?

His green eyes were intense. "Remember when I said earlier I wanted to come after you, but something happened and I couldn't? There was something wrong with me yesterday after I left you. I went back to the apartment and practically passed out. Stef stopped off just long enough to give me your message. Then I seem to recall Simon being there, too. That's the last thing I remember before waking up at midnight. It's been bothering me. I don't even remember going to bed. I just remember sitting in the living room, thinking it was odd that Simon was there, then waking up in bed when Stef shook me."

He hesitated. "I was pretty well out of it. Maybe there was someone else there, too. Maybe I said something about your message, and I can't remember."

He was looking for help from her, but she had none to give. He waited a moment, then leaned forward. "When are you scheduled to fly back to Chicago?"

"Today, at four-thirty."

He nodded. "Good. Get on that plane and get out of here. We have to do something to disrupt the flow of things, something to sidetrack this dream. Getting you out of here is the first step. I'll nose around a little and see what I can learn. Maybe I can uncover something. If I can't, I'll leave, too. I've got a few days coming. I'll just take them. If neither of us is here, the events in the dream won't happen."

She studied him. "You'll leave before dark, before tonight's celebration?"

His lips compressed tightly. "I won't go anywhere near the Seattle Art Museum. I'll stay far away."

She was thinking about the promise she had made to herself to see things through to the end. But if she insisted on staying, he would stay, too. She couldn't allow that. And if they both left, then the matter was ended— for the moment, at least. If Ross accepted he was in danger, that there was a demon out there working to subvert him, he would be on his guard. That ought to be enough. She had delivered the Lady's message, and that was all she was expected to do.

"All right," she said. "I'll go."

"Now?"

"As soon as I can pack my bag and check out. I'll catch a taxi to the airport. You won't have to worry about me anymore."

He exhaled slowly. "Fair enough."

"Just promise me you won't forget to keep worrying about yourself. This isn't going to end until you find out who the demon is."

"I know," he said.

And it wouldn't end then either, and they both knew it.

It wouldn't end, because even if he unmasked this demon, there would be another, and another, until one of them succeeded in destroying him. It wouldn't end until he either found a way to give back the staff or agreed to resume his life as a Knight of the Word. It was not a choice that would be easily resolved, and neither one of them wanted to examine it too closely.

"Will you call me in Hopewell and at least leave a message?" she asked him in the ensuing silence.

"Yes."

She sighed. "I hate leaving this business unfinished." She saw the sudden look of concern in his eyes. "But I'll keep my bargain, John. Don't worry."

"That's just the trouble. I do."

She stood up. "I'd better go. Good-bye, John. Be careful."

He rose, as well, and she walked around to embrace him, kissing his cheek. The gesture was stiff and awkward and uncertain.

"Good-bye, Nest," he said.

She stepped back. "I'll tell you something," she said. "I don't know that saying good-bye feels any better this time than it did the last. I'm still not sure about you."

His smile was bitter and sad, and he suddenly looked older than his years. "I know, Nest. I'm sorry about that. Thanks for coming. It means a lot that you did."

She turned and walked out of the bar, crossed the lobby to the elevators, and did not look back.

CHAPTER 20

Andrew Wren woke early that same morning despite the fact he had been up very late tracing the transfers of funds from the corporate accounts of Fresh Start and Pass/Go to the private accounts of Simon Lawrence and John Ross. It was well after midnight by the time he completed his work and satisfied himself he knew exactly how all the withdrawals and deposits had been made and the routes through which various funds had traveled. He was exhausted by then, but a little bit of sleep did wonders for him when he was hot on the trail, and he felt energized and ready to go once more shortly after first light.

Nevertheless, he took his time. He had calls to make and faxes to send. He wanted to check on balances and signatures. He wanted to make very sure of what he had before he started writing anything. So he showered and shaved at a leisurely pace, thinking things through yet again, formulating his plans for the day.

It wasn't until he went downstairs for breakfast and was engaged in perusing Wednesday's *New York Times* that he overheard a conversation at an adjoining table and learned Fresh Start had burned down during the night.

At first he couldn't quite believe what he was hearing, and he paused in his reading to listen more closely as the conversation revealed the details. The building was a total loss. There was only one fatality, an employee. Arson wasn't thought to be the cause. Simon Lawrence would be holding a press conference on the future of the program at two o'clock that afternoon.

Andrew Wren finished his breakfast and bought a copy of the *Post-Intelligencer*, Seattle's morning paper. There were pictures and a short piece on the fire on the front page, but it had happened too late for an in-depth story.

Wren walked back to his room with the papers and sat down at his work desk with his yellow pad and notes and the packet of documentation on the illegal funds transfers spread out before him. He tried to decide if the fire had anything to do with what he was investigating, but it was too early to make that call. If it wasn't arson, then it wasn't relevant. If it was arson, then it might be. He stared out the window, deciding what to do next. It was only nine-fifteen.

He made up his mind quickly, the way he always did when he was closing in on something. He sent his faxes to the home office and to various specialists he worked with from time to time, requesting the information he needed, then began calling all the banks at which personal accounts had been opened in the names of Simon Lawrence and John Ross for the deposit of Fresh Start and Pass/Go funds. He used a time-tested technique, claiming to be in accounting at one or the other of the nonprofit corporations, giving the account number and the balance he had before him, and asking to verify the amounts. From there he went on to gather other information, building on the initial rapport he had established with whoever was on the other end of the line to complete his investigation. It was practically second nature to him by now. He knew all the buttons to push and all the tricks and ploys.

He was done by a little after ten-thirty. He called the number at Pass/Go and asked for Stefanie Winslow. When she came on the line, he told her he was coming over to see the Wiz. She advised him that Simon wouldn't be available until late in the day, if then. He assured her he understood, he had heard about the fire and knew what Simon must have been going through, but he needed only a few minutes and it was imperative they meet immediately. He added it involved the matter they had discussed yesterday, and he was sure Simon would want to see him.

She put him on hold. When she came back on, she said he could come right over.

Andrew Wren put down the phone, pulled on his rumpled jacket with the patches on the elbows, picked up his briefcase, and went out the door, humming softly.

Ten minutes later, he was climbing out of a taxi in front of Pass/Go. The educational center was situated right next door to Fresh Start, but separated by a narrow alleyway. Before last night, the two buildings had looked substantially the same—1940s brick buildings of six stories facing on Second Avenue with long glass windows, recessed entries with double wooden doors, and no signs. But Pass/Go had survived the fire where Fresh Start had not. Fresh Start was a burned-out, blackened shell surrounded by barricades and yellow tape, its roof and floors sagging or collapsed, its windows blown out by the heat, and its fixtures and furnishings in ruins.

As he stood staring at the still-smoking wreck, Stefanie Winslow came out the front door of Pass/Go.

"Good morning, Mr. Wren," she said cheerfully, her smile dazzling, her hand extended.

As he offered his own hand in response, he was shocked to see the marks on her arms and face. "Good heavens, Ms. Winslow! What happened to you?"

She gave a small shrug. "I was involved in getting people out last night, and I picked up a few bumps and bruises along the way. It's nothing that won't heal. How are you?"

"Fine." He was somewhat nonplussed by her attitude. "You seem very cheerful given the circumstances, if you don't mind my saying so."

She laughed. "Well, that's my job, Mr. Wren. I'm supposed to put a good face on things, my own notwithstanding. We lost the building, but all the clients got out. That doesn't help much when I think about Ray, but it's the best I can do."

She filled him in on the details of Ray Hapgood's death and the efforts of the fire department to save the building. Ross had been present when it took place, but he had been sleeping earlier and she'd had to wake him to help her, so it didn't look like he was involved in any way. Wren listened without seeming overly interested, taking careful mental notes for later.

"The building was fully insured," she finished, "so we'll be able to rebuild. In the meantime, we've been given the use of a warehouse several blocks away that can be brought up to code pretty easily for our purposes and will serve as a temporary shelter during the re-building. We've been given a number of donations already to help tide us over and there should be more coming in. Things could be much worse."

Wren smiled. "Well, I'm very glad to hear that, Ms. Winslow."

"Stefanie, please." She touched his arm. "Ms. Winslow sounds vaguely authoritarian."

Wren nodded agreeably. "Do you suppose I could see Mr. Lawrence now for those few minutes you promised me? Before he becomes too tied up with other things? I know he has a news conference scheduled for two o'clock."

"Now would be fine, Mr. Wren." She took his arm as she might an old friend's. "Come with me. We've got him hidden in the back."

They went inside through a lobby decorated with brightly colored posters and children's drawings, past a reception desk, and down a hall with doors opening into classrooms and offices. Through tall glass windows, Wren could see a grassy play area filled with toys and playground equipment shoehorned between the surrounding buildings.

"The nursery, kitchen facilities, dining rooms, Special Ed, and more classrooms are upstairs," Stefanie informed him, waving to one of the teachers as she passed by an open door. "Life goes on."

Simon Lawrence had set up shop in a tiny office at the very back of the building. He sat at an old wooden desk surrounded by cartons of supplies and forms, his angular frame hunched forward over a mound of papers, files, notepads, and pens and pencils. He was on the phone talking, but he motioned Wren through the open door and into a folding chair identical to the one he was occupying. Stefanie Winslow waved good-bye and went out the door, closing it softly behind her.

The Wiz finished his conversation and hung up. "I hope this isn't bad news, Andrew," he said, smiling wearily. "I've had just about all the bad news I can handle for the moment."

"So I gather." Wren glanced around at the boxes and bare walls. "Quite a comedown from your last digs."

Simon snorted derisively. "Doesn't mean a thing compared to the cost to Fresh Start. It will take a minimum of three to four weeks to get the warehouse converted and the program up and running again. How many women and children will we lose in that time, I wonder?"

"You'll do the best you can. Sometimes that has to be enough."

Simon leaned back. His handsome face looked worn and haggard, but his eyes were bright and sharp as they fixed on the reporter. "Okay, Andrew, what's this all about? Lay it out on the table and get it over with."

Andrew Wren nodded, reached into his briefcase, took out the copies he had made of the documents with which he had been provided, and placed them on the desk in front of the Wiz. Simon picked them up and began scanning them, quickly at first, then more slowly. His face lost some color, and his jaw tightened. Halfway through his perusal, he looked up.

"Are these for real?" he asked carefully. "Have you verified they exist?"

Wren nodded. "Every last one."

The Wiz went back to his examination, finishing

quickly. He shook his head. "I know what I'm seeing, but I can't believe it." His eyes fixed on Wren. "I don't know anything about this. Not about the accounts or any of the transfers. I'd give you an explanation if I could, but I can't. I'm stunned."

Andrew Wren sat waiting, saying nothing.

The Wiz leaned back again in his folding chair and set the papers on the desk. "I haven't taken a cent from either program that wasn't approved in advance. Not one. The accounts with my name on them aren't really mine. I don't know who opened them or who made the transfers, but they aren't mine. I can't believe John Ross would do something like this, either. He's never given me any reason to think he would."

Wren nodded, keeping silent.

"If I were going to steal money from the corporations, I would either steal a lot more or do a better job of it. This kind of petty theft is ridiculous, Andrew. Have you checked the signatures to see if they match mine or John's?"

Wren scratched his chin thoughtfully. "I'm having it done professionally. I should know something later today."

"Who brought all this to you?" The Wiz indicated the incriminating papers with a dismissive wave of his hand.

Wren gave a small shrug. "You know I can't tell you that."

Simon Lawrence shook his head in dismay. "Well, they say these things come in threes. Last night I lost a good friend and half of five years' hard work. Today I find I'm about to lose my reputation. I wonder what comes next?"

He rose from the desk and paced to the door and back again, then turned to face Wren. "I'm betting that when you check the signatures, you won't find a match."

"Quite possibly not. But that doesn't mean you aren't involved, Simon. You could have had someone else act for you."

"John Ross?"

"Ross, or even a third person."

"Why would I do this?"

"I don't know. Maybe you were desperate. Desperate people do desperate things. I've given up trying to figure out the reasons behind why people do the things they do. I've got all I can handle just uncovering the truth of what's been done."

The Wiz sat down again, his eyes smoldering. "I've spent five years building this program, Andrew. I've given everything I have to make it work. If you report this, it will all go down the tubes."

"I know that," Wren acknowledged softly.

"Even if there's nothing to connect me directly, even if an inquiry clears me of any wrongdoing, the program will never be the same. I'll quit in order to remove any lingering doubts about the possibility of impropriety, or I'll stay and fight and live with the suspicion that something is still going on, but either way Fresh Start and Pass/Go will always be remembered for this scandal and not for the good they've accomplished."

Andrew Wren sighed. "I think maybe you're over-stating your case a bit, Simon."

The Wiz shook his head. "No, I'm not. You know why? Because the whole effort is held together by the slenderest of threads. Helping the homeless isn't a program that attracts support naturally. It isn't a program people flock to just because they believe in aiding the homeless. What happens to the homeless is a low priority in most people's lives. It isn't a glamorous cause. It isn't a compelling cause. It's balanced right on the edge of people's consciousness, and it could topple from view with just a nudge. It took me years to bring it to people's attention and make it a cause they would choose to support over all the others. But it can lose that same support in the blink of an eye."

He sighed. "I know you're just doing your job, Andrew," he said after a moment. "I wouldn't ask you to do anything less. But be thorough, please. Be sure about this before you act. An awful lot rides on what you decide to do."

Andrew Wren folded his hands in his lap and looked down at them. "I appreciate what's at stake better than you think, Simon. That's why I came to talk with you first. I wanted to hear what you had to say. As far as making any decisions, I have a lot more work to do first. I won't be rushing into anything."

He rose and held out his hand. "I'm sorry about this. As I told you earlier, I admire the work you've done here. I'd hate to think it would suffer for any reason."

Simon Lawrence took his hand and shook it firmly. "Thank you for coming to me about this. I'll do what I can to look into it from this end. Whatever I find, I'll pass along."

Andrew Wren opened the door and walked back down the hall to the reception area. There was no sign of Stefanie Winslow, who was probably out working on preparations for the press conference. He paused as he neared the front door, then turned back.

The young woman working the intake desk looked up as he approached, smiling. "Can I help you?"

"I was wondering," he said, returning the smile, "if you know where I could find John Ross."

CHAPTER 21

It was nearing two o'clock by the time Nest packed her bag, checked out of the Alexis, and caught a taxi to the airport. She rode south down I-5 past Boeing Field on one side and lines of stalled traffic heading north on the other. She stared out the window, watching the city recede into the distance, wrestling with the feeling that her connection with John Ross was fading with it.

She was riddled with doubt and plagued by a sense of uneasiness she could not explain.

She had done everything she had come to do and a little more. She had found John Ross, she had given him the Lady's warning, she had persuaded him he was in danger, and she had extracted his solemn promise he would take whatever steps were necessary to protect himself. She kept telling herself there was really nothing else she could do—nothing else, in fact, that she could justify—but none of the monolog seemed to help.

Maybe it had something to do with the fact that Ariel and Audrey and Boot were still dead and some part of the guilt for that was still hers. Maybe it had something to do with her discomfort at having done so little to help them. She knew she was dissatisfied with the idea of leaving the demon who had killed them loose in the city of

Seattle. But what was she supposed to do? Track it down and exact revenge? How would she do that and what difference would it make now? It wouldn't bring back the forest creatures. It wouldn't make things whole or right in any meaningful way. Maybe it would give her a measure of satisfaction, but she wasn't even sure of that.

Mostly, she decided, she was bothered by the prospect of leaving behind so many loose ends. She was a runner, a competitor, and she was used to seeing things through to the finish, not giving up halfway. And that's what her leaving felt like.

For a time she managed to put it aside and think about what waited at the other end of her flight. Northwestern University, with classes first thing in the morning, three days of homework waiting to be made up, and her lapsed training regimen. Her grandparents' home, now hers, and the papers sitting on the kitchen counter, which would permit its sale. Pick, with his incessant questions about her commitment to Sinnissippi Park. Robert, waiting patiently for a phone call or letter telling him everything was all right.

As she would wait for a phone call or a letter from John Ross telling her the same thing.

Or would she never hear another word?

The taxi took the airport exit, wound its way along a series of approaches, and pulled onto the ticketing ramp. She looked over at the big airplanes parked at the boarding gates and contemplated the idea of flying home. It didn't seem real to her. It didn't seem like something that was going to happen.

She got out at the United terminal, paid the driver, and walked inside. She checked in at the ticketing counter and received her boarding pass and gate assignment. She decided to keep her bag with her because it was not very big and she did not want the hassle of trying to retrieve it through baggage claim at O'Hare. She walked toward the shops and gate ramps, remembering suddenly, incongruously, she still hadn't replaced her windbreaker. She had thrown on her sweatshirt, but that wasn't going to provide her with enough warmth when she had to go outside in Chicago.

She glanced around, then walked into a Northwest Passage Outdoor Shop, a clothing store that sold mostly logo products. After rooting around in the parkas for a while, she found a lightweight down jacket she could live with, carried it up to the register, and paid for it with her charge card.

As she carried it out of the store, under her arm, she found herself wondering if the dead children's memories that had helped make up Ariel would be used to make another tatterdemalion or if they would be blown about by the wind forever. What happened to tatterdemalions when their lives ended? Little more than scraps of magic and memories to begin with, did they ever come together again in a new life? Pick had never said.

She moved to a seating area facing a security check and sat down. She was back to thinking about John Ross. Something was very wrong. She didn't know what it was, but she knew it was there. She was trying to pretend everything was fine, but it wasn't. On the surface maybe, but not down deep, beneath the comfortable illusion she was trying to embrace. She held up her anxiety for examination, and it glared back at her defiantly.

What was it she was missing?

What was it she needed to do in order to make the discomfort go away?

She began to examine the John Ross situation once again. She went through all of its aspects, stopping abruptly when she came to his dream. The Lady had warned Nest about the dream, that it would come to pass in a few short days, and that to the extent Ross was a part of the events it prophesied, he risked becoming ensnared by the Void. The dream foretold that Ross would kill Simon Lawrence, the Wizard of Oz.

It also foretold that he would kill her. But it hadn't done that until last night.

Because until these past few days, she hadn't been a part of his present life at all, had she?

She stared at the lighted window of a newsstand across the way, thinking. John Ross had told her about his dreams five years earlier. His dreams of the future were fluid, because the future was fluid and could be changed by what happened in the present. It was what he was expected to accomplish as a Knight of the Word. It was his mission. Change those events that will hasten a decline in civilization and the fall of mankind. Change a few events, only a few, and the balance of magic can be maintained and the Void kept at bay.

What if, in this instance, the Lady was playing at the same game? What if the Lady had sent Nest to John Ross strictly for the purpose of introducing a new element into the events of his dream? Ross would listen to Nest, the Lady had told her through Ariel. Her words would carry a weight that the words of others could not. But it hadn't worked out that way, had it? It wasn't what she'd said to Ross that had made a difference. It was what had happened to her in the park. It was the way in which her presence had affected the demon that, in turn, had affected him. Like dominos toppling into one another.

Could that have been the Lady's purpose in sending her to Ross all along?

Nest took a slow, deep breath and let it out again. It wasn't so strange to imagine there were games being played with human lives. It had happened before, and it had happened to her. Pick had warned her the Word never revealed everything, and what appeared to be true frequently was not. He had warned her to be careful.

That triggered an unpleasant thought. Perhaps the Lady knew Nest's presence would affect John Ross's dream, would change it to include her, jolting Ross out of his complacent certainty he was not at risk.

If so, it meant the Word was using her as bait.

When John Ross left Nest, he didn't go back to Pass/Go or to his apartment. He walked down First Avenue to a Starbucks instead, stepped inside, bought a double-tall latte, took it outside to a bench in Occidental Park, and sat down. The day was still sunny and bright, the cool snap of autumn just a whisper on the back of the breezes blowing off the sound. Ross sipped at his latte thoughtfully, warmed his hands on the container, and watched people walk by.

He kept thinking he would have a revelation regarding the demon's identity. He was certain that if he thought about the puzzle hard enough, if he looked at it in just the right way, he would figure it out. There were only a handful of possibilities, after all. A lot of people worked at Fresh Start and Pass/Go, but only a few were close to him. And once you eliminated Ray Hapgood and Stef and certainly Simon, there weren't many candidates left.

But each time he considered a likely suspect, some

incongruity or contradictory piece of evidence would in-
tervene to demonstrate he was on the wrong track. The
fact remained that no one seemed to be the right choice.
His confusion was compounded by his complete failure
to understand what his dream about killing Simon Lawrence had to do with anything. The demon's subterfuge
was so labyrinthine he could not unravel it.

He finished the latte and crumpled the empty container. He was running out of ideas and choices. He
would have to keep his promise to Nest and subtract
himself from the equation.

Dumping the latte container in a trash can, he began
walking back to his apartment. He wouldn't even bother
going in to work. He would just pack an overnight bag,
call Stef, have her meet him, and walk down to the ferry
terminal. Maybe they would go up to Victoria for a few
days. Stay at the Empress. Have high tea. Visit the
Buchart Gardens. Pretend they were real people.

He was almost to the front door of his apartment
building when he heard his name called. He turned to
watch a heavyset, rumpled man come up the sidewalk
to greet him.

"Mr. Ross?" the man inquired, as if to make sure.

Ross nodded, leaning on his walking stick, trying to
place the other's face.

"We haven't met," the newcomer said, and extended
his hand. "I'm Andrew Wren, from *The New York
Times*."

The investigative reporter, Ross thought warily. He
took the proffered hand and shook it. "How do you do,
Mr. Wren?"

The professional face beamed behind rimless glasses.
"The people at Pass/Go thought I might find you here. I

came by earlier, but you were out. I wonder if I could speak with you a moment?"

Ross hesitated. This was probably about Simon. He didn't want to talk to Wren, particularly just then, but he was afraid that if he refused it would look bad for the Wiz.

"This won't take long," Wren assured him. "We could sit at one of those tables in the little park right around the corner, if you wish."

They walked back to the entrance to Waterfall Park and took seats at a table on the upper level where the sound of the falls wasn't quite so deafening. Ross glanced across the street at the offices of Pass/Go, wondering if anyone had seen him. No, he amended wordlessly, not if anyone had seen him. If the demon had seen him.

He grimaced at his own paranoia. "What can I do for you, Mr. Wren?"

Andrew Wren fumbled with his briefcase. "I'm doing a piece on Simon Lawrence, Mr. Ross. Last night, someone dropped off some documents at my hotel room." He extracted a sheaf of papers from the case and handed them across the table. "I'd like you to take a look."

Ross took the packet, set it before him, and began to thumb through the pages. Bank accounts, he saw. Transfers of funds, withdrawals and deposits. He frowned. The withdrawals were from Fresh Start and Pass/Go. The deposits were into accounts under Simon Lawrence's name. And under his.

He glanced up at Andrew Wren in surprise. Wren's soft face was expressionless. Ross went back to the documents. He worked his way through, then looked up again. "Is this some sort of joke?"

Wren shook his head solemnly. "I'm afraid not, Mr. Ross. At least not the sort anyone is laughing at. Particularly Simon Lawrence."

"You've shown these to Simon?"

"I have."

"What did he say?"

"He says he's never seen them."

Ross pushed the packet back across the table at Wren. "Well, neither have I. I don't know anything about these accounts other than the fact they're not mine. What's going on here?"

Andrew Wren shrugged. "It would appear you and Simon Lawrence have been siphoning funds from the charitable corporations you work for. Have you?"

John Ross was so angry he could barely contain himself. "No, Mr. Wren, I have not. Nor has Simon Lawrence, I'm willing to bet. Those signatures are forgeries, every last one of them. Mine looks pretty good, but I know I didn't sign for any of those transfers. Someone is playing a game, Mr. Wren . . ."

The minute he said it, he knew. The answer was there in ten-foot-high neon lights behind his eyes, flashing.

"Do you have any idea who that someone might be, Mr. Ross?" Andrew Wren asked quietly, folding his hands over the documents, his eyes bright and inquisitive.

Ross stared at him, his mind racing. Of course, he did. It was the demon. The demon was responsible. But, why?

He shook his head. "Offhand, I'd say whoever provided you with the information, Mr. Wren."

The other man nodded thoughtfully. "I've considered that."

"Someone who doesn't like Simon Lawrence."

"Or you."

Ross nodded. "Perhaps. But I'd say Simon is the more likely target." He paused. "But you've thought this through already, haven't you? That's what an investigative reporter does. You've already considered all the possibilities. Maybe you've even made up your mind."

Wren grimaced. "No, Mr. Ross, I haven't done that. It's too early for making up one's mind about this mess. I have tried to consider the possibilities. One of those possibilities relies on your analysis that the Wiz is the primary target. But for that to be true, it must also be true that someone is setting him up. That requires a motive. You seem to have a rather good one. If you were looking for a way to protect yourself in the event your own theft was discovered, salting an account or two in Simon Lawrence's name might just do the trick."

Ross thought it through. "Oh, I get it. I steal a little for me, a little for him, then claim it was all his idea if I get caught. That gets me a reduced sentence, maybe even immunity."

"It's happened before."

"You know something, Mr. Wren?" Ross looked off at the waterfall for a minute, then back again. His eyes were hard and filled with a rage he could no longer disguise. "I'm just about as mad as I've ever been in my life. I love my work with Fresh Start. I would never do anything to jeopardize that. Nor would I do anything to jeopardize a program I strongly believe in and support. I've never stolen a penny in my life. Frankly, I don't care much about money. I've never had it, and I've never missed it. Nothing's happened to change that."

He rose, stiff-legged and seething. "So you go right ahead and do what you have to do. But let me tell you something. If you don't find out who's behind this, I will. That's a promise, Mr. Wren. I will."

"Mr. Ross?" Andrew Wren stood up with him. "Could you just give me another minute? Mr. Ross?"

But John Ross was already walking away.

Bait.

Nest Freemark considered the implications of the word as calmly as she could, which wasn't easy to do. The thought that she had been dispatched to Seattle to find John Ross, not with any expectation she could influence him by virtue of well-reasoned argument, but solely for the purpose of influencing his dreams and forcing him to rethink his position at the same time she was being put at risk was almost more than she could bear.

She fumed for a moment, then wondered how the Lady could know how her presence would affect things. Could she know the dream would be changed in a way that would make Ross reconsider? If the Lady knew what the dream was, it wasn't such a long shot she knew how to change it.

Nest put her face in her hands and closed her eyes. She was jousting with shadows. She was just guessing.

She left behind the dream and its implications and went back to what she knew. There was a demon. The demon was in Seattle. The demon was after Ross. The demon was someone he knew, probably well. The demon was determined to claim him—so determined it had been willing to attack and kill another demon who challenged it for possession of his soul.

So far, so good. Nest nodded into her hands. What else?

The demon had recognized Nest and decided she was a threat. But not enough of a threat to do anything about her until after she had gone to Lincoln Park to speak with Boot. Boot was going to tell her something when the demon attacked, something about the demon changing again, only not in the same way.

She backed off, knowing all she could do with that approach was to speculate, that the answers she needed had to be reached from another direction.

She glanced at her watch. Three-thirty. Her plane would begin boarding around four. She looked down at her bag, glanced over at the security check and the people lined up to go through the metal detector, and went back to thinking.

The demon had been present when she had gone to Fresh Start to find John Ross. Her magic, into whatever form it had evolved, had reacted to the demon and made Nest physically sick. The demon had tracked her or followed her or intercepted her message and found her later at Lincoln Park. Which? It had killed Boot, Audrey, and Ariel, and had tried to kill her. And then it had gone back to the city and set fire to Fresh Start. Why?

Her head hurt. Nothing fit. She walked down the concourse with her bag to an SBC stand and ordered a decaf cappuccino. Then she found a different seat and thought about the demon some more.

What was she missing?

Stay away from him, Ariel had warned her of John Ross. He has demon stink all over him. He is already lost.

Seemed right to her, given his refusal to accept the

possibility he was in danger, that he might be fooling himself about his vulnerability. But John Ross genuinely seemed to believe that he was a different person, no longer a Knight of the Word, no longer a keeper of the magic. He was shattered by San Sobel, and now he was in love with Stefanie Winslow and committed to the work of Simon Lawrence, and his life was all new.

Like her own was new, she thought suddenly. She had left the past behind as well, back in the park of the Sinnissippi, back with the passing of Gran and Old Bob, back with the end of her childhood.

She thought suddenly of her mother. There was no reason for it, but all of a sudden she was thinking about how much she missed not having her there while she was growing up. Gran and Old Bob had done the best they could, which was pretty good, but the gap in her life that her mother's death had left wasn't something anyone could fill. She wondered if that was how John Ross had felt before Stef had come into his life. He had wandered alone for more than ten years in service to the Word, living with his terrible dreams of the future and the responsibility they forced on him in the present. It was so hard to be without someone who loved you. Everyone was affected by the absence of love. Even her father, who was a demon . . .

The words froze in midsentence, crystallized in her mind, and hung there like shards of ice. She had been trying to think of something earlier, something that spoke to the issue of the demon's behavior with Ross, something from her past. Now she knew what it was. It was her father's behavior toward Gran, years ago.

It was the same. It was exactly the same.

In a moment's time, everything came together, all the

loose ends, all the answers she had been unable to locate, all the missing clues. She felt her breath catch in her throat as she thought it through, trying it out, seeing if it fit.

She knew who the demon was.

She knew why John Ross could not escape it.

A wave of heat rushed through her. Maybe she had been wrong about the Lady after all. Maybe the Lady knew Nest would see what Ross could not.

But was there still time enough to save him?

She was on her feet, her bag flung over one shoulder, running for the exit and the taxi stand.

CHAPTER 22

John Ross went up to his apartment and stood at the
window looking down at the ruins of Fresh Start, fum-
ing. A crew from the fire marshall's office was picking its
way carefully through the debris, searching for clues. He
scanned the busy streets for Andrew Wren, but the reporter was nowhere to be seen.

Why was the demon working so hard to discredit him?
What did it hope to gain?

Where the Wiz was concerned, the answer was obvious. The demon hoped that by discrediting Simon, it
would derail the progress of his programs. If enough
doubt was cast and suspicion raised as to the integrity of
the work being done at Fresh Start and Pass/Go, donors
would pull back, political and celebrity sponsors would
disappear, and support from the public would shift to another cause. Worse, it would reflect on programs assisting
the homeless all across the country. It was typical demon
mischief, a sowing of discontent that, given enough time
and space, would reap anarchy.

The more difficult question was why the demon had
chosen to paint him with the same brush. What was the
point? Was this phony theft charge supposed to send him

into a tailspin that would lead to an alliance with the Void? Given that the demon intended to subvert him and claim his magic, this business of manipulating bank accounts and transfers seemed an odd way to go about it.

He chewed his lip thoughtfully. It might explain the fire, though. Burning down Fresh Start at the same time Simon Lawrence was being discredited would only add to the confusion. If the plan was to bring down Simon and put an end to his programs, an attack from more than one front made sense.

He shoved his hands in his jeans pockets angrily. He wanted to walk right over to Pass/Go and deal with his suspicions. But he knew there wasn't really anything he could do. Andrew Wren was still in the middle of his investigation. He was checking signatures and interviewing bank personnel. Maybe the signatures wouldn't match. Certainly the bank people wouldn't remember seeing either him or Simon.

Except, he remembered suddenly, the demon was a changeling and could have disguised itself as either of them.

He turned away from the window and stared at the interior of the apartment in frustration. The best thing he could do was to follow through on his promise to Nest and get out of town. Do that, put a little distance between himself and whatever machinations the demon was engaged in, and take a fresh look at things in a few days.

Don't take any chances with the events of the dream.

He glanced at his watch. It was already approaching four o'clock, and the festivities at the Seattle Art Museum were scheduled to begin at six sharp.

Dropping into his favorite wing chair, he dialed

Pass/Go and asked for Stefanie. Told that she was in a meeting, he left a message for her to call him.

He went into the bedroom, pulled his duffel bag out of the closet, and began to pack. It didn't take long. There wasn't much packing to do for this sort of trip, and he didn't have much to choose from in any case. It gave him pause when he realized how little he owned. The truth was, he had never stopped living as if he were just passing through and might be catching the morning bus to some other place.

He was reading a magazine when the door burst open and Stefanie stalked into the room and threw a clump of papers into his lap.

"Explain this, John!" she demanded coldly, standing rigid with fury before him.

He looked down at the papers, already knowing what they were. Photocopies of the bank transfers Andrew Wren had shown him earlier. He looked up again. "I don't know anything about these accounts. They aren't mine."

"Your signature is all over them!"

He met her gaze squarely. "Stef, I didn't steal a penny. That's not my signature. Those aren't my accounts. I told the same thing to Andrew Wren when he asked me about it an hour ago. I wouldn't do anything like this."

She stared at him silently, searching his face.

"Stef, I wouldn't."

All the anger drained away, and she bent down to kiss him. "I know. I told Simon the same thing. I just wanted to hear you say it."

She put her hands on his shoulders and ran them down his arms, her tousled black hair falling over her battered face. Then she knelt before him, her eyes lifting to find his. "I'm sorry. This hasn't been a good day."

You don't know the half of it, he thought to himself. "I was thinking we might go away for a few days, let things sort themselves out."

She smiled up at him sadly. "A few days, a few weeks, a few months, we can take as much time as we want. We're out of a job."

He felt his throat tighten. "What?"

"Simon fired you. When I objected and he wouldn't change his mind, I quit." She shrugged.

He shook his head in disbelief. "Why would Simon fire me without giving me a chance to explain?"

"He's cutting his losses, John. It's the smart thing to do." Her dark eyes studied him. "He's frightened. He's angry. A lot of bad things are happening all at once, and he has to do something to contain the damage. If word of this leaks to the mayor's office or the local press, it's all over for Simon."

"So his solution is to fire me?"

"That's what I asked him." She brushed her hair aside, her mouth tight and angry. Then she stood up and walked across the room and threw herself on the couch, staring up at the ceiling. "There's nothing back yet on the transfer signatures, and no one he's talked to at the banks involved remembers anything about who opened the accounts. But when Wren suggested the possibility that you were trying to set Simon up, Simon bought into it. He thinks you're responsible, and he wants to distance himself from you right now before you become a liability he can't explain."

She looked over at him. "There's more. He claims he

came by last night after I left. He claims he found you
drunk and irrational, and you threatened him. I told him
that wasn't possible, that you weren't drinking. I told
him you were sick and half asleep when I left you, so
maybe he misinterpreted what he heard. He refused to
listen." She exhaled sharply, her bitterness evident. "He
fired you, just like that. So I quit, too."

Ross was staring at the space between them, stunned.
First the business of the demon hunting him, then Andrew Wren's accusations, and now this. He felt as if he
was caught in some sort of diabolical whirlpool that was
sucking him under where he couldn't breathe.

"This isn't like Simon, John," Stef was saying. "This
isn't like him at all. He hasn't been the same lately. I
don't know what the problem is, but it's almost as if he's
someone else completely."

Ross was thinking the same thing. A glimmer of suspicion had surfaced inside, hot and fierce. It couldn't be, he
was thinking. Not Simon. Not the Wiz.

Stef crossed her long legs and stared down the length
of her body at her feet. "I don't understand what he's
thinking anymore."

Ross looked at her. "How did his TV interview go last
night?" he asked casually.

She pursed her lips. "It didn't. He canceled it. I didn't
even find out until I showed up and no one was there.
That's when I came back here and found you collapsed
on the couch. I hauled you off to bed and read my book in
the living room until around midnight, when I woke you
about the fire."

His suspicion burned inside like an inferno. "You
know that message you got over the phone from Nest
Freemark? The one about meeting her in West Seattle?

Did you mention it to anyone else? Or could anyone else have overheard?"

Stefanie sat up slowly, puzzled. "I don't know. Why?"

"Just think about it. It might be important."

She was silent a moment. "Well, Simon knew, I guess. He was there talking with me when I took Nest's call. He asked me afterward what it was about, and I said it was from Nest and she wanted you to meet her in Lincoln Park. He laughed, said it was an odd place to meet someone. I said it had something to do with a friend of somebody named Pick."

Ross felt the blood drain from his face.

Stef sat up slowly, her brow furrowing with concern. "John, what's going on?"

He shook his head. Simon Lawrence knew about the meeting with Nest. If he was the demon, he had time and opportunity to get over there, intercept her at her meeting with the forest creatures, and still get back to set the fire at Fresh Start.

He almost laughed out loud. No, this was ridiculous!

But the idea had taken root. Who was in a better position than Simon Lawrence to sabotage the work of Fresh Start and Pass/Go? Simon was the whole program. If he came under suspicion, if he was forced to quit, if—just suppose now—he disappeared at a crucial juncture in the investigation, everything would go down the drain. There would be national coverage. Every homeless program in the country would be adversely affected.

"John?" Stef was on her feet. She looked frightened.

He smiled. "It's all right, I'm just thinking. Would you mind getting me a root beer from the fridge?"

She nodded, smiling back at him uncertainly. He

waited until she was out of the room, then resumed his deliberation. Simon Lawrence as the demon—it made a certain amount of sense. Simon could ruin his own programs. He could sabotage homeless programs nationwide by wrecking his own. And he was in a great position to wreck Ross's life, as well. He could implicate him in the theft of corporate funds, terminate his job, maybe even have him sent to prison. If the demon intended to turn him to the Void's service, it would be a perfect place to begin.

It might even cost him his relationship with Stef.

His head throbbed fiercely. One misstep was all it took, the Lady had cautioned. One misstep that led to another. He considered the possibility that the demon might take that step for him. It wasn't too difficult to imagine.

But Simon Lawrence? He still couldn't bring himself to accept that the Wiz was a demon.

Stefanie reentered the room. He came to his feet, facing her. "Stef, I can't go away just yet. I have to do something first. I have to see Simon."

She sighed. "John, no."

He took hold of her arms and held her gently, but firmly, in place. "I can call him up right now or I can just go over. It won't take but a moment."

She shook her head, her eyes angry. "It won't do you any good, John. He's made up his mind. I already argued your case for you, and it didn't change anything."

He studied her face, thinking she was right, that it was pointless. "I have to try," he insisted anyway. "I have to make the attempt myself. I'll be right back."

She grabbed his arm as he started to turn away. "John,

he's not even there. He's already gone down to the art museum to help put things in place for tonight's benefit. He's doing interviews and . . . Look, forget this. Let it go. Give me five minutes to pack a bag and we're out of here. We'll deal with it when we get back, okay?"

But he was already committed. He could not just walk away, not even for three or four days. He had to know the truth about Simon. He had no idea how he was going to find it out, but he could at least speak with him face-to-face and see how he responded.

Then a very strange thought occurred to him. What if the dream about killing the Wizard of Oz wasn't a warning at all? What if it were an admonition? Perhaps he had been mistaken about the purpose of the dream, and he was having it not because he was supposed to avoid the Wiz, but because he was supposed to go after him. His dreams of the future had been windows into mistakes that had been made in the present and might yet be corrected. He had assumed this was the case here. But he was no longer a Knight of the Word, and it was possible this dream, the only dream he was having anymore, the one he had experienced so often, was meant to work in a different way.

Maybe he was supposed to kill Simon Lawrence because Simon was a demon.

It was a stretch, by any measure, and he had no way of knowing if it were so. But if Simon was a demon, it would give new meaning to his dream. It would lend it a purpose and a reason for being that had been missing before.

Stefanie was still holding the root beer. He looked down at it and shook his head. "I've changed my mind. I don't want it after all."

She put her free hand on his arm. "John . . ."

"Stef, I'm going down to the art museum to find Simon. I won't be long. I just want to ask him why he didn't wait a little longer. I just want to hear him tell me why he won't give me the benefit of the doubt."

She set the can of root beer down on the table. "John, don't do this."

"What can it hurt?"

"Your pride, for one thing." She was seething. Her exquisite features were calm and settled, but her eyes were angry. "You don't have anything to prove to Simon Lawrence, certainly not anything more than he should have to prove to you. Those are his signatures on those bank accounts, too. Why isn't it just as likely he's to blame?"

Ross put his finger to her lips. "Because he's the Wiz, and I'm not."

She shook her head vehemently, her anger edging closer to a breakout. "I don't care who he is. You don't have to prove anything."

"I just want to talk with him."

She didn't say anything for a moment, studying him with a mix of resignation and dismay, as if realizing all the arguments in the world had been suddenly rendered useless. "I'm not going to change your mind on this, am I?"

He smiled, trying to take the edge off the moment. "No, but I love you for trying. Go pack your bag. Wait for me. I'll be back inside of an hour, and then we'll go."

He kissed her mouth, then walked over to the front closet and pulled on his greatcoat. She was still standing there, staring after him, as he went out the door.

*   *   *

Nest Freemark rode back into the city from the airport in impatient silence, staring out at the sun as it dropped westward toward the Olympics. It was already growing dark, the days shortened down to a little more than eight hours, the nights lengthening in response to the coming of the winter solstice. Shadows crept and pooled all across the wooded slopes of the city's hills, swallowing up the last of the light.

She had thought to call ahead, to reach Ross by telephone, but what she had to say would be better coming from her in person. He might believe her then. She might stand a chance of convincing him.

She exhaled wearily, peering out at the descending dark. This was going to be a much harder task than the one the Lady had given her.

The taxi rolled onto the off-ramp at Seneca and down to Pioneer Square. The district's turn-of-the-century lamps were already lit, the shadows of the city's tall buildings stretching dark fingers to gather in dwindling slivers of daylight. The taxi pulled up at the curb beside the burned-out hulk of Fresh Start, and she paid the driver and jumped out, bag in hand. The taxi drove away, and she stood there, gathering her thoughts. She realized how cold it had gotten, a brisk wind whipping out of the northwest down Second Avenue's broad corridor, and she slipped hurriedly into her new jacket.

She turned and looked across the intersection at Waterfall Park and the apartment building where John Ross lived with Stefanie Winslow. The wind buffeted her gangly form as she stood there and tried to decide what she should do.

Finally, she picked up her bag and turned the corner to walk up Main Street to Pass/Go. She entered the reception area and glanced around. Except for the lady working the intake desk, the room was empty.

She moved over to the desk, taking several deep breaths to slow the pounding of her heart, masking her trepidation and urgency with a smile. "Is John Ross here?" she asked.

The woman at the desk shook her head without looking up. She seemed anxious to stick with her paperwork. "He didn't come in today. Can I help you?"

"My name is Nest Freemark. I'm a friend. I need to speak with him right away. It's rather urgent. Can you give him a call for me at his apartment? Or would you let me have his number?"

The woman smiled in a way that let Nest know right off the bat she wasn't about to do either. "I'm sorry, but our policy is—"

"Well, look who's back!" Della Jenkins strolled into the room, smiling like this was the best thing that had happened all day. "I thought you was flying home, Nest Freemark. What're you doing, back in my kitchen?"

She saw Nest's face, and the smile faded away. "Good gracious, look at you! If I didn't know better, I'd say you'd been in a cat fight with Stef Winslow! She looks just the same!"

Nest flinched as if she had been struck. "I'm sorry to barge in like this, but something's come up and I really need to find John."

"Lord, if this isn't a day for finding John! Everyone wants to find John! You'd think he'd won the lottery or something. He hasn't, has he? 'Cause if he has, I want to be sure and get my share. Marilyn, let me use the phone there, sweetie."

Della moved the woman at the intake desk out of the picture with an easy exercise of authority that didn't leave much room for doubt as to who was boss. She picked up the receiver, punched in a number, and waited, listening. After a long time, she set the receiver down.

"John's been home all day, far as I know. He's stayed clear of here, and I don't expect him in. Stefanie's gone, too. Left here a short time ago. There's no answer at the apartment, so maybe they're out together somewhere."

Nest nodded, her mind racing over the possibilities. Had they left town? Had John Ross done as he promised? She didn't think so. She didn't think there was a prayer of that happening. He would still be in the city . . .

"Is Mr. Lawrence here?" she asked quickly.

"Oh, no, he's gone, too," Della answered, surrendering her seat to Marilyn once more. She came around the desk and put her finger to the side of her cheek. "You know, Nest—oh, I do love that name! Nest! Anyway, Nest, John might be down at the art museum, helping set up for tonight. That's where Simon's gone, so maybe John's gone there, too."

Nest was already starting for the door, shouldering her bag. "Thanks, Della. Maybe you're right."

"You want me to call and ask?"

"No, that's okay, I'll just go down. If John shows up here or calls in, tell him I'm looking for him and it's really important."

"Okay." Della made a face. "Here, where are you going with that bag? You don't want to be carrying that all over the place. You leave it with me, I'll keep it safe."

Nest came back and handed her bag to the big woman. "Thanks again. I'll see you."

She raced across the lobby, thinking, *I'm going to be too late, I'm not going to be in time!*

"Slow down, for goodness' sake, this ain't the fifty-yard dash!" Della called after her, but she was already out the door.

Andrew Wren spent the remainder of the afternoon following investigative roadways that all turned into dead ends. He was not discouraged, though. Investigative reporting required patience and bulldog determination, and he had an abundance of both. If the research took until Christmas, that was all right with him.

What wasn't all right was the way his instincts were acting. He trusted his instincts, and up until this morning they had been doing just fine. They had told him the anonymous reports of wrongdoing at Fresh Start were worth following up. They had told him the transfer records that had been slipped under his door were the real thing.

But what they were telling him now, barely eighteen hours later, was that something about all this was screwy.

For one thing, even though he had proof of the funds transfers from the corporate accounts of Fresh Start and Pass/Go to the private accounts of Simon Lawrence and John Ross, he couldn't find a pattern that made any sense. The withdrawals and deposits were regular, but the amounts transferred were too low given the amounts that might have been transferred from the money on hand. Sure, you wouldn't take too much, because you didn't want to draw attention. But you wouldn't take too little either, and in several cases it appeared this was exactly what the Wiz and Mr. Ross had done.

Then there was the matter of identifying the thieves. No one at any of the various banks could remember ever seeing either Mr. Lawrence or Mr. Ross make a deposit. But some of the deposits had been made in person, not by mail. Andrew Wren had been circumspect in making his inquiries, cloaking them in a series of charades designed to deflect the real reason for his interest. But not one teller or officer who had conducted the personal transactions could remember ever seeing either man come in.

But it was in the area of his personal contact with the two men he was investigating that his instincts were really acting up, telling him that the two men didn't do it. When someone was guilty of something, he could almost always tell. His instincts lit up like a scoreboard after a home run, and he just knew. But even after bracing both Simon and John Ross on the matter, his instincts refused to celebrate. Maybe they just weren't registering the truth of things this time out, but he didn't like it that they weren't flashing even a little.

Well, tomorrow was another day, and tonight was the gala event at the Seattle Art Museum, and he was anxious to see if he might learn something there. It wasn't an unrealistic expectation, given the circumstances. He would have another shot at both the Wiz and Ross, since both were expected to attend. He would have a good chance to talk with their friends and maybe even one or two of their enemies. One could always hope.

He reached the Westin just after five and rode up to his room in an otherwise empty elevator. He unlocked his door, slipped out of his rumpled jacket, and went into the bathroom to wash his face and hands and brush his teeth.

When he came out again, he located his invitation, dropped it on top of his jacket, and poured himself a short glass of scotch from what remained of last night's bottle.

Then he sat down next to the phone and called Marty at the lab in New York. He let it ring. It was three hours later there, but Marty often worked late when there was no one around to interrupt. Besides, he knew Wren was anxious for a quick report.

On the seventh ring, Marty picked up. "Lab Works."

"Hello, Marty? It's Andrew. How are you coming?"

"I'm done."

Wren straightened. He'd sent Marty the transfer records by fax for signature comparison late that morning, marked "Urgent" in bold letters, but he hadn't really expected anything for another day.

"Andrew? You there?" Marty sounded impatient.

"I'm here. What did you find?"

"They don't match. Good forgeries, very close to the real thing, but phony. In some cases the signatures were just tracings. Good enough to pass at first glance, but nothing that would stand up in court. These boys are being had."

Andrew Wren stared into space. "Damn," he muttered.

Marty chuckled. "I thought you'd like that. But hang on a second, there's more. I checked the forgeries against all the other signatures you sent—friends, acquaintances, fellow workers, so on and so forth."

He paused meaningfully. "Yeah, so?" Wren prodded.

"So while there isn't a match there either, there is a singular characteristic in one other person's writing style that suggests you might have a new suspect. Again, not enough to stand up in court, but enough to make me sit up and take notice. It only appears on the signatures copied freehand, not on the ones traced, which is good because it's their freehand writing we're interested in."

Wren took a long drink of his scotch. "Enough with the buildup, Marty. Whose signature is it?"

CHAPTER 23

John Ross stepped out of the bus tunnel onto Third Avenue, walked right to University Street, and started down the steep hill. The evening air was brittle and sharp, tinged with a hint of early frost, and he pulled the collar of his coat closer about his neck. He moved slowly along the sidewalk, his gaze lowered to its surface, conscious of a slippery glaze encrusting the cement, relying on his staff for support.

Still bound to my past, he thought darkly. *Crippled by it. Unable to escape what I was.*

He tried to organize his thoughts as he passed close by the imposing glass lobby of the symphony hall, brilliant light spilling out across the promenade and planting areas to where he walked. But his mind would not settle. The possibilities of what he might discover when he confronted Simon Lawrence did not lend themselves readily to resolution. He wanted to be wrong about Simon. But a dark whisper at the back of his mind told him he was not and warned him he must be careful.

At the next intersection, he paused, waiting for the light to change, and allowed himself his first close look at his destination. The high, curved walls of the Seattle Art Museum loomed ahead, filling the entire south end of the

block between Second and First. The Robert Venturi–
designed building had a fortresslike look to it from this
angle, all the windows that faced on First hidden, the
massive sections of exposed limestone confronting him
jagged, rough, and forbidding. In the shadowy street
light, the softening contours and sculpting were invisible,
and there was only a sense of weight and mass.

He crossed with the light and began his descent of a
connecting set of terraces and steps that followed the
slope of the hill down to the museum's primary entrance.
He limped uneasily, warily, seeing movement and shadows
everywhere, seeing ghosts. He peered into the brightly lit
interior, where service people were bustling about in
preparation for the night's festivities. He could see a
scattering of tables on the broad platform of the mezzanine outside the little café, and more on the main floor of
the entry. Stacks of trays and plates were being set out
along with bottles of wine and champagne, chests of ice,
napkins, silver, and crystal. The waiters and waitresses
were dressed in skeleton suits, their painted bones shimmering with silver incandescence. One or two had already donned their skull masks. It gave the proceedings
an eerie look: no guests had arrived yet, but the dead
were making ready.

Ahead, the *Hammering Man* rose fifty feet into the
night, stark and angular against the skyline of Elliott Bay
and the mountains. A massive, flat steel cutout painted
black, it was the creation of Jonathan Borofsky, who
had intended it to reflect the working nature of the
city. A hammer held in the left hand rose and fell in
rhythmic motion, giving the illusion of pounding and
shaping a bar that was held firmly in the right. The head
was lowered in concentration to monitor the work being

done, the body muscular and powerful as it bent to its endless task.

Ross stopped at the sculpture's base and looked up at it. An image of the dream that had haunted him these past six months clouded his vision, the old man accusing him anew of slaying the Wizard of Oz, in the glass palace of the Emerald City, where the Tin Woodman kept watch. He had recognized the references instantly, known them to be the museum and the *Hammering Man*. He had sworn to stay away, to do anything required to keep the dream from becoming reality. Yet here he was, as if in perverse disregard of all he had promised himself, because now there was reason to believe the dream was meant to happen.

He stood rooted in place then, thinking desperately. If he entered the museum, he was accepting he might not be meant to foil the dream, but to facilitate it. Such logic flew in the teeth of everything he had learned while he was a Knight of the Word, and yet he knew the past was not always an accurate measurement for the present and what had once been reliable might no longer be so. If he turned around now and walked away, he would not have to find out. But he would be left with unanswered questions about the demon who sought to destroy him and about Simon Lawrence, and he would have no peace.

He held the staff before him and stared into its rune-scrolled length. He gripped it in frustration, as if to break it asunder, giving way to an inner core of rage and heat that sought to drag the recalcitrant magic from its hiding place. But no magic appeared, and he was forced to consider anew that perhaps it was forever gone. As he had often wished, he reminded himself bitterly. As he had often prayed.

Cars moved past him on the streets in a steady line of headlights, rush-hour traffic heading home. Horns honked, more in celebration than in irritation. It was Halloween, and everyone was feeling good. Some passersby wore masks and costumes, waving their hands and yelling, holding up plastic weapons and icons against the night. Ross gave them a momentary glance, then faced the museum anew. The magic of the staff was a crutch he did not require. He would not have to do more than ask Simon why. There need not be a confrontation, a struggle, or a death. The dream need not come about. It was the truth he was seeking, and he thought it would make itself known quickly when he had Simon Lawrence before him.

But still he hesitated, torn in two directions, caught between choices that could change his life inalterably.

Then he took a deep breath, hefted the staff, set the butt end firmly on the ground, and walked into the museum.

It was loud and cavernous in the lobby, where the servers were scurrying about in final preparation. He stood in the doorway, glancing about for an indication of where to go. Ahead and to his left was a reception desk, the museum shop, and doors opening into an auditorium where the announcement of the dedication of city land for a new building for Fresh Start would be made. To his right, the Grand Stairway climbed through a Ming dynasty marble statuary of rams, camels, and guardians past the mezzanine to the upper floors. The prominent, distinctive arches draped from the ceiling were spaced at regular intervals so that Ross could imagine how the inside of the whale must have looked to Jonah. Where the rough-edged exterior was formed of limestone, sandstone, and terra-cotta, the softer interior was comprised of polished floors of terrazzo set in cement and of walls of red oak. Ross had visited the museum only once during the time he had lived in Seattle. He admired the architectural accomplishments, but still preferred the green, open spaces of the parks.

One of the security guards walked up to him and asked to see his invitation. Staying calm when he felt anything but, he said he had forgotten it, but he was employed at Fresh Start and was on the guest list. The guard asked for identification, which Ross produced. The guard seemed satisfied. Ross asked him if he had seen Simon Lawrence, but the guard said he had been working the door and hadn't seen anyone who might have entered another way.

Ross thanked him and walked past, eyes scanning the lobby, then the upper levels. There was no sign of Simon. He was feeling edgy again, thinking Stef had been right, he shouldn't have come, he should have let it go.

One of the servers came up to him with a mask. "Everyone gets a mask at this party," she enthused, handing him his. "Do you want me to take your coat?"

Ross declined her offer, not expecting to stay beyond talking with Simon, and then, because she seemed to expect it, he slipped on the mask. It was a black nylon sheath that covered the upper half of his face. It made him feel vaguely sinister amid the skeleton suits and Halloween trimmings.

He looked around some more without success for Simon and was about to move on to the reception desk when a security guard from the upper mezzanine area came down the steps toward him, waving to catch his attention.

"Mr. Ross?" he asked. When Ross nodded, the guard said, "Mr. Lawrence is waiting for you on the second floor in the Special Exhibition Hall. He said to go on up."

Ross caught himself staring at the guard in surprise, but then thanked him quickly and moved away. Simon was waiting for him? He began to climb the Grand Stairway without even considering the elevator, the broad steps leading up from the brightness of the lobby and mezzanine to the more shadowy rooms of the display halls above. He ascended at a steady pace through the rams and camels, through the civilian and military guardians, their eyes blank and staring, their expressions fixed, sculptures warding artifacts and treasures of the dead. Servers bustled by, skeleton costumes rippling, masks in place. He glanced at his watch. The evening's events were scheduled to begin in less than thirty minutes.

At the top of the stairs, he stopped and looked around. Below, the Grand Stairway stretched downward in a smooth flow of steps, arches, and glass windows to the array of finger foods, drinks, and serving people. Ahead, the hallway wound back on itself up a short flight of stairs to the exhibition rooms. Simon Lawrence was nowhere to be seen.

A ripple of apprehension ran down his spine. What was Simon doing up here?

He climbed the short flight of stairs and walked down the hallway into the exhibition rooms. The lights were dim, the red oak walls draped with shadows. There was a display of Chihuly glass that shimmered in bright splashes of color beneath directional lighting. Fire reds, sun-bright yellows, ocean blues, and deep purples lent a festive air to the semidark. Ross walked on, passing other exhibits in other areas, searching. The sound of his footfalls echoed eerily.

Then abruptly, shockingly, Simon Lawrence stepped out from behind a display directly to one side and said, "Why are you here, John?"

Ross started in spite of himself, then took a quick breath to steady the rapid beating of his heart and faced the other man squarely. "I came to ask you if what Stef told me was true."

Simon smiled. He was dressed in a simple black tuxedo that made him look taller and broader than Ross knew him to be and lent him an air of smooth confidence. "Which part, John? That I fired you for stealing money from the project? That I chose to do it without talking to you first? That I did it to distance myself from you?" He paused. "The answer is yes to all."

John stared at him in disbelief. Somehow, he hadn't expected Simon to find it so easy to say it to his face. "Why?" he managed, shaking his head slowly. "I haven't done anything, Simon. I didn't steal that money."

Simon Lawrence moved out of the shadows and came right up to Ross, stopping so close to him that Ross could see the silvery glitter of his eyes. "I know that," Simon said softly. "I did."

Ross blinked. "Simon, why—"

The other man interrupted smoothly, dismissing the question with a wave of his hand. "You know why, John."

John Ross felt the ground shift under his feet, as if the stone had turned to quicksand and was about to swallow him up. In that instant of confusion and dismay, Simon Lawrence snatched away his staff, wrenching it from his grasp with a sudden, vicious twist, then stepped back swiftly out of reach, leaving Ross tottering on his bad leg.

"I set fire to Fresh Start as well, John," Simon went on smoothly, cradling the staff beneath one arm. "I killed Ray Hapgood. Everything you think I might have done, I probably did. I did it to destroy the programs, to undermine the Simon Lawrence legend, the mystique of the Wiz, which, after all, I created in the first place. I did it to further the aims I really serve and not those I have championed as a part of my disguise. But you guessed as much already, or you wouldn't be here."

Ross was fighting to keep from attempting to rush Simon—or the thing that pretended at being Simon. An attack would only result in Ross falling on his face. He had to hope the other might come close enough to be grappled with, might make a mistake born of overconfidence.

"You fooled us all," he said softly. "But especially me. I never guessed what you really were."

The demon laughed. "I hired you in the first place, John, because I knew what *you* were and I was certain I could make good use of you. A Knight of the Word fallen from grace, an exile by choice, but still in possession of a valuable magic. The opportunity was too good to pass up. Besides, it was time to abandon this charade, to put an end to Simon Lawrence and his good works. It was time to move on to something else. All I had to do was to destroy the persona I had created by discrediting him. You were the perfect scapegoat. So willing, John, to be seduced. So I used you, and now you will take the blame, I will resign in disgrace, and the programs will fail. If it works as I intend, it will have a ripple effect on homeless programs all over the country. Loss of trust is a powerful incentive for closing up pocketbooks and shutting off funds."

The demon smiled. "Was that what you wanted to hear, John? I haven't disappointed you, have I?"

It took the staff from beneath its arms and flung it into the space behind, where it skidded across the stone floor and clattered into the wall. Then it reached out and took Ross by his shirt front and dragged him forward. Ross fought to escape, but the demon was too strong for him and backhanded him across the face. The blow snapped Ross's head back, and a bright flash of pain left him blinded and stunned. The demon lifted Ross and held him suspended above the floor. Ross blinked to clear his vision, then watched as the demon lifted its free hand. The hand began to transform, changing from something human to something decidedly not. Claws and bristling hair appeared. The demon glanced at its handiwork speculatively, then raked the claws across Ross's midsection. They tore through coat and shirt, shredding the flesh beneath, bringing bright welts of blood.

The demon threw John Ross down, sending him sprawling back onto the floor. "You really are pathetic, John," it advised conversationally, walking to where he lay gasping for breath and bleeding. "Look at you. You can't even defend yourself. I was prepared to offer you a place in service to the Void, but what would be the point? Without your staff, you're nothing. Even with the staff, I doubt you could do much. You've lost your magic, haven't you? It's all dried up and blown away. There's nothing left."

The demon reached down, picked Ross up, and slashed him a second time, this time down one shoulder. It struck Ross across the face again, dropping him as it might a thing so foul it could not bear to hold him longer. Ross collapsed in a heap, fighting to stay conscious.

"You're not worth any more of my time, John," the demon sneered softly, standing over him once more. "I could kill you, but you're worth more to me alive. I've still use for you in destroying Simon Lawrence and his fine works. I've still plans for you."

It bent down, leaning close, and whispered, "But if I see you again this night, I will kill you where I find you. Don't test me on this, John. Get out of here and don't come back."

Then it rose, pushed Ross down with its foot, held him pinned helplessly against the floor as it studied him, then turned and walked away.

For a long time Ross lay where the demon had left him, a black wave of nausea and pain threatening to overwhelm him with every breath he took. He lay on his back, staring up at a ceiling enveloped in layers of deep shadows. He might have given in to the despair and shame that swept through him if he were any other man, if he had not once been a Knight of the Word. But the seeds of his identity ran deeper than he would have thought possible, and amid the darker feelings wound an iron cord of determination that would have required him to die first.

After a while, he was strong enough to roll onto his side and sit up. Dizziness threatened to flatten him anew, but he lowered his head between his legs, braced himself with his hands, and waited for the feeling to pass. When it did, he lurched to his knees, dropped back to his hands, and began to crawl. Streaks of blood from his wounds marked his slow passage, and shards of fire traced the deep furrows the demon's claws had left on his body. The hallway and exhibit areas were silent and empty of life, and he worked his solitary way across the polished stone with only the sound of his breathing for company.

He had been a fool, he told himself over and over again. He had misjudged badly, been overconfident of what he could accomplish when he would have been better served by being more cautious. He should have listened to Stef. He should have trusted his instincts. He should have remembered the lessons of his time in service to the Word.

Twice he slipped in pools of his own excretions and went down. His arms and hands were wet from blood and sweat, and every movement he made trying to cross the museum floor racked his body with pain.

Damn you, Simon, he swore silently, resolutely, a litany meant to empower. *Damn you to hell.*

When he reached the staff, he rose again to his knees and wiped his bloodstained palms on his pants. Then he took the staff firmly in his hands and levered himself back to his feet.

He stood there for a moment, swaying unsteadily. When the dizziness passed, he moved to an empty bench in the center of the hall, seated himself, slipped off the greatcoat, then the tattered shirt, and used the shirt to bind his ribs and chest in a mostly successful effort to slow the flow of his blood. He sat staring into space after that, trying to gather his strength. He didn't think anything was broken, but he had lost a lot of blood. He could not continue without help, and the only help he could count on now would have to come from within.

Hard-eyed and ashen-faced, he leaned forward on the

bench, wrapped in the tatters of his shirt, his upper torso mostly bare and red-streaked with his blood. He straightened with an effort and tightened his grip on the staff, his abandoned choices swirling around him like wraiths, his decision of what he must do fully embraced. He no longer cared about consequences or dreams. He could barely bring himself to think on the future beyond this night. What he knew was that he had been driven to his knees by something so foul and repulsive he could not bear another day of life if he did not bring an end to it.

So he called forth the magic of the staff, called it with a certainty that surprised him, called it with full acceptance of what it meant to do so. He renounced himself and what he had become. He renounced his stand of the past year and took up anew the mantle he had shed. He declared himself a Knight of the Word, begged for the right to become so once more, if only for this single night, if only for this solitary purpose. He armored himself in his vow to become the thing he had tried so hard to disclaim, accepting as truth the admonitions of Owain Glyndwr and O'olish Amaneh. He bowed in acknowledgment to the cautions of the Lady as delivered by Nest Freemark and her friends, giving himself over once more to the promises he had made fifteen years earlier when he had taken up the cause of the Word and entered into His service.

Even then, the magic did not come at once, for it lay deep within the staff, waiting for the call to be right, for the prayer to be sincere. He could sense it, poised and heedful, but recalcitrant. He strained to reach it, to make it feel his need, to draw it to him as he would a reluctant child. His eyes were closed and his brow furrowed in concentration, and the pain that racked his body became a white-hot fury at the core of his heart.

Suddenly, abruptly, the Lady was before him, there in the darkness of his mind, white-gowned and ephemeral, her hands reaching for him. Oh, my brave Knight Errant, would you truly come back to me? Would you serve me as you once did, without reservation or guilt, without doubt or fear? Would you be mine as you were? Her words filtered like the slow meandering of a forest stream through rocks and mud banks, soft and rippling. He cried at the sound of her voice, the tears filling his lids and leaking down his bloodied face. I would. I will. Always. Forever.

Then she was gone, and the magic of the staff stirred and gathered and came forth in a swift, steady river, climbing out of the polished black walnut into his arms and body, filling him with its healing power.

Silver light enfolded the Knight of the Word with bright radiance, and he was alive anew.

And dead to what once he had hoped so strongly he might be.

John Ross lifted his head in recognition, feeling the power of the magic flow through him, rising out of the staff, eager to serve. He let it strengthen him as nothing else could, not caring what it might cost him. For the cost was not his to measure. It would be measured in his dreams, when they returned. It would be measured in the time he would spend unprotected in the future he had sworn to prevent and, as a Knight of the Word once more, must now return to.

But before that happened, he vowed, climbing to his feet as the damage to his body was swept aside by the sustaining magic, he would find Simon Lawrence, demon of the Void.

And he would destroy him.

Nest Freemark arrived at the museum with the first crush of invited guests, and it took her a while just to get through the door. When she was asked for her invitation and failed to produce it, she was told in no uncertain terms that if her name wasn't on the guest list, she couldn't come in. She tried to explain how important this was, that she needed to find John Ross or Simon Lawrence, but the security guards weren't interested. People behind her were getting impatient with the delay, and she might have been thwarted altogether if she hadn't caught sight of Carole Price and called her over. Carole greeted Nest effusively and told the security guards to let her through.

"Nest, what are you doing here?" the other woman asked, steering her to an open spot amid the knots of masked guests and skeleton-costumed servers. "I thought you'd gone back to Illinois."

"I postponed my flight," she replied, keeping her explanation purposefully vague. "Is John here?"

"John Ross?" A waiter came up to them with a tray filled with champagne glasses, and Carole motioned him away. "No, I haven't seen him yet."

"How about Mr. Lawrence?"

"Oh, yes, Simon's here somewhere. I saw him just a little while ago." Her brow furrowed slightly. "You heard about the fire, didn't you, Nest?"

Nest nodded. "I'm sorry about Mr. Hapgood." There was an awkward silence as she tried to think of something else to say. "I know John was very upset about it."

Carole Price nodded. "We all were. Look, why don't you go on and see if you can find him. I haven't seen him down here, but maybe he's up on the mezzanine. And I'll tell Simon you're here. He'll want to say hello."

"Thanks." Nest glanced around doubtfully. The lobby was filling up quickly with guests, and everyone was wearing a mask. It made recognizing people difficult. "If you see John," she said carefully, "tell him I'm here. Tell him it's important that I speak with him right away."

Carole nodded, a hint of confusion in her blue eyes, and Nest moved away before she could ask any questions.

A passing server handed her one of the black nylon masks, and she slipped it on. All around her, people were drinking champagne. Their talk and laughter was deafening in the cavernous space. Eyes scanning the crowd, she moved toward the wide staircase with the massive stone figures warding its various levels and began to climb. As she did so, a troubling realization came to her. She had forgotten about the dream, the one that had haunted Ross for months, the one in which the old man accused him of killing the Wizard of Oz—and perhaps of killing her as well. She had been thinking so hard about Ross and the demon and what she suspected about both that it had slipped her mind. It was supposed to happen here, in the Seattle Art Museum, on this night. He had wanted her far away from this place, so it could never happen. He had wanted himself far away as well. But she suspected events and demon schemes were at work conspiring to thwart his wishes. Simon Lawrence was already here. She was here. If he wasn't already, soon John Ross would be here too.

She reached the mezzanine and glanced around anew.

She did not see Ross. She felt a growing desperation at her inability to locate him. The longer he remained ignorant of what she suspected, the greater the risk his dream would come to pass. But all she could do was to keep looking. She walked over to a security guard and asked if he had seen John Ross. He told her he didn't even know who Ross was. Frustrated with his response, she asked if he'd seen Simon Lawrence. The guard said no, but asked her to wait and walked over to speak with a second guard. After a moment he came back and told her the second guard had sent a man upstairs not long ago to talk with Mr. Lawrence—a man who walked with a limp and carried a walking stick.

Stunned by her blind good luck, she thanked him and moved quickly to the stairway. She had never even thought to ask if a man with a walking staff and a limp had come in. Stupid, stupid! She tore off the nylon mask and went up the stairs in a rush, wondering what Simon and Ross were doing up there, wondering if somehow she was already too late. There was still too much she didn't know, too much about the circumstances surrounding the events portended in Ross's dream that was hidden from her. There was a tangle of threads in this matter that needed careful unraveling before it ensnared them all.

She reached the second-floor landing and wheeled left to where a dozen steps rose to a dimly lit corridor and the exhibition rooms beyond. She was halfway up this second set of stairs when she drew up short.

John Ross walked out of the shadows, a luminous, terrifying apparition. His clothes were torn and bloodied, and his tattered coat billowed out from his half-naked body like a cape. The black, rune-scrolled staff that was the source of his magic shimmered with silver light, and the radiance it emitted ran all about him like electricity. His strong, sharply angled face was hard-set and drawn, and his green eyes were fierce with determination and rage.

When he saw her, he faltered slightly, and with recognition came a hint of fear and shock. "Nest!" he hissed.

Her breath caught in her throat. "John, what happened?" When he shook his head, unwilling to answer, she wasted no further time on the matter. "John, I had to come back," she said quickly. "I took a chance I might find you here. I have to talk with you."

He shook his head in horror, seeing something that was hidden from her, some truth too terrible to accept. "Get out of here, Nest! I told you to get away! I warned you about the dream!"

"But that's why I'm here." She tried to get closer, but he held up one hand as if to ward himself against her. "John, you have to forget about the dream. The dream was a lie."

"It was the truth!" he shouted back at her. "The dream was the truth! The dream is meant to happen! But some of it can still be changed, enough so that you won't be hurt! But you have to get out of here! You have to leave now!"

She brushed back her curly hair, trying to understand what he was saying. "No, the dream doesn't have to happen. Don't you remember? You're supposed to prevent the dream!"

He came forward a step, wild-eyed and shining with silver light, the magic a living thing as it raced up and down his body and across his limbs. "You don't understand!" he hissed at her in fury. "I'm supposed to *make* it happen!"

There were footsteps and voices on the Grand Stairway, and Nest turned in surprise. She heard Simon Lawrence speaking, and she rushed to where she could see him climbing out of the brightly lit mezzanine toward the second-floor shadows.

She wheeled back to find John Ross striding toward her. "Get out of the way, Nest."

She stared at him, appalled at what she saw in his eyes and heard in his voice. "No, John, wait."

The footsteps stopped momentarily, the voices still audible. Nest could hear Simon Lawrence distinctly, calling to someone below. A woman. Carole Price? Nest went back toward Ross, holding out her hands pleadingly. "John, it isn't him!"

His laugh was brittle. "I saw him, Nest! He did this to me, moments ago, up there!" He gestured back in the direction from which he had come. "He told me everything, admitted it! Then he attacked me! He's the demon, Nest! He's the one who stalked you in the park, the one who destroyed Ariel and Audrey and Boot! He's the one who set fire to Fresh Start! He's the one who killed Ray Hapgood!"

He slammed the butt end of his black staff against the stone floor, and white fire ran up its length like a rocket, searing the dark. "This dream isn't like the others, Nest! It's a prophecy!" His voice was ragged and uneven, choked with anger. "It's a revelation meant to put things right! It's a window into a truth I was trying wrongly, foolishly to ignore! I have to act on it! I have to make it happen!"

She held up her hands to slow his advance. "No, John, listen to me!"

The footsteps were approaching again, the voices growing stronger. She could hear Simon joking with someone, could hear muffled responses, sudden laughter, the clink of glasses. Ross was staring past her, the staff's magic gathering about his knotted hands, growing brighter as he waited for Simon to come into view so that he could unleash it.

"Step aside, Nest," he said softly.

In desperation she backed away from him, but slowly and with measured steps, so he did not advance immediately, but stood watching to see what she intended. She backed until the sweep of the stairway came into view, then wheeled on the knot of people approaching. Simon Lawrence was foremost, smiling, at ease, exchanging remarks with Carole Price and three weathered, worn-looking men who looked to have seen hard times and few respites. They had not seen her yet, and she did not wait for them to do so. She acted on instinct and out of need. She called on her own magic, on the magic she had been born with but had forsworn since the death of Gran. She called on it without knowing whether it would come, but with certainty that it must. She drew Simon Lawrence's gaze to her own, just a glimpse and no more, just enough to bind them for an instant, then used the magic to buckle his legs and drop him nerveless and limp upon the stairs.

She stepped quickly from view as his companions gathered around him, kneeling to see what had happened. It surprised her how quickly she was able to regain her use of a skill she had not tested for so long. But calling on it had an unexpected side effect. It had awakened something else inside of her, something much larger and more dangerous. She felt it stir and then rise, growing large and ferocious, and for a terrifying moment she felt as if it might get away from her completely.

Then she recovered herself, all in an instant, and turned back to face Ross. He hadn't moved. He was standing where she had left him, a puzzled look on his face. He had seen something that had escaped her, and whatever it was, it had left him confused and momentarily distracted.

She did not wait for him to recover. She went to him immediately, crossed the open space between them, and came right up to where he stood, aswirl in his magic, enfolded by the staff's power, the rage and fierce determination returning to his eyes as he recovered his purpose.

"No, John," she said again, quickly, firmly, taking hold of his arms, ignoring the feel of the magic as it played across her skin. She was not afraid. There was no place for her fear in what he required of her. Her eyes met his and she held him bound. "You've been tricked, John. We've all been tricked."

"Nest," he whispered, but there was no force behind the speaking of her name, only a vague sort of plea.

"I know," she replied softly, meaning it without understanding how exactly, knowing mostly that he needed to feel it was true. "But it isn't him, John. It isn't Simon. He isn't the demon."

And then she told him who was.

CHAPTER 24

So now, with his memory of the dream that had started it all fading like autumn color, John Ross began to cross the shadowed cobblestone expanse of Occidental Park in Pioneer Square, his topcoat pulled close about his battered, bloodied torso, a wraith come down out of Purgatory to find the demon who had sentenced him to Hell. The night air was cold and sharp with the smell of winter's coming, and he breathed in the icy scents. Wooden totems loomed overhead as he passed beneath their watchful, fierce gaze, and the homeless who scurried to get out of his way cast apprehensive glances over their shoulders, wary of the silver glow that emanated in a faint sheen from the long black staff that supported him. On the hard surface of the cobblestones, the butt end of the staff clicked softly to mark his progress, and a sudden rush of wind blew debris in a ragged scuttle from his path. The feeders who had gathered at his return trailed silently in his wake, eyes watchful, movements quick and furtive. He could sense their anticipation and their hunger for what lay ahead.

He was a Knight of the Word once more, now and forever, bound by the pledge he had given in persuading the magic to return to him. He was become anew what he had sought so hard to escape, and in his recognition and acceptance of the futility of his efforts he found a kind of solace. It was the home he had looked for and not found in his other life. It was the reality of his existence he had sought to deny. In his renunciation of the Word, he had lost his way, been deceived, and very nearly given himself over to a fate that even on brief reflection made his skin crawl.

But all that was past. All of who he had been and sought to be in these last twelve months was past. His life, the only life he would ever have now, he supposed, was given back to him, and he must find a way to atone for casting it aside so recklessly.

Even if it meant giving it up again as payment for the cost of setting things right.

Street lamps burned with fierce bright centers through the Halloween gloom. All masks were off, all secrets revealed, the trickery finished. By dawn, there would be an accounting and a retribution and perhaps his own death. It would depend on how much of himself he had rescued, how much of the warrior he had been he could summon anew.

He looked ahead to the lights of his apartment, and beyond to the smoking ruins of Fresh Start and the mostly darkened bulk of Pass/Go. The buildings lined the corridor of Main Street, safeholds hiding the secrets of the people within. Ross experienced a sense of futility in thinking of the disguises that obscured the truths in human existence. It was so easy to become lost in the smug certainty that what happened to others really mattered very little to you. It was so easy to ignore the ties that bound humanity on its collective journey in search of grace.

A solitary car passed down the broad corridor of Second Avenue and disappeared. In the distance rose voices and music, laughter and shouts, the sounds of celebration on All Hallows' Eve. For those people, at least, the dark side of witchery and demons was only a myth.

He passed Waterfall Park, the rush of the waterfall a muffled whoosh in the dark confines of the park's walls, the courtyard a vaguely defined spiderweb of wrought-iron tables, chairs, and trellises amid the blockier forms of the stone fountains and sculptures. He turned on hearing his name called, looking back the way he had come. Nest Freemark was running toward him, her unzipped parka flying out behind her, her curly hair jouncing about her round, flushed face. Feeders melted away into the darkness at her approach, into the rocks of the park, into the tangle of tables and chairs, but she seemed heedless of them. She came up to Ross in a rush and stood panting before him, eyes quickly searching his own.

"I came to help," she said.

He smiled at her earnest expression, at the determination he found in her young voice. "No, Nest," he told her quietly.

"But I want to. I need to."

He had left her behind at the museum when he had departed. She had gone down the stairs to intercept Simon Lawrence and his companions, to delay them long enough for Ross to slip out a side door so he wouldn't be seen. Even so, in leaving another way besides the main entrance he set off an alarm that brought security guards from the lower level. As he crossed the street toward a dark alleyway, he watched them stumble unaccountably in their efforts to navigate the Grand Stairway, Nest studying them intently from her position beside a recovering Simon.

"For Ariel," she said firmly. "For Boot and Audrey."

He felt a rush of hot shame and anger, the revelations she had provided burning through him in a fresh wave of shock and disbelief. But truth has a way of making itself known even to the most skeptical, and he had stripped away the blinders that had kept him deceived and was empowered by his new knowledge and the determination it generated.

"For myself, John," she finished.

But she had not seen herself as he had, back at the museum, in the shadowy confines of the Exhibition Hall, where the two of them had come face-to-face in a confrontation that might have led to the horrific fulfillment of his dream. She did not realize yet what she had revealed to him that even she did not know, of the way her magic had evolved, of the secret she now held inside. Powerful forces were at work in Nest Freemark that would change her life yet again. He should tell her, of course. But he could not bring himself to do so now, when the secrets of his own life weighed so heavily on his mind and demanded their own resolution.

He stepped closer to her and put his hands on her shoulders. "I am a Knight of the Word, Nest. I am what I was always meant to be, and I owe much of that to you. But I cannot claim the right to serve if I do not resolve first the reason I lost my way. I have to do that. And I have to do it alone. This is personal to me, so close to the bone that to settle it in any other way would leave me hollowed out. Do you see?"

She studied his face a long time. "But you're hurt. You've lost a lot of blood."

He took his hands away from her shoulders and settled them on the polished length of his staff. "The magic will give me the strength I need for this."

She shook her head. "I don't like it. It's too dangerous."

He looked at her, thinking it odd that someone so young should speak to him of what was too dangerous. But then the dangers in her own life had been, on balance, no less than his.

"Wait for me here, Nest," he told her. "Keep watch. If I don't come out, at least one other person will know the truth."

He didn't wait for her response but wheeled away quickly and went down the sidewalk to the corner, turned left along Second, and walked to the apartment entrance. Feeders reappeared in droves, creeping over the walls of Waterfall Park, coming up from the gutters and out of the alleyways between the buildings. They materialized in such numbers that he experienced an unexpected chill. Their yellow eyes were fixed on him, empty of everything but their hunger. So many, he mused. He could feel the weight of their expectations in the way they pressed forward to be close to him, and he knew they understood with primal instinct what was at stake.

He entered the foyer, using his key, walked to the elevator, and took it up to the sixth floor. The feeders did not follow. He imagined them scaling the outside wall, climbing steadily, relentlessly closer to the windows of his apartment. He envisioned an enormous tidal wave washing toward a sleeping town.

He exited the elevator and moved to his apartment door, used his key again, and entered.

The apartment was shadowy and silent, with only a single lamp burning at one end of the old couch. Stefanie sat reading in the halo of its light, her exquisite face lifting to greet him, her strange, smoky eyes filling with shock as he closed the door and came into the light.

"John, what happened?" she whispered, rising quickly.

He put out his hand, a defensive gesture, and shook his head. "Don't get up, Stef. Just stay where you are, please." He leaned heavily on his staff, studying her perplexed face, the way she brushed back her dark hair, cool and reserved, watchful. "Simon Lawrence isn't dead," he said quietly.

He saw a flicker of something dark in her eyes, but her face never changed. "What do you mean? Why *would* he be dead? What are you talking about, John?"

He shrugged. "It's simple. I went to the museum to speak with him. He was waiting for me. He admitted everything—firing me without giving me a hearing, stealing the money himself, working to destroy Fresh Start, all of it. Then he attacked me. He overpowered me, threw me down, and walked away. When he left, I went after him. I wanted to kill him. I would have, too, except for Nest Freemark. She came back from the airport to warn me. It wasn't Simon Lawrence I was looking for at all, she said." He paused, watching her carefully. "It was you."

She shook her head slowly, a strange little smile playing over her lips. "I have no idea what you are talking about."

He nodded indulgently. She was so beautiful, but everything about her was a lie. "The fact of the matter is, I was ready to believe everything you wanted me to believe. That Simon Lawrence was the demon. That he was responsible for all the bad things happening. That he was intent on ruining my life, on using me, on breaking me down. I had convinced myself. Then, when you tricked me into coming upstairs at the museum, when you disguised yourself as Simon and attacked me, humiliated me, taunted me, and cast me aside as if I were worthless, I was primed and ready to kill him the moment I found him again. And I would have killed him, too, if not for Nest."

"John—"

"She told me it was you, Stef, and after I got past the initial shock that such a thing could possibly *be*, that I could have been fooled so *completely*, that I could have been so *stupid*, I began to realize what had happened. You were so clever, Stef. You used me right from the beginning. You let me approach you in Boston, played me like a fish on a line, and then reeled me in. I was hooked. I loved you. You made yourself so desirable and so accessible I couldn't help myself. I wanted to believe you were the beginning, the cornerstone, of a new life. I was through being a Knight of the Word; I wanted something else. You understood what that something was better than I did, and you gave it to me. You gave me the promise of a life with you.

"But you know, what really made it all work was that I couldn't imagine it wasn't real. Why would it be anything else? Why wouldn't you be exactly who you said you were? When Nest first suggested you might be the demon, I dismissed the idea out of hand. It made no sense. If you were the demon, why wouldn't you just kill me and be done with it? Of what possible use was I alive? A former Knight of the Word, an exile, a wanderer—I was just further proof you had made the right choice a long time ago when you embraced the Void."

She wasn't saying anything. She was just sitting there, listening attentively, waiting to see if he had really worked it out. He could tell it just by looking at her, by the way she was studying him. It infuriated him; it made him feel ashamed for the way he had allowed himself to be used.

"Nest figured it out, though," he continued. "She explained it to me. She said you saw me in the same way her father had seen her grandmother, when her grandmother was a young girl. Her father was drawn to her grandmother's magic, and you were drawn to mine. But demons need to possess humans, to take control of them in order to make the magic their own, and sometimes they mistake this need to possess for love. Their desire for the magic confuses them. I think maybe that's what happened to you."

"John—"

"No. Don't say a word to me. Just listen." His fingers knotted about his staff more tightly. "The fact remains, I was no good to you dead. Because if I were dead you couldn't make use of the magic trapped inside the staff. And you wanted that magic badly, didn't you? But to get it, you had to do two things. You had to find a way to persuade me to recover it from the dark place to which I had consigned it and then to use it in a way that would make me dependent on you. If I could be tricked into killing Simon Lawrence, if I could be made to use the magic in such a terribly wrong way, then I would share something in common with you, wouldn't I? I would have taken the first step down the path you had chosen for me. I was halfway there, wasn't I? I was already very nearly what you wanted me to be. You'd worked long and hard to break me down, to give me the identity you wanted. Only this one last thing remained."

He shook his head in amazement. "You killed that demon in Lincoln Park to protect your investment. Because it wanted me dead, so it could claim victory over a Knight of the Word. But you wanted me alive for something much grander. You wanted me for the magic I might place at your command."

She stared at him, her perfect features composed, still not moving. "I love you, John. Nothing you've said changes that."

"You love me, Stef? Enough that you might teach me to feed on homeless children, like you've been feeding on them?" He spit out the words as if they were tinged with poison. "Enough that you might let me help you hunt them down in the tunnels beneath the city and kill them?"

Her temper flared. "The homeless are of no use. No one cares what happens to them. They serve no real purpose. You know that."

"Do I?" He fought down his disgust. "Is that why you killed Ariel and Boot and Audrey? Because they didn't serve any real purpose either? Is that why you tried to kill Nest? That didn't work out so well, did it? But you were quick to cover up, I'll give you that. Burning down Fresh Start, that was a nice touch. I assumed at first that you burned it down just to undermine its programs. But you did it to hide the truth about what happened in Lincoln Park. You marked yourself up pretty good going after Nest, smashing down doors and hurtling through windows. You couldn't hide that kind of damage. So you killed two birds with one stone. You'd drugged me earlier so I wouldn't be able to meet Nest. When you woke me, after you'd set fire to Fresh Start, you did so in the dark so I couldn't see your face, and while I was still barely coherent, you ran on ahead on the pretext of waking the women and children sleeping on the upper floors on the building, thereby providing yourself with a perfect excuse for the cuts and bruises on your face and hands."

His laugh was brittle. "It's funny, but Nest figured that out, too. When she came looking for me, she stopped by Pass/Go, and Della told her she looked just like you. Nest got the connection immediately. She knew what it meant."

She leaned forward. "John, will you listen . . . ?"

But he was all done listening, and he pushed relentlessly on. "So you set me up with this story about Simon firing me, and you quitting, and how strangely he's been acting, and how every time something bad happens, he's among the missing, and I'm just like a loaded gun ready to go off. I take the bus down to the museum, which you know I'll do, and it takes me a while because I don't walk very well with my bad leg, and you catch a cab, and there you are, waiting, disguised as Simon, ready to point me in the right direction."

He was so angry now he could barely contain himself, but his voice stayed cool and detached. "I really hate you, Stef. I hate you so much I can't find the words to express it!"

She studied him a moment, her perfect features composed in thoughtful consideration, and then she shook her head at him. "You don't hate me, John. You love me. You always will."

His shock at hearing her say it left him momentarily speechless. He had not expected her to be so perceptive.

She was right, of course. He loved her desperately, even now, even knowing what she was.

"You aren't as honest with yourself as you think," she continued calmly, her dark eyes locking on his own. "You don't want any of this to be so, but even knowing it is, you can't get around how you feel. Is that so bad? If you want me, I'm still yours. I still want you, John. I still love you. Think about what you're doing. If you give me up, you become the thing you fought so hard to escape being. You become a Knight of the Word again. You give up everything you've found this past year with me. You go back to being solitary and lonely and rootless. You become like the homeless you've spent so much time trying to help."

She rose, a smooth, lazy motion, and he tensed in response, remembering how strong she was, what she was capable of doing. But she didn't try to approach him. "With me, you have everything that's made you happy these past twelve months. I can be all the things I've been to you from the beginning. Are you worried you might see me another way? Don't be. You never will. I'll be for you just what you want. I've made you happy. You can't pretend I haven't."

He smiled at her, suddenly sad beyond anything he had ever known. "You're right," he acknowledged softly, and all the rage seemed to dissipate. "You have made me happy. But none of it was real, was it, Stef? It was all a sham. I don't think I want to go back to that."

"Do you think other people live any differently than we do?" she pressed. She took a step away from the couch, then another, moving out of the circle of lamplight, edging into the shadows beyond. Ross watched, saying nothing. "Everyone keeps secrets. No one reveals everything. Even to a lover." He winced at the words, but she didn't seem to notice. She brushed back her hair, seemingly distracted by something behind him. He kept his eyes on her. "We can do the same," she said. "You won't ever find anyone else who feels about you the way I do."

The irony of that last statement must have escaped her entirely, he thought. "How you feel about me is rooted mostly in the ways you hope to use me, Stef."

He was moving with her now, a step and then two, a slow circling dance, a positioning for advantage.

"You can make your own choices about everything, John," she said. "I won't interfere. Just let me do the same. That's all I require."

His laugh was brittle. "Is that all it would take to make you happy, Stef? For me to ignore what you are? For me to let you go on feeding on humans? For me to pretend I don't care that you won't ever stop trying to turn the Word's magic to uses it was never intended for?" She was shaking her head violently in denial. "Just forget about the past? Forget about Boot and Audrey and Ariel and Ray Hapgood and several dozen homeless people? Forget about everything that's gone before? Would that do the trick?"

He saw a glimmer of something dark and wicked come into her eyes. He took a step toward her. "You crossed the line a long time ago, and it's way too late for you to come back. More to the point, I don't intend to let you try."

She was silhouetted against the bay window that looked down on Waterfall Park, her slender body gone suddenly still. Outside, feeders were pressed against the glass, yellow eyes gleaming.

There was a subtle shift in her features. "Maybe you can't stop me, John."

He straightened, clasping the staff in both hands, the magic racing up and down its length in slender silver threads.

Her smile was faint and tinged with regret. "Maybe you never could."

In a single, fluid motion she dropped into a crouch, wheeled away, and catapulted herself through the plate glass of the window behind her. Before he could even think to try to stop her, she had dropped from sight and was gone.

Nest Freemark was standing on the sidewalk outside Waterfall Park when the apartment window exploded as if struck by a sledgehammer, raining shards of glass into the night and sending feeders scattering into the shadows like rats. She turned toward the sound, her first thoughts of John Ross, but the dark thing that plummeted through the gloom was screaming in another voice entirely. Nest stood frozen in place, watching as it began to twist and re-form in midair, as if its flesh and bones were malleable. It had been human at first, but now it was something else entirely. It struck the jumble of rocks midpoint on the waterfall, bounced away, and tumbled into the catchment.

Nest raced for the narrow park entrance, her heartbeat quick and hurried and anxious. She burst through the ungated opening as the dark thing climbed free of the trough, a two-legged horror that was already losing what remained of its human identity, dropping down on all fours and shape-shifting into something more primal. Its legs thinned and lengthened and turned crooked, its torso thickened from haunches to chest, and its head grew elongated and broad-muzzled.

Stefanie Winslow, she thought in horror. The demon.

Re-formed into something that most closely resembled a monstrous hyena, the demon shook itself as if to be rid of the last of the disguise that had confined it and lifted its blunt snout toward the heights from which it had fallen. Feeders leaped and scrambled about it in a frenzy, like shadows flowing over one another, eyes bright against the dark. The demon snarled at them, snapped at the air through which they passed, and started to turn away.

Then it caught sight of Nest and wheeled quickly back again.

Even in the scattered light of the street lamps, Nest could see the hard glitter of its eyes fix on her. She could see the hate in them. The big head lowered, the muzzle parted, and rows of hooked teeth came into view. A low-pitched, ugly snarl rose from its throat. Maybe it intended to finish what it had started in Lincoln Park. Maybe it was just reacting on instinct. Nest held her ground. She felt her magic gather and knot in her chest. She had fled from this monster once; this time she would stand and face it. The demon, it seemed, had made up its mind as well. It could have turned away from her, could have scaled the park fence and escaped without forcing a confrontation. But it never wavered in its approach.

In a scrabbling of claws on stone and with a bone-chilling howl, it attacked. Feeders converged in its wake, leaping and darting through the shadows in a wave of yellow eyes. Nest had only a moment to react, and she did so. She locked eyes with the demon and threw out the magic she had been born with, her legacy from the

Freemark women, thinking to stun it, to throw it off stride, to cause it to falter. She need only delay it long enough for John Ross to reach her. He would be coming; the demon was clearly in flight from him. A few moments was all she needed, and her magic would give her that. She had used it on Simon Lawrence and the security guards at the museum not two hours earlier. It was an old and familiar companion, and she could feel its presence stir deep inside even before she called it forth.

Even so, she wasn't prepared for what happened next.

The magic she had called upon did not respond.

Another magic did.

It came from the same place as the magic she had been born to, from inside, where her soul resided in a conjoining of heart and mind and body. It exploded out of her in a rush of dark energy, taking its own distinctive form, unleashed by instincts that demanded she survive at any cost. Its power was raw and terrifying, and she could not control it. It did not release from her as she had expected, but swept her along, borne within its storm-racked center, and it was as if she were caught inside a whirlwind.

She was seeing the demon now through darker, more primitive eyes, and she realized suddenly, shockingly, that those eyes belonged to Wraith. She was trapped inside the ghost wolf. She had become a part of him.

Then she was hurtling into the demon, with no time left to think. Claws and teeth ripped and tore, and snarls filled the air, and she was fighting the demon as if become Wraith, herself grown massive through the shoulders and torso, rough-coated with fur, gimlet-eyed and lupine.

Back against the rocks she drove the demon, steeped

in the ghost wolf's strength and swift reactions. The demon
twisted and fought, intertwined so closely with her she
could feel the bunching of its muscles and hear the hissing
of its breath. The demon tried to gain a grip on her throat,
failed, and leaped away. She gave pursuit, a red veil of
hot rage and killing need blinding her to everything else.
They rolled and tumbled through the wrought-iron furni-
ture, against the maze of rocks and fountains, and she no
longer thought to wonder what was happening or why,
but only to gain an advantage over a foe she knew she
must destroy.

Perhaps she would have succeeded. Perhaps she would
have prevailed. But then she heard her name called. A
sharp cry, it was filled with despair and anguish.

John Ross had reached her at last.

White fire lashed the air in front of her, turning her
aside. But the fire was not meant for her. It struck the
demon full on, a rope of searing flame, and threw it
backward to land in a bristling heap. She caught sight
of Ross now, standing just inside the park entrance, his
legs braced, the black staff bright with magic. Again
the fire lanced from the Knight of the Word into the
demon, catching it as it tried to twist away, knocking it
down once more. Ross advanced, his face all planes
and sharp edges, etched deep with shadows and grim
determination.

The demon fought back. It counterattacked with a
stunning burst of speed and fury, snapping at the scorched
night air. But the Word's magic hammered into it over
and over, knocking it back, flinging it away. Ross closed
the distance between himself and his adversary, ignoring
Nest, his concentration centered on the demon. The
demon wailed suddenly, as if become human again, a cry

so desperate and affecting that Nest cringed. Ross screamed in response, perhaps to fight against the feelings the cry generated somewhere back in the dark closets of his heart, perhaps simply in fury. He went to where the demon lay broken and writhing, a thing barely recognizable by now. It was trying to change again, to become something else—perhaps the thing Ross had loved so much. But Ross would not allow it. The black staff came down, and the magic surged forth, splitting the demon asunder, ripping it from neck to knee.

Feeders swarmed over it, rending and digging hungrily. The winged black thing that formed its twisted soul tried to break free from the carnage, but Ross was waiting. With a single sweep of his staff, he sent it spinning into the darkness, a tiny, flaming comet trailing fire and fading life.

What remained of the demon collapsed on itself and scattered in the wind. Even when the last of its ashes had blown away, John Ross stayed where he was, silhouetted against the shimmer of the waterfall, staring down at the dark smear that marked its passing.

THURSDAY,
NOVEMBER 1

CHAPTER 25

It was a little after ten-thirty the following morning when Andrew Wren walked into the offices of Pass/Go, announced himself to the receptionist, and was told Simon Lawrence would see him. He thanked her, advised her that he knew the way, and started back. He proceeded down the hall past the classrooms and offices, contemplating a collage of children's finger paintings that decorated one section of a sun-splashed wall. He was dressed in his corduroy jacket with the patches at the elbows and had worn a scarf and gloves against the November chill. He carried his old leather briefcase in one hand and a newsboy cap in the other. His cherubic face was unshaved, and his hair was uncombed. He had overslept and been forced to forgo the niceties of personal grooming and had simply pulled on his clothes and headed out. As a result, he looked not altogether different from some of the men standing in the soup line at Union Gospel Mission up the street.

Rumpled and baggy, he shuffled through the doorway of the Wiz's cramped office and gave a brief wave of his hand. "Got any coffee, Simon?"

Simon Lawrence was immersed in paperwork, but he gestured wordlessly toward a chair stacked with books, then picked up the phone to call out to the front desk to fill Wren's order and one of his own.

Wren cleared the chair he had been offered and sat down heavily. "I watched you perform for the assembled last night with something approaching awe. Meeting all those people, shaking hands, answering questions, offering prognostications, being pleasant. To tell you the truth, I don't know how you do it. I couldn't possibly keep up the kind of pace you do and stay sane."

"Well, I don't do it every night, Andrew." Simon stretched and leaned back in his chair. He gave Wren a suspicious look. "I'm almost afraid to ask, but what brings you by this time?"

Wren managed to look put upon. "I wanted to see how you were, for one thing. No more episodes, I hope?"

The other man spread his hands. "I still don't know what happened. One moment I was standing there on the stairs, talking with Carole and those workers from Union Gospel, and the next I was down on the floor. I just seemed to lose all my strength. I'm scheduled to see a doctor about it this afternoon, but I don't think it's anything more than stress and a lack of sleep."

Wren nodded. "I wouldn't be surprised. Anyway, I also wanted to congratulate you on last night. It was a huge success, as you know. The gift of the land from the city, the offer of additional funding, the pledges of support from virtually every quarter. You should be very pleased about that."

Simon Lawrence sighed, arching one eyebrow. "About that, yes, I'm very pleased. It helps take the edge off a few of the less pleasant aspects of the day's events."

"Hmmm," Wren murmured solemnly. "Speaking of which, have you seen her today?"

Simon didn't have to ask who he was referring to. "No, and I don't think I'm going to. Not today or any other. I went by her apartment early this morning, thinking I might surprise her with the news, but she was gone. Her clothes, luggage, personal effects, everything. The door to the apartment was wide open, so I had no trouble getting in. At first I thought something might have happened to her. A chair had been thrown through the living room window. It was lying down in the park with pieces of glass all over the place. But nothing else in the apartment seemed disturbed. There was no sign of any kind of violence having occurred. I called the police anyway."

Wren studied him thoughtfully. "Do you think she suspected we were onto her?"

Simon shook his head. "I don't see how. You and I were the only ones who knew the lab results—and I didn't know until after the dedication, when you told me." He paused, reflecting. "I tell you, Andrew, I'd never have guessed it was her. Not in a million years. Stefanie Winslow. I still can't believe it."

"Well, the handwriting analysis of the signatures on the deposit slips were pretty conclusive." Wren paused. "Why do you think she did it, Simon?"

Simon Lawrence shrugged. "I can't begin to answer that question. You'll have to ask her, if she ever resurfaces from wherever she's gone to ground."

"Maybe John Ross can tell us something."

Simon pursed his lips sourly. "He's gone, too. He left this. It was on my desk when I came into work this morning, tucked into an envelope."

He reached into his desk and produced a single sheet of white paper with a handwritten note. He handed it to

Wren, who pushed up his glasses on the bridge of his
nose and began to read.

Dear Simon,

I regret that I am unable to deliver this in person,
but by the time you read it I will already be far away.
Please do not think badly of me for not staying.
I am not responsible for the thefts that occurred
at Fresh Start. Stefanie Winslow is. I wish I could
tell you why. As it is, I feel that even though all the
money will be returned, my continued involvement
with your programs will simply complicate matters.
I will not forget the cause you have championed so
successfully and will endeavor in some small way to
carry on your work wherever I go.

I am enclosing a letter authorizing transfer back
to Fresh Start of all funds improperly deposited to
my accounts.

John

Wren looked up speculatively. "Well, well."
The coffee arrived, delivered by a young volunteer,
and the two men accepted the cups and sat sipping at the
hot brew in the silence that followed the intern's
departure.
"I think he was as fooled as the rest of us," the Wiz
said finally.
Wren nodded. "Could be. Anyway, there's no one left
who can tell us now, is there?"
Simon put down his coffee cup and sighed. "If you
want to have dinner tonight, I can try to fill you in on the

details of this mess so you can keep your article for the *Times* as accurate as possible."

Wren smiled, relinquished his own cup, and rose to his feet. "I can't do that, Simon. I'm flying out this afternoon, back to the Big Apple. Besides, the article's already written. I finished it at two this morning or something like that."

The Wiz looked confused. "But what about . . ."

Wren held up one chubby hand, assuming his most professional look. "Did you get all the money transferred back to Fresh Start out of Ross's accounts?"

Simon nodded.

"And your own?"

Simon nodded again. "First thing this morning."

"Then it's a story with a happy ending, and I think we ought to leave it at that. No one wants to read about a theft of charitable funds where the money is recovered and the thief is a nobody. It doesn't sell papers. The real story here is about a man whose vision and hard work have produced a small miracle—the opening of a city's stone heart and padlocked purse in support of a cause that might not gain a single politician a single vote in the next election. Besides, what point is there in writing about something that would serve no other purpose than to muddy up such beautiful, pristine waters?"

Andrew Wren picked up his briefcase and donned his cloth cap. "Someday, I'll be back for the story of your life. The real story, the one you won't talk about just yet. Meantime, go back to work on what matters. Just remember, for the record, you owe me one, Simon."

Then he walked out the door, leaving the Wizard of Oz staring after him in bemused wonder.

*   *   *

Nest Freemark spent the first day of November traveling. After spending another night at the Alexis, she caught a midmorning flight to Chicago, which arrived shortly before four in the afternoon. She had debated returning to Northwestern for the one remaining day of the school week and quickly abandoned the idea. She was tired, jittery, and haunted by the events of the past few days, and not fit company for herself, let alone anyone else. Her studies and her training would have to wait.

Instead, she chartered a car to pick her up at the airport and drive her to Hopewell. What she needed most, she decided, was to just go home.

She slept most of the way there, on the airplane and in the car, curled up in the warmth of her parka, drifting in and out of a light, uneasy sleep that mixed dreams with memories, so that by the time her journey was over, with daylight gone and darkness returned, with Seattle behind her and Hopewell at hand, they seemed very much the same.

Nest, as a part of Wraith, as a part of a magic different from anything she knew, returned slowly to herself on the empty walkway in Waterfall Park. She felt the magic withdraw and her vision change. She felt Wraith slip silently away on the night breeze. She stood swaying in the wake of his departure, feeling as if she had returned from a long journey. She drew in deep gulps of air, the cold burning down into her lungs, sending a rush of adrenaline through her body and sharp-edged clarity to her dizzied head.

Oh, my God, my God! she whispered soundlessly, and

she hugged herself against the first onslaught of willful despair.

John Ross turned from the demon's remains and limped to her side. He reached for her, drew her into the cradle of his arms, and held her close. Nest, it's all right, he whispered into her hair, stroking it softly, comfortingly. It's all over. It's finished.

Did you see? Did you see what happened? She gasped, broke down, and could not finish.

He nodded quickly. I know. I saw it begin at the museum. It didn't happen there, but I saw that it could. Wraith is inside you, Nest. You said he just walked into you and was gone, that last time you saw him. It's like Pick said. Magic doesn't just cease to exist. It takes another form. It becomes something else. Don't you see? Wraith has become a part of you.

She was shaking now, enraged and despairing. But I don't want him inside me! He's got nothing to do with me! He belongs to my father! Her head jerked up violently. John, what if my father's come back to claim me? What if Wraith is some part of him trying to reach out to me still!

No, no, he said at once, holding her away from him, bracing her shoulders with his strong hands. He released the black staff, and it clattered to the concrete. His eyes held her own. Listen to me, Nest. Wraith wasn't your father's. He was never that. He saved you from your father, remember? Gran made him over with her own magic to protect you. He was yours. He belonged to you.

The lean, weathered face bent close. Perhaps he's only done what he was supposed to do. When you became of age and strong enough to look after yourself, perhaps his job as your protector was finished. Where does magic go

*when it has served its purpose and not been fully ex-
pended? It goes back to its owner. To serve as needed.*

So maybe, he whispered, Wraith has just come home.

She spent every waking moment of her journey back
to Hopewell wrestling with that concept. Wraith had
come home. To her. To become part of her. The idea was
terrifying. It left her grappling with the prospect that at
any moment she might jump out of her skin. Literally. It
made her feel as if she were a character out of *Alien*,
waiting for that repulsive little head to thrust out of her
stomach, all teeth and blood.

But the image was wrongly conceived, and after a
while it diminished and faded, giving way to a more
practical concern. How could she control this newfound
magic? It didn't seem as if she had done much of a job so
far. What was to prevent it from reappearing again
without warning, from jeopardizing her in ways she
couldn't even begin to imagine?

Then she realized this image was wrongheaded, as
well, that Wraith's magic had lived inside her for a long
time before it had surfaced. What had triggered its appearance last night was the presence of other magic, first
the magic of John Ross and then the magic of the demon.
She remembered how strangely she had felt that first day
at Fresh Start, then later that night in Lincoln Park, both
times when she was in close proximity to the demon. She
hadn't understood that it was Wraith's magic, threatening to break free. But in each instance, his magic was
simply responding to the perceived threat another magic
offered.

Realizing that gave her some comfort, but she still
struggled with the idea that the big ghost wolf was
locked inside her—not just as magic, but as the creature

in which the magic had been lodged. Why did it still exist in that form?

It wasn't until she was almost home, the lights of the first cluster of outlying residences breaking through the evening darkness, that she decided she might still be misreading things. In the absence of direction, magic took the form with which it was most familiar. It didn't act independently of its user. Pick had taught her that a long time ago, when he was instructing her on the care of the park. If Wraith had still been whole, still her shadow protector, he would have come to her defense instinctively. It was not strange to think that bereft of form and independent existence, his magic would still do so. After all, the magic had been given to her in the first place, hadn't it? And in making its unexpected appearance, absent any direction from her, was it surprising it would assume the same form it had occupied for so many years?

What was harder for her to reconcile, she discovered, was that in seeking its release it had required her to become one with it.

She rode through the streets of Hopewell, slumped in the darkness of the car's rear seat, curled into the cushions like a rag doll, looking out at the night. She would be a long time coming to terms with this, she knew.

She found herself wondering, somewhat perversely, if the Lady had known about Wraith in sending her to John Ross. She wondered if she had been sent with the expectation that in aiding Ross she would discover this new truth about herself. It was not inconceivable. Any contact with a strong magic would have released Wraith from his safehold inside her. Knowledge of his continued existence was something Nest would have had to come to grips with sooner or later. The Lady might have believed it was better she do so now.

As they passed the Menards and the Farm and Fleet, she gave the driver directions to her house. She sat contemplating the tangled threads of her life, of what was known and what was not, until the car turned into her driveway and parked. She climbed out, retrieved her bag, signed the driver's receipt, said good-bye, and walked into the house.

It was dark and silent inside, but the smells and shadows of the hallways and rooms were familiar and welcome. She turned on some lights, dropped her bags in the living room, and walked back to the kitchen to fix herself a sandwich from a jar of peanut butter and last week's bread.

She sat eating at the kitchen table, where Gran had spent most of her time in her last years, and she thought of John Ross. She wondered where he was. She wondered how much success he was having at coming to terms with the truths in his life. He had not said much when they parted. He thanked her, standing there in the shadowy confines of Waterfall Park, his breath billowing out in smoky clouds as the cold deepened. He would never forget what she had done for him. He hoped she could forgive him for what he had done to her, five years earlier. She said there was nothing to forgive. She told him she was sorry about Stefanie. She told him she knew a little of how he must feel. He smiled at that. If anyone did, it was she, he agreed.

Did he feel trapped by being what he was? What was it like to be a Knight of the Word and realize your life could never change?

She had not told him of Two Bears. Of the reason O'olish Amaneh had come to Seattle for Halloween. Of the terrible responsibility the last of the Sinnissippi bore for having given him the Word's magic.

She finished the sandwich and a glass of milk and carried her dishes to the sink. The contracts for the sale of the house still sat on the kitchen counter. She glanced down at them, picked them up, and carried them to the table. She sat down again and read them through carefully. In the hallway, the grandfather clock ticked steadily. When she was finished reading, she set the contracts down in front of her and stared off into space.

What we have in life that we can count our own is who we are and where we come from, she thought absently. For better or worse, that's what we have to sustain us in our endeavors, to buttress us in our darker moments, and to remind us of our identity. Without those things, we are adrift.

Her gaze shifted to the darkness outside the kitchen window. John Ross must feel that way now. He must feel that way every day of his life. It was what he gave up when he became a Knight of the Word. It was what he lost when he discovered the truth about Stefanie Winslow.

She listened to the silence that backdropped the ticking of the clock. After a long time, she picked up the real estate contracts, walked to the garbage can, and dropped them in.

Moving to the phone, she dialed Robert at Stanford. She listened to four rings, and then his voice mail picked up.

At the beep, she said, "Hey, Robert, it's me." She was still looking out the window into the dark. "I just wanted to let you know that I'm home again. Call me. Bye."

She hung up, stood looking around her at the house for

a moment, then walked back down the hallway, pulled on her parka, and went out into the cold, crisp autumn night to find Pick.

It was just after four in the morning when John Ross woke from his dream. He lay staring into the empty blackness of his room for a long time, his breathing and his heartbeat slowing as he came back to himself. On the street outside his open window, he could hear a truck rumble by.

It was the first dream he had experienced since he had resumed being a Knight of the Word. As always, it was a dream of the future that would come to pass if he failed to change things in the present. But it felt new because it was his first such dream in a long time.

Except for the dream of the old man and the Wizard of Oz, of course, but he did not think he would be having that dream anymore.

He closed his eyes momentarily to gather his thoughts, to let the tension and the fury of this night's dream ease. In the dream, he had been stripped of his magic, as he knew he would be, because he had chosen to expend his magic in the present, and when he made that choice, the price was always the same: For the span of one night's sleep, there was no magic to protect him in the future. He often wondered how long the loss of magic lasted in real time. He could not tell, for he was given only a glimpse of what was to be before he came awake. If he used the magic often enough in the present, he sometimes wondered, would he at some point lose the use of it completely in the future?

His eyes opened, and he exhaled slowly.

In his dream, he had run through woods at the edge of a nameless town. He had a vague sense of being hunted by his enemies, of being tracked like an animal. He had a sense of being at extreme risk, bereft of any real protection, exposed to attack from all quarters without being able to offer a defense, at a loss as to where he might go to gain safety. He moved swiftly through the darkened trees, using stealth and silence to aid him in his flight. He tried to make himself one with the landscape in which he sought to hide. He burrowed into the earth along ditches and ravines, crawled through brush and long grasses, and edged from trunk to trunk, pressing himself so closely to the terrain he traversed that he could feel and smell its detritus on his skin. There was a river, and he swam it. There were cornfields, and he crept down their rows as if navigating a maze that, if misread, would trap him for all time.

He did not see or hear his pursuers, but he knew they were back there. They would always be back there.

When he awoke in the present, he was still running to stay alive in the future.

He rose now and picked up the black staff from where it lay beside the bed. He limped over to the window, leaning heavily on the staff, and stood for a time looking down at the street. He was in Portland. He had come down on the train early this morning and spent the day walking the riverfront and the streets of the city. When he was so tired he could no longer stay awake, he had taken this room.

Thoughts of Stefanie Winslow crowded suddenly into the forefront of his mind. He let them push forward, unhindered. Less painful now than yesterday, they would be less painful still tomorrow. It was odd, but he still thought of her as human, maybe because it made thinking of her at all more bearable. Memories of a year's time spent with someone you loved couldn't be expunged all at once. The memories, he found, were bittersweet and haunting. They marked a rite of passage he could not ignore. If not for Stefanie, he would have no sense of what his life might have been were he not a Knight of the Word. And in an odd sort of way, he was better off for knowing. It gave him perspective on the worth of what he was doing by revealing what he had given up.

He studied the empty street as if it held answers he could not otherwise find. He might have been a decent sort of man in an ordinary life. He might have done well over the years working with Simon Lawrence on the programs at Fresh Start and Pass/Go. He might have made a difference in the lives of other people.

But never the kind of difference he would make as a Knight of the Word.

His eyes drifted from empty doorway to empty doorway, through shadows and lights. He had been wrong in thinking that successes alone were the measure of his worth in the Word's service. He had been wrong in fleeing his mistakes as if they marked him a failure. It was not as simple as that. All men and women experienced successes and failures, and their tally at death was not necessarily determinative of one's worth in life. This was true, as well, for a Knight of the Word. It was trying that mattered more. It was the giving of effort and heart that lent value. It was the making of sacrifices. Ray Hapgood had said it best. Someone has to take responsibility. Someone has to be there.

That was the real reason he was a Knight of the Word.

Such a hard lesson, in retrospect, but Stefanie Winslow had taught him well the price for not understanding it.

He thought back to last night. When he left Nest, he had gone back up to the apartment to write Simon a short note of explanation and a letter of authorization for transfer of the misplaced funds. He had packed his duffel bag, then packed Stefanie's suitcases, removing everything of a personal nature from the apartment. Tossing the wooden desk chair out the window to provide an explanation for the glass breakage had been an afterthought. He had taken the note and authorization, put them in an envelope, and carried them over to Pass/Go.

Then he had gone down to the train station with his duffel and Stefanie's bags in hand to wait for the six-ten commuter. When he reached Portland, he disembarked and dumped Stefanie's bags in a Dumpster not a block away from the station.

He turned away from the window and looked around the little room. He wondered how Nest Freemark was doing. She had come to Seattle to help him, to give him a chance he might not otherwise have gotten, and it had cost her a great deal. He was sorry for that, but he did not think it his fault. The Lady had sent her, knowing to some extent the likely result. The Lady had placed her in a dangerous situation, knowing she would be forced to use her magic and would discover the truth about Wraith. It would have happened at another time in another place if not here. And it had saved his life. It did not make him feel better knowing this. But recognizing truths seldom achieved that result anyway.

He thought about how much alike they were, both of them gifted with magic that dominated their lives, both of them pressed into service by an entity they would never fully understand or perhaps ever satisfy. They were outsiders in a world that lacked any real comprehension of their service, and they would struggle on mostly alone and largely unappreciated until their lives were ended.

There was one glaring difference, of course. In his case, the choice to be what he was had been his. In hers, it had not.

He went into the bathroom, showered and shaved, and came out again and dressed in the light of the bedside lamp. When he was finished, he packed his duffel bag. He went downstairs to the lobby, dropped his key on the desk, and walked out.

Sunrise was brightening the eastern sky, a faint, soft glow against the departing night. The day was just beginning. By nightfall, John Ross would be in another town, looking to make a change in the way the world was going. His dreams would begin to tell him again what he could do that would make a difference.

It wasn't the worst sort of way to live one's life. In his case, he concluded hopefully, perhaps it was the best.

ANGEL FIRE EAST
by Terry Brooks

As a Knight of the Word, John Ross has struggled against
the tireless dark forces of the Void for twenty-five years.
But for all his power, John Ross is only one man, while the
demons he hunts—and which hunt him in turn—are legion.

Then Ross learns of the birth of a gypsy morph, a rare and
dangerous creature formed of wild magics spontaneously
knit together. If he can discover its secret, the morph could
be an invaluable weapon against the Void. But the Void,
too, knows the value of the morph, and will not rest until
the creature has been corrupted—or destroyed.

Desperate, Ross returns to the town of Hopewell, Illinois,
home of Nest Freemark. Together they must face an
ancient evil beyond anything they have ever encountered.
As a firestorm of good and evil erupts, threatening to consume lives and shatter dreams, Ross and Nest have but a
single chance to solve the mystery of the gypsy morph—
and of their own profound connection.

*He stands at the edge of a barren and ravaged orchard look-
ing up from the base of a gentle rise to where the man hangs
from a wooden cross. Iron spikes have been hammered
through the man's hands and feet, and his wrists and ankles
have been lashed tightly in place so he will not tear free. Slash
wounds crisscross his broken body, and he bleeds from a deep
puncture in his side. His head droops in the shadow of his long,
lank hair, and the rise and fall of his chest as he breathes is
shallow and weak.*

*Behind him, serving as a poignant backdrop to the travesty
of his dying, stands the fire-blackened shell of a tiny, burned-
out country church. The cross from which the man hangs has
been stripped from the sanctuary, torn free from the metal
brackets that secured it to the wall behind the altar, and set
into the earth. Patches of polished oak glisten faintly in the
gray daylight, attesting to the importance it was once
accorded in the worshipping of God.*

*Somewhere in the distance, back where the little town that
once supported this church lies, screams rise up against the
unmistakable sounds of butchery.*

*John Ross stands motionless for the longest time, pondering
the implications of the horrific scene before him. There is
nothing he can do for the man on the cross. He is not a doctor;
he does not possess medical skills. His magic can heal and sustain only himself and no other. He is a Knight of the Word, but
he is a failure, too. He lives out his days alone in a future he
could not prevent. What he looks upon is not unusual in the
postapocalyptic horror of civilization's demise, but is sadly
familiar and disturbingly mundane.*

*He can take the man down, he decides finally, even if he
cannot save him. By his presence, Ross can give the man a
small measure of peace and comfort.*

*Beneath a wintry sky that belies the summer season, he
strides up the rise to the man on the cross. The man does not
lift his head or stir in any way that would indicate he knows
Ross is present. Beneath a sheen of sweat and blood, his lean,
muscular body is marked with old wounds and scars. He has
endured hardships and abuse somewhere in his past, and it*

seems unfair that he should end his days in still more pain and desolation.

Ross slows as he nears, his eyes drifting across the blackened facade of the church and the trees surrounding it. Eyes glimmer in the shadows, revealing the presence of feeders. They hover at the fringes of his vision and in the concealment of sunless corners, waiting to assuage their hunger. They do not wait for Ross. They wait for the man on the cross. They wait for him to die, so they can taste his passing from life into death—the most exquisite, fulfilling, and rare of the human emotions they crave.

Ross stares at them until the light dims in their lantern eyes and they slip back into darkness to bide their time.

A shattered length of wood catches the Knight's attention, and his eyes shift to the foot of the cross. The remains of a polished black staff lie before him—a staff like the one he carries in his hands. A shock goes through him. He stares closely, unable to believe what he has discovered. There must be a mistake, he thinks. There must be another explanation.

But there is neither. Like himself, the man on the cross is a Knight of the Word.

He moves quickly now, striding forward to help, to lower the cross, to remove the spikes, to free the man who hangs helplessly before him.

But the man senses him now and in a ragged, whispery voice says, Don't touch me.

Ross stops instantly, the force of the other's words and the surprise of his consciousness bringing him to a halt.

They have poisoned me, the other says.

Ross draws a long, slow breath and exhales in weary recognition: Those who have crucified this Knight of the Word have coated him in a poison conjured of demon magic. He is without hope.

Ross steps back, looking up at the Knight on the cross, at the slow, shallow rise and fall of his breast, at the rivulets of blood leaking from his wounds, at the shadow of his face, still concealed within the curtain of his long hair.

They caught me when I did not have my magic to protect

me, the stricken Knight says softly. I had expended it all on an effort to escape them earlier. I could not replenish it quickly enough. Sensing I was weak, they gave chase. They hunted me down. Demons and once-men, a small army hunting pockets of resistance beyond the protection of the city fortresses. They found me hiding in the town below. They dragged me here and hung me on this cross to die. Now they kill all those who tried to help me.

Ross finds his attention drawn once more to the shrieks that come from the town. They are beginning to fade, to drain away into a deep, ominous silence.

I have not done well in my efforts to save mankind, the Knight whispers. He gasps and chokes on the dryness in his throat. Blood bubbles to his lips and runs down his chin to his chest.

Nor have any of us, Ross says.

There were chances. There were times when we might have made a difference.

Ross sighs. *We did with them what we could.*

A bird's soft warble wafts through the trees. Black smoke curls skyward from the direction of the town, rife with the scent of human carnage.

Perhaps you were sent to me.

Ross turns from the smoke to look again at the man on the cross, not understanding.

Perhaps the Word sent you to me. A final chance at redemption.

No one sent me, Ross thinks, but does not speak the words.

You will wake in the present and go on. I will die-here. You will have a chance to make a difference still. I will not.

No one sent me, Ross says quickly now, suddenly uneasy.

But the other is not listening. In late fall, three days after Thanksgiving, once long ago, when I was on the Oregon coast, I captured a gypsy morph.

His words wheeze from his mouth, coated in the sounds of his dying. But as he speaks, his voice seems to gain intensity.

It is my greatest regret, that I found it, so rare, so precious, made it my own, and could not solve the mystery of its magic. The chance of a lifetime, and I let it slip away.

The man on the cross goes silent then, gasping slowly for breath, fighting to stay alive just a few moments longer, broken and shattered within and without, left in his final moments to contemplate the failures he perceives are his. Eyes reappear in the shadows of the burned-out church and blighted orchard, the feeders beginning to gather in anticipation. Ross can scorch the earth with their gnarled bodies, can strew their cunning eyes like leaves in the wind, but it will all be pointless. The feeders are a part of life, of the natural order of things, and you might as well decide there is no place for humans either, for it is the humans who draw the feeders and sustain them.

The Knight of the Word who hangs from the cross is speaking again, telling him of the gypsy morph, of how and when and where it will be found, of the chance Ross might have of finding it again. He is giving Ross the details, preparing him for the hunt, thinking to give another the precious opportunity that he has lost. But he is giving Ross the chance to fail as well, and it is on that alone that his listener settles in black contemplation.

Do this for me if you can, the man whispers, his voice beginning to fail him completely, drying up with the draining away of his life, turning parched and sandy in his throat. Do it for yourself.

Ross feels the implications of the stricken Knight's charge razor through him. If he undertakes so grave and important a mission, if he embraces so difficult a cause, it may be his own undoing.

Yet, how can he do otherwise?

Promise me.

The words are thin and weak and empty of life. Ross stares in silence at the man.

Promise me . . .

John Ross awoke with sunshine streaming down on his face and the sound of children's voices ringing in his ears. The air was hot and sticky, and the smell of fresh turned earth and new leaves rose on a sudden breeze. He blinked and sat up. He was hitchhiking west through Pennsylvania, and he had stopped at a park outside Allentown to rest, then fell asleep beneath the canopy of an old hardwood. He had thought only to doze for a few minutes, but he hadn't slept well in days, and the lack of sleep had finally caught up to him.

He gazed around slowly to regain his bearings. The park was large and thickly wooded, and he had chosen a spot well back from the roads and playgrounds to rest. He was alone. He looked down at his backpack and duffel bag, then at the polished black staff in his hands. His throat was dry and his head ached. A spot deep in his chest burned with the fury of hot coals.

His dream shimmered in a haze of sunlight just before his eyes, images from a private hell.

He was a Knight of the Word, living one life in the present and another in the future, one while awake and another while asleep, one in which he was given a chance to change the world and another in which he must live forever with the consequences of his failure to do so. He had accepted the charge almost twenty-five years ago and had lived with it ever since. He had spent almost the whole of his adult life engaged in a war that had begun with the inception of life and would not end until its demise. There were no boundaries to the battlefield on which he fought—neither of space nor of time. There could be no final resolution.

But the magic of a gypsy morph could provide leverage of a sort that could change everything.

He reached in his backpack and brought forth a battered water bottle. Removing the cap, he drank deeply from its lukewarm contents, finding momentary relief for the dryness in his throat and mouth. He had trouble fitting the cap in place again. The dream had shaken him. His dreams did so often, for they were of a world in which madness ruled and horror was commonplace. There was hope in the present of his waking, but none in the future of his sleep.

Still, this dream was different.

He climbed to his feet, strapped the backpack in place,

picked up the duffel bag, and walked back through the park toward the two-lane blacktop that wound west toward Pittsburgh. As always, the events of his dream would occur soon in his present, giving him a chance to affect them in a positive way. It was June. The gypsy morph would be born three days after Thanksgiving. If he was present and if he was quick enough, he would be able to capture it.

Then he would have roughly thirty days to change the course of history.

That challenge would have shaken any man, but it was not the challenge of the gypsy morph that haunted Ross as he walked from the park to begin his journey west. It was his memory of the man on the cross in his dream, the fallen Knight of the Word. It was the man's face as it had lifted from the shadow of his long hair in the final moments of his life.

For the face of the man hanging on the cross had been his own.

* * *

Sunday, December 21

Nest Freemark had just finished dressing for church when she heard the knock at the front door. She paused in the middle of applying her mascara at the bathroom mirror, and glanced over her shoulder, thinking she might have been mistaken, that she wasn't expecting anyone and it was early on a Sunday morning for visitors to come around without calling first.

She went back to applying her makeup. A few minutes later the knock came again.

She grimaced, then glanced quickly at her watch for confirmation. Sure enough. Eight forty-five. She put down her mascara, straightened her dress, and checked her appearance in the mirror. She was tall, a shade under five-ten, lean, and fit, with a distance runner's long legs, narrow hips, and small waist. She had seemed gangly and bony all through her early teens, except when she ran, but she had finally grown into her body. At twenty-nine, she moved with an easy, fluid model's grace that belied the strength and endurance she had acquired and maintained through years of rigorous training.

She studied herself in the mirror with the same frank, open stare she gave everyone. Her green eyes were wide-set beneath arched brows in her round, smooth Charlie Brown face. Her cinnamon hair was cut short and curled tightly about her head, framing the small, even features of her face. People told her all the time she was pretty, but she never quite believed them. Her friends had known her all her life and were inclined to be generous in their assessments. Strangers were just being polite.

Still, she told herself with more than a trace of irony, fluffing her hair into place, you never know when Prince Charming will come calling. Best to be ready so you don't lose out.

She left the mirror and the bathroom and walked through her bedroom to the hall beyond. She had been up since five-thirty, running on the mostly empty roads that stretched from Sinnissippi Park east to Moonlight Bay. Winter had set in a month before with the first serious snowfall, but the snow had melted during a warm spot a week ago, and there had been no further accumulation. Patches of sooty white still lay in the darker, shadowy parts of the woods and in the culverts and ditches where the snowplows had pushed them, but the blacktop of the country roads was dry and clear. She did five miles, then showered, fixed herself breakfast, ate, and dressed. She was due in church to help in the nursery at nine-thirty, and whoever it was who had come calling would have to be quick.

She passed the aged black-and-white tintypes and photographs of the women of her family, their faces severe and spare in the aged wooden picture frames, backdropped by the dark webbing of trunks and limbs of the park trees. Gwendolyn Wills, Carolyn Glynn, and Opal Anders. Her grandmother's picture was there, too. Nest had added it after Gran's death. She had chosen an early picture, one in which Evelyn Freemark appeared youthful and raw and wild, hair all tousled, eyes filled with excitement and promise. That was the way Nest liked to remember Gran. It spoke to the strengths and weaknesses that had defined Gran's life.

Nest scanned the group as she went down the hallway, admiring the resolve in their eyes. The Freemark women, she liked to call them. All had entered into the service of the Word, partnering themselves with Pick to help the sylvan keep in balance the strong, core magic that existed in the park. All had been born with magic of their own, though not all had managed it well. She thought briefly of the dark secrets her grandmother had kept, of the deceptions Gran had employed in the workings of her own magic, and of the price she had paid for doing so.

Her mother's picture was missing from the group. Caitlin Anne Freemark had been too fragile for the magic's demands. She had died young, just after Nest was born, a victim of her demon lover's treachery. Nest kept her pictures on a table in the living room, where it was always sunlit and cheerful.

The knock came a third time just as she reached the door and opened it. The tiny silver bells that encircled the bough wreath that hung beneath the peephole tinkled softly with the movement. She had not done much with Christmas decorations—no tree, no lights, no tinsel, only fresh greens, a scattering of brightly colored bows, and a few wall hangings that had belonged to Gran. This year Christmas would be celebrated mostly in her heart.

The chill, dry winter air was sharp and bracing as she unlatched the storm door, pushed it away, and stepped out onto the porch.

The old man who stood waiting was dressed all in black. He was wearing what in other times would have been called a frock coat, which was double-breasted with wide lapels and hung to his knees. A flat-brimmed black hat sat firmly in place over wisps of white hair that stuck out from underneath as if trying to escape. His face was seamed and browned by the wind and sun, and his eyes were a watery gray as they blinked at her. When he smiled, as he was doing, his whole face seemed to join in, creasing cheerfully from forehead to chin. He was taller than Nest by several inches, and he stooped as if to make up for the disparity.

She was reminded suddenly of an old-time preacher, the kind that appeared in southern gothics and ghost stories, railing against godlessness and mankind's paucity of moral resolve.

"Good morning," he said, his voice gravelly and deep. He dipped his head slightly, reaching up to touch the brim of his odd hat.

"Good morning," she replied.

"Miss Freemark, my name is Findo Gask," he announced. "I am a minister of the faith and a bearer of the holy word."

As if to emphasize the point, he held up a black leather-bound tome from which dangled a silken bookmark.

She nodded, waiting. Somehow he knew her name, although she had no memory of meeting him before.

"It is a fine, grand morning to be out and about, so I won't keep you," he said, smiling reassuringly. "I see you are on your way to church. I wouldn't want to stand in the way of a young lady and her time of worship. Take what comfort you can in the moment, I say. Ours is a restless, dissatisfied world, full of uncertainties and calamities and impending disasters, and we would do well to be mindful of the fact that small steps and little cautions are always prudent."

It wasn't so much the words themselves but the way in which he spoke them that aroused a vague uneasiness in Nest. He made it sound more like an admonition than the reassurance it was intended to be.

"What can I do for you, Mr. Gask?" she asked, anxious for him to get to the point.

His head cocked slightly to one side. "I'm looking for a man," he said. "His name is John Ross."

Nest started visibly, unable to hide her reaction. John Ross. She hadn't seen or communicated with him for more than ten years. She hadn't even heard his name spoken by anyone but Pick.

"John Ross," she repeated flatly. Her uneasiness heightened.

The old man smiled. "Has he contacted you recently, Miss Freemark? Has he phoned or written you of late?"

She shook her head no. "Why would he do that, Mr. Gask?"

The smile broadened, as if to underline the silliness of such a question. The watery gray eyes peered over her shoulder speculatively. "Is he here already, Miss Freemark?"

A hint of irritation crept into her voice. "Who are you, Mr. Gask? Why are you interested in John Ross?"

"I already told you who I am, Miss Freemark. I am a minister of the faith. As for my interest in Mr. Ross, he has something that belongs to me."

She stared at him. Something wasn't right about this. The air about her warmed noticeably, changed color and taste and texture. She felt a roiling inside, where Wraith lay dormant and dangerously ready, the protector chained to her soul.

"Perhaps we could talk inside?" Findo Gask suggested.

He moved as if to enter her home, a subtle shift of weight from one foot to the other, and she found herself tempted simply to step aside and let him pass. But she held her ground, the uneasiness become a tingling in the pit of her stomach. She forced herself to look carefully at him, to meet his eyes directly.

The tingling changed abruptly to a wave of nausea.

She took a deep, steadying breath and exhaled. She was in the presence of a demon.

"I know what you are," she said quietly.

The smile stayed in place, but any trace of warmth disappeared. "And I know what you are, Miss Freemark," Findo Gask replied smoothly. "Now, is Mr. Ross inside or isn't he?"

Nest felt the chill of the winter air for the first time and shivered in spite of herself. A demon coming to her home with such bold intent was unnerving. "If he was, I wouldn't tell you. Why don't you get off my porch, Mr. Gask?"

Findo Gask shifted once more, a kind of settling in that indicated he had no intention of moving until he was ready. She felt Wraith stir awake inside, sensing her danger.

"Let me just say a few things to you, Miss Freemark, and then I'll go," Findo Gask said, a bored sigh escaping his lips. "We are not so different, you and I. When I said I knew what you are, I meant it. You are your father's daughter, and we know what he was, don't we? Perhaps you don't care much for the reality of your parentage, but truth will out, Miss Freemark. You are what you are, so there isn't much point in pretending otherwise, though you work very hard at doing so, don't you?"

Nest flushed with anger, but Findo Gask waved her off. "I also said I was a minister of the faith. You assumed I meant your faith naturally, but you were mistaken. I am a servant of the Void, and it is the Void's faith I embrace. You would pretend it is an evil, wicked faith. But that is a highly subjective conclusion. Your faith and mine, like you and I, are not so different. Both are codifications of the higher power we seek to comprehend and, to the extent we are able, manipulate. Both can be curative or destructive. Both have their supporters and their detractors, and each seeks dominance over the other. The struggle between them has been going on for eons; it won't end today or tomorrow or the day after or any time soon."

He stepped forward, kindly face set in a condescending smile that did nothing to hide the threat behind it. "But one day it will end, and the Word will be destroyed. It will happen, Miss Freemark, because the magic of the Void has always been the stronger of the two. Always. The frailties and weaknesses of mankind are insurmountable. The misguided belief that the human condition is worth salvaging is patently ridiculous. Look at the way the world functions, Miss Freemark. Human frailties and weaknesses abound.

Moral corruption here, venal desires there. Greed, envy, sloth, and all the rest at every turn. The followers of the Word rail against them endlessly and futilely. The Void embraces them, and turns a weakness into a strength. Pacifism and meek acceptance? Charity and goodwill? Kindness and virtue? Rubbish!"

"Mr. Gask—"

"No, no, hear me out, young lady. A little of that famous courtesy, please." He cut short her protestation with a sharp hiss. "I don't tell you this to frighten you. I don't tell it to you to persuade you of my cause. I could care less what you feel or think about me. I tell it to you to demonstrate the depth of my conviction and my commitment. I am not easily deterred. I want you to understand that my interest in Mr. Ross is of paramount importance. Think of me as a tidal wave and yourself as a sand castle on a beach. Nothing can save you from me if you stand in my way. It would be best for you to let me move you aside. There is no reason for you not to let me do so. None at all. You have nothing vested in this matter. You have nothing to gain by intervening and everything to lose."

He paused then, lifting the leather-bound book and pressing it almost reverently against his chest. "These are the names of those who have opposed me, Miss Freemark. The names of the dead. I like to keep track of them, to think back on who they were. I have been alive a very long time, and I shall still be alive long after you are gone."

ANGEL FIRE EAST
by Terry Brooks

Published by Del Rey Books.
Coming in hardcover October 1999 to bookstores everywhere.